I0761671

Advance Praise for
MOTHER OF BOURBON

"Unsung bourbon distiller—and force of nature—Mary Dowling overcame family tragedy, discrimination, and Prohibition, to achieve extraordinary success. Her story comes to life in this page-turning novel."

—**Susan Reigler**, author of *Kentucky Bourbon: The Essential Guide to the American Spirit*

"Mother of Dragons? Give me the Mother of Bourbon! In this historical fiction, Kaveh Zamanian and Eric Goodman break the boundaries of traditional bourbon books, just like the woman it's based on—Mary Dowling. From love to business, this bourbon soap opera is a must read, will keep you entertained, and make you question everything you thought you knew about America's Spirit."

—**Fred Minnick**, author of *Bourbon: the Rise, Fall and Rebirth of an American Whiskey*, *Bourbon Curious*, and *Whiskey Women: The Untold Story of How Women Saved Bourbon, Scotch and Irish Whiskey*

"Imagine a woman, born before the Civil War, running a distillery by herself at the turn of the 20th Century, decades before women had even won the right to vote. As far-fetched as this seems, Mary Murphy Dowling was that woman in real life. Unfortunately, because she was too busy getting shit done, little record of her accomplishments exists today. Her name has been whispered throughout the Kentucky bourbon industry for years, particularly at Louisville's Vendome Copper & Brass Works, where her original pot still doubler sits on display, a relic of her highly successful Juarez, Mexico distillery, which she built during the throes of American Prohibition. If not for that physical reminder of her work, Mary Dowling's legacy might have been lost forever. Kaveh Zamanian and Eric Goodman took the scraps of her legacy and wove them into an historical fiction based on her life, giving a voice to one of Kentucky bourbon's nearly forgotten bourbon barons."

—**Maggie Kimberl**, Content Editor, *American Whiskey Magazine*

"Mary Dowling cut a formidable character across bourbon history, but she has been largely forgotten—until now. *Mother of Bourbon* not only gives her the spotlight she deserves, but it does so with intelligence and grace. Whether you love whiskey or just want a good yarn about a life well lived, this book is for you."

—**Clay Risen**, author of *American Whiskey, Bourbon & Rye: A Guide to the Nation's Favorite Spirit* and *Bourbon: The Story of Kentucky Whiskey*

MOTHER OF BOURBON

MOTHER OF BOURBON

THE GREATEST AMERICAN WHISKEY STORY NEVER TOLD

ERIC GOODMAN
with **KAVEH ZAMANIAN**

A POST HILL PRESS BOOK

Mother of Bourbon:
The Greatest American Whiskey Story Never Told

ISBN: 979-8-88845-812-9
ISBN (eBook): 979-8-88845-813-6

Cover design by Savannah Graham, CRZY Design
Interior design and composition by Greg Johnson, Textbook Perfect

Post Hill Press
New York • Nashville
posthillpress.com

Published in the United States of America
1 2 3 4 5 6 7 8 9 10

To all the amazing women in our lives who nurtured and guided us with their strength and fortitude. We would not be where we are without you.

Murphy and Dowling Family Tree

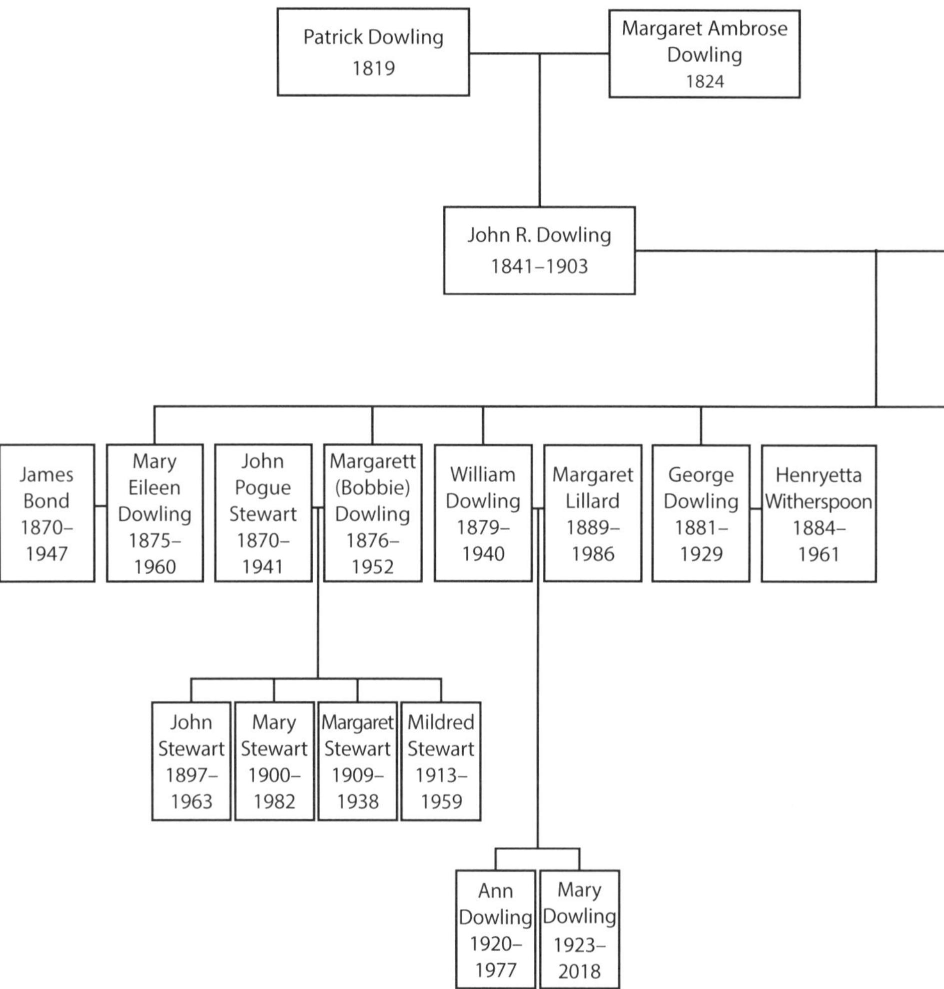

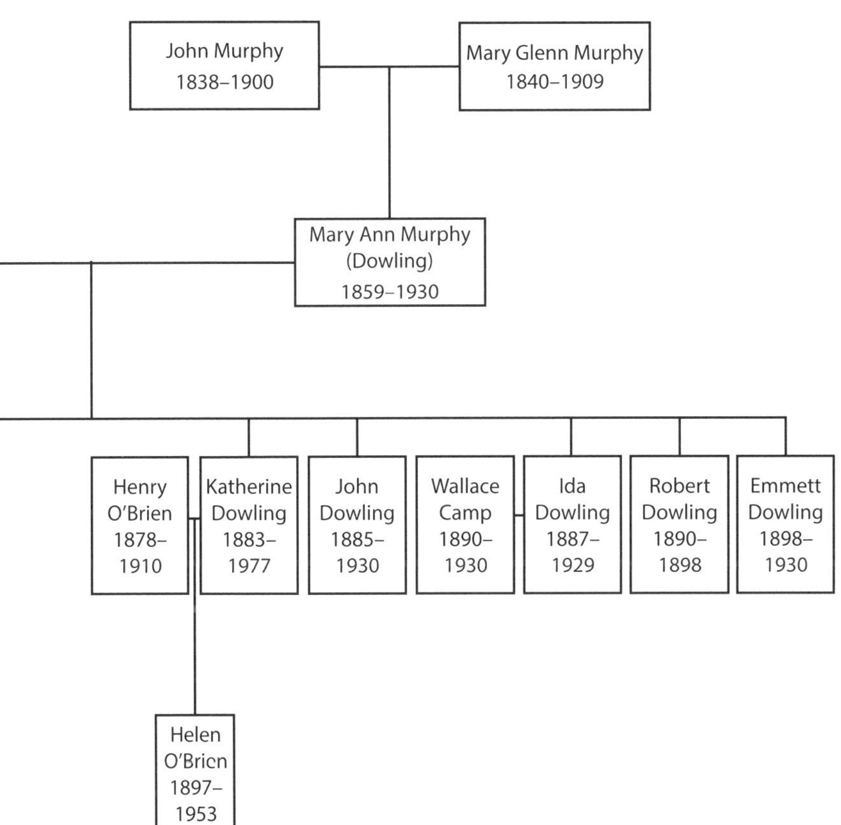
John Murphy
1838–1900
Mary Glenn Murphy
1840–1909
Mary Ann Murphy
(Dowling)
1859–1930
Henry
O'Brien
1878–
1910
Katherine
Dowling
1883–
1977
John
Dowling
1885–
1930
Wallace
Camp
1890–
1930
Ida
Dowling
1887–
1929
Robert
Dowling
1890–
1898
Emmett
Dowling
1898–
1930
Helen
O'Brien
1897–
1953

Introduction

Because of the Irish potato famine of 1845 and the period of struggle that followed, one-quarter of the population of Ireland left the English colony in hopes of food, jobs, religious freedom, and class advancement in America. Ireland then was in fact an exporter of butter, honey, vegetables, fish, and livestock, but those commodities were for the few rich; instead, the general population subsisted on potatoes at every meal. Hence "The Great Hunger" that caused one million of the poor to die of starvation.

The ships that conveyed the Irish to America were often called "Coffin Boats" because so many in steerage died of starvation or disease during an ocean voyage that could last up to ten weeks. And once the survivors arrived in cities like Boston, New York, and Philadelphia, they frequently faced hostility from the established classes who disparaged the Irish as ill-mannered Catholic loafers and drunkards, forcing them to find housing in foul ghettos rife with crime, cholera, tuberculosis, and typhus. So, like the Murphy and Dowling clans featured here, many Irish immigrants sought greater freedom and opportunity farther west in frontier states like Illinois, Ohio, and Kentucky.

The jobs they took were generally menial at first. Soldiery in the Civil and Indian wars was a go-to for many hungry Irish men who welcomed the "three hots and a cot." But 50 percent of the United States then was dedicated to agriculture, so there was a good deal of work as hired hands or tenant farmers in Kentucky, the "Bluegrass State," where corn, hay, wheat, and tobacco were the main crops. We find out here that the immigrant Murphy family ran a general store in Kentucky, and their oldest daughter, Mary Ann, the focus of Eric Goodman and Kaveh Zamanian's fine novel, worked there as a girl. The far older John Dowling, who would marry her, was a cooper who crafted whiskey barrels from American Oak for many distilleries, including Waterfill and Frazier, which he would eventually own.

The Irish immigrants had left behind their Guinness stouts and Jameson Irish whiskey in the Old Country and in America sought replacements in Yuengling lager and varieties of Kentucky bourbon. The prime ingredient in Irish whiskey was malted barley, and the brew was aged in old casks for at least three years. Its greatest affinity was with Scotch, whereas the prime ingredients in Kentucky bourbon were corn mash, malted barley or rye, and sometimes wheat, and the liquor was aged in new, charred, or toasted oaken barrels, gaining character as it felt the heat of summer and cold of winter. Aging often took four years, though some deluxe whiskeys could become more complex and flavorful after a quarter century or more. The high quality of the product is said to be due to Kentucky's peerless limestone-filtered groundwater, which connoisseurs claim is superior to any tap water in the land.

In 1917, Congress drafted an Eighteenth Amendment to the Constitution banning intoxicating liquors and duly sent the measure to the states for ratification. Within thirteen months, the measure passed. Some voting in favor of the legislation thought its intent was restrictions against hard liquors, not wine or beer, but the Volstead Act codified that it would hereafter be illegal to "manufacture, sell, barter, transport, import, export, furnish, deliver, or possess" any drink containing more than one-half of 1 percent alcohol. President Woodrow Wilson vetoed the Volstead Act, but the Senate and House overrode his veto, and so the Roaring '20s became an era of lawlessness as thirsty citizens defied Prohibition with bathtub gin, speakeasies, and sly commerce with bootleggers.

Some of the most exciting scenes in *Mother of Bourbon* occur in this period when Mary and her children were forced to contend with corrupt public officials, grand theft of their whiskeys, highly selective prosecutions, and the miscarriage of justice in the courts.

"The Mother of Bourbon" had become a widow in 1903, but she was undaunted as she continued whiskey-making. Mrs. Dowling had little formal education, but she was shrewd, canny, and intelligent, with amazing business acumen, an enterprising spirit, and the fierce courage of her convictions. She must have seemed a force of nature to competitors then: a mother of eight who vied within a world of condescending men and achieved successes that could only have made them envious. When Prohibition shut down most whiskey-makers in Kentucky, she dismantled her distillery, shipped it to Juarez, Mexico, to avoid federal agents, and made another fortune.

She became a civic leader and philanthropist in Lawrenceburg until she passed away in 1930. But like most founders and donors whose names are on buildings, her well-earned fame lasted for only a generation. This book hopes to restore it.

Eric Goodman and Kaveh Zamanian are excellent at telling a factual, thrilling, rags-to-riches story with such zest, insight, and alacrity. Mary Dowling has been mostly lost to history, but she has come alive again with this account. And now it's time for the world to get to know and love her.

—***Ron Hansen***

PROLOGUE

No Dogs, No Irish

When we began the research for Mother of Bourbon, *we weren't sure what we'd find or what sort of book we'd write. Almost everything published about Mary Dowling was inaccurate, and much remained hidden. We'd assumed a prominent woman who gave birth nine times in the late nineteenth century would have scads of direct heirs. We also assumed we'd find diaries or at least substantial correspondence.*

Wrong and wrong. After extensive online and in situ *research, and with the assistance of the direct descendants of Mary's second and third eldest children, as well as the descendants of an African American family who worked for her, an image of this extraordinary woman began to emerge. While filling it in, we enjoyed some remarkable moments as writer-researchers. We found contemporaneous newspaper accounts of KKK rallies in Lawrenceburg, corroborating Dowling family stories. In the 1880 US Census, we came upon a young African American servant girl named Ida living with John and Mary Dowling. And quite late in the writing process, a Dowling heir resurrected Mary Dowling's inscribed rosary and shared it with us.*

Because the known facts of Mary's life assembled from family anecdotes, county records, and newspaper accounts proved so compelling, and because she left no words of her own to help us understand who she was or why she made the choices she did, we wrote Mother of Bourbon *as historical fiction rather than nonfiction or biography. The historic photographs that enrich this text are authentic: Mary Dowling, her husband and children, their possessions. While we have imagined scenes and dialogue, we have not invented major characters or created composites. We'd like to think the liberties we've taken have helped bring Mary Dowling to life as she was: a powerful, complicated woman, who made her way in a man's world, not just years, but decades ahead of her time.*

Mary Ann Murphy was the eldest of ten born to Mary Glenn and John Murphy, Irish-Catholic immigrants. Her parents left Ireland as young adolescents to escape the Famine, arriving in America at the height of another plague: anti-immigrant, anti-Catholic fervor led by the nativist Know-Nothing Party. In 1855, in Louisville and Cincinnati, mobs torched Catholic neighborhoods and murdered dozens of Irish immigrants, who at that time weren't considered white. Mary was born four years later in 1859, in Clark County, Kentucky, east of Lexington. She had dark hair and a high forehead shuttering intense, intelligent eyes, which, even when she was a girl, peered out with considerable boldness.

In later years, after she'd become Mrs. John Dowling, dowager of Dowling Hall in Lawrenceburg, her gaze was formidable. If her eyes engaged yours, whether you were man or woman, you tended to look away first. She was not demure, Mary Dowling, though she was modest, as befit a woman of her era. Once she became John's widow, never to remarry though she was just forty-four with eight dark-haired, dark-eyed children (except for blue-eyed Emmett, her youngest and favorite, born when she was thirty-nine), Mary Dowling's gaze was not just formidable but had acquired the *Don't mess with me* look that informed her later life. She'd need that attitude to walk her singular path.

She did not suffer fools, yet she was kind-hearted, civic-minded, and generous. She was a force of nature until the end, acknowledging no man's authority (well, maybe John's), and certainly not the government's, but only God's. Mary Dowling had flaws. She was domineering and ran her family with the same iron grip with which she ran her distilleries. But she possessed grit, a nineteenth-century virtue in excess. This is her story, long forgotten, but fully researched and presented in these pages, returning to the light of a new century a truly remarkable woman: Mary Dowling, Mother of Bourbon.

PART ONE

John and Mary Dowling

CHAPTER ONE

Opening Moves
1874

In the first decade after the Civil War, the United States, especially the breakaway southern ones, strove to recover. Immigrants moved west from eastern cities, drawn by cheap land and new opportunities. Unsurprisingly, the whiskey business exploded, fueled by inexpensive labor, the cessation of hostilities, and by a generation of Union soldiers who'd learned to appreciate Kentucky bourbon during the years they'd spent in the South.

Murphy Dry Goods needed her. Mary Ann had worked beside Father since she was eight years old. Mother rarely came downstairs into the store; she was too busy attending whichever of Mary's nine younger sisters and brothers had been born that year. When she wasn't nursing, and sometimes even when she was, Mother washed, cooked, and baked till exhaustion darkened her visage. Fortunately for the family, Mary was adept at figuring, sharp as the pins and scissors the dry goods sold. She bustled from early to late, measuring, cutting, weighing, and bagging, then it was upstairs to supervise the washing up and putting away. Some of the younger girls, especially Katie and Margaret, six and eight, shirked if you let them, which Mary took upon herself to ensure didn't happen. Young or old, every Murphy girl needed to pull her weight; the boys, Lawrence and James, were too young to help. Mother could barely stand by evening's end, and Father was old and hadn't been strong, she was told, since the shipwreck on the way from Ireland, in which his brother and sister perished. She felt so sorry for Father, and when she saw a certain weariness slip over his features, she'd send him upstairs to rest.

Late one Thursday, when Mary was sweeping up, the bell jingled and cold air rushed in. It was October 5, and nearly dark. Mary looked past the bins and barrels to the open door. Beneath a bowler's brim, she glimpsed a face dimly remembered. Thick brown moustache, eyes dark and bold.

"Doan remember me, do ye?"

"No."

His lips split in a smile. "John Dowling. Me and my brother Ed are friends of your da's."

"We're closed."

"Then you should bolt the door," John Dowling laughed.

At her, Mary thought, which she did not take to.

"I remember you, Mary Ann, though you were a wee small girl. Tell your da I'll be back in the morning."

John Dowling was as good as his word, arriving early the following day in the same brown suit, black bowler, and bowtie. Mary was helping Mrs. Mooney with her order, far too busy, she told herself, to glance his way as Father exclaimed, "Johnnie Dowling, look at you in that suit!"

They were five foot eight, both Johns, Murphy and Dowling, their speaking voices like songbirds, unlike Mary Ann's, the first Murphy born in Kentucky, her speech slower and with gentler vowels.

"We're owners now, me and Ed. Dowling Brothers Cooperage in Lawrenceburg, Anderson County, west of the Kentucky. And just last spring, we bought half of Waterfill and Frazier, distillers of fine bourbon. It's in a nearby village, once called Steamville, but now Tyrone, for all the Irish living there."

Mary felt his eyes on her and turned again to Mrs. Mooney.

Father asked, "You wouldn't have a sample now?"

"Don't I?"

He set a quart Mason of amber whiskey on the counter. Father unhinged the frame that secured the glass lid, raised the bottle, and sipped.

"Say, join us for supper? A bite to accompany your lovely whiskey."

"Love to." Dowling started towards the door. "What time?"

"We'll expect ye at six. And Johnnie, this is my eldest, Mary Ann."

"I know."

She hoped he wouldn't mention he'd stopped by yesterday. She looked quickly in Dowling's direction, and he smiled as if to say, *Your secret's safe with me*. Then he turned to Father.

"How many children do ye have now?"

"An even ten. And you?"

"Just one distillery and one cooperage." Dowling winked. "But I'm expecting."

The bell tinkled and the door closed behind him.

John Dowling came to supper that night and the next one too. In the kitchen, ladling pork-and-leek pie into bowls her army of sisters marched to the table. Mary heard bites of the men's conversation through the door. Dowling had procured a half load of dry goods and promised to buy more after he sold the final barrels in his wagon.

The purpose of his trip was to find new tavern owners for his whiskey. Mary filled the last bowls and carried them in herself, then sat in the empty chair on Father's left, opposite John Dowling. He fisted a tumbler, as did her father.

Father sipped, then said, "Let us now say Grace."

The Murphy family bowed and held hands, even the youngest, each with the next.

"Let your blessing, almighty God, descend on this portion of your bounty," Mary's mother, also Mary, intoned from the far end of the table. "And on us, your unworthy servants; through Jesus Christ, our Lord. And let us say, Amen."

Father and Dowling clinked tumblers.

"That's fine," Father said.

"Glad ye think so." John Dowling smiled in her direction.

The party set upon the pork-and-leek pie, even James, who could barely work a spoon. Two bites in, Dowling said, "Fantastic, Missus Murphy." Turning to Mary, he asked, "Did you help your ma with the cooking?"

Before she could frame an answer, Father said, "Not *our* Mary Ann! She could run the dry goods herself, but she can't scald water."

Mary's cheeks burned, and she peered into her pie. "I could if I wanted." She looked up at Dowling. "But I don't."

The next day was Sunday, which meant Mass at St. Paul's Church on Short Street. Mary loved the grand new church, a red-bricked Greek Revival, which had been completed and consecrated when she was six, replacing St. Peter's. The soaring space fed her spirit, as did the pealing bells and the dark wood of the pews and confessionals. While Father Horrigan conducted the Latin Mass, which none of the Dowlings understood, she knelt beside Mother, watching her lips move as she prayed her rosary. Mother often fingered the wooden beads during Mass, but this morning her lips and fingers moved faster and with greater urgency. Mary wondered what was wrong. What was Mother praying for? Was the dry goods failing?

She remembered her parents talking in shocked tones about the cost of St. Paul's, what a struggle it had been for Lexington's Catholics, many of them poor Irish, come over during the Famine, to raise funds so soon after the War Between the States. Two hundred thousand Irishmen, it was said, fought in the War, three-quarters for the Union.

"'Twas a way," Father said, "for a poor man off the boat to earn a living. And if he died, his wife and kids, or his family in Ireland, received the pension. Not so for the Irish who fought for the rebels, or the soldiers on either side who lost a leg and not their life, like the sad singer in 'Paddy's Lamentation.'"

Money was a constant problem, her parents said, and Mary felt it in her bones as she watched them squeeze every penny. But she also knew how chuffed they were to worship as they wished in the great Commonwealth of Kentucky, now that the Know-Nothings and their hateful doctrine were no more. *Amen.*

On the altar, Father Horrigan raised his arms and announced Communion. Beside him, the Ambrose brothers, who lived down the street, swung their censers, and a fragrant cloud of incense ascended. Mary joined the line for Communion, waiting for the wafer that symbolized the body of Christ. Stepping forward, she recalled John Dowling smiling at her across the dinner table. What a handsome moustache he had, full and dark. She knew he was older but wasn't sure *how* old. Yet she couldn't ask her parents. They'd want to know why she cared. And maybe it signified naught, but she remembered the way Dowling said *he remembered her*, and the way his eyes laughed when he teased her. Something fluttered inside her, but as she knelt and accepted the host, every foolish notion floated away, and she thought only of the Blessed Mother and Her Son, whose holy sacrifice had redeemed them all.

Later, after supper had been served, the table cleared and dishes put away, her parents called her into the front room. Though the afternoon was gray and dismal, their single lamp wouldn't be lit for hours. Across from Mother and Father, above the sideboard that Mother often said was her single decent stick of furniture, Jesus hung on His Cross, wrists and ankles bound, daubed red with painted blood. Mother balanced James on her knee, but the other children were elsewhere, either down for a nap or outside under the supervision of her second sister Sallie. Mary would soon realize Mother had deliberately sent them away.

"We've got something to tell you," Father said.

"Something I've been praying for," added Mother.

"John Dowling asked for your hand in marriage." Father glanced at Mother. "And I've given my blessing."

Mary's cheeks heated and blood pounded in her ears.

"But I'm fifteen, and he lives so distant."

"That's what I said to your mother."

"And I said," Mother broke in, blue eyes flashing, "when I was *thirteen*, I left County Tyrone and crossed the Atlantic in the stinking hold of a coffin ship. Your father, but twelve, lost his siblings in a shipwreck. So doan cry about being young or Lawrenceburg too far away."

"Father needs me in the dry goods."

Father coughed into his fist, which he did when something made him anxious. "Dowling offered to hire us a shopgirl."

Mary tried not to, she did, but then her thoughts, as so often happened, exploded unfiltered through her lips. "You sold me!"

"You ungrateful girl," said Mother. "John Dowling's a good man, and for years, we've known he'd be a rich one. There's something about him, his brothers too. He told us of a fire last year in Lawrenceburg, and now the ground's been cleared, so to speak, and property's cheap."

"Why Mary," Father added. "I thought you'd be happy. He fancies you, and I saw how you smiled at him at dinner."

"I did not!"

"He's coming to dinner again tomorrow," Mother said, "and Father's given his word."

"Then let Father marry him!"

The flat of Mother's hand slammed hard into Mary's cheek. Tears sprang to her eyes, and she rushed from the room, calling over her shoulder, "I bet he didn't offer half enough for the shopgirl!"

That night, after the younger girls were asleep, Mary crept from the bedroom in her nightgown. She found her parents where she expected: in the front room, balancing account books. That's where and how they spent Sunday nights, preparing for Monday, with just the one lamp lit to save on oil. Mother saw it was she and dropped her gaze to the ledger. Mary waited, hands behind her back, determined to speak judiciously. Apologies did not come easily; they never would. She was almost always right.

"I'm sorry I lost my temper."

"And what else?" Mother asked.

"I apologize for the rashness of my speech."

Father's gray brows rose into his thin hair. "Mary," he said softly, meaning Mother.

Mother's blue eyes engaged her brown ones. "You're not a little girl, Mary Ann."

I've never been a little girl, Mary thought.

"You've got a woman's body and mind."

She wanted to melt at the mention of her body in front of Father.

"It's just that Father needs me in the dry goods."

Mother replied, "When my own ma was dying in the Famine, yet still sharing her portion with the children, she sent me away, though I was much younger than you, so I could *live*." Mother's eyes blazed. "Well, I'm not dying, Mary Ann; I'm leading my life, and it's a good one, even if hard. Now I'm telling you, go live your own damn life. Father and I, we have ours."

"But I won't see you."

"'Twill be a good life. I always told your father: Johnnie Dowling, him and his good-looking brother Ed, with their big moustaches, silky hair, and blarney, will fill pots with gold. You may not see us now, but in years to come, we'll visit in your big fine house."

Mary bowed her head. She could get around Father, who was kinder and gentler, but once Mother had made up her mind, there was no gainsaying her.

"And doan tell me you don't fancy Dowling." Mother took Mary Ann's hands. "A mother knows what she knows."

When John Dowling arrived next morning, Mary couldn't look his way. She felt stirred up like Mother's roiling jam pot in summer. And flummoxed, that was it, flummoxed! She could hear him talking with Father, ordering bolts of curtain cloth, bed sheets (*Oh my God, bed sheets!*), blankets, towels, and shams. She'd catch him glancing her way, a twinkle or perhaps an unanswered question lighting his eye, and she'd turn away quickly. He angered her so, and yet there was no denying he intrigued her. A bit of this, a bit of that, while she feigned indifference, then she heard Dowling tell Father he'd sold his last three barrels and needed to deliver them but expected to return in time for dinner. *Just listen to him*, she thought, *acting like we're a public house*.

His bootheels approached, and she busied herself filling a jar with half-penny candies. When she looked up, John Dowling stood before her, hat in his hands.

"I'll look forward to seeing you at dinner." He grinned then added in a whisper, "You look lovely, Miss Mary. But then, you always do."

When dinner ended, Mary hurried to the kitchen to supervise the washing up. She'd worn a clean apron and fussed more than usual with her dark hair, which was thick and prone to obstinate curls, but had said not one word to John Dowling, nor he to her, the entire meal. The next she knew, he stood beside her sisters Sallie, Jessie, and Margaret, Margaret and Jessie assigned the rinsing, and Sallie the drying, the way she'd organized them earlier this year. As for Mary, her arms were submerged to the elbow in a tub of warm, soapy water.

"Miss Mary," he said. "What's this about turning me down when your father has already said yes?"

"I haven't turned you down."

"Well, you haven't said *Yes* to me, now, have you?"

She could feel the water on her arms and her sisters' eyes peeking at her, like baby birds from the nest.

"Mary Ann," he began, as if it were the first words of a song. "I know you have feelings for me!"

Her eyes blazed. "I do not!"

Dowling shook his head. "Doan say ye don't when ye do." He looked her full in the eyes. "You must know how much I care for you!"

She looked up from the sudsy tub. "Then why didn't you ask me? Why didn't YOU ask ME?"

A smile spread like sunlight from his eyes to his lips. "You're right." He dropped to a knee. "Mary Ann Murphy, I love ye with all me poor heart. Since that first night in the dry goods, when you glared at me with such fire in your eye and told me you were closed. I thought, *That's the girl for me. We'll do* fine *together!*"

Still kneeling, he glanced up at her. "So, Mary Ann, will YOU marry ME?"

Teetering on the edge of *Yes*, Mary drew back and demanded, "What about my awful cooking? And twenty-five dollars for a shop-girl? That's barely half enough."

"Fifty then." He laughed and took her hand in both of his, and his touch both thrilled and shocked her. "And doan worry, darling, we'll hire a cook."

Her heart sprang open, and joy rushed in. "Then I will marry you, John Dowling. And love you for all our days."

He rose and kissed her in front of her gaping sisters.

They set their wedding for Sunday next, October 11, 1874. He'd remain in Lexington prospecting new business for spring; it was two days by horse and cart to the ferry at Tyrone, so there was nothing to be gained by leaving only to return. He confessed his brother Ed had expected him ten days ago. Grain was in, and it was mashing weather; the still and doubler were running twenty-four hours; but he'd lost his heart, he had, and Ed would have to carry on a bit longer. When he telegraphed his news, Ed had responded, "*Congratulations, now hurry home.*"

Mary spent the next days gathering her things and preparing to be wed at St. Paul's morning Mass, then a wedding lunch and off to Versailles, thirteen miles west, where they'd spend their first night. Her sisters, especially Sallie, second-born and dearest to her heart, had been teasing her about the wedding night, for none of the Murphy girls had ever had a suitor, or knew what to expect, except what they knew of stallions and mares. Sallie had many bawdy notions, while Jessie, third-born, was full of romantic airs. As for Mary, she hadn't given marriage a solitary thought, occupied as she was by sales and orders.

"What do you think *it* will be like?" Sallie whispered in the quiet of their room, the next three younger girls insensible in their bed; she and Sallie shared their own. "With John Dowling having such a bushy moustache?"

Mary had no idea. "I'm sure it will be fine. Nothing more, nothing less."

"Oh, you're no fun," Sallie whispered. And then, "Sister, I'll miss you so!"

Mary rolled towards Sallie and embraced her. "I'll miss you too, I will." Not wishing to succumb to emotion, fearing she might blubber if she did, Mary said, "Let's try to sleep. Morning will come soon enough."

But it was quite some time before her eyes remained closed.

In the morning, everything changed. Father Horrigan sent word there had been a fire at Saint Paul's, and the sanctuary was closed for several weeks. What to do? John had promised to return to Lawrenceburg by Monday next, and after not giving it a thought all her life, Mary's heart was set on a church wedding. So instead of posting their marriage bond in Lexington, John and her father galloped off to Mount Sterling, seat of Montgomery County, where her parents had once lived, and posted the hundred-dollar marriage bond there.

Mary organized her things once, a second, and then a third time; when finished, she turned her attention to the shelves in the dry goods. "Enough," Mother said, bringing her upstairs. "We'll be fine without you."

Mary wondered, *But will I be fine without you?*

Sunday morning the Murphy family and John Dowling set out long before the sun. They arrived in Mount Sterling and found their way to St. Patrick's, which turned out to be a small house bought and converted to the Lord's service by Father Lambert Willie, who would marry them. Mary reminded herself that wherever two gathered in His name, Christ dwelled, but it was a terrible long way to come for just a house. Father Lambert Willie was stout and gray and spoke with an accent, likely French, in both Latin and English, and Mary wasn't sure she liked that either.

Then John took her hand, and her mind quieted. Such strong fingers. They stood together, heads bowed, surrounded by her family, perhaps for the last time. And in that moment, touched equally by grief and joy, she allowed herself to think, not for the first time, *Mrs. John Dowling. I'm going to be Mrs. John Dowling.*

They arrived at the Rose Hill Inn, village of Versailles, in the frosty midnight dark. John knocked not once but three times before Mrs. Terrell, the innkeeper's wife, arrived at the door in a long white gown with a taper in her hand.

"What do you want?" she demanded. "It's the damn middle of the night."

"Aye," John said. "Our wedding night. We're sorry to be tardy, but we've traveled a fierce long way."

Murmurous voices within, while Mary glanced around the balustraded porch on which columns supported a second-story balcony. The door opened wide, and Mrs. Terrell and a young Black maid admitted them. John excused himself to attend their wagon, anxious the team receive an extra portion of grain. They'd be up early and traveling again; they dared not miss the final ferry at Tyrone. Mary followed Mrs. Terrell's candle up the wide staircase, with its fine turned banisters and stained-glass oculus at the first landing, where the banister and staircase doubled back before rising to the second floor. Mary had never entered such a big fine house, like a church, with its row of four-panel doors, lighter on the frames, darker in the framing, bringing to her tired mind the confessionals in St. Paul's. If ever John made the living her parents predicted, she'd ask for a house grand as this one.

Mrs. Terrell led her to a door at the end of the corridor. "Our finest," she said. "Fit for a bride's first night." Candle-lit from below, her smile turned ghoulish. "'Tis a featherbed. Have you never slept in one?"

Mary shook her head.

"There's no hot water. The night's half gone, and if I'd listened to Mister Terrell, you wouldn't have been admitted at all. He's particular about his sleep, he is." Mrs. Terrell smiled again. "Not that you're likely to get much."

Mary blushed, grateful for the dark.

"Clara will bring up towels and a basin of water. And mind you, no blood on the sheets or your husband will be charged."

Will she never stop?

Mrs. Terrell pressed her small hand against Mary's more substantial one.

"Tell you a secret, child. Close your eyes, it'll be over soon enough."

She'd recall the bristle of his whiskers, John warning her this might hurt at first so he'd endeavor to be gentle. Then his hands on her breasts, fingers where she'd never been touched. Sharp, piercing pain, and she gasped, trying not to cry out. *This can't be right,* she thought, *it can't,* and closed her eyes. When she opened them again, she watched John rise above her in the dark. The rapture on his face, like a painting of the saints.

In the morning, not as early as planned, they woke and embraced. Mary pressed her cheek against her husband's chest. She'd known nothing of men, and now this.

Downstairs, they discovered Mrs. Terrell had laid a fine table, which Clara, the young maid, served. One plate begat the next, and they didn't finish till half-ten. A boy hitched their team. John settled the bill. Mrs. Terrell found her outside the parlor door and announced with a grin, "Don't worry about the sheets, Clara's soaking them now."

The post road was hilly and rutted. They chatted of this and that. John's team was so well-matched they responded to a light right hand, and from time to time his left would land upon her knee. At first, she startled. *What was he doing?* Mary Ann Murphy, fifteen and eldest of ten, was suddenly, remarkably, a wife.

They sat the laden wagon, stopping only to water the horses. Shadows lengthened and heat rose until it again felt like summer, though it was the Ides of October. At four o'clock on his pocket watch, the sky darkened.

"How much still to go?"

"Another mile." He peered up at the clouds. "Maybe two."

A half mile on, she heard thunder, then lightning split the western sky. No matter. They hurried towards the storm and their new life. The wind picked up. Treetops doubled. Leaves swirled and eddied around them. Then they were inside the storm, and she was drenched to the skin. John drove on, hands steadying the team.

"Are ye all right?" he called over wind and rain.

"I'm fine!"

When the rain abated, the late sun returned, but not its warmth.

John muttered, "We should have made do with less breakfast."

She knew he feared there'd be no ferry, and where would they sleep? And what would they do with their things, and the dampness of their clothes? "We'll be fine," she said.

"I'm glad ye think so."

She couldn't ken his meaning. He clicked his tongue and snapped the reins; the team sprang forward. Ten minutes more, and the track started to descend. She smelled the river now.

"We're there," she said.

"Not quite." He turned her way and smiled, the first she'd seen in quite some time. "But soon enough."

When they reached the pier on the eastern shore, there was no ferry. They stared across the Kentucky at the limestone cliffs on the other side and a few small buildings of the Village of Tyrone. And there, at the end of the guide wire that traversed the river east to west and west to east, was the flat-decked ferry more than big enough for their wagon and team.

John climbed down, strode to the end of the dock, withdrew his revolver, and fired two shots in the air. Before the last echo faded, a shot answered from the opposite shore. John turned and faced her, nodding.

She sat close beside him in the fading light while they crossed, two ferrymen at their oars. Beneath them, the broad Kentucky flowed, swollen by the storm. Beyond lay their future, Tyrone and Lawrenceburg, all unseen. She held her husband's hand, Mary Dowling, eager to reach the other shore.

CHAPTER TWO

Resurrection 1882-1884

When Mary arrived in Lawrenceburg, she joined a world struggling to rise from its own ashes. Her mother had mentioned the fire, and John had told her of the rebuilding, but the devastation was beyond comprehension. The great fire of 1873 had leveled a city, now scarcely a village. Would she have come if she'd known? *Yes*. She had little choice. John had wooed and swept her parents off their feet, but to be honest, she'd agreed. Still, she told him flat out that first week, "Spare me the rose-colored glasses, John. From now on, tell me plain."

He smiled. "Maybe I was describing what will be, not yet what is. But you and me, Mary Ann, our eyes are fixed on the future."

The Anderson County courthouse had been spared, along with ten or twelve houses. Everywhere else, ruin and the cacophony of hammering, above which Fortune sang a siren song to those who heard her: the hungry and the driven. And none were hungrier or more driven than John and his brother Ed. By day, the brothers commanded a rough crew of Irish coopers and former slaves. There were long hours and little sleep; the Dowlings drove their men hard. Mary slept even less. Mary Eileen was born in November 1875, a year and a few days after they married. Margaret May followed nineteen months later, just long enough to escape the sobriquet of Irish twins, which Mary detested. She was sensitive to all slights of the Irish, for there were many in the early days, and freely voiced too. Catholics, she never forgot, had been down-talked as the late-arriving few amongst the many, ranked with Blacks, whom the white townspeople had known, and often owned, for decades.

John's early life had been different from his brothers', which accounted for his ambition. To escape the Famine, he'd been put on a ship bound for New Orleans with a family friend in 1853, when but twelve. Watching his neighbors starve while the English Protestant landlords took their crops, John had been eager to leave and make something of himself and his family. He rarely spoke of those hard, lonely years.

Ed and Mike Dowling had remained in Ireland until after the War Between the States, while John worked his way up the Mississippi to Ohio and learned the cooper's trade. By the time he'd saved enough for his brothers' passage, he was in Cincinnati; the brothers had been partners ever since. From Cincinnati, it was an easy move to Lexington, where John had met her parents, and thank goodness for that. Being on his own so young, expected not only to feed himself but to bring his brothers over, had made John hard and ambitious. "Nothing like hunger," he liked to say, "to get you up before dawn."

Making barrels, at which the brothers excelled, was how they'd come to own distilleries. Instead of cash, they'd accept a share of ownership. Whiskey men, Mary had observed, often lacked the sense Christ gave chickens, in direct proportion to their skill with a still. It was lucky, she sometimes thought, that barrels could not be drunk, only the whiskey inside them. Over time, and not much time, really, John and Ed had acquired stakes in several Tyrone distilleries, and the Dowlings were on their way.

Mere months after the conflagration had "fired out" the old order—as the locals said—John purchased a large parcel for his cooperage on the north end of College Street. College ran north and south, east of Main, on the poorer side of town. Dotson's Grocery lay just south, while the Negro Baptist Church and several Black cottages bordered Dowling & Co to the north. Like the cooperage, the Baptist Church was newly constructed. Following the shameful lead of Baptist congregations around the South, Lawrenceburg's First Baptist Church, which had permitted slaves to worship from a separate balcony, expelled its Black members after the War. Apparently, Mary thought with disdain, Protestants would worship under the same roof with slaves, but not free Blacks. No wonder she mistrusted them.

John, Ed, and their roughnecks worked from dawn till dusk and sometimes later, while Mary ran the accounting side of the business, as well as the Dowling household. In years to come, their cooperage would face the train tracks and depot. Early on, barrels were moved by men and wagons. If John wasn't at one of their distilleries, he was supervising barrel-making and loading, six days a week. If not for Mary, he would have worked Sundays, but she protested vehemently against disrespecting the Sabbath. In time, John relented, although no Mass was served closer than Bardstown, forty miles distant, a journey too lengthy to contemplate. *We're not beasts of burden*, she'd insist, although she often felt like one.

The lack of a Latin Mass, which soothed her soul, and the grueling hours both worked led to fearsome quarrels, loud and long, during their first years of marriage. John was convinced he knew best, while Mary believed—and would her entire life—that her judgment was practically infallible. With John so much older, it took time and tenacity for Mary to retrain her husband's eyes to see what she saw. They were both early-born, at the head of large families, after all. Mary had helped ramrod her sisters and brothers since she was six. John was on his own from twelve onward. Both were undaunted and accustomed to their own way. And a good thing too. In the 1870s and 1880s, when every other Catholic family in Lawrenceburg and Tyrone was headed by a laborer, being Irish Catholic required a deep well of endurance.

For the first four years, they lived adjacent to the cooperage in a two-bedroom cottage shared with Ed. The privy was out back, and she saw more of Ed than ever she wanted; she wasn't sure he forgave her for having come between him and his beloved big brother. Some of her worst fights with John were about living with Ed, who was gregarious and loud, and liked a dram or three at the end of the day.

To be fair, the problem lay not so much in her brother-in-law but in Mary's desire for a place of her own. Both children slept in their room, or didn't sleep, as was the case many a night. The next day Mary would be exhausted and short-tempered, prone to behavior she wasn't proud of, for her husband worked as hard as she. Through the fall of 1878, she fumed and fretted yet held her tongue, except when rage bubbled up and out of her. But on Christmas Day, after she'd missed her second monthly—so knew for certain they'd have three children by summer—she told John without explaining why. Enough was enough; she must have her own home.

"What am I to do, boot me own brother into the street?"

"No, John, there's a house coming open on East Woodford, large enough for a family of five."

His eyes widened, as comprehension dimly dawned.

"And a wee maid's room, so Erna can live in. And a baby nurse too, which we'll be needing."

"So, this is how you tell me."

"It is."

"You're a wily one, Mary Dowling."

"And let me tell you something else. If we keep having babies as we planned, in a few years we're going to need a house far grander than this one on Woodford. So, we best be saving our money."

"Since you've taken charge of our books, ye know we are."

He tried to kiss her, but she moved her mouth.

"Not for the *business*, John. For the fine mansion you promised me, with stained-glass windows on the first landing."

He got a far-away look in his eyes, and she knew he was remembering their honeymoon at the Rose Hill Inn. As was she.

"Just as soon as we've secured the whole of Waterfill, we'll commence saving for your mansion."

She threw her strong arms around his neck and kissed him.

"I suppose," he whispered, "you've already picked out where to build."

She smiled and settled in his arms.

They moved onto East Woodford in April. Erna Nicholas, who'd cooked for John and Mary since they arrived in Lawrenceburg, moved in too. Erna was seven years older than Mary, widowed and childless. Her husband had been kicked in the head by a mule, and she'd moved home with her parents into one of the Black cottages near the cooperage. From there, she'd walked to work and cooked three meals, but now she'd live in and help with the little girls. Her food was simple but tasty, especially her biscuits and dumplings. With John's encouragement, she was learning to prepare Irish dishes, especially shepherd's pie, which John had missed, he said, since he left the auld sod. Short and stout, Erna was easygoing and easy to live with. If she missed her husband, she never spoke of him. Or sought another.

In June, when Mary was eight months gone and laboring under considerable baby weight, with days so hot she thought she'd descended to Hell and nights so close and humid she'd wake dreaming she was suffocating, John arrived home trailed by a Black girl as tall as he, yet so thin her eyes looked over-large for her face.

"Mary," John began. "This is Ida Leyter, granddaughter of Mose, who works at Waterfill."

"Ma'am," the girl said, eyes on the ground.

Mary heaved herself to her feet. Her daughters, three and a half and not quite two, played on the floor with a calico kitten and a ball of yarn.

"John," Mary said, "come with me."

He followed her to the kitchen where Erna was frying chicken.

"Why'd you bring her home?"

"To help with the children."

"She's but a child herself."

"Mose says she's a hard worker and excellent with kids."

Mary snapped, "What else would he say?" Then, moving faster than she had in days, she returned to the front room and stood over Ida, who knelt beside her daughters.

"Tell me, child," Mary began.

Ida stood, three inches taller than Mary herself, eyes averted.

"How old are you?"

"Fourteen." Then, faltering, she confessed, "My next birthday."

"Have you cared for young children?"

"I'm eldest of eight, been caring for young'uns my whole life."

"Speak up," Mary said, her heart softening. She well knew the demands faced by the oldest girl in a large family. "Have ever you cared for white children?"

"No, ma'am," Ida answered. "There be no white children in our family."

Was she impudent or dense? Then Mary spied the smidge of a spark in Ida's eyes, and thought, *She's not as scared and simple as she seems.*

"All right, you're hired for two weeks, and we'll see how you do. Did you bring your things?"

Ida shook her head. "Mister Dowling said not to till you agreed."

"Mister Dowling's a smart man, isn't he?" Mary smiled, and Ida allowed herself a small smile too.

"Can you cook?"

"Just a little."

"Erna will teach you. Now go home and collect your things."

Ida slipped out the door and closed it behind her.

On July 23, 1879, Mary gave birth to William Edward Dowling, whom John had chosen to endow with his brother's name, rather than that of his father back in Ireland. John would never say why, maybe some bad blood before he left, and she asked but once. Will looked so much like her firstborn, Mary Eileen, it sometimes felt as if she'd given birth to the same child twice.

That same year, Ed Dowling married Frances Cronin, daughter of his former landlady in Lexington, and moved her into the cottage adjacent to the College Street cooperage. The brothers worked longer hours than ever, and Mary's sister-in-law, who went by Frankie, spent most of her days with Mary on East Woodford. Somehow John and Mary found time to conceive George, who was born the ninth of April 1881.

To give John his due, Ida excelled as a baby nurse. Mary had been right too. There was greater depth and intelligence to Ida than met the eye, and Mary soon depended on her. But with two active baby boys and the two older girls to contend with, Mary, and especially Ida, were literally run off their feet, and the poor girl couldn't put on weight. Her large, expressive eyes seemed to pop out of her cheeks, and though her body filled out, her face remained excessively thin, as if she were starving, though Mary and Erna made sure she filled her plate.

Sometimes, when Mary walked uptown to buy groceries, she'd take Ida with her. She'd grown accustomed to servants, and now that money was pouring in, she didn't mind letting people know. Some of the wealthy wives, the McGregors, the Bonds, the McBrayers, the Lillards, and especially the Ripys, whom John was in business with, spoke to Mary on the street, used her first name too, and had started inviting her to lunch.

In the dry goods and green grocers, the owners and shopgirls treated her with grudging respect, encouraging her to open accounts and buy on credit, since they knew the Dowlings could afford to. And sometimes, when they thought she wasn't looking, she'd catch the clerks and shopgirls regarding her with resentment, because she was Irish but no longer poor, while they still were. She could afford the best cuts from steers and hogs mash-fed at Waterfill. She wore new silk dresses over fine petticoats and owned not one but many. She walked through town with her head high, Ida beside her carrying the bundles, or on wet days, two paces behind, holding up the long skirts of Mary's dresses to keep them out of the mud and slop of Lawrenceburg's unpaved streets.

Mary saw the envy in the shopgirls' eyes but chose not to notice. No longer poor Irish, she didn't need to. She could rise above, or pretend to, because the day she'd been dreaming of was coming soon. They'd signed a contract to buy the rest of Waterfill in October 1881, seven years from the month they married. Who would have believed it? Not many, but John and Mary both.

Walking home with Ida holding up her long dress, with deliveries scheduled from the butcher, from Dotson's, and the dry goods too, Mary remembered last night's conversation with John in bed.

"We'd best keep the name Waterfill and Frazier on our bourbon, don't you think, John?"

"I suppose."

He looked perturbed and sulky, like the little boy she'd never known but could see in Will and George; she knew he'd wanted to call it Dowling Whiskey. Or Old Dowling. Maybe Dowling Brothers.

"But we'll change the company name to Waterfill, Dowling."

"Aye," he said.

"And we'll call the mansion we'll be building Dowling Hall. We'll hire the same builders and architect as TB. Ours will be the finest in town."

John grinned. "You're a marvel, Mary Dowling. Have ever I told you?"

"Aye, but not often enough."

"Ha!"

Then he'd kissed her. And now, walking home through the muddy streets, trailed by Ida, Mary smiled as she had the night before, dreaming of their bright and fearsome future.

CHAPTER THREE

John and Mary, Ascendant
1886

So much had changed.

But Mary hadn't. Still pigheaded. Still convinced she knew best.

It certainly helped that early on John had both the good sense to recognize Mary was better organized than any woman or man had the right to be and also the self-assurance to put his wife in charge of his company's finances. Not many men of his day had the strength of character and the self-confidence to do such. But very few men were married to a woman like Mary Dowling.

At forty-five, twelve years into their marriage, John remained strong and trim, moustache luxuriant though salted and peppered, twinkling eyes and lilting voice still able to charm birds out of summer trees. Twelve years his wife, Mary still wasn't certain why he'd chosen her. Must have been love, as he claimed. Or the fierce look in her eyes when riled, as he also claimed. Lord knows the Commonwealth was flush with prettier, more docile women. But John didn't value docile. He must have loved her as she was—sharp-tongued and strongly opinioned—and she took warm comfort in that.

Seated at her dressing table in the pale light of dawn, Mary pinned her curls, then checked her face in the glass. Hardly beautiful, but beauty faded—good sense did not. She no longer minded not being a beauty, at least most days. She stood and exited the master suite, leaving John abed; Sunday was the only morning he slept in. So much to manage, so many barrels to fill. There was no getting off the carousel they'd set in motion, and why would they want to? The Dowlings were rich. Their marriage and their businesses had prospered. Dowling Hall, an immense brick Queen Anne—ten thousand square feet, a dozen bedrooms, and two front parlors, on ample grounds with a side entrance for carriages—was the second largest home in Lawrenceburg. Completed just months ago, it lay across Southern Avenue from the mansion of TB Ripy, John's friend and sometimes partner; only TB, who owned Cliff Spring outright and partnered in Clover Bottom and J.M. Walker, distilled more whiskey than they.

In the row of Protestant mansions on Southern Avenue, Dowling Hall, built by and filled with Catholics, did not quite belong. Maybe it would someday. John had warned her when they purchased the parcel she'd selected that theirs was on the *wrong* side of the street, closer to the rough part of town, where their cooperage was situated. Poor whites and Blacks also lived east of Main.

"No matter," she'd replied. Their parcel was a savvy purchase, and she foresaw a day when which side wouldn't matter, only its location on Southern Avenue. Dowling Hall was a palace, and it was *theirs*.

Mary started down the grand, mahogany-appointed staircase, pausing to admire the stained-glass windows John had ordered from Tiffany Glass to remind them of Rose Hill. She looked up the open staircase to the third floor where all six children slept, tended by Erna, Ida, and Kinky, who'd been hired for two weeks as a seamstress but had never left. Blue the yardman lived on the fourth floor, as did Henry who tended their horses and drove the carriage.

All their servants except Kinky were Black. Blue, Henry, and Erna were older than Mary, born before the War, the children of slaves, enslaved themselves. They signed with an X, not having had even the three years of schooling Mary had completed. She barely remembered slavery, having been born just before it ended. But she saw its evil everywhere, and she was old enough to remember the most virulent hatred of the Irish. *No dogs, no Irish,* and of course, *No Colored.* As the mother of six, the idea that someone could own your children enraged her.

Kinky, who'd worked for the Lillards and McGregors before Mary, had emigrated from a small city in Sweden, the name of which Mary could neither remember nor pronounce. Kinky's husband died of cholera soon after they arrived, and instead of becoming a farmer's wife, Kinky had supported herself ever since with her clever needle. She educated Mary about brocaded silks and satin, the shocking cost—to Mary, raised on homespun and cotton—of dresses from a dress shop, which was another reason, the first being their mutual fondness, that Kinky would remain employed at Dowling Hall until she died.

Kinky was Mary's height but twenty years older, angular, prim, and reserved. She spoke strongly accented English and, at first, didn't mix with the Black servants, perhaps because they barely understood each other. Mary picked Kinky's mind about sterling tea sets, French champagne flutes—though she didn't like champagne—and the proper setting of a dinner table. Anyone could learn to be rich, Mary thought, if they set their mind to it, and if they had the money. Mary had both, money and mind, and a fine teacher in Kinky.

Later, Kinky befriended Ida, or perhaps Ida befriended her. Kinky would always live with them—she had no family in Kentucky—and she seemed resigned to life without a man.

Today was not only the Fourth of July but First Sunday. After they'd moved into Dowling Hall, Bishop McCloskey, the first ever Irish American bishop of Louisville, had granted permission for Mass to be held in their living room; there weren't sufficient Catholics in Lawrenceburg to warrant a resident priest. But now, with Father Ronald visiting once a month, the older children could study for confirmation: Mary Eileen, eleven; Margaret, nine; and Will, nearly seven. *Just in time*, she thought. For years, she'd fretted about their religious education, surrounded as they were by a blond sea of Protestants.

Mary found Erna in the kitchen. Bacon sizzled on the griddle, from a hog slopped at their distillery on Bailey's Run. Biscuits formed from Sifted Snow, the flour mill they owned with TB, cooled on the stone table.

Erna smiled from under her cap. "Morning, ma'am."

It no longer felt strange to be *ma'am*-ed.

"Morning to you too." And then, all business, Mary continued, "Father Ronald will want to start promptly, so we'll need to finish by half-eight."

"Then we'd better have the children down."

"Aye," Mary said, thinking of the struggle to rouse the littlest girls. "And don't forget, John's brothers will be attending the party with all the others."

Just then she heard her brood on the stairs, her eldest daughter scolding the younger ones.

Erna's eyes met her own. They both knew Mary Eileen was too full of herself, not just firstborn, but over-praised for her pretty face, dark hair, and sparkling eyes: John's spitting image minus a moustache.

The children bustled in, accompanied by Ida. Despite working for them for seven years, Ida remained taciturn and soft-spoken, although no longer so thin. She'd married at sixteen and had two children at home.

After Ida came Emilie, Baby John's wet nurse. George, their second boy, looked just like Will, while Katherine, not yet three years old and two years younger than George, was petite and fine-boned like Margaret. Each of them dark-haired, brown-eyed, and fair-complected. Black Irish, one and all, produced as she and John had agreed when they began, eighteen to twenty-four months apart, preferably in summer or fall, growing their family like their business, everything ordered and planned by Mary, who ran a very tight ship indeed.

Mary's brother-in-law, Ed, and her sister-in-law, Frankie, arrived for Mass with their three children. They lived nearby in Lawrenceburg. Herbert, Frankie's youngest, was four months younger than Mary's John, and they were dispatched straightaway to the nursery. Major Mike, the third and youngest Dowling brother in Kentucky, was a bachelor and not expected for Mass.

With only four years between them, the same height and with similar features, John and Ed looked very much alike: dark-haired Irishmen with big moustaches and even bigger personalities. Everyone loved the Dowling brothers, including Mike, who was eight years younger than John and had joined the US Army when he arrived. He retired a major and now managed one of their distilleries: Dowling Bros, twenty miles away in Mercer County. He lived alone on the distillery grounds, a strange and solitary man.

"He'll never find a wife," John liked to say, "out there in the boonies."

"Nor is he looking," she would answer.

Major Mike rarely bathed, and the sour yeasty smell of mash got into his hair, his clothes, and his skin. Since they'd moved into Dowling Hall, she'd leave towels, clean clothes, and a bar of lye soap near the pump and require Mike to wash up before entering. He obliged with a smile, joining them for most Sunday dinners. That's how he was—kind, sweet, and pliable. Or maybe she was just too hard to say no to, which everyone around her had surely learned.

On this July 4, the people of Lawrenceburg celebrated all day. After a parade the length of Main ended in front of the courthouse, where bleachers had been erected and red, white, and blue bunting bearing the inscription "1776 Welcome 1886" had been strung; after speechifying and a reading of the Declaration of Independence by Judge McBrayer; after insults hurled at old King George; after prayers by two different ministers, though none by a priest; after a patriotic saxophone solo and another on cornet; after wheelbarrow and sack races, the climbing of a greased pole, and the sending up of paper balloons; after all this, the Dowlings, the Ripys, the Bonds, and some of the Lillards and McGregors returned to Dowling Hall, where Erna and Ida, with help from Blue and Henry, had set up tables on the back lawn to serve the feast of roast pig they'd been prepping since morning.

Later, when the women and children had gone home and the men were sipping bourbon, Mary joined them in the front parlor. The conversation had shifted to the topic of the hour: a proposal to link Lawrenceburg west by rail to Louisville and east to Lexington. The price: $100,000, a goodly sum. Judge Feland, editor of the *Anderson News*, had extolled the tax in the name of progress in several of his weekly editorials. John agreed. He looked to the future and frequently shared his views with Mary. *Ye have to spend money to make money*. So, she was surprised to hear Ed, loudly and angrily, advocating the opposing view.

"Listen to me, Johnnie. I *doan* want the government's hand in me pocket. *Doan* they tax our whiskey hard enough?"

They did, Mary thought. She didn't like the government either. But she trusted John's vision of the future, bound not just by affection, but by how often he was right.

"Listen, Ed," she said, and the men's eyes swung towards her. She'd never been adept at keeping still, as was expected of her sex in a roomful of men. Judge McBrayer, TB Ripy, Judge Feland, and two local bankers, Charles Bond and John McGregor, waited for her to speak.

Looking straight at Ed, she continued, "If the road doesn't come through Lawrenceburg, it'll go elsewhere, and then where will *we* be?" She spied John's smile from the corner of her eye, while in front of her, Ed turned red-faced as a fool. "We'll be left out and left behind, that's where. Is that really what you want?"

The judges and bankers murmured assent, but from the look on Ed's face, she feared she'd made an enemy of him. After a moment, she excused herself to see after the children, thinking she'd best let the brothers work this out alone.

Later, in the sitting area of their grand new bedroom, winding down from the day as they had for years and would continue to do for many more—with a glass of their own bourbon in their hands—John said, "You carried the day with your talk about the road."

"You think so?"

"Aye." He sipped. "And not just I thought so. Both judges and TB too."

"What about your brother?"

John's look darkened. He drained his dram and poured himself another, then moved the bottle towards her; she waved it off.

"Ye scored no points with Ed. Ye knew you wouldn't, but still ye spoke your mind."

"A familiar failing of mine."

He smiled. "And a virtue not many have.'

"Thank you, John." She sipped. "I fear I've made an enemy of your brother."

"Perhaps that can't be helped. Ed can be a fool."

"You shouldn't say that about your brother."

"Even if it's true?" John looked at her angrily, although she soon saw the anger wasn't directed at her. He sipped his bourbon. "I want ye to know, I've decided to change my will, so that if anything should happen to me, you'd take over Waterfill, Dowling, not Ed."

"Oh, John, I'll not come between you and your brother." They looked at each other, hard and long. "Nor should you act out of anger."

"It's not anger—I decided this months ago. Truth is..." He reached for her hand, and she gave it to him more willingly than when she'd wed him twelve years ago. "You've a better head for business than Ed.

If ye weren't a woman, any fool could see that plain. But because ye are…" He grinned and pointed at himself with the hand that wasn't holding hers. "I'm the only one. Lucky me."

And with the hand that wasn't holding his, she raised her glass and drank it down. "Maybe I'll have that second one," she said.

He smiled.

We've come a long way from our first night at the Rose Inn, she thought.

She was twenty-seven, mother of six, and in every way, her husband's partner.

They celebrated their first Thanksgiving in Dowling Hall on November 25, 1886, and they had much to give thanks for. Six children. A mansion. The thousand head of cattle mash-fed at Waterfill, Dowling, then sent to market. The soaring revenues from their businesses. They planned a grand feast and invited everyone for two p.m. Just before the first guests arrived, little Johnnie, two years old and, as his proud poppa liked to say, "Full of piss and vinegar, that one," took off running as he was prone to, towards the open pit in the backyard, where turkeys were turning on a spit. Unmindful of anything except outrunning his older brothers, Johnnie raced towards the banked coals and open fire, his head craned back towards his pursuers.

"Johnnie, stop!" Ida shouted from the far side of the fire, where she was turning the spit. "Stop, Johnnie!"

Mary saw the tableau plain from the kitchen porch, fifty feet away, her attention seized first by the fear in Ida's voice. She started running but was too distant to save her son. Ida hesitated but, seeing she had no choice, plunged through the banked coals and open fire, emerging from the other side to scoop Johnnie up and save him. Mary arrived a moment later and took him in her arms, delivering a swift clap to his bottom, then setting him down to roll Ida on the ground and extinguish her burning dress. Ida screamed in pain,

Johnnie screamed because he'd been spanked, and Mary screamed for help. She could smell Ida's burning flesh.

From that day on, Mary included Ida in her prayers for saving Johnnie from serious burns or worse, in the same breath she prayed to the Blessed Mother of God to protect her own children. She gave Ida two paid weeks off to recover and $200 to help her buy a house in the area on East Lincoln called The Grove.

When Ida returned to work, Mary asked to see her in the front parlor where she'd set up a desk to do paperwork.

"How are you feeling, Ida?"

"Jes' fine."

"Your burns are healed?"

Ida nodded. "Thank you for asking, Missus Dowling."

"I want you to know," Mary began. "You're part of our family now." She looked in Ida's eyes, which no longer seemed too large for her face. "If you need something, just ask. Mister Dowling and I owe you more"—Mary hesitated—"than we can ever pay."

Mary never again asked Ida to walk behind her and hold up her skirts. And eleven months later, on October 10, 1887, the day before her thirteenth wedding anniversary, when Mary delivered her seventh child and fourth girl, she insisted they name her Ida, to honor the maid who'd saved her sixth from injury or worse. At first John protested. He wanted to use the name of some maiden aunt in Ireland Mary had scarce heard of, much less met. And maybe the baby would be a boy, so there'd be no issue to decide or argument to pursue. But as she lay in bed, suckling her newborn girl, she told John plain she'd not yield on this.

"But Mary," John protested, "no white family names their child for a Negro."

"Why not?" She could feel her eyes burning with a furious light, the *Doan mess with me look* as John called it, although sometimes, when she'd really angered him, he called it her *Doan foock with me look*.

"Why not?" she repeated.

He shouted, "You think the Ripys would name their daughter for a Negro maid? You think the McGregors would?"

"Don't you shout at me," she shouted at him. "I just birthed your daughter."

He took a calming breath, and she endeavored to take one too. After a moment, more quietly but with no less intensity, she continued, "I don't give a damn what *they* would do." And from the way she said *they*, she knew he'd take her meaning: all the Protestants in whose midst they lived. "And neither should you."

"You're an impossible woman, Mary Dowling. And so have you been since the evening I fell in love with you in your parents' dry goods." He grinned. "Ida she shall be."

Mary pressed the child to her breast, and with her other hand reached for John. She knew it was the giving birth and the river of hormones rushing through her. She was both exhausted and wound up like a spring. In a moment she could be crying or laughing, or both at once. Then John grasped her hand, and she asked again, "Why not? Under the skin, aren't we the same in God's loving eyes?"

"Mary, I already agreed."

He had, hadn't he?

Moments later, Mary felt someone lift the child from her arms as she slipped into sleep.

CHAPTER FOUR

Dowlings At the Top 1888-1897

Mary and John planned everything together, business and family, although it was hard to see where one left off and the other began. Years ago, they'd decided on eight children, four boys, four girls, no more than two years apart. Miraculously, which is to say with the help of the Blessed Virgin, patron saint of all mothers, they were spot on schedule. John's friends, to whom he'd boasted of Mary's plan, would inquire, "How do you do it, Johnnie?" And he'd respond with a grin, "Just luck, I guess."

Although more than once, when he thought she was out of hearing, she'd heard him add, "I twist right for a lad, left for a lass."

Men, she thought. *As if they had more than twenty seconds to do with producing children.*

After delivering Ida, with the eighth and last planned for the fall of '89, Mary was ready to put childbearing behind her. It wasn't so much the toll on her body, although at twenty-nine, she wasn't nearly as slim as once she was. It was more that she was eager for the next phase of her life in the changing world of Lawrenceburg. She was John's partner, in work as well as at home, one of the "important" ladies of the town, ready to assume her place as a civic and social leader, and more than ready to act on some of her many ideas on developing their business.

Fifteen hundred people now called Lawrenceburg home, treble what there was when they arrived. Although a road tax had been voted down two springs ago—Ed Dowling was one of the leading *No* voices—a group of businessmen, including John, rallying around the motto, "Don't give up the road," had raised enough via subscription to begin the Louisville-Lawrenceburg line. For a full year now, 150 men had been laying track in Anderson County, with the big day coming soon: April 5, 1888.

Mary had planned a reception. As Dowling Hall had been designed for entertaining, they did so frequently. John said it was good for business, but it was more than that. Now regarded as one of the Five Families, they believed it was their civic duty to maintain "a certain standard." But there was more to it even than the standard. The other leading families, the Bonds, Lillards, Ripys, and McGregors, had been in Lawrenceburg for decades, many of them since before Anderson became its own county in 1827. Most importantly to Mary, of all the bourbon barons living on Southern Avenue—now officially South Main, but familiarly known as *Cream Street* because its residents had risen to the top of Lawrenceburg society—only the Dowlings were Catholic. The Ripys might have been generations ago, but no longer. Yet 90 percent of the distillery workers in Tyrone were Catholic. And that was the point in the minds of their neighbors. Dirty Irish=distillery workers=drunkards.

No one would ever say that about the Dowlings, at least not to their faces.

The first train ever to stop in Lawrenceburg was scheduled for ten a.m. Thursday morning. Judge McBrayer and his wife were to be honored as first passengers, along with the mayor of Harrodsburg. School was cancelled, and the Five Families had gathered on the platform with their children. Mary held little Ida in her arms. The two older boys stood beside John, while adult Ida kept a firm grip on Johnnie to keep him from running.

It was a warm, bright morning, and inside her black dress—she chafed sometimes at all the somber clothes women were expected to wear—Mary felt the first sticky beads of perspiration. *Would the train never come?* Everyone was here, except Ed and his family. Although in many ways the most genial of men, Ed had remained steadfast in his opposition to the road. John had offered many times to pay Ed's share, and just as often Ed refused. Once, when John announced at Sunday supper that he was simply going to make the contribution in the name of the Dowling Brothers, they nearly came to blows.

"Like hell!" Ed bellowed. "Who do ye think ye are?"

"Senior partner, Dowling Brothers!"

"Not in my name, ye *bastid*!"

And they glared at each other, standing nose to nose, in profile so much alike she could scarcely tell them apart.

"I've got a position to uphold!"

"Subscribe in your name but leave me out!"

"No, ye goddamn fool!"

Ed turned to his wife. "Come on, Frankie, we're going home."

John backed down, subscribed in his own name only, and the brothers patched things over, but relations were never the same. Ed already wasn't much talking to Mary, often pretending she wasn't in the room when she was, especially when business came up. Ed and Frankie began to talk of relocating to Lexington, where Frankie's sisters and widowed mother lived. Mary didn't see how that would work, not with John and Ed being partners. For the past year, Ed and Frankie had dined with them less frequently, and they certainly wouldn't be coming tonight. She'd understood for quite some time it might be difficult to be the younger Dowling brother in Lawrenceburg, the one without Dowling Hall, father of four, not seven, children.

Just then, the platform began to shake, and she put her troubling thoughts aside. Peering down the track she saw the locomotive fast approaching. Three blasts blew. Baby Ida wailed. Cinders flew. Children squealed. Mothers secured their toddlers, and the band played "Dixie" as the first train to Lawrenceburg rattled into town.

Mary gave birth to their eighth child on August 8, 1890, a year later than planned. They named him after John's brother Robert, who'd remained in Ireland with their mother. John always said that without Robbie, the others couldn't have come to the States and prospered, so every year until this one, Dowling Bros had gifted Robbie a round sum to thank him, even after their mother passed. This year there'd be no such gift because John and Ed had dissolved their partnership, announcing the split in the *Lexington Register* on April 21. Hard feelings had lingered after the road tax fight, although even Ed had ultimately agreed trains were a good idea.

Who could argue, especially after Young's High Bridge was completed in '89? Two hundred and eighty feet above the Kentucky River, with a span of more than five hundred feet! Oh, hadn't it thrilled Mary when the first passenger train connecting Louisville to Lexington had rumbled across it. After the first came a torrent. According to the *Anderson News*, riders now averaged one thousand a day, which led to a building boom, with everyone repeating a quip some wag had made: "Lawrenceburg is a large town for its size!"

She liked that. And she liked thinking of a brighter future for Lawrenceburg, a future she and John were helping to shape.

But there had been losses along the way, Mary thought, while nursing Robbie in the third-floor nursery. Ed and Frankie had pulled up stakes and moved to West Main Street in Lexington. The brothers put the best face on matters and said they'd continue to work together, but Mary knew it wasn't so. Although Ed retained his third of the Dowling Bros distillery in Burgin, he'd needed cash to commence a new life in Lexington. She and John had bought his share of Dowling Brothers Cooperage and Waterfill, Dowling.

Ed used the cash to start his own cooperage in Lexington and to invest in what he said would be his primary occupation: coal merchant. It was better all around, Mary thought, although bittersweet; she'd miss having family in Lawrenceburg, but Ed needed to be out from under John's considerable shadow. She and John wanted to follow their own vision for the business, and she'd heard, from Ed and others, that there was a fortune to be made in the coal fields in eastern Kentucky, so it was better for Ed as well.

Mary shifted Robbie from her left breast to her right. Instead of an eighteen-month to two-year interval, dependable as the morning sun, three years had passed since Ida's birth. She didn't know if the delay reflected her age, or John's, or how busy their lives had become, but for a year, despite marrying relations to her monthly cycle, no baby had come. Now that she held Robbie in her arms, it was strange to think he'd be her last. At thirty-one, she'd been giving birth for half her life. She wouldn't miss the nursing and being up all hours of the night. In fact, for the last few and now Robbie, she'd arranged for a wet nurse to begin at three months and let her milk dry up.

But never again to hold a newborn? Or feel tiny fingers grasp her own? *It was too much*, she thought, and suddenly Mary found herself shedding tears. Her body was still stirred up, her hormones all in a pickle. She sniffed and sighed, felt the baby's mouth lose the nipple. He was dozing off.

She shifted Robbie to her shoulder and rubbed his back. If he were her last, she thought, rocking, it shouldn't be too many years before Mary or Margaret made her a nana. Mary would soon turn fifteen; Margaret was already thirteen. Both were pretty girls, especially Mary, for they favored John. As a rich man's daughters, the girls would neither wed nor bear children nearly so young as she.

In Lawrenceburg, young women didn't enter society until seventeen. What had her parents been thinking? *One less mouth to feed.*

Of course, when Mary had been Mary Eileen's age, there was no "society" to enter, just the struggle of the working poor. Instead, her knight in Irish shining armor had come along, and they'd made a very different life. And here in her arms lay the youngest member of the clan, all thanks be to the Mother of God.

Mary rubbed and patted, patted and rubbed, and just when she feared he'd fallen asleep, Robbie burped, and his innocent breath blessed her neck. Mary rocked her infant son long and slow until he slumbered.

Mary Eileen married James Chandler Bond on November 6, 1895, the day before she turned twenty. Everyone oohed and aahed over the match. The Bonds were one of the oldest and wealthiest Lawrenceburg families, and Jim Bond, as he was known, or sometimes Gentleman Jim because he had such exquisite manners, was widely considered the handsomest bachelor in town. Mary Eileen made a lovely bride. Society columns in the *Anderson News* and *Lexington Register* praised her rich complexion, classic figure, and raven hair. The praise delighted Mary Eileen, that and being married before twenty, which in Lawrenceburg, was the official beginning of spinsterhood.

Although she spoke of it to no one, Mary had significant misgivings about her eldest daughter. Mary Eileen so admired her own appearance and opinions, there was no reasoning with her. Mary blamed John for doting so completely on his first child; she was spoiled to the core, like a pear left too long on the tree. Nothing, really, and no one, was good enough. That's likely why she'd lingered on the maiden vine. She was sharp-tongued and caustic, but unlike her mother, who realized she might be the origin of her daughter's biting wit, Mary Eileen lacked the sense to know when to keep her opinions private. Nor did she value anyone's opinion unless it supported hers. If she had, Mary would have been more forceful in expressing her opinion of Gentleman Jim Bond, who was twenty-five, and though extremely good-looking and possessed of the finest tenor in Lawrenceburg, brought neither career nor ambition to the marriage.

When he was younger, Jim had window-shopped in one or another of the Bond family businesses, but during his courtship of Mary Eileen, he was a man of leisure. Dark-haired and blue-eyed, with a well-trimmed moustache, Gentleman Jim hadn't worked a day nor earned a dollar in several years and showed scant inclination towards either. Rumors had reached John's ears, who'd shared them with Mary, that Jim had been involved with and possibly engaged to a girl of good family in Louisville, but the engagement had ended badly.

"I'd like you to talk to her," Mary said one night in their bedroom, "before this goes any further."

John set down the bourbon he'd been tippling. "Why don't ye?"

"She doesn't listen to me, and you know it."

"I believe she's set her cap for him." John drained the dram. "She means to marry a Bond."

"Couldn't she find one who works?"

John shrugged and refilled his glass, then poured one for Mary. She sipped, then asked, "Maybe you should ask how she plans to live?"

"I doubt she's thought of that."

"Do you intend for us to support them?"

John shot her a look, sipped, then sipped again. "Maybe he'll work for us."

"You think we'll have more success than the Bonds? Don't be a fool."

"You're a hard case, Mary Dowling."

"Always have been." Mary finished her drink. "So, you'll talk to her?"

"That I will."

But he didn't, at least not so she ever heard.

Several months after Mary Eileen and Gentleman Jim started keeping company, Mary took her daughter aside after Jim dropped her home in the Bond's horse and buggy in the middle of a Tuesday afternoon. The younger children were still at school. John was at Waterfill.

"Isn't he something, Mother?"

Mary bit her tongue.

Mary Eileen continued, "I didn't tell you, but at the McGregors' masquerade on Saturday? All the girls wanted to dance with Jim, but he saved every one for me."

Mary thought about how that must have appeared to the other guests. "Wasn't that indiscreet?"

"Everyone knows how we feel about each other."

"Has Jim proposed?"

Her daughter nodded.

"Have you accepted him?"

Mary Eileen's eyes sparked and fired. "Of course."

"Without consulting me or your father?"

"Jim intends to ask Father tonight. I wasn't going to say anything, but you forced it out of me."

"I did what?"

"*Forced* it. By claiming we were indiscreet."

"What would you call it?" They glared at each other, mother and daughter equally angry. Mary remembered her own mother slapping her face all those years ago, and how she'd asked John to talk to Mary Eileen, but he hadn't. "So, you've said yes to this *loafer*? Who has no career and takes you for carriage rides on a workday afternoon?"

Mary Eileen's cheeks were a rainbow of rage, first pink, then red, then purple. "He's *not* a loafer, Mother. He's a gentleman, from one of the oldest and best families in Lawrenceburg."

"By oldest and best, you mean Protestant."

"What of it?"

Mary considered her words carefully, then asked, "If you have children, will you promise to raise them Catholic?"

Mary Eileen's eyes blazed. "We haven't decided."

"If you don't," Mary's own temper was raging, "don't expect my blessing to marry that loafer."

"*Mother!* If you don't take that back, I may never talk to you again!"

"Take what back? That he's never made a penny? How will you live?"

"Quite happily!"

"And *what* will you live on? His good manners?"

Her daughter sneered. "All you care about is money."

"That's because your father and I were given none and had to make our own. My parents squeezed every penny—"

"I know, until it was flat." Her daughter drew herself up proudly. "Father has changed with your fortunes, Mother, but though you dwell in Dowling Hall, you might as well live in a shanty!"

Mary slapped her daughter's cheek. Mary Eileen tossed her pretty head, then stomped out of the parlor, slamming the door, not giving her mother time to apologize or take any of it back. Not that she would have.

When Gentleman Jim asked John for his daughter's hand in marriage, he said they planned to raise their children Catholic, which was enough to secure John's blessing. As for Mary and Mary Eileen, they didn't speak for a month. Even after the silence ended—through the rest of the young couple's courtship and their first ten months of marriage—Mary kept the vow she'd made to herself after she slapped her daughter's face for the first and only time. A family tradition, or so it seemed, passed down the maternal line. Mary Eileen had made her bed and now she must lie in it. As for how Gentleman Jim and Mary Dowling Bond, as she would insist on being called, would afford their expensive clothes and dinner parties, she had nary a clue. Let John pay for their life if he wanted. Until her daughter brought it up, however, Mary would save her breath to cool her porridge.

Margaret, the Dowlings' second daughter, would be known as Bobbie after marriage. She was smaller, quieter, and less striking than Mary Bond, but made a far more advantageous match. Educated, as was her older sister, at a finishing school in Cincinnati, Margaret had met, been wooed by, and agreed to marry Dr. John Pogue Stewart, son of Dr. John Stewart of Frankfort, who'd formerly served as the Kentucky commissioner for the feeble-minded. The elder Dr. Stewart owned and administered Stewart Home, a private sanitorium for the physically and mentally handicapped. Stewart Home occupied the former estate of the Kentucky Military Institute, seven miles north of Lawrenceburg.

The younger Dr. Stewart, though only twenty-six, had already completed his medical training and established a specialty in the treatment of mental and nervous disorders. He worked with his father and would someday, Mary foresaw, take over Stewart Home, which was already ranked the best sanitorium for the feeble-minded west of the Alleghenies, and quite possibly in the entire country. Although Mary hadn't gone beyond third grade because she needed to help her parents, she valued education. She especially admired the Stewarts' work with the weak and afflicted, for it made her think of Jesus serving lepers, filling her with pride that Margaret, soon to be Bobbie, was marrying into such a distinguished family.

So, who could blame her for sparing no expense for this wedding? And because their distilleries, the cooperage, and John's investment with Ed in Kentucky oil fields were all booming—things were much better between the brothers now that they didn't work together—it hadn't been hard to convince John.

As the hot days of September wound down, and her daughter's wedding day, October 7, 1896, approached, Mary turned her considerable organizational skills to the thousand details of the joyous event. Her parents were attending, as well as her two closest sisters, Sallie and Jessie, with their husbands. They'd stay the weekend in Dowling Hall, which would be full to bursting. Weddings and confirmations were the only times Mary saw her family. It was just too far and her life too busy, so she'd taught her heart not to miss them.

The ceremony would take place in the bay window of the front parlor. Ed's daughter Frankie and Ida, both nine, would serve as flower girls, dressed all in white. They'd enter first, carrying yellow roses. Following them, Bishop McCloskey of Louisville and Father Thomas of Danville would perform the nuptials. Then little Robbie, just six and small for his age, would enter in a miniature day coat, carrying a basket of flowers in which the wedding rings would be hidden. Will was the best man; Dr. John had no brothers. Mary Bond was the matron of honor, and she looked so elegant beside her brother, Mary almost forgave her bad temper.

Last came the bridegroom and bride; Margaret had chosen a wedding dress of accordion-plaited Paris muslin. The dress was the only detail Mary had allowed Margaret-soon-to-be-Bobbie to choose herself, and only after Margaret, an agreeable and pliant child, had protested, with tears in her brown eyes, "Mother, I'm getting married, not you!"

Mary couldn't help herself. She wanted everything to be just so, and everyone knew—even John admitted—that she was better at managing details than any two other people put together. No matter. She relented and spared no expense. Bobbie would have her Paris muslin, pleated just the way she wanted.

John walked Margaret down the aisle formed from chairs in the center of their parlor. He wore a long coat just like little Robbie and the groom. Though John was fifty-five, and his hair and moustache riven with gray, he remained handsome and full of life. Her mind flew back to her own simple wedding twenty-two years ago. Next, she'd be crying, and Mary Murphy Dowling never cried in public—and rarely in private. It was a point of pride. And yet, and yet, and yet!

Once her second-born had slipped the gold band on the ring finger of Dr. John P. Stewart, and he had slid the more elaborate bejeweled one on hers, both carried down the aisle by little Robbie, and the charming young couple had exchanged their *I do's*, and gray-haired Bishop McCloskey had said, "I now pronounce you man and wife. May the Holy Spirit of God fill your hearts with love!"—for she'd insisted that the wedding be Catholic, and insisted, too, that any issue be raised Catholic, though the Stewarts were Presbyterians—her own John took her hand, and she smiled up into his eyes.

We've done all right, she thought.

When her son-in-law raised his wife's veil and bent low to kiss her, for the former Margaret May Dowling, now Bobbie Dowling Stewart, was just a slip of a girl, Mary couldn't help herself, she began to weep. John squeezed her hand and smiled at her with love and surprise in his eyes.

"My, my, Mary. My, my."

Then the flower girls and Robbie led the wedding march out of the parlor. Mary Dowling, mother of the bride, dried her tears and felt her thoughts return to a more comfortable concern: the thousand details of a wedding breakfast on the lawn for a well-heeled mob of fifty.

CHAPTER FIVE

Angel of Death, Angel of Light 1898

In early April, after she'd missed her second consecutive monthly, her breasts began to ache in a familiar way. She was having difficulty eating breakfast and keeping it down when she did. She'd felt like this before. In fact, eight times before. But this time. *This* time! She was thirty-nine. Unlike the others, this was wholly unplanned. If you're pregnant—*Of course, you're pregnant, you silly goose; you've been craving peppers and ice cream again*—you'll give birth just shy of forty. John will be fifty-seven! What's he going to say? What's everyone going to say?

My God, she thought, startling and sitting up in bed. *Our baby will be younger than Bobbie's. If a boy, he'll be younger than his own nephew!*

Then she remembered. The Saint Valentine's masquerade at TB Ripy's. John had been drinking with the men, and when they stumbled home across the street—well, John stumbled, she supported him—he'd persuaded her to share a dram and then a second of their specially aged Waterfill and Frazier. One thing must have led to another. And then she did remember and placed her hand over her lips and laughed. *You randy old man. Aren't you going to be pleased with yourself.*

Mary lay down, placed her hand on her husband's shoulder, and wished him a fond goodnight a second time. In the morning, after the children had departed for school, she joined John in the breakfast room, where he was finishing coffee, toast, and jam, already garbed in the white shirt and bowtie he wore on workdays.

"John," she began, sitting down. "Do you remember the Valentine masquerade at TB's?"

He grinned. "Not very well."

"I warrant you'll remember it better in years to come."

"How's that? If I doan remember now?"

She never knew how the question popped into her head, then out her lips. "That night, did you twist right for a lad or left for a lass?"

"What? I didn't know… *What?*"

A dim flame flickered then fired in his eyes. John dropped his toast into what remained of his coffee, which splashed up and stained his white cuff.

"Mary!" Then louder, "*Mary!* Have you seen the doctor?"

"Not yet, but ask if I'm sure?"

"I guess by now ye would be." He laughed. "How do ye feel?

"I feel…" She thought a moment. "Wonderful. And silly. But mostly wonderful."

They grinned at each other, long on long.

"But I can tell you, that's the last time I'll be drinking late at night with you, Mister Dowling."

"Aye."

And then he kissed her.

She was eleven weeks along Friday afternoon, April 29, when Robbie came home from first grade and complained his head and neck hurt. He looked unwell, somehow both pale and flushed, but when she lay the back of her hand against his forehead, it barely felt warm. Robbie had the most delicate features of all her children. Hair slightly reddish, like Ida's, but blessed with long lashes the older girls complained were wasted on a boy. She gave him a glass of cool water then sent him upstairs to nap.

An hour later, she was seated at her desk in the side parlor, entering figures in the Waterfill ledger. *Another splendid month.* Kinky, who'd now been with her for twenty-two years, burst into the parlor and blurted, "Missus Dowling, you'd best come quick and see about Robbie."

They rushed upstairs, Mary lifting her long skirts to free her legs. She hadn't gained much weight yet and barely showed, certainly not through her voluminous petticoats and dress. They hadn't told anyone she was expecting; they never did until three months. And certainly not this time, doctor's orders. She'd been cautioned not to exert herself, but there had been such fear in Kinky's quiet voice, and she wasn't an impressionable girl but a trusted, older woman.

They dashed into Robbie's room, and when Mary placed her hand against Robbie's forehead, it was like touching an iron.

"Quick," Mary said, "fetch the mercury thermometer. And call Doctor Thomas." *No,* she thought and shouted after Kinky, "I'll call the doctor, just come back quick!"

When Kinky returned, Mary raced downstairs to the parlor phone, trying to calm herself, thinking, *This can't be good for the baby!* Dr. Thomas arrived soon; by then she knew the worst. Robbie's temperature was 105, even after she and Kinky applied cold compresses using chips from their icehouse. When she first read out Robbie's temperature, Kinky's pale lips trembled. She loved the boy, had helped raise him, and had naught of her own. To get her out of the room, Mary again dispatched her to the icehouse. Then she sent Bill James, their new yardman, to fetch John from Waterfill but didn't expect him for an hour at best. And Robbie, poor Robbie, babbled away, drifting in and out of sleep and fever dreams, complaining of his head and demons only he could see.

"When did it start?" Dr. Thomas asked.

"Not an hour ago. When he returned from school."

"You did well to apply cold."

"Doctor Thomas, don't tell me what I already know. What do you think it is?"

"With the fever coming on so fast and high?"

She looked straight at him, and his voice tailed off. After a long moment, his eyes came to hers.

"It could be meningitis. I've heard of two cases in Harrodsburg."

"What is that exactly?"

"Swelling of the membranes around the spine and brain. The first symptoms are fever and neck pain."

Mary felt her heart blacken. "Robbie said his neck hurt."

Dr. Thomas tried to meet her gaze but failed again.

"Doctor," she asked. "What's to be done?"

"I have tincture of willow bark for fever."

"That's all?"

"Pray it's not meningitis."

Kinky was so upset she had to be sent to bed. In her place, Ida joined Mary in a bedside vigil.

"Missus Dowling," Ida said, after they'd been alone for some time. "Is there anything you want me to do?"

"Pray with me."

Ida sat on the other side of Robbie's bed. She nodded and lowered her head.

Mary said, "You saved Johnnie. Maybe a Baptist and a Catholic praying together can yet save Robbie."

Their prayers went unanswered. At ten p.m., Dr. Thomas returned and advised Mary to send for a priest. But Dr. Thomas was Church of Christ and could not be expected to know. Until a child turned eight, which the Church considered the age of reason, he dwelled in innocence, incapable of distinguishing between good and evil, and therefore, incapable of sin. So, there was no need of Extreme Unction. But what of her own sinning heart? And John's? And the other children, who'd never known such sorrow? And her unborn child? Oh, she thought, remembering and amending the famous poem by Ben Johnson. *O, could I lose all mother now!*

She and John sat by Robbie's bed through the night, and in the great, still blackness he slipped away. Weeks later, when she could think again and feel more than her own grief, Mary prayed to the Blessed Mother of God, who'd known the terrible sorrow of losing a son, to give her strength. Mother Mary must have known Robbie would be taken by this terrible disease, and that's why she'd gotten pregnant. How else to understand Robbie's death, which was otherwise senseless and cruel, when the Virgin and her son embodied love?

But she knew better than to mention this to John, whose own faith was less profound than hers. To the end of his days, he would rage with sacrilegious anger, mourning the child named for his brother.

Mary's ninth pregnancy was uneventful, and the baby came early. Not in mid-November when she was due, but on November 1, 1898, All Saints Day, commemorating the loss of his brother Robbie, whom Mary believed with all her heart had joined the saints in Heaven. She and John named their ninth child and fifth son Emmett Ambrose Dowling. In later years, he would be known to most as their eighth child and fourth son, but Mary believed Emmett was both their eighth and ninth child, their fourth and fifth son: Robbie reborn through Emmett. Even his middle name honored the past. Ambrose was the maiden name of John's mother, whom he never again saw after he left Ireland.

Emmett would grow up to be, by far, the tallest of the clan, nearly six-one, and the only child blessed with his Grandmother Murphy's blue eyes.

CHAPTER SIX

Along Comes the Modern World 1899-1903

When it came time to hire a wet nurse, Mary demurred. After the loss of Robbie and the gift of Emmett, she couldn't. She was still nursing on her fortieth birthday, and a year later as well, when the twentieth century burst over Lawrenceburg like a Fourth of July rocket. At meetings of the Commercial Club, business leaders discussed constructing a water plant on the Salt River, three miles distant, to pipe water into town. Another popular proposal, endlessly debated, was to raise funds for an electric plant to replace Lawrenceburg's old-fashioned oil lamps, which were a fire hazard. And once electricity arrived, could an ice plant be far behind?

John brought all these plans home to discuss with his blunt and foresightful wife. Mary's opinion? "It will take them years to rise from their duffs and fund anything." Their own plans for the new century were something else again. Typical of John and Mary, their projections weren't just blather. In the decade since they'd become sole owners of Waterfill, Dowling, they'd doubled mashing from 125 to 250 bushels a day, while expanding warehouse capacity from nine to twenty-one thousand barrels. And they weren't stopping there. In January, after the JR Walker Distillery, once owned by JB Walker, TB Ripy, and Judge McBrayer, burned to the ground, they purchased the ten-acre site—a mile from the courthouse on Main Street—then signed contracts to rebuild. They'd already selected a name: John Dowling Distillery, with an initial mashing capacity of one hundred bushels a day. They planned to call their new brand Old Dowling.

As for the children, Will had graduated from college in Lexington and been accepted at the University of Louisville law school. They were enormously proud and praised Will to the stars: the first Dowling with a four-year degree. On a warm June afternoon, Mary stood beside John on the banks of Bailey's Run, a hundred yards from the front stone steps of Waterfill, Dowling. The crick flowed quickly; there'd been storms the last three afternoons. Sunlight sparkled on the rifling surface, amplified by reflection from the limestone banks behind it. Birds chirruped, and in the near distance, cattle lowed, eager for their feast of mash. John grasped her hand, and she recalled how late last night, after his bedside whiskey, John had announced in a wondering whisper, "Our Will's to be a lawyer, Mary! And neither me nor you completed fourth grade!"

She'd replied, "Don't say it loud, or they might take back Will's admission!"

"Ha!"

Now, beside the burbling stream, she said, "You remember Bobbie and Doctor John are coming to Sunday dinner with both grandbabies?"

"Of course." He turned from the sparkle of Bailey's Run, and they started towards the distillery, its limestone walls block-quarried from local stone decades ago. "Ye know, Mary, I'm pretty sure the good doctor doan believe we're genteel enough to be his kin."

"He does think highly of himself. While we're just poor, uneducated Irish, who don't know which fork to use with the fish course."

"Ha! Poor, *rich* Irish."

"That helps, John, don't it? But I forgive him."

"Why?"

"Because of how well he treats our daughter."

"No question. I just wish he wouldn't run on so."

"Don't listen, that's my secret."

"He doan talk much to you."

"I'm a woman, not worth talking to."

"Ha, again!"

They walked on in easy silence to the stone steps leading up and into the distillery. Inside, she could hear men's voices and the bark of laughter.

"That shows he ain't nearly so smart as he thinks," John said.

"Thank you for thinking so."

"Any fool would think the same."

"But you're no fool."

"I'm a fool for ye, Mary Dowling. Always have been."

He started up the steps, calling over his shoulder, "I'll be right back." Then he turned to her. "Why doan ye come in too?" He winked. "Time to show Milo who the real boss is."

Inside the thick stone walls, it was ten, maybe fifteen degrees cooler than outside. When her eyes adjusted to the dim light, she smiled up at John. "Maybe now," she said quietly, "it's time to discuss the yield with Milo."

They'd been talking about this at home. Going back through the careful records she'd kept the past two years, she'd noticed that the yield per ton of grain had slipped, though the mash bill she and John had agreed to when Waterfill and Frazier became fully theirs had remained the same: 70 percent corn, 15 percent each rye and malted barley.

Milo, a burly man with a reddish beard, greeted them when they stepped from the front room onto the main distillery floor. They were not yet mashing for the season—grain wasn't in—but Milo was readying the tanks and piping, as they knew he would be.

"John," cried Milo heartily. And then, looking askance at her—for she was seldom in the distillery, and everyone knew, at least the men all thought, it was no place for a woman—Milo said coldly, "Missus Dowling."

With its rough-cut limestone walls, dirt floor, and open tanks, the large room looked and smelled ancient and mysterious. A dungeon or cellar like the one at Dowling Hall. And the scent, leaching from the stone walls, reminded Mary of her brother-in-law Mike, who carried it with him everywhere.

John said, "Looks like you'll be ready to start mashing when the grain's in."

"Aye," Milo answered, "The work's near done."

John continued, "Mary and I have noticed." He glanced at her, and she nodded, "That the yield's been down a bit the past two years, not much, but enough to matter."

Milo asked, "Are you sure?"

Mary answered, "I keep careful records."

"What is it you're saying? Is this an accusation?"

"Now, Milo," John said, "ye know me better than that. Maybe we change the yeast."

"Or check the weight of the grain more carefully," Mary said. "Perhaps it was delivered short."

"I see," said Milo.

"Through no fault of your own," Mary added.

That hung in the cool and bitter-smelling room. After a moment, Mary said, "John, I'll wait for you outside. Milo, it was a pleasure talking. I'll look forward to this year's yield."

Milo nodded, warily. Mary turned and walked towards the front room, then started down the steps to the out of doors. John called after her, "I won't be long."

Mary smiled into her hand. Once John got talking to Milo, they could go on for quite some time. So be it. She thought the conversation just completed had gone well. No direct accusation made, and none needed; Milo had clearly gotten the message.

Mary walked towards Bailey's Run. The sun shone brightly, filtered by the canopy of oaks and poplars. Birds chorused in the higher limbs. Mary inhaled contentedly. She loved owning a business. Loved the planning and execution, loved the making of money. She considered her many blessings, and how Emmett's birth had cushioned the terrible loss of Robbie. The conversation *had* gone well, despite the anxious undertones. Mary hummed a hymn of praise, harmonizing with the innocent creatures, resigned to wait for her loquacious husband, however long that might be..

On March 27, 1903, barely two months after they'd waltzed at the fancy dress party he'd hosted for her forty-fourth birthday, John suffered a paralyzing stroke. He was sixty-one, had showed no signs of weakness or failing health until he collapsed in their bedroom and couldn't rise, his right side frozen, hand curled in a bird's claw, mouth agape, lips twisted, tongue suddenly too large to speak. Panicked and panicking, though projecting her usual *sangfroid*, she'd sent for Dr. Kavanaugh, and with her sons' help, hoisted John onto their bed. For the nine days since, he'd been unable to walk, barely able to speak.

Emmett, four and a half, blue-eyed and precocious, kept asking when Father would be better, and why he didn't want to play?

The older children kept vigil with her; Will returned from Louisville, where he was completing his last semester of law school. *Good,* she'd thought. *He can put his education to use and re-draft John's will.* Which he had, still leaving everything to Mary but removing Robbie's name and adding Emmett's. Unlike the previous draft, however, John couldn't sign his own name; instead, with Will's hand guiding his own, he slashed a crude X.

She had no illusions, Mary. She did not dissemble nor sugarcoat, which had never been her way or John's. The man she loved remained inside. She could see him through his frightened eyes. But he would not survive this. Nor, she knew, would he care to linger, unable to walk or converse—John who had always been so strong and vital.

She'd known, though she had tried not to dwell, that this day would come. When a fifteen-year-old marries a man thirty-three, she'd have to be a fool or self-deluded, and Mary was neither, not to know that someday she'd wear a young widow's weeds.

She'd hoped it would be much later. She had planned they'd still be waltzing. That John would attend Emmett's confirmation, if not his graduation. Ten days ago, that hadn't seemed too much to hope for. Now, for John's sake, she prayed the end was near.

To give John his due—and she did, *she did!*—he'd insisted, the night he turned sixty, that they talk of this.

"When I pass," he began.

They were sitting up in bed, *Collier's Weekly* in her hands. John sipped his bedtime whiskey.

"Don't be morbid."

"I'm not. I'm sixty. So, when I pass, don't be afraid to run the business as ye think best."

"I won't."

"And don't let any of them tell ye what to do because you're *only* a woman."

"You can count on that."

"That's my Mary Ann. That's the girl I fell in love with." He grinned. "And it's a lucky man I've been all these years."

Her heart melted. He could still con birds out of summer trees. He gulped his whiskey and poured a second. "And if ye wish to remarry."

"Hush, John."

"I need to say this. If ye remarry, that's fine. But the money's for our children, and our children only."

"I said, 'Hush, John.' And I meant it."

He'd nodded and tossed back the second dram.

Sitting beside him now, on the morning of April 6, 1903, the date to be carved on his headstone, holding the cup of black coffee he loved to begin his days with but could no longer manage himself or even sip from her hands without liquid drooling down his chin, she said, "There will be no second marriage for me, John Dowling. I'm a one-man woman and you're that one man. And don't you know it."

Then she was crying, and he was too. *So, you* are *still in there,* she thought, and squeezed John's hand. She willed him to squeeze back. She needed to feel his strength one last time. But he couldn't. His face slackened, and she thought, *Thank God.*

Yet John remained. He moaned, softly.

Mary sent for Dr. Kavanaugh. She sent for the bishop, although John had already been given Extreme Unction. And she sent for their children because she knew the end was near.

PART TWO

Mary Dowling, Sole Proprietor

CHAPTER SEVEN

And the World Falls Apart 1903

In May, a month after John died, Will graduated from the Jefferson School of Law in Louisville. Sometime that winter, John had arranged for Will to join a friend's law firm in Louisville. He'd long boasted of his firstborn son. College graduate. Soon to be a lawyer. Responsible and even-tempered, with a solid character.

Thinking about Will, and about John too, whose image and presence so filled her days and nights she had to push her memories into a wee corner of her mind to do what needed doing, Mary waited for Will to knock on her home office door. She'd been dreading this conversation. *Dreading,* but it could no longer be avoided. Partially to staunch her guilt for what she intended to ask, Mary was indulging a mother's natural fondness. Not only was Will smart and solid, he was exceptionally good-looking.

She couldn't help herself. She'd never been beautiful, but Will and Mary Eileen, who insisted on being addressed as Mary Dowling Bond, as if it were her title, still turned people's heads. Such lovely dark hair, John's high-boned cheeks, and vibrant eyes. So much alike that even now, at twenty-seven and twenty-three, strangers mistook them for twins.

Their resemblance was skin-deep. Will possessed John's easy charm and fine character, while Mary Bond, sharp-tongued and judgmental, did not. She had recently moved back into Dowling Hall. Two weeks ago, on a sun-splashed April afternoon, Mary returned from a day's work at Waterfill—part of her project to know all the employees better but especially to make Milo understand he'd be taking orders from her now—and discovered Mary Bond and all her things in the front hall: hatboxes, trunks, and hanging bags of dresses. Mary Bond was directing the servants charged with carrying her possessions upstairs.

"What's all this?" Mary asked.

"What does it look like?"

"Are you and Jim seeking a divorce?"

"Mother, I'm *Catholic*."

"So, he's moving here with you?"

Mary Bond's dark eyes flashed. "Absolutely not."

"May I ask *why* you're moving home?"

Just then, Gentleman Jim came through the front door, sporting a straw boater and red bowtie.

"Good afternoon, Missus Dowling," he said, touching the brim of his hat. "Lovely afternoon, isn't it?"

"The day your wife moves back into her mother's house is a *lovely* afternoon?"

"I referenced the weather."

Ida, Kinky, and Bill James descended the main stairs for another load of clothing. As they started up again, Mary Bond called after them, "Mind, don't wrinkle my dresses!"

When the servants were out of earshot, Mary inquired, "If you don't mind my asking, Jim, where will you be living?"

"Mother, that's none of your business!"

"I don't mind," Jim replied. "Temporarily, I'll move home to my parents."

He smiled in the gracious way he affected. Or maybe it was real, Mary thought, and Jim was nothing more than his handsome face and fine manners.

"It's just for now." Jim touched Mary Bond's hand. "Isn't it, dear?"

Mary Bond nodded, then she and her husband started up the main stairs headed for her old suite of rooms. Mary could make little sense of her daughter's marriage. For eight years, she'd watched in amazement. Frequent musical soirees at which Jim showed off his tenor and a young woman named Elsa accompanied him on the piano. Elegant dinner parties, no expense spared, but no children, and as far as Mary could tell, few signs of physical affection. Several years ago, Mary had inquired after the frequency of her daughter's marital relations, thinking that might explain the dearth of children, and that with a bit of motherly advice, things might change for Mary Bond and Jim. Instead, her daughter had screamed, "*Mother!*" turned royal purple, and departed.

As it turned out, Mary Dowling Bond and Gentleman Jim would remain married and good friends their entire lives. Although his mother-in-law never saw them kiss and he never spent the night in her daughter's bed, Jim often stopped for dinner and stayed to socialize on the front porch, before returning to his parents' house to sleep. If there were rumors about Jim's dalliances, either with women, or possibly, other men in Lexington, Mary refused to credit them. In her mind, they simply couldn't afford their own establishment, and Mary Bond would later confess—though not to her mother—that if someone's family must pay her expenses, it wouldn't be the Bonds. Dinner was free and ample at Dowling Hall, and Jim excelled at pleasant conversation. As for connubial relations, Mary assumed that either or both of them found it distasteful.

A knock on her office door returned Mary to the here and now. When Will settled in the chair opposite her desk, she began, "I'm afraid I must ask a favor."

Will smiled. He was five-eight, the same height as his father, but clean-shaven.

"No need to be afraid, Mother."

"As you know, your father and I ran our business like a family. And some would say we've run our family like a business."

Will smiled again. "I've heard Mister Ripy say that it's hard to tell where one ends and the other begins."

"Your father would be gone at the distilleries and cooperage. At first, I worked beside him, but as the family grew, I stayed home with our ledgers and the children. Still, we decided everything together." She looked straight at her son. "As you know, Will, not many men appreciate a woman in a distillery, telling them what to do. Even if she's paying the bills and making the decisions."

Will met her eyes then glanced away.

"I'm going to change that." Mary waited for Will to look back at her, then continued, "But I need you to do some things I can't. To be the face of Waterfill, Dowling in the world."

"What about Uncle Mike or Uncle Ed?"

"We're not partners, except in Dowling Brothers. To be frank, Mike's a bit of a fool as a businessman. As for Uncle Ed, you're too young to remember, but it didn't work before. That's why he's in Lexington."

"So, what's the favor, Mother?"

"I need you to move home and not take the law job in Louisville. The family needs you."

She watched strong feeling dash across Will's cheeks and brows before being swallowed by his eyes. After a moment, he asked, "What about my law career?"

"This won't be forever. You can study for the bar with Judge McBrayer. And practice law on the side."

Will didn't speak for quite some time. She needed him, and he'd always been a dutiful son. She waited. Will looked up at her and nodded.

She hadn't told Will everything. She would, but not yet; she didn't want to alarm him. As it turned out, John couldn't have died at a worse time, not that there was a good time for your own true love to pass. Still, 1903 was a brutal year for Mary to find herself on her own. Ever since President McKinley was assassinated and Teddy Roosevelt had taken over, promising to break up the trusts, the country had been moving towards and finally falling into a recession, known as the Rich Man's Panic. The shares of US Steel John had left were down 35 percent. More importantly, banks everywhere, including Lawrenceburg National, started by the McGregors, another of the Five Families, were identifying risky loans and cutting back on credit.

For more than twenty years, John and Mary had done all their banking with the McGregors. Mary didn't know for certain, but she believed they were among the bank's largest depositors. That hadn't stopped the bank from summoning Mary barely two months after John died to inform her that although they were terribly sorry, and meant nothing personal by it, they were cutting off Waterfill, Dowling's line of credit.

"Why is that Mister McGregor?"

She was facing two Mister McGregors, an uncle and a nephew. The younger one, still in his twenties, chose to answer. "I think you know why, Mary."

She was offended he'd dared to use her first name. "I don't, Mister McGregor. Enlighten me."

Nephew turned to uncle, then back to her. "John's name is on these lines of credit. And you've never run a business."

As she'd thought. "Now, Mister McGregor, or should I call you Jimmy, as I did when you played at my house in short pants. You know as well as I or your uncle that my late husband and I ran Waterfill, Dowling together, going on fifteen years."

Jimmy McGregor replied, "Running it together is not the same as running it yourself."

Mary glanced from Jimmy to John McGregor, older than she and something of a dandy. His ostentatious mutton chops extended into a green ascot.

Mary continued, "As you also know, without a line of credit, a distillery can't remain in business."

Neither McGregor replied. Looking from one to the other, Mary could feel her temper rising. Finally, the older McGregor said, "We've also heard you've lost your distributor, which is the other thing a distiller needs."

"Nonsense," Mary said. "Who told you that?"

Jimmy McGregor, who was Will's age, replied, "I don't want to be talking out of school."

"I should hope not." Mary shot him a withering glance. "You're barely out of school."

"I'm not sure what my age has to do with this."

"I'm not sure what being a woman has to do with you calling our loan, but apparently, quite a lot."

"Mary," Jimmy McGregor began, "that's not true."

"Don't lie to my face, Jimmy McGregor. And call me, *Missus Dowling*." She turned towards his uncle. "You should teach your nephew more respect for his elders."

And his betters, Mary thought, but did not say.

The air sizzled. After a moment, John McGregor said, "We heard it *from* your distributor."

"The hell you did."

Mary looked from one McGregor to the other. Then Jimmy smiled and said, "We *did*."

Caught out, Mary seethed but said nothing. They talked of this and that. Rather, the McGregors talked, while Mary plotted her next move. Soon it was time to go, and the elder McGregor, who knew Mary and John's reputation as honest but no-holds barred business owners, tried to smooth things over. Lawrenceburg was a small town, with considerable intermarriage and socializing amongst the upper classes. She barely looked at them. In the conversational lull that followed, young Jimmy, who lacked the sense Christ gave chickens, had the temerity to suggest that if she were ever interested in selling her business, he could help find a buyer.

"I won't be needing a buyer, *Jimmy*."

While stroking his preposterous facial hair with the fingers of his left hand, John McGregor allowed that because she was such a valued customer they'd give her thirty days to make new financial arrangements. And he sincerely hoped she'd maintain her personal accounts at Lawrenceburg National.

"In a pig's eye, John. Good day, gentlemen."

Unfortunately, her bankers' intelligence about her distributor proved accurate. As soon as the tax-paid barrels in their bonded warehouse were sold—likely by September—her current Cincinnati distributor, James Levy & Bro., a Jewish firm, was dropping her. From the time he'd come north, John had been associated with the Queen City. For years, one of their Tyrone warehouses had been designated for another of their brands, Pilgrim Distilling, which maintained offices in Cincinnati. John had worked with many Jews in Cincinnati, admiring their drive and ambition, their entrepreneurial spirt.

That was one of the unfortunate things about Lawrenceburg, John always said: not enough Jews. That wasn't so in Louisville, and certainly not in Cincinnati, where there was a Jewish cathedral. In Louisville, Jewish immigrants Isaac Wolfe Bernheim and his brother Bernard owned and ran I.W. Harper. There were many similarities between the Bernheims and Dowlings. Like John, Isaac Bernheim had arrived first and saved to bring over a younger brother. Like John, he first acquired a distillery in 1872 and married in 1874. Like John, he was the target of anti-immigrant and religious discrimination.

In fact, Bernheim intentionally left his name off the brand that made him wealthy: I.W. Harper. I.W. were his first two initials, but he chose "Harper" because it *didn't* sound Jewish, a common decision by Jews in the late nineteenth and early twentieth centuries. Bourbon had always been marketed as an *American* whiskey, and Jewish distillers in Louisville, Cincinnati, and elsewhere didn't want to lose anti-Semitic customers.

Because they had owned Pilgrim Distilling—since merged into Waterfill, Dowling—John and Mary had remained loyal to James Levy & Bro. But loyalty, Mary was learning, didn't extend beyond her deceased husband. Specifically, it didn't extend to women. "Nothing personal, Missus Dowling. We hope you understand."

Mary understood, all right. It was personal. She lay awake many a night searching for a solution. Emmett had his own troubles sleeping, and once or twice a week, he'd elude the servants and find his way in the dark to her bedside, crying, "I want Daddy." Some nights she'd return him to the third floor, but others, like this one, she'd lay him down beside her, mostly for his sake—not yet five, Emmett cried so hard he shook—but also because she missed John. Such sorrow. First Robbie, then John, and she wasn't sure she could bear it. But she had no choice. The family and businesses depended on her.

Mary sat up in the dark, listening to Emmett's gentle exhalations. John had been gone a little more than four months; she thought she'd feel better by now. Lord alive, she didn't have time to feel this way. She told herself she'd feel better come morning. In the morning, she'd FEEL BETTER. If only she could find a path back into the pale arms of sleep.

Just when she thought things couldn't get worse, on Sunday night, November 22, 1903, fire broke out in the Dotson grocery on College Street. The flames, propelled by strong winds, spread rapidly to the Dowling cooperage. The Lawrenceburg fire department telegraphed to Lexington for aid but cancelled the request when their only fire engine broke down and it was clear the cooperage would be lost. The adjacent Negro Baptist Church also burned to the ground, as did several Black cottages. Mary's loss in the cooperage was $21,000, partially insured. According to newspaper reports, Dotson's was valued at $1,000, the Baptist Church at $1,500. Despite regular discussions at the Commercial Club, there was still no electricity or a water plant in Lawrenceburg, and buildings burned frequently.

Just three months later, on Valentine's Day, 1904, disaster struck again. The Sunday watchman at Waterfill, Dowling in Tyrone sent word that a fire had broken out in the yeast room, and the distillery was in flames. Bucket brigades from Lawrenceburg and Tyrone battled the blaze but soon realized the distillery was too far gone and focused their efforts on saving neighboring buildings, including a warehouse in which twelve thousand barrels were stored. *Thank the Lord,* Mary thought later, trying to mine light from darkness—the warehouse was saved. Twelve thousand barrels would be a loss from which they might never recover, because it would slay the future, as well as the present.

Did someone set the blaze? A disgruntled employee? She didn't believe so. In fact, she prayed no one had, because if so, she'd be consumed by vengeance. She'd never learned to turn the other cheek. It was a failing, she knew, but one she'd never overcome. She'd grown up too poor, too hard, too fast.

As it was, Mary considered herself lucky. The distillery could be rebuilt. All she needed was time and money. *Time and money*. In the days immediately after the second blaze, her many losses felt like barrels strung from her neck. In that darkness, when she didn't know what to do first or last, or if she'd ever sleep through the night again, she found comfort in the soft music of Emmett's breathing, and in remembering how John had said, "I'm a fool for you, Mary Dowling."

She'd respond, *That was some Valentine's Day gift you gave me, John,* and imagine his laughter. Things could be worse, she told herself one sleepless night. I could be one of the twenty men burned out of a job at Waterfill, Dowling. Or a member of the church that included several of her servants, left with no place to worship, but still not welcomed by the white Baptists in Lawrenceburg. *For shame! Blessed Mother,* she prayed, *help me to help them as I help myself.* And in that darkest night, she promised to contribute to the church fund, if ever she solved her own problems.

Mary took comfort in the example of the Blessed Mother, which helped her to accept her own sorrows. And in the story of Job, that proud, obstinate man who'd lost everything, yet somehow climbed back into God's pure light.

CHAPTER EIGHT

Out of the Ashes, Hope Glimmers 1904

When she asked her neighbors to recommend a distributor, the Bonds and Ripys were surprisingly circumspect. If Mary were feeling charitable, which she wasn't—she was feeling murderous—she might have told herself they feared to offer bad advice. They knew how much she'd lost and what she yet faced. Robbie's death. John's death. Rebuilding the cooperage. Rebuilding Waterfill. She also believed—although she wouldn't breathe her suspicions to anyone, not even Will—that in a town as small and inbred as theirs, her neighbors knew Lawrenceburg National had cut her off.

Were they surreptitiously kicking her while she was down? Had the other inhabitants of Cream Street long envied the upstart Irish their enormous success, and with John gone, were they exacting their revenge? Was it possible the other distillers, all men, wished her gone? Damn right it was. This much she knew. If she insisted on continuing, the other distillers would simply ignore her, at least until she showed she could make it on her own.

The only neighbor to come to her aid was Will Saffell, known as WB, husband of Mary's friend Frankie. The Saffells had raised six daughters. Their only boy died an infant. Maybe that's how Frankie convinced WB to help; both families knew what it was like to lose a son. Or maybe WB, who'd earned his fortune instead of inheriting it, wasn't jealous of the Dowlings' success. Maybe he didn't care who was Protestant and who Catholic, or realized his Irish workers were neither lazy nor drunks.

For many years, WB had worked as superintendent for Judge McBrayer at the Cedar Brook Distillery. Not until 1889, three years after she and John had built Dowling Hall, did he open his own distillery, WB Saffell, near the southern rail stop in Alton. WB didn't become wealthy until the mid-1890s, which is when the Saffells moved into their own Cream Street mansion: two doors down and across from Dowling Hall, on the "better" side of the street. Many an afternoon after Frankie and WB had moved in with their bounty of girls, Mary would cross Main to visit with Frankie, who was small and sharp as a whip, but had nothing to do with the Saffell distillery.

"I don't know how you do it," Frankie would say. "Or why?"

That was before John died and left her to carry on alone. How could she explain, without insulting Frankie, that she'd been working since she was six years old, and she *liked* it?

WB, who was also vice president and a director of the other bank in town, sent word two days after the Waterfill, Dowling fire. "I hear you need a distributor. Try Grommes and Ulrich in Chicago. They have a reputation for quality. And tell them I sent you." His advice was a gift from heaven.

Mary considered going herself to Chicago, or accompanying Will, before deciding Will should go alone as her agent. The Grommes brothers were German immigrants, incredibly astute, but Old

World businessmen who wouldn't want to discuss terms with a woman. Better to send her very presentable lawyer son. She knew he'd be nervous; he'd never been to Chicago, or run a meeting on his own, but better for Will to travel alone to get his feet beneath him, and to know she trusted him.

All she had to do was prep Will, which she did: three grueling days of study, quizzing, and rehearsing. Capacity and pricing. Mash bill. Yeast. The cost of bottles and caps. The price advantage conferred by making her own barrels. Acceptable credit terms. The age and quantity of whiskey held in bond. How she planned to maintain reserves using production from John Dowling and Dowling Brothers until she rebuilt Waterfill. Three days to learn the entire business. Mary hoped he'd gleaned some things along the way and would prove himself to be his father's and his mother's son.

After she put Will on the train in Versailles with samples of her best bourbon, a line of credit for his Chicago expenses, and instructions to buy himself a fine dinner on the train and in Chicago, Mary returned home and ate with Ida, who was not quite sixteen, and Emmett, who'd turn five in November. Emmett chattered away, but Ida was painfully shy and thin and had not yet developed any bosom to speak of; Mary wondered if the phenomena were connected. Her mind percolated with worry, and the evening was close and warm. Then Ida went out to visit with Margaret Lillard, her one close friend, and Emmett was sent upstairs with his tutor. He was advanced for his age, already reading. She'd go up at eight to kiss him goodnight and hoped she wouldn't see him again at midnight, but of that she wasn't quite sanguine.

Mary retired to her office to pore over account books. If all went well, she'd need six, perhaps nine, months to rebuild Waterfill, Dowling. Assuming twelve to be safe, she decided, meant completion next August or September, still in time to begin mashing next year's grain. Until then, she'd have to cover expenses, both household and business. There was ample whiskey in her warehouses, but no one to market it, nor a line of credit. The funds in Lawrenceburg National would last six months, and she could sell John's US Steel shares and their investments in Kentucky oil fields purchased with Ed Dowling, though she'd hate to liquidate either; everything had lost so much value this year. As a last resort, she could attempt to sell her third of Dowling Bros in Burgin, but she doubted Ed or Mike had enough ready cash to pay a fair price.

Mary rang for Erna and asked for a pot of tea. She foresaw a long, anxious night as she navigated this thicket of worry. She hoped Emmett would sleep the night through, though she'd be lying to herself not to admit she'd miss his presence in her lonely room.

Godspeed, Will. Let me hear from you soon.

She heard nothing from Will the next day or the day after, when he should have met with Grommes and Ulrich. She'd asked him to send word before starting home, but perhaps he'd forgotten. Or didn't know how. Or the news was vexing, and he'd decided to deliver disappointment face-to-face.

That afternoon, she met with her insurance broker Mr. Pars and confirmed what she'd long known. Few distillers were as wise or prudent as her John. Waterfill, Dowling was 60 percent insured, and she'd be able to use the settlement to rebuild and perhaps to tide her over until she secured a new line of credit. *To hell with those back-stabbing McGregors,* she thought. *To hell with them and back.* Now, if Will somehow reached terms with Grommes and Ulrich, all might not be lost.

She sent Bill James with her carriage and team to meet Will's train, scheduled to arrive at Versailles at half-seven. Just past eight, she heard the carriage approach the side porch; then footsteps that could only be Will's entered through the carriage door. She closed her black ledger and straightened her desk. She didn't want to appear anxious by rushing into the hall in case the meeting had ended badly. Nor would it do to appear indifferent. This was, after all, Will's first business responsibility.

"Mother!" he called. "I'm home."

She swept out of her office and following Will's voice, found him in the kitchen, hunting a bite to eat.

"Why didn't you send word?" she demanded. "As I instructed?"

"The meeting finished late," he replied, a buttered biscuit near his lips. "I scarcely had time to catch my train."

"And?"

"I believe it went well." He aimed his shoulder at her and smiled a boyish version of his father's smile. "You'll have to check the terms, I'm really not sure."

"Did they treat you with respect?"

"They did, Mother."

"And your presentation? As we practiced?"

"Every word, Mother." Will grinned and reached for a second biscuit. "*Famished*. But I think it went well."

In later years, when he'd tell the story, Will would always begin, "Never was a country boy so green as I, going up to the big city. Maybe Mister Grommes took pity on me, having just lost my father. Or maybe it was his third dram of our eight-year reserve."

Then Mary would break in. "Will doesn't give himself enough credit. Next morning when Will and I took the paper over for Mister Saffell to read, he was astonished. 'Why, Will,' he declared. 'This is the best contract ever signed by an Anderson County distiller. Well done, lad. Well done, indeed!'"

Grommes and Ulrich would distribute Dowling whiskey until Prohibition's curtain descended.

CHAPTER NINE

Mary on the March 1904

In April 1904, Mary met with the board of the State Bank of Anderson County: C.E. Bond, President; WB Saffell, Vice-President; J.W. Rice, T.J. Ballard, and A.B. McAfee, Directors. She knew them socially. She'd been to their houses, and she and John had entertained them frequently, but this was the first time she'd met with these men in their official capacity, and she in hers: Mary Dowling, sole proprietor. Her friend and neighbor, WB Saffell, had arranged the meeting; nevertheless, she mistrusted the board. Stepping down from her carriage, then waiting for the uniformed guard to open the bank's heavy glass door, she reminded herself she was the one with available funds, which the bank needed, and there were plenty other banks in Anderson County, although no other in Lawrenceburg save the one she endeavored to leave.

The board awaited her in the conference room. A seat had been left vacant at the foot of the long table, directly opposite Charles

Bond, current bank president. His father, Will Bond, former president, now deceased, had been a friend of John's. Charles was cousin to her daughter's idle husband, Gentleman Jim Bond, and Mary allowed herself, just for a second, to wonder what might have been if her daughter had married a more ambitious member of the family.

Charles was a few years younger than Mary, but his hair was already white. "Missus Dowling," he began. "Thank you for coming in to see us."

She nodded.

"I believe WB has explained our intention to reorganize under a national charter."

She smiled at her neighbor. "He has."

"And he's told us of your interest not only in moving your business and personal accounts, but in purchasing a significant number of the new shares we'll be issuing as part of applying for our new charter."

She wondered why Charles, whom she'd never regarded as the cleverest of men, was rehashing information he must know she was aware of.

"Yes, Mister Bond," she replied. "All of that is so."

"I wanted to make sure." Charles Bond moistened his lips from a cut-glass water goblet. "You understand we will not be able to offer a seat on the bank's board."

Ah, she thought. "We hadn't discussed that."

"We assumed"—Charles sipped again—"you'd be too busy with your own affairs to desire a seat, but since you're purchasing a substantial number of shares…"

Mary interrupted, "You thought I might *expect* a seat?"

Charles Bond met her gaze across the long table, then glanced away. Mary felt a rush of rage. Her whole life she'd fought her temper, struggling not to blow up and tell these men exactly what she thought of them. But she was also damn sick and tired of being patronized by these pale Protestant bankers. She could almost feel their hands on hers, gently patting. *Now, Mary, don't worry your pretty little head.*

Well, her head wasn't little or pretty, never had been, and she was the sole proprietor of two distilleries and partner in a third.

"Mister Bond," she began. "I *will* be busy, both overseeing the rebuilding of Waterfill, Dowling, and at the same time, ramping up production at John Dowling." She glanced from one bearded banker to the next, their necks rising out of identical collars. "But I am hardly naïve. While we all *know* my shares merit a board seat, I see no other women at this table. Until there are"—she glanced around, daring anyone to hold her gaze—"the board may vote my shares as it sees fit, so long as my line of credit is set a quarter point below standard. I assume that will be acceptable compensation for being denied a board seat?"

Charles Bond and the others looked surprised. It hadn't occurred to them that the widow would know she had room to maneuver and demand more favorable terms. But they needed her money so had little choice. When Charles and then the others nodded, Mary allowed herself a small, satisfied smile.

To purchase the bank shares that secured her line of credit, Mary sold John's US Steel shares and most of their holdings in Kentucky oil fields, which they'd purchased through Ed. If her brother-in-law questioned her decision, he did not do so to her face. After many a long session with her ledgers, she saw no other solution. She retained enough cash to see her through the end of the year, *if* the rebuild of Waterfill, Dowling went as planned. If not, she'd be forced to sell the remaining oil shares, and who knew what else.

Mary admitted her concerns to no one, not even Will, who'd turned twenty-five in July, the same month he was admitted to the Kentucky bar. After his triumph with the Grommes and Ulrich contract, she had taken over business arrangements with their distributor. Mary was looking forward to the first on-site visit with their representative, Heinrich Heinsohn, who would come to town in September. Will had moved into day-to-day management of the John Dowling Distillery, while her third son, Johnnie, saved in infancy by Ida, had grown into a practical young man of twenty. He was overseeing the rebuild of Waterfill, Dowling, which was ahead of schedule. Her second oldest, George, eighteen months younger than Will, had no head for business and couldn't be trusted to oversee anything, not even his own wallet. Give George a dollar, or even five or ten, on Monday morning, and the money would be gone before Tuesday dawned. After starting but failing to complete university studies at Notre Dame, George was living and working in Cincinnati.

It had given Mary considerable satisfaction to think about withdrawing all her funds from the McGregors' bank. She arrived at eleven a.m. on a Monday, when she believed both men would be in the building, and stood in the line of teller Matthew Still, with whom she'd been working for years. When it was her turn, she announced loudly, so that other customers could hear clearly, "I'd like to close all my accounts. Please provide a certified check for each, payable to the Anderson Bank."

"*All* your accounts?"

She nodded.

"I'll need to have them counter-signed by Mister McGregor."

"If you please."

Her teller hurried towards John McGregor's office and disappeared inside. Moments later, John McGregor of the ludicrous muttonchops emerged. Without addressing her, he followed Matthew Still behind the cashier window. They spent some time preparing her checks, five in all, one for each account, which McGregor signed. When he stepped forward to present them to her, she said, "Thank you, John. It's been a *pleasure* doing business with you. Especially today."

He nodded.

"Please tell young Jimmy I won't be needing his help finding a buyer, or for that matter, with anything. Somehow…" She stopped and told herself to hush, but that had never been her style. "I managed to muddle on myself."

Mary left with her checks and never entered the McGregors' bank again.

On the evening of September 11, Heinrich Heinsohn of Grommes and Ulrich checked into the Commercial Hotel in Lawrenceburg. He intended to stay for ten days, familiarizing himself with Mary's businesses. Fifty-six years old, a German Catholic widower with grown sons, he was tall and thin, with sober gray eyes.

In the morning, Mary sent her horse and carriage to pick him up. After Mister Heinsohn declined her offer of breakfast—he'd already eaten, hours ago, he said—they set out for Waterfill, Dowling, proceeding north on Main, past the courthouse and the Commercial Hotel before turning east on Woodford. It was a fine morning, not as oppressively humid as the past few, perhaps a hint that the worst of the summer's heat might be ending.

Mary hadn't ridden in the back of this carriage with any man except John and her sons. Or for that matter, with anyone not named Dowling except her married daughters. Unfortunately, she was finding Mister Heinsohn difficult to converse with. Perhaps it was his accent. Or maybe, she admitted to herself, he was the first person, other than John, with whom she planned to discuss the real state of her businesses. She didn't consider what had transpired with her bankers, either the hateful McGregors or even the Bonds, to be conversations. More nearly boxing matches.

She turned to Heinrich Heinsohn, "If I'd known you were such an early riser, we would have picked you up much earlier."

"*Vell*, I'm here ten days." He smiled. "We *haf* much time to adjust our schedule."

Before John died, she'd visited Waterfill, Dowling at most once or twice a month. Since the fire and just-completed reconstruction—

Johnnie brought it in two weeks early and $400 under budget—she'd been several times a week. She now looked forward to the carriage ride, especially the last leg once they'd left the main road and started down through the trees. The ride not only helped clear her mind, but for some reason, in the woods around the distillery, she most felt John's spirit. As if this was where he'd chosen to abide.

They rode in silence except for the clicking and whispering of Bill James to the team, the click-clatter of the wooden wheels, and the horses' hooves on the stony track. When they stopped, one hundred feet or so above Bailey's Run, and about the same distance from Waterfill, Dowling, Mister Heinsohn said, stepping down from the carriage, "It must be a pleasure to come to *vork* each day. Like a cathedral, it is."

That showed good sense, she thought.

The creek rifled below them, while in a nearby tree, a cardinal trilled: two long, then a series of short whistles. She was grateful Mister Heinsohn hadn't said much on the ride down; he was appreciating his surroundings. Without the lowing of hungry cattle—a thousand steers would be moved into the pens downstream of the distillery once there was spent mash to feed them—it was so peaceful here. And the air certainly smelled much fresher than it would in a few weeks' time.

She led Mister Heinsohn into the distillery. Everything looked perfect. New three-eighth-inch gravel floors. Pushed out walls allowing for two additional tanks. New piping from Bailey's Run. New doubler and tower ordered from and installed by Hoffman, Ahlers. And a larger office with space for two desks, one for Mary and one for her new distiller, Sean Malloy, hired away from Cedar Brook after she let Milo go.

On the distillery floor, four mash hands were paddling fresh grain into the tanks. Mary led Heinrich Heinsohn to the new office and introduced him to Sean Malloy, who was making notes in a ledger. He was ginger-haired and had brought a new strain of yeast with him from Cedar Brook.

"Sean Malloy," Mary said. "Say hello to Heinrich Heinsohn of Grommes and Ulrich. They're our new distributors, just as you are my new distiller."

The men shook hands, Sean Malloy not yet forty, Heinrich Heinsohn gray and closer to sixty than fifty. *It's a new day and a new team*, Mary thought, tapping a mental foot as the men made small talk; she was anxious to get on with the tour. After a few minutes, she said, "Mister Heinsohn, I'd like to show you the warehouse now."

"Do you want me to come with, Missus Dowling?"

"No need, Sean," Mary answered. "I'm sure there's much to occupy you here."

The men shook hands a second time, then Mary led Heinsohn out of the new distillery and into the vast warehouse that the merciful Mother of God had spared during last summer's fire. Once they were safely inside, and alone with her twelve thousand barrels of aging bourbon, Mister Heinsohn asked, with a knowing gleam in his eye, "What happened to your old distiller, Missus Dowling? Milo Barnes, if I'm not mistaken?"

She considered her response, then decided to plunge ahead. This would either work with Heinsohn or not. "He was my *husband's* distiller, Mister Heinsohn, not mine. He made fine whiskey, but he was loyal to John Dowling, not to me." Their eyes met. "I couldn't have that, you know."

"As I thought." Heinsohn smiled, just slightly, lips pressed together, so the smile was mostly in his eyes, and she would have missed it if she hadn't been looking right at him. "You're in charge now, so you *vant* men loyal to you."

"You understand me."

"I believe I do." He reached into the inside pocket of his suit coat for the small notebook she would never see him without in all the years they'd work together. "And please," he said, "call me Heinrich, if you don't mind. I *vould* be happy for you to do so."

She nodded, but did not ask him to call her Mary, though in the months to follow she would. "And now," she said, "let me show you the barrels. For we have much to do."

Mary hosted a formal Sunday dinner to celebrate Johnnie's impressive achievement and to introduce her family and friends to Heinrich Heinsohn. She invited the Saffells, the Ripys, and all her grown children. Bobbie and her husband, Dr. John, arrived with her grandchildren, Dowling, seven, and Mary Hall, four.

The little ones stayed around long enough to be admired by their aunts and uncles, then were fed in the kitchen with Emmett, not yet six and younger than his nephew Dowling. After eating, they were dispatched to the playroom under the care of Emmett's tutor, while Mary, her neighbors, and her family celebrated the successful reconstruction of Waterfill, Dowling with champagne donated by Grommes and Ulrich.

With Will on her right and Johnnie to her left, Mary raised her flute towards Heinrich, who sat in the center of the long table between her daughters, Mary Bond and Katherine. In response, Heinrich raised his own flute and, turning towards her, then glancing around the table, began in a loud voice, "To the success of the Dowling family endeavors. And to the partnership between Dowling *vhiskies* and Grommes and Ulrich." He turned towards her and smiled. "I predict great things and a long, profitable future."

"Hear, hear!" cried the men. "Hear, hear!"

Mary sipped her champagne, which she did not much care for.

"Thank you, Mister Heinsohn."

She sipped again. The bubbles tickled her nose, and she did her best not to sneeze. Then, to demonstrate her mastery, she sipped again.

CHAPTER TEN

Success and More Success 1905-1910

Mary's distilleries increased mashing capacity and production every year, and Grommes and Ulrich proved adept at marketing her bourbon. Mary convinced her brothers-in-law, Ed and Mike, to transfer Dowling Brothers' distribution to Grommes, and revenue shot up in Burgin as well. Heinrich visited Lawrenceburg twice a year to audit her warehouses and to plan marketing campaigns. Mary valued his advice and sought his opinion on trends in the spirits business. After five years, she regarded Heinrich as a friend and looked forward to his visits. And why not—her businesses were booming.

In November 1905, the Pierian Club replaced the Magazine Club as the Lawrenceburg Woman's Club. Mary Bond was a charter member, while Mary, entirely focused on business, didn't join until a year later. Unlike the Magazine Club, the Pierian Club not only had affiliated chapters in other cities, but its charter outlined a strong civic mission. In 1906, the Pierians established Lawrenceburg's first public library in rooms above the Lawrenceburg National Bank. Two years later, the club received grants from Andrew Carnegie: $5,000 to build a library building and $800 to furnish it. In later years, when she served as Pierian president, Mary would play a significant role in the developing civic life of Lawrenceburg.

In November 1907, Mary's third daughter, Katherine, already twenty-four, wed Henry O'Brien in Dowling Hall. Henry hailed from Westchester County, New York, and had met Katherine through family friends in Lawrenceburg. His grandfather, originally from South Carolina, fought in the first battle of the Civil War: the attack on Fort Sumter. A special train car brought Henry's family, including Lewis O'Brien, his best man, and several of his friends directly to Lawrenceburg for the wedding.

Mary liked her new son-in-law. To her surprise, Mary Bond, who rarely liked anyone, approved of his deep Southern roots. Henry was sharp-witted and seemed very much in love with Katherine, who was overjoyed to be his bride. Mary shared Katherine's happiness, although the marriage meant Katherine would be moving to New York where Henry had business interests. Watching Will walk his younger sister down the aisle in the front parlor, Mary's mind rushed back to her own simple wedding and how little she'd seen of her parents in the years that followed.

Katherine swore that wouldn't happen. "Don't you worry, Mother," she'd promised before leaving on her honeymoon trip to Niagara Falls, Boston, and Maine, before settling in Tarrytown, New York, near her husband's family. "I won't be a stranger."

"Sure, you will," Mary Bond interjected. "How often do you think you'll visit? Once a year, twice at most?" Mary Bond smiled in the cruel way she had. "Enjoy your honeymoon, Katherine. It's the best part of a marriage. And we'll see you next year."

Mary shot back, "Just because your own marriage is ridiculous, don't be cruel to your sister."

Mary Bond colored and stomped up the main staircase.

Katherine repeated, "I won't be a stranger. I promise."

Mary believed her. After all, trains were so much faster and frequent. And Katherine wouldn't be employed. Henry was a real estate broker and politician, able to support Katherine in the style to which the Dowling children had grown accustomed, including paying for Katherine's trips to Lawrenceburg. If not, Mary would be happy to subsidize her trips home. Her distilleries, rolling mill, and rebuilt cooperage earned considerably more than when John was alive. She'd been able to cut costs—her particular expertise—while producing and selling more, which was Heinrich's contribution to the Dowling empire.

Throughout this period of expansion, although Mary maintained that nothing was more important to her than her children, she'd sometimes travel for business on one of their birthdays. And there was the unfortunate occasion, which neither Will nor Mary Bond tired of teasing her about, when the entire family had gathered at Dowling Hall to commemorate the anniversary of John's death, and she neglected to come home until two hours after the party began.

Still, if her family were a business, then her children and grandchildren were its most valuable assets. She'd had little choice regarding Katherine's decision to marry and move out of state; Katherine was twenty-four and eager to escape Mary Bond and Bobbie's considerable shadows. But Mary endeavored to keep her other children close. Maybe this was because she'd married John so young and lost her first family. Or maybe it was because she'd lost John too soon. Maybe it was both. Materially, she was blessed, but in her heart of hearts, the children were all she had, and she'd fight to hold onto them.

The year 1909 brought two wonderful additions to the Dowling family. Katherine gave birth to a little girl she and Henry named Helen Staunton O'Brien, with the middle name honoring Henry's maternal grandparents. Mary was disappointed that neither Helen's first nor middle name referenced the Dowlings, but that didn't stop her from opening a substantial savings account in her granddaughter's name and traveling east for her christening. On the same trip, Mary visited Manhattan for the first time and took a boat tour of New York Harbor to see Lady Liberty close up. She also sat for a formal portrait in the Fifth Avenue photographic studio of Theodore Marceau, whom Henry and Katherine assured her was the preferred photographer of New York society. Mary didn't know anything about New York society, but she knew one important thing about the photograph. Marceau had captured her with a no-nonsense look in her eye. Not exactly a glare, but certainly not a smile. A look, Mary thought, pleased with the image, that declared, *Don't mess with me.*

Mary's fourth grandchild, Margaret Morrow Stewart, was also born in 1909. Maggie, as Bobbie and Dr. John's third child came to be known, was exceptionally pretty. Now that her businesses were flourishing and didn't require constant attention, Mary spent more time at Sunnyside, the house Bobbie and Dr. John had completed in 1905 on the grounds of the Stewart Home School. The Stewarts' estate was renowned for its beauty: five hundred rolling bluegrass acres, with a small lake adjacent to Sunnyside, which itself was constructed just below the historic administration building. It was seven miles, give or take, from Dowling Hall to the Stewart Home School, and on sunny Saturdays or any day during the summer, Mary would bundle Emmett into the carriage with her so he could play with his nephew, known to one and all as Dowling.

Through the end of 1908, they'd either spend the night or start out early in the morning to allow time for the visit and return carriage ride. But in April 1909, Mary purchased a 1908 Packard Model 30 touring car with side curtains and hired her first chauffeur, Pat Tierney, a young Irishman from Belfast, who'd somehow learned to drive a motorcar. The Packard cost $4,000, and while she could have chosen a less costly vehicle, the Model 30 was large and impressive.

Although she never allowed Pat to challenge the top speed of sixty-five miles per hour, they could easily drive from Dowling Hall to Sunnyside in fifteen minutes. What fun! Just have Erna pack a lunch, ring for Pat, and away they'd go in her Packard.

One afternoon in late September, after she'd returned from visiting Katherine, Mary was having herself driven to Stewart Home on a perfect Indian summer day. Suddenly, the sky darkened, and one of the summer downpours for which Kentucky was notorious began to pelt the Packard. Pat pulled over, put up the side curtains, getting drenched in the process, and resumed the drive.

With Emmett beside her, and rain sluicing down the front glass, Mary was overcome by a feeling of longing for John, sudden as the storm, though it had been more than six years since he passed. She remembered approaching Tyrone and the Kentucky River for the first time with him, a newlywed, a mere girl, soaked to the skin, her homespun dress plastered to her arms, not knowing what the future might bring.

Oh, John, she thought. *Oh, John! I still can't believe you're gone. I wish you were here to share this, I do! A horseless carriage in the rain!*

CHAPTER ELEVEN

Civic Leaders 1906-1913

Mary loved her children equally; at least she believed she ought to. But it was difficult not to feel a surge of pride when she considered Will. Not only had he helped save the family business by successfully negotiating with Grommes and Ulrich, but he'd also worked full time at John Dowling Distillery until everything was humming along, only then transitioning into his first love: law and politics. In 1906, he was appointed police judge for Lawrenceburg. Ever since—he turned twenty-seven in 1906—his official title was: Honorable William E. Dowling.

A year later, Will was elected to the Kentucky House of Representatives. Not long afterwards, in January 1908, Mary clipped a short article from the *Lexington Herald-Leader*, which read, in part, "...two young orators in the House are causing the feminine world to sit up and take notice. We refer to the Hon. William Dowling...and to the Hon. Henry Schobert, of Versailles. Both are young, fluent speakers, and just good enough looking to escape the banality of being called handsome."

Will's brothers teased him about the article, but he was a good speaker, and he was handsome. Mary, who'd always felt insecure about her own looks, took inordinate pride, she knew, in her children's appearances. What was there to be so proud about? Mary Bond's beauty had brought little of value—just Gentleman Jim—while Will seemed oblivious to his appearance and claimed to be too busy even to consider marriage. With the Kentucky State Capitol just twelve miles from Dowling Hall, Will regularly attended society parties in Lawrenceburg and in Frankfort, but he hadn't found a special someone yet. Or maybe he was too engaged and ambitious; after two years in the Kentucky House, Will was elected to the Kentucky Senate in 1909 and again in 1911. After spending his first term learning how the Senate functioned, Will had been appointed to the Building and Monuments Committee in January 1912 and introduced his first bill. One evening over supper, Will said that if they wanted, Mary and other family members could attend the debate and final vote in the General Assembly scheduled for the end of the month, though they might not find it interesting.

"Of course, I'll attend." Mary smiled at Will over her meatloaf. "Nothing could keep me away."

On February 1, 1912, with Mary, Ida, George, Bobbie Stewart, and Mary Bond watching from the gallery, Will's bill was debated and passed. It was all so thrilling! Mary had never felt so pleased with any of her children, except maybe when Bobbie gave birth to her third child. Afterwards, his pale face flushed with excitement, Will took her aside and whispered, "You know, Mother, it really wasn't a very important bill."

"It's important to me." Mary hugged her son, adding softly, "Your father would be so proud."

Will strode off to join his fellow legislators on the floor of the General Assembly, while Mary and her other children watched the beginning of the next debate. Finding it boring, they excused themselves and left.

Two days later, Mary learned Pat from Belfast, who'd been her driver since she bought the Packard, had been thieving from her. A little here, a little there, but it added up. He inflated the cost of gasoline and motor oil. He didn't return change when he picked up orders at the butcher and greengrocer, and it turned out he'd been charging his own food and supplies to Mary's accounts around town. After confirming the accusations brought by her two older and trusted servants, Mary asked Pat to stop by her office on Friday morning.

"Good morning, Missus Dowling," he said, removing his cap upon entering.

"Good morning, Pat. Close the door and sit down."

Pat did as he was told and sat in the green leather chair in front of her desk, a nervous smile playing on his lips.

"It grieves me to say this, Pat, but I'm letting you go." She pushed an envelope across the desk. "Here's your final wages."

"Why?"

"I think you know why."

"I swear on my mother's grave, I don't."

"Don't add lying to stealing in the assay of your sins, and don't swear on your mother's name. For shame, Patty."

"Who says I've been stealing?"

"That's not the point now, is it? And I bet you wouldn't have the stones to steal from a man."

He glared at her. What could he say, *I would!*

"I've been dealing with men like you my entire life. Bigger thieves, and bigger liars. I won't have it."

"Wait a minute."

"No, you wait. I checked myself with the filling station and the butcher. I know what you've been doing. You ought to be ashamed."

"What about you?" he cried. "Paying the staff so little when you've got so much! I swear, you're like the English lairds during the

Famine, my grandda told me about. Starving the poor to feed your own greedy gut."

She leapt to her feet. "Get off my property, Patty Tierney, before I press charges with the sheriff, you thieving bastard!"

He looked at her with such hatred, she thought he meant to circle her desk and hit her. "Come on then," she said. "I'm not afraid of you."

He didn't move.

"Get out," she said.

And he did.

On February 22, Mary's youngest daughter, Ida, already twenty-four, was set to accompany Will to a black-tie affair hosted by Kentucky Governor McCreary in Frankfort. The dinner-dance at the governor's mansion not only celebrated the birthday of founding father George Washington, it honored legislative accomplishments of the winter session. Mary was waiting in the front hall when her children descended the main stairs, dressed to the nines. Will looked as handsome as ever in his tuxedo. Ida wore a long, lime-green dress, with a brocaded and beaded top that ill-suited her complexion. She owned a closetful of gowns, but none of them made her look as attractive on the outside as Mary knew her to be inside. While she had lovely Dowling hair, dark with auburn highlights, Ida was so slender she appeared frail, with nary a womanly curve. She often looked faded, as she did tonight, as if the bloom was off the flower of her youth, although Ida had never bloomed. Mary didn't know why. Her first two girls were vivacious and popular, Katherine less so, but still she had suitors. Now here came Ida, last and least, with her hand on Will's arm, like a rose that had failed to open.

"Don't you look beautiful," Mary said, when Ida stood beside her in the hall.

"Thank you, Mother," Ida replied softly, not meeting her mother's eyes.

"You too, Will," Mary added.

Her self-assured son nodded. "Ida," he said. "Mother's right. That dress is most becoming."

Ida said, softly, "I'm not sure the color is right."

Mary wondered, *Then why are you wearing it?* But knowing how insecure her daughter was, she said, "Nonsense. It suits you."

Will headed towards the side carriage door to see if the new driver, John Cody Cunningham, a short, dark-complected Black man, had brought the Packard around. Bill James, the yardman, and Ida Leyter, although she no longer worked for Mary, had recommended him. They knew him from church. "A godly man," Ida had said. "A deacon."

"Remember to smile," Mary said to Ida. "You have such a beautiful smile."

"I do smile, Mother."

"Not enough, if you ask me."

Ida looked down.

"And talk to them when you're dancing."

"I'm not often dancing, except with Will. And when I am, I can't think of a thing to say."

"Just ask them about themselves." Mary smiled. "Men love that."

"Yes, Mother." Ida cocked her head like a small bird. "Why didn't I think of that?"

"You probably did, you're just too shy. Trust me, men like to be flattered."

"I don't hear you doing it, Mother."

That brought Mary up short, and she smiled. "Well, maybe I used to. I'm a battle-scarred old woman now." She touched Ida's smooth cheek. "Do what I say, not what I do. And remember to have fun."

Ida nodded, then she was out the door, following Will's voice, who'd announced the car was ready.

Mary watched the Packard proceed up the driveway, then retired to her study. For years, although she tried never to say so directly to Ida, she'd feared her youngest would never find a husband. She was just so shy and retiring, as if the pilot light of her life force was set too low. She'd shared this concern many times with Bobbie, who was too busy with young children to help, and with Will, which is why he so often brought Ida to state functions.

Still, Mary worried. When Ida was young, Mary was too busy running the business on her own to pay her youngest much attention. Whatever energy she had for childrearing after John died flowed to Emmett. And so, it had come to this. At twenty-four, Ida was not only unmarried but without prospects. Mary calculated. At Ida's age, she already had five children.

Later, Mary sat at her desk, account books open. She ran half a dozen successful businesses but still felt responsible for planning her children's lives, even though Emmett, now thirteen, was the only Dowling still in school. He was her favorite, tall for his age, with her own mother's blue eyes. Mary had decided that, as the last of the Dowlings, without a phalanx of brothers and sisters around him, it would benefit Emmett to attend an Eastern preparatory school. She'd been told years ago by her son-in-law Henry O'Brien that Phillips Exeter was the best, and she'd always aimed high for Emmett. She hadn't told him yet, but she dreamed he would graduate from Harvard then take over the family business.

Mary sipped mint tea from her Havilland rose cup and saucer. When John was alive, she often joined him for an evening whiskey. He never missed a night, and sometimes the first begat a second or third, as it had the night they conceived Emmett.

Most nights, John drank Waterfill and Frazier, neat, but he sometimes tippled their competitors' just to see what they were up against. Research, he'd called it, winking. But with John gone nine years come April, she indulged much less frequently at home, mostly sampling barrels at her distilleries to decide which to preserve for extra aging. There was something about drinking alone—maybe she'd heard her mother rail against it—that rankled. She supposed she could share a glass with one of her grown children after dinner or bridge. Mary Bond was home most evenings, as were Johnnie, Ida, and, less frequently, Will. But she'd never befriended her children, not so she'd want to drink with them.

And so, Mary had grown accustomed to tea, which the night girl brewed and delivered to the parlor. Most nights mint, but sometimes chamomile, purchased at the apothecary at the corner of Main and Woodford. *You're fifty-three,* Mary thought and smiled, a *tea-drinking widow.* With enough money in the bank to last her lifetime and the children's if they needed it, and it seemed some of the girls would. Mary Bond was thirty-six and showed no signs of divorcing Jim, who still stopped frequently for dinner, although that seemed to be his only connubial duty. What a waste. She wondered sometimes if they'd ever had relations, even when they lived together. Her daughter was strange, beautiful, and cold, while Jim seemed more interested in his appearance than anything else. In that regard they were well matched.

Considering herself a leader of Lawrenceburg society, and never having wanted for anything, Mary Bond wouldn't consider joining a Dowling business, which she regarded as beneath her. And she could make herself so disagreeable, who would want her? She was, however, president of the Pierian Club, so not completely idle. She also contributed articles on local history and early settlers to the weekly Lawrenceburg newspaper, the *Anderson News*. As for money, she knew how to spend it.

And then there was poor Katherine, whose prospects had looked so bright when she married Henry in 1907. Two years later, Helen was born, and Katherine's life seemed to spread happily before her. Then, tragically—Mary rarely used that word because people were always losing the ones they loved—Henry died in 1910 at the age of thirty-four, widowing Katherine and leaving Helen without a father. Mary urged Katherine to return to Lawrenceburg, but she refused. "New York," she said, "offered so much more than a backwater Kentucky town." When Mary Bond heard that, she was outraged. She loved living in Lawrenceburg at the top of the heap. Although Mary rarely agreed with her eldest, she concurred about Lawrenceburg.

However, despite Katherine's poor judgement, Mary transferred one hundred dollars each month to her account. There was Helen to consider.

As for Ida, if she hadn't attracted an appropriate suitor and preferably a fiancé by this summer, Mary had decided to send her on a grand tour of Europe for her twenty-fifth birthday, in October. What was the point of having money if not to lavish on her children? She may have grown up poor Irish, but she was hardly poor today. She'd developed an eye for Persian carpets, which Mr. Shahrokh Shahi, a dealer based in Manhattan, offered on semi-annual visits to Kentucky. She'd bought more than a dozen, including several very fine and rare ones, both for herself and for Bobbie's new house on the Stewart estate.

In fact, the distilleries and other Dowling businesses were doing so well, they half-ran themselves. Over the past five years, she'd bought so many rugs and so much fine furniture—including a set of intricately carved dragon chairs, which both fascinated and frightened her grandchildren—that Mary was sick of shopping, preferring the challenges of making money to the pleasures of spending it. It was time, she thought, to develop other interests and causes or she'd turn into one of the ladies of leisure she had so little respect for.

Maybe, she thought, refilling her teacup, she'd run for president of the Pierian Club after Mary Bond's term was up. If she sent Emmett to Exeter and Ida somehow found a husband, there'd be no one at Dowling Hall who needed her. If she were a man, she'd sit on the bank's board, be active in the Masons and Rotary or run for office like Will. As it was, she'd have to content herself with the Pierians, since she had scant interest in bridge and none in the United Daughters of the Confederacy (UDC), although she'd served as third vice president when the Lawrenceburg chapter was organized in 1901. John had thought it was good for business, and perhaps he was right, but several of the UDC ladies held strongly negative feelings about Black people, which she did not share. *Lazy, stupid, shiftless;* growing up, she knew those words well. The same insults were applied to the Irish.

The Black folks who worked for her worked hard. That's why she'd replaced thieving Pat Tierney with John Cody. And of course, there was Ida, no longer with her, to whom she owed a debt she could never repay. In her experience, Black servants were as honest and reliable as whites, maybe more so, and so she paid them equally. A year after John died, she quietly left the UDC, though Mary Bond remained active. In fact, she was talking about standing for state chairperson. She never could talk sense to that girl, who spurned everyone's advice and opinions except her own. And her own were generally unkind and wrong-headed.

Mary thought about the Black men and women who worked for her. Bill James, the yard man, had been with her many years. Because he was so light and his eyes such an odd blue gray, she suspected his grandfather, back in slave days, must have been his grandmother's owner, or perhaps some other white man. She'd been told there was a lot of that back then, owners forcing relations. How shameful.

That clearly hadn't happened in John Cody's family; his skin was extremely dark. In the short time he'd worked for her, he'd proved himself trustworthy, arriving early twice a week to wash and polish the Packard. John Cody never used two words when one would do, but that was her only complaint. He drove impeccably and remained reserved around her. As she saw it, that was his right. He was paid to drive not socialize.

And then there was Rose, who lived in the Grove on East Lincoln, where many Black folks lived. Rose was Ida's niece, and Ida had recommended her, when she decided to stay home and care for her grandchildren. Rose was thirty-five or so, with several children of her own. Rose resembled Ida: tall and thin, with large, intelligent eyes. She didn't say much, and only when spoken to, but what she did say, implied good sense. She'd been hired to clean but was also helping the new cook, Mary Margaret.

Mary smiled, remembering John's pledge that if she married him, she wouldn't have to cook a day in her life. He'd kept that promise and many more, but that hadn't stopped him from teasing her about her lack of culinary skills. As time went on, it became a joke. "My Mary," he'd say, "can do everything a man or woman can. Except boil water."

For years she'd answer, "I could if I wanted." But in the last years of his life, she'd smile and say, "*Damn right.*"

The mantle clock chimed ten. Mary wondered when Will and Ida would return from the reception, and if Ida had met anyone suitable? She hoped so. Why didn't she worry that her sons remained single? Will would turn thirty-three in July—John's age when they married. Maybe she'd worry after Will's birthday. For now, she'd sip tea, wait up for her children, and hope she didn't float away.

In August 1913, Mary delivered Emmett to Phillips Exeter Academy, the venerable institution she'd chosen for him. In years to come, after he'd become an Old Exonian, Emmett would gaze back fondly at his four years in New Hampshire preparing for university. He'd learn a great deal about himself and others. How to talk *Yankee*. How to roll *R*s and conjugate verbs in Spanish, French, and German. How to sneak out without getting caught and how to conceal a flask in his room. He learned there were families far wealthier and more important than the Dowlings. He befriended the only Jewish member of his class; they were both outsiders in the Protestant halls of Exeter. He learned to kiss a girl. He learned New Hampshire winters were nothing to trifle with, and in the spring of his junior year, he learned how to shave without nicking his chin.

But that first steamy August, during the long and tedious train ride, all Emmett knew was he was being sent a thousand miles from home where he'd know no one and no one would know him. He wasn't good with strangers. He was shy and physically awkward, and as the journey stretched into a second day, Mary watched her youngest and dearest grow increasingly withdrawn. When they were less than hour from Exeter, she asked, "Emmett, what's the matter?"

"What if no one likes me?"

"How could anyone not like you?"

"I'm hopeless at sports, and little better at making friends."

"Do you know why I'm sending you to Exeter?"

"Not really."

"I have big plans for you. After Exeter, you'll go to Harvard."

This surprised him.

"And after Harvard"—she smiled—"you'll join me in the distilleries and warehouses. And when you've learned how, you'll run our businesses."

"What about Will and Johnnie?"

She wondered how much was too much to share with a fourteen-year-old but plunged ahead. "Neither of them wants it. Will prefers politics, while Johnnie lacks the ambition to run a large enterprise. So, it's you, Emmett, and that's why you must apply yourself and work hard to fit in."

He considered what she'd said. There had always been a precocious seriousness about him, a maturity, she thought proudly, beyond his years.

"I'll try, Mother, but I doubt there will be anyone in my class from Kentucky, nor many Catholics. I will be," he announced, with the sort of rhetorical flourish that endeared him to her, "the classic fish out of water. I could well die of loneliness before Christmas."

She tried not to smile. "I'm sure you'll learn to swim in strange waters. And if you're lonely, write every night, and I'll write you back."

He did write every night, but only the first week. Subsequently, they corresponded twice a month, and Mary saved all his letters.

Back in Lawrenceburg, she involved herself in the campaign of Mrs. Lee Campbell, the suffragette, who stood for Anderson County school superintendent. The incumbent Democrat had been implicated in a terrible scandal—helping to rig county exams and sell the answers—which opened the door to Lee's candidacy.

She was a few years younger than Mary and had taught for many years in the Lawrenceburg schools. She wore her hair short, and her eyes sparkled. She enjoyed a stellar reputation as a teacher—several Dowling children had been her students—and Mary admired Lee tremendously, not only because of her intelligence and education, but for her fine character. She'd grown up in Lawrenceburg; her maiden name was Mattox. When young, like Mary, she was certain she knew better than everyone, and over her parents' objections, married the wrong young man.

Lee's husband, Mr. Campbell, proved a drunk and a gambler. After several mordantly unhappy years, Lee fled with her infant daughter to El Paso, Texas, where her older sister lived with her husband, Judge Julius Augustus Buckler. Buckler also hailed from Kentucky, just not Lawrenceburg. After a few years, Lee felt the pull of home and returned to Lawrenceburg. She bravely sued for divorce, nearly unheard of at the time, but the judge—a man, of course—denied her petition. Ever since, Lee had lived on her own, in a small house paid for with her teacher's salary. She'd been a strong voice for progress in Lawrenceburg, an advocate for women's rights and suffrage.

When Lee stood for Anderson County school superintendent, Kentucky women could only vote in school elections; they wouldn't gain the right to vote in general elections until January 1920, when Kentucky ratified the Nineteenth Amendment. Because Lee Campbell was so admired, and because they viewed the election as a step towards full suffrage, many Pierian Club women joined her campaign. Yet despite the dark cloud of corruption hanging over the incumbent, many men were outraged a woman dared to run for office. Young Tom Ripy, the son of John's old partner TB Ripy, was the Anderson County attorney, and he pulled every dirty trick he could think of to prevent women from voting, filing one motion on top of another.

But young Tom failed, and on Election Day, like several of her friends, Mary helped get out the vote; she had John Cody drive women to the polls from the time they opened until they closed. And when, against all odds, Mrs. Lee Campbell won a four-year term, how proud Mary was of her friend. How proud all the women were. And what a party they threw.

In 1914, when Mary became president of the Pierians, she broke precedent and announced she didn't want a banquet in her honor. Instead, she convinced the club to redirect its entertainment budget and a great deal more to mount a campaign to wipe out trachoma, a leading cause of blindness in Anderson County. She had read articles in the Lexington and Owensboro newspapers about how contagious trachoma was now known to be, so much so that any child with symptoms was barred from school. That horrified her. Trachoma, after all, could be cured. All it took was money, and not very much. Left unchecked, however, trachoma scarred the cornea and led to blindness.

By the spring of 1915, under Mary's determined direction, the ladies of leisure who made up the membership of the Pierian Club had accepted that their funds and energy must be directed to goals more substantial than socializing. The Pierians organized a Health and Welfare League, which converted a house on Fairmont into a temporary trachoma hospital, the first in Kentucky. Civic-minded citizens donated cots, linens, and furniture. A resident nurse was retained, and for five months Dr. McMullen, a trachoma specialist, arrived twice weekly from Lexington with two trained nurses.

All treatment was gratis, as Mary believed it should be. Most trachoma sufferers were countrified and impoverished. They needed help, and news of the free hospital spread quickly. Soon, children from neighboring counties were also receiving treatment: wholesome food, skilled care, clean blankets—everything necessary for a full recovery. In all, more than fifty indigent children were treated, and Lawrenceburg's program became a model for other Kentucky counties and other Southern states.

The success of the program made Mary feel as if she were following the example of her Savior. Terrible things were happening in Europe, where men were dying in trenches, mustard-gassed by their enemies. But at home in Lawrenceburg, Mary and the Pierians were making the world a better place. If only, she thought, emulating the Blessed Mother and Her Son was enough.

Mary didn't realize it yet, but she would soon face and, in many ways desired, larger challenges. Much as she enjoyed the Pierian women and their projects, men still controlled power and money. And since John died, Mary had wielded as much money and power as any man in Lawrenceburg.

CHAPTER TWELVE

Mary Bond, the UDC, and The Rise of the Second Klan 1913-1915

At its 1913 convention in Winchester, the United Daughters of the Confederacy (UDC) elected Mary Bond Kentucky state president. Founded in 1894 by Caroline Goodlett of Tennessee and Anna Raines of Georgia, the UDC devoted its first twenty years to raising funds for Confederate monuments. Mounted on a massive granite pedestal inscribed with the names of local casualties, Lawrenceburg's memorial, an eight-foot-high Johnny Reb, defended the courthouse. Leading the honored dead was Captain Gus Dedman, for whom the Lawrenceburg UDC was named. Dedman had organized one of Lawrenceburg's four Confederate companies and died in the Battle of Chickamauga, a decade before John Dowling marched into Lawrenceburg.

Mary Bond, who qualified for UDC membership through marriage to Gentleman Jim (being a Dowling most certainly did not qualify her) had, ironically, become well-known in Lawrenceburg for her articles about early Anderson County settlers. Like the rest of the Dowlings, Mary Bond was a relative newcomer in every way: Irish-Catholic, with parents born into poverty. But she was rich, beautiful, and had married into one of the leading Protestant families. Their heritage, she believed, was now hers.

Quite simply, Mary Bond was a snob and considered herself the leader of the younger branch of Lawrenceburg society. Never mind that the Bonds, Lillards, Ripys, and McGregors had lived in Lawrenceburg for eighty years or more. By marrying Gentleman Jim, whether or not they lived together, Mary Bond felt she was one of them. And blessed with her mother's determination but without the burden of children, a career, her own house, or a full-time husband to manage, she had a deep well of untapped energy and threw herself into organizing UDC functions.

Mary Bond prevailed upon Kentucky Governor McCreary, a Confederate veteran she knew through Will, to host the 1914 UDC convention in the new capitol building in Frankfort. On October 14, 150 delegates arrived from all around the Commonwealth to pursue their traditional agenda: reviewing local chapters' fundraising, planning monuments, and selecting the location of the next convention—which would turn out to be Fulton, in the southwest corner of the state, close to the borders with Tennessee and Missouri.

Most exciting, however, was a planned discussion of *The Ku Klux Klan or The Invisible Empire*, a new book by Laura Martin Rose, president of the Mississippi state chapter. Mrs. Rose's book began as a fundraising pamphlet for a monument at Beauvoir, the Mississippi mansion of Jefferson Davis. The pamphlet proved so popular, Mrs. Rose expanded it into a textbook, which was unanimously endorsed at the UDC's 1913 National Convention. Not everyone knew, but Mary Bond certainly did, that Jefferson Davis, the Confederacy's only president, had been born in Fairview, Kentucky, not far from Fulton, reason enough to site the 1915 UDC convention there.

The Invisible Empire promoted the narrative that the Confederacy was a glorious "Lost Cause," and the Civil War had been fought over states' rights, not slavery. According to this revisionist history, in the years immediately after Appomattox, members of the first Klan heroically defended the virtue of white Southern women against lusty, "emancipated Negroes." The UDC's mission, and the discussion Mary Bond looked forward to leading, was how to arrange for Mrs. Rose's wonderful book to be accepted by Kentucky school boards so that the true history of the War Between the States, would be taught to children all around the Commonwealth.

Mary Bond arrived home with several copies of *The Invisible Empire*, buoyed by her success. UDC chapter heads had voted unanimously to work on getting Mrs. Rose's textbook adopted by local school boards. Mary Bond gave her mother a copy and asked her to recommend it to her friend Lee Campbell, the superintendent of Lawrenceburg schools. A week later, Mary and Mary Bond settled in for Sunday supper joined by Will, Emmett, Ida, Johnnie, and Gentlemen Jim, whose perfect features—except for his moustache—looked as if they'd been lifted from a porcelain doll. Will sat at the head of the table, where his father used to sit, opposite Mary, who sat at the foot, closest to the kitchen door. Mary Bond was at her mother's right hand, Gentleman Jim on her right, with Ida beside him. Emmett and Johnnie were seated on the other side of the table, Emmett closest to Mary, with Johnnie adjacent to Will. Even as grown men, Will and Johnnie remained best friends.

Ida's niece Rose, the maid who'd become Mary's confidante among the servants, bustled about bringing in plated meals from the kitchen: pork tenderloin, scalloped potatoes, and brussels sprouts. After everyone had started eating, Mary Bond set down her cutlery, patted her lips dry with a napkin, then asked, "Mother, have you had a chance to read the book I gave you?"

Mary had been dreading this conversation. With a forkful of pork balanced halfway to her mouth, she looked at her troublesome namesake. "I have."

Mary Bond glanced at Gentleman Jim, then back at her mother. "What did you think?"

Mary chewed slowly, endeavoring to frame her response with care. "Why don't we discuss this later?"

"No, *Mother*." Mary Bond spoke in the querulous tone the family dreaded. "I meet tomorrow at nine a.m. with Missus Campbell. I've been waiting a week for you to tell me you support me."

Mary Bond's tone had acquired the attention not only of her siblings, but of her husband, who looked anxious. All other table conversation ceased.

"Since you insist." Mary glanced at her other children, then back at her eldest. "In my opinion, that book is a reeking pile of hateful lies, and I've told Missus Campbell what I believe: whoever wrote that awful book should be ashamed. I won't have it used to poison the minds of innocent children."

Anger distorted Mary Bond's features. "Well, Mother," she snapped. "I see we disagree, as always. Every once in a while, you could support me."

"I lived through those days, Mary, and let me tell you, the Klan were not knights in armor defending white women from Black men. You weren't born yet. You have no idea the lies they peddle."

"I *do* have an idea!" She threw down her fork, which bounced off her plate and clattered to the parquet floor. "Jim," she commanded. "We're leaving now."

She strode from the room. Gentlemen Jim sighed, consumed a final forkful of pork, then one of potatoes. He stood and looked around the long table, an embarrassed smile on his lips. His eyes came to Mary.

"I'm sorry, Missus Dowling. But you know how she can be," he said before exiting.

Do I ever, Mary thought.

"That went well," Will said. "Why didn't you tell her what you really thought?"

The others laughed nervously. Then Rose, who'd witnessed the ugly scene, circled the table, offering second helpings. When she stopped on Mary's right, behind Mary Bond's empty place, their eyes met. And in that moment, before her maid's eyes dropped respectfully to the floor, Mary glimpsed a new and unguarded Rose who appeared surprised and grateful.

After dinner, Mary sought out Rose and asked to speak to her privately on the kitchen porch. It was late October, but the air remained warm.

"Rose," Mary began. "About the conversation you overheard." Their eyes met. "Or let's be honest and call it an argument."

"I'll call it whatever you want, Missus Dowling."

Mary smiled. "As I'm sure you know, once children grow up, you can't control what they think or say."

"I have four—the eldest sixteen, the youngest eight. To be honest, I can't control now what they think or say."

"I want you to know, I don't agree with what Missus Bond says."

Rose nodded.

Mary continued, "But because she's my daughter, I ask that anything you hear, no matter how misguided, stays within these four walls."

"I'm no gossip, Missus Dowling."

"I guess I knew that. But I'm glad we had this conversation." Mary paused, then added, "I want you to know, as I told your Aunt Ida years ago. If you or your family need anything, ask me."

"I guess I knew that too." Rose looked at Mary with her large, expressive eyes. "Aunt Ida told me how you helped when our church burned."

The same month the Dowlings were arguing about the *The Invisible Empire*, *The Birth of a Nation*, originally called *The Clansman*, was being filmed in California. Directed by D.W. Griffith and starring Lillian Gish, *The Birth of a Nation* would premiere in early 1915 and be hailed as the first great American movie. Three hours long, Griffith's landmark silent film was the first American blockbuster, ground-breaking and innovative, the first feature to include realistic battle scenes. It earned vast sums, and it was completely racist.

The Birth of a Nation sparked civil rights protests in several Northern cities and led directly to the founding of the second Ku Klux Klan in November 1915, days before its Atlanta premiere. Emboldened by the film's immense popularity, William Simmons, a former Methodist preacher, led fourteen horsemen in full Klan regalia up Stone Mountain, just outside Atlanta, where they burned a large cross. A few days later, the same founding members paraded in hoods on white shrouded horses past the Atlanta premiere of *The Birth of a Nation*.

The first Klan, formed immediately after the Civil War, was a Southern organization. It was relatively short-lived, mostly eradicated by the federal government by the mid-1870s. Simmons' second Klan, however, hired publicists to promote chapters all around the United States. At its height of popularity in 1924-25, there were nearly four million members.

There was another major difference between the first and second Klans, mostly obscured by the march of history, but terribly significant in Mary Dowling's story. The post–Civil War Klan directed its hatred almost entirely towards freed slaves. The second Klan was more ambitious. While they certainly preached hatred of and lynched African Americans, their bigotry was much broader. The rhetoric of the KKK of the 1920s and 1930s reached back to the Know-Nothing Party of the 1850s. Blacks, Catholics, and Jews equaled scum and vermin. In the minds of second Klan members, only white Protestants were genuine Americans. Significantly, in the first decade of the Klan's rebirth, its members would become vocal, and frequently violent, backers of Prohibition.

The Klan's racist agenda was actively promoted by the leaders of the UDC. At its 1915 national convention in San Francisco, UDC delegates unanimously endorsed—as they had in 1913—the teaching of *The Invisible Empire* in schools. A year later, in 1916, its author, Mrs. Rose, was named historian-general of the UDC.

It was against this political backdrop, on September 23, 1915, that Mary Bond convened the Kentucky state UDC convention in the Methodist church in Fulton. Over the next two days, highlighted by a speech by Maj. General Haldeman of Louisville, Mary Bond controlled the gavel, rallying support for teaching *The Invisible Empire*. Her final act as state president would be leading the grand march at the second night's fancy dress ball. She was thirty-nine, still a beauty, and she and Gentleman Jim danced the night away, much admired by the UDC ladies.

Two months later in Stone Mountain, Georgia, the second Klan would be founded, with grave consequences for Mary and the Dowling family.

CHAPTER THIRTEEN

Men and Their Doings 1917-1918

On March 12, 1917, Mary sent John Cody to meet the six p.m. train in Versailles. After working with Heinrich for more than a decade, she considered him a good friend and advisor, perhaps her first and only male friend. Like her, Heinrich had lost a beloved spouse and never remarried. Mary knew her own reasons. Eight children. Her age: fifty-eight. And even if she were interested, how could she trust a man's intentions when she'd have so much more money? And then there was her heart, still wedded to John's. But what were Heinrich's reasons? Why hadn't he taken another wife? Every other man did. He was a little Germanic, she supposed, but smart and cultured, with good sense and a kind heart.

Just then, a car started up the circular drive, tires crunching over the freshly raked gravel. Mary closed her ledgers. Heinrich's train must have been on time.

They dined alone, with Heinrich on her right and the rest of the long table empty. After soup, Heinrich's lean face lit with pleasure when Rose set a plate of schnitzel with mushroom gravy, spaetzle, and braised red cabbage in front of him.

"Mary," he said, after the first bite. "*Haf* you hired a German cook?"

"It's all right?"

"Better than all right, as I'm sure you know."

"Mary Margaret, our new cook, is Irish. But I sent her for lessons to our neighbor where the cook is named Helga."

Heinrich fed a substantial square of schnitzel through his lips, followed by a forkful of spaetzle, then one of cabbage. "Please tell your neighbor Helga's a treasure."

After dinner, they retired to her office where she served Heinrich twelve-year Waterfill and Frazier, barreled when John was yet alive.

"Excellent." Heinrich set his glass on her desktop. "Tell me, Mary, is *Vill* still considering a move to New York?"

"If he can find an appropriate job."

Heinrich raised a bushy eyebrow, untrimmed and unruly. "He has one *vith* you."

Heinrich always knew her mind. "He wants to try New York before settling down. He's seeing one of the Lillard girls."

Heinrich's eyebrow rose again. "Of Bond and Lillard?"

"A granddaughter, on the side that hasn't any money."

Heinrich sipped his whiskey. "And *vhat* about Emmett, how is he getting on at Exeter?"

"These days he rarely writes, but I'm told he'll be accepted at Harvard."

"I'm not surprised. Just imagine *vere* you *vould haf* gone if a man."

"And if I'd finished fourth grade."

Heinrich smiled. "I *haf* something for you." He reached into the pocket of his suit coat, withdrawing a small, black velvet box.

"What's this?" It looked very much like a jeweler's box.

"A token of Grommes and Ulrich's esteem and affection. Our thanks for eleven years of partnership."

Mary opened her present: a glittering diamond and sapphire ring. "Oh no," she said, flushing. "I couldn't."

"You don't like it?"

"It's lovely, but—"

"You know Grommes is well-known in our industry for presenting filigreed sterling plates and bowls to our best clients. You've received some."

"I have."

"I convinced Mister Grommes jewelry *vould* be more appropriate and appreciated."

"Receiving the same gift as every other account would be appropriate."

Heinrich looked at her severely. "But you are not every other account." That hung awkwardly. "You're my best account. Missus Grommes accompanied me to her jeweler and helped pick this out."

Mary didn't know if Mrs. Grommes's involvement made matters better or worse. "She has good taste."

Heinrich's expression changed from concern to pleasure. "So, you *do* like it?"

"Very much. Thank you, Heinrich."

A short while later Heinrich announced he was tired, and Mary directed John Cody to drop him at the Commercial Hotel. They arranged to meet in the morning to begin the obligatory inspections and inventories of her distilleries and warehouses. Later, seated at her dressing table after having changed into her nightgown, Mary slipped Heinrich's present onto the ring finger of her right hand and held it up to the mirror. The large stone sparkled like a blue star. She especially liked sapphires, but Heinrich couldn't have known that. Or perhaps he'd noticed her other sapphire jewelry. No matter, she hadn't received such a gift since John died. Mrs. Grommes, or quite possibly Heinrich, had chosen well.

Friday, after touring the final warehouse—Heinrich was departing in the morning—they were returning from Burgin; she always saved Dowling Brothers, of which she owned only one-third, for the final inventory of the week. It was a warm afternoon, more like May than mid-March, and John Cody had folded the windows down into the door of her new Twin Six Packard. Wind gusting into the car tousled her hair and ruffled the sleeves of her black dress. She wondered if Heinrich had noticed she was wearing the sapphire ring.

She'd spent more time than she'd care to admit contemplating whether to wear it. At last, she decided, *If it really was from the company, it would be rude if she didn't.* Still, it was odd to receive such a personal item from a business associate, and odder still that Heinrich hadn't said anything. Maybe he hadn't noticed. Many a man didn't, but Heinrich had always been so observant.

Later, while they finished up in her office, Heinrich said, "We should discuss the eight-hundred-pound gorilla in the room."

"Come again?"

"It's a German joke. *Vhere does an eight-hundred-pound gorilla sleep?* Answer: *Anyvhere he vants.*"

"I hope you don't mind my saying; I've never thought Germans were funny."

"Not like the Irish." Heinrich laughed, then gazed at her intently. "The gorilla means the big subject people don't discuss."

She wondered if he meant the possibility of Prohibition, which had been worrying her. Then she decided, *No. It is the ring.* Perhaps Heinrich had misinterpreted her intention in wearing it, or she had misinterpreted his in giving it to her.

"What is that?" she asked.

"Prohibition. I fear it's coming."

She should have known. Mary took a moment to shift her thoughts from Heinrich's possible affection for her to business. She certainly preferred business.

"I've been meaning to talk to you about this. I don't know why we haven't."

"*Ve* should *haf.* I'm very *vorried,* as is Mister Grommes. No longer does the Women's Christian Temperance Union lead the charge. Its members have moved on to suffrage. Today it's the Anti-Saloon

League, much better funded and more dangerous. Their first move back in '09, *ven ve veren't* paying attention and didn't understand how dangerous they *vere, vas* to support a Federal Income Tax, ratified by the states in '13 as the Sixteenth Amendment. Its secret goal *vas* to replace lost income from the Federal *Vhiskey* Tax, ploughing the ground for Prohibition. And now, puffed up *vith* their success, no longer *vorking* in the shadows, they've helped ban alcohol in North Carolina."

"I know," Mary said, feeling sick.

"They control the money, Mary. And come November, they'll be supporting a strong slate of candidates from both parties for the House and Senate. Vote Dry, they tell these politicians, or no money for you. It looks bad, Mary."

She was suddenly feeling anxious and angry. Heinrich glanced around her empty office, as if he feared being overheard.

"They claim," Heinrich continued, "they're against politicians buying votes in saloons, *vile* they're buying votes in Congress. Truth is, they're anti-immigrant and anti-Catholic. Just consider. *Vunce* again, Protestants are trying to impose their beliefs on Catholics. And who else leads the fight, supporting the same Prohibition candidates? Those Ku Klux Klan devils. They *haf* a big chapter in Chicago."

Heinrich poured himself another inch of bourbon, sipped, and put his glass down. She'd never seen him so agitated, and she thought back to her arguments with Mary Bond, two years earlier, when she headed up the UDC. Thank God, Lee Hamilton had agreed with her advice and kept *The Invisible Empire* out of Lawrenceburg schools.

Heinrich's face was flushing red, and his accent was growing stronger. He tapped her wrist with a blunt finger. "Italians make *vine*, Irish distill *vhiskey*, Germans brew beer. So, who *vill* Prohibition hurt? And *vith* talk of America entering the *Var*, and maybe a draft, there comes more anti-German feeling. I've had friends beaten up by these hooligans."

"Why haven't I heard about this?"

"It's more the big cities, *vhere* there are more immigrants. My point is, no one *vill vant* to hear *vhat* Germans say, as if belonging to the spirits industry makes us anti-American. As if only Protestants are real Americans." Heinrich raised her whiskey to his lips, drained the glass, and set it down. "If you ask me, it's again the Reformation, Luther nailing his Manifesto to the church door, except now the Klan swings the hammer."

Mary had never heard Heinrich speak so passionately, and while it might be the whiskey, she felt caught out and foolish for not being more prepared. Her mind flashed back to her parents' fear and hatred of the Know-Nothing Party. She should have known better. She *did* know better. And she thought of her own foolish daughter and the UDC women trumpeting that evil book. Not to mention *Birth of a Nation,* which she'd hated and told everyone who would listen how evil it was, no matter what they thought. After a moment, Mary said, "Without distilleries and whiskey tax, Anderson County will go bankrupt."

"Do they care? *No!*" Heinrich's eyes looked as if they were going to pop out of his skull. "In a year or two, likely *vhen* this damn *var* ends, the Anti-Saloon League, the Klan, and all the Protestants they represent, *vill* try to shut down all sale and production of alcohol."

Mary let the seriousness of what Heinrich was saying sink in. For months, she'd been worried but trying not to think about these things, and it was a relief to discuss her concerns with another professional. "That will be terrible for our business."

"Mary, you *vill* have no business. So, *ve* must look ahead and prepare."

"You're right, Heinrich. And we will." Mary smiled at her friend. "I really mean that. And now, may I offer another whiskey? Or a cigar?"

"Since *vhen* do you smoke cigars?"

"I don't. My sons do."

"I better not. I *haf* an early train and still must pack." He looked into her eyes. "By the *vay,* the ring looks lovely on your finger."

She raised her hand to display her gift, and the sapphire flashed. "Thank you, Heinrich. I like it very much."

He hesitated, then said, "I'll tell Missus Grommes."

They sat in comfortable then not so comfortable silence while a million thoughts swirled in Mary's head. What Heinrich was thinking, she could not guess. After another moment, she added, "There's a great deal to consider. But I agree, we need a plan."

"Yes."

Heinrich shook her hand, or rather, she shook his. Maybe she'd been wrong not to consider becoming involved with him. She could do worse, and so could he. But that time of life had passed. Besides, she told herself, what they really shared was passion for the whiskey business and a deep knowledge of how it worked. She smiled at Heinrich, then rang for John Cody and walked Heinrich to the side door. After the Packard disappeared down the dark drive, she returned to her office. Just as well, she decided, that Heinrich had declined her offer of another drink. It was late, and she had much to consider. These days, and from long habit, she did her best thinking alone.

CHAPTER FOURTEEN

War and Prohibition 1917-1918

Heinrich proved prescient. The United States entered the war against Germany in April 1917; in response, sauerkraut was renamed "liberty cabbage," hamburgers became "liberty steak," and dachshunds transitioned to "liberty pups." German language newspapers closed or began publishing in English. All around the country new anti-sedition and espionage laws targeted German Americans, who were pressured to buy liberty bonds to prove their patriotism. In May, to support the war effort, the US approved a military draft. Fortunately, for the long-term health of Mary and her sons, Will, George, and Johnnie were too old and Emmett, then in his final term at Exeter, was too young. Only men between the ages of twenty-one and thirty participated in the first National Registration Day, held on June 5, 1917.

A few days later, Emmett graduated from Exeter, taking with him, in addition to his diploma, three distinctive nicknames: Hick, Bird, and Tweedy. *Hick* was easy to understand. His accent, *y'all*. More generally, Lawrenceburg, Kentucky, was so culturally distant from Phillips Exeter Academy (founded in 1781 in Exeter, New Hampshire), that in the 1917 yearbook, under his picture, Emmett's hometown was listed as *Lawrenceville, KY*, and no one noticed except possibly Emmett and his family, but by then it was too late. (It's also possible the "error" was a schoolboy prank in which Emmett participated; Lawrenceville was the name of a prominent preparatory school in Lawrenceville, New Jersey, five miles from Princeton University.)

Bird referenced Emmett's appearance: tall (nearly six-one), sandy-haired, long-limbed, and blue-eyed, physically distinct from every other child of John and Mary Dowling, as if the eleven-year gap between Ida, the youngest girl, and Emmett, the Dowling baby, rendered him a late-born family of one. *Tweedy* might have referred to his style of dress, but in Exeter slang, *tweedy* signified understated and upper-class, which was likely Emmett's response to being called *Hick*. Not surprisingly, Emmett's self-selected motto (every Exeter senior chose a phrase to appear beneath his photo) was: "Discretion of speech is more than eloquence."

While at Exeter, Emmett achieved moderate academic success: Honorable Mention for Exeter's honor society. He'd belonged to the Southern Club and served as church monitor. He wore his hair center-parted and learned to play the mandolin. Above all, he fulfilled Mary's top-line ambition for him. Having joined the Harvard Club during his first term at Exeter, he graduated into Harvard's Class of 1921.

By January 1918, three of Mary's eight children were living in the Northeast. Emmett was in Cambridge. Katherine lived in Tarrytown,

New York, with her daughter Helen. After finishing a second term in the Kentucky House, Will had proposed to Margaret Lillard from Lawrenceburg, ten years his junior, then moved alone to New York City promising to send for her as soon as he found work as an attorney.

Mary liked her future daughter-in-law. Margaret was sensible, smart, and smitten with Will. *As well she should be.* And there was this. Although the Lillards were one of the Five Families, and therefore, socially acceptable, Margaret's grandfather had frittered away his share of the family wealth, and Margaret grew up in a small house on the outskirts of town. For some women, having their adored firstborn son propose marriage to a girl whose parents couldn't afford a society wedding might have turned her against the match.

Not Mary. The Dowlings had enough for both families, and it was time, in fact, past time in Mary's opinion, for Will, who would turn thirty-nine in July, to settle down. Shortly after Will left for New York, Mary invited her dear friends, Frankie Saffell and Lee Campbell, to lunch and asked what they thought of the match.

Frankie said, "I like Margaret. She's friends with two of my girls."

"And a good student," Lee added. "I taught her twice."

"Speaking of teaching," Mary said. "What's it like being back in the classroom?"

A shadow of annoyance crossed Lee's face. She'd lost her bid for a second term as superintendent, and Mary knew it was a sore topic, but there was no point ignoring it.

"Well," Lee said, blinking rapidly. When she was angry or annoyed, she blinked. *Better than screaming,* Mary thought.

"Let's just say," Lee continued. *Blink, blink, blink.* "It's a good thing I like teaching—"

"You're so good at it," Frankie added.

"—because the old boys who run things will do their damndest never to let me back in."

"That's for sure," Mary said.

Just then, Rose came in to clear their luncheon dishes and to offer cups of coffee.

"Cookies, anyone?" Mary asked. When her friends hesitated, Mary added, "Come on, you know you want them."

Later, over coffee and jam-filled thumbprints, Mary said, "I like Margaret too. But you know her parents can't afford a proper wedding."

"Will you make one?" asked Frankie.

"I don't think so." Mary glanced at Lee, who had considerably less money than she or Frankie. "They'll have a small wedding after Will gets settled and Margaret joins him."

"That makes good sense," Lee said.

"I think so too," added Frankie.

"Here's something I'd like to ask," Mary said. "Well, it's more a conjecture than a question, but I'd appreciate your thoughts."

Her friends nodded.

"It occurs to me," Mary began, "that maybe the children of the rich in small towns don't grow up to be sensible. I mention no names, but look around my house; you can see why I might be concerned."

Neither of her friends would meet her eyes.

"Come on, Lee," Mary began, "you've taught the children of the rich and the poor. You must have an opinion."

Lee fixed Mary with her bright button eyes. "It's true. Sometimes money makes them idle."

Frankie, who disliked discord and had married off six daughters, some successfully and some to bounders, shook her head. "You just can't say."

Mary said, "I've come to think it's just as well Margaret's family hasn't much, because she's got a good head on her shoulders." Mary sipped her coffee and popped another of the luscious thumbprints into her mouth. "When I think of how John and I scrimped to get ahead, I wonder we never thought, poor as we were, what it would be like to raise rich children."

"Oh, come on, Mary." Lee laughed. "Don't tell me you're having second thoughts about all your money. If you are," she laughed again, "you can give some to me!"

"I've no regrets about making money." She paused, marveling, as if she'd never thought of this before. "It's just some things you don't see coming."

Six months later, on September 28, 1918, Mary and Margaret, her daughter-in-law to be, disembarked at New York's Pennsylvania Station. They'd made the long train trip together from Louisville. Mary had packed for a week, but Margaret brought her entire trousseau and who knew what else? They'd required two porters to carry their baggage at the Louisville station and two again in New York, even with Will helping. After two days in Manhattan sightseeing and recuperating from the journey, the three of them would train to Washington, DC, where Will and Margaret would be married on October 2.

It was terribly exciting yet a bit irregular. In the view of Lawrenceburg society, Will and Margaret were eloping. Yet it wasn't *that* irregular; they were eloping accompanied by the groom's mother.

The day after Mary and Margaret arrived in Manhattan, Katherine and Helen, now nine, caught the train in from Westchester to join them for a celebratory lunch in the Empire Room of the Waldorf Astoria. The entire family had taken rooms in the Waldorf wing. Emmett arrived from Cambridge a few minutes after their lunch reservation, looking grown-up and dashing. Will ordered champagne and toasted his bride in flowery language, while Margaret, to her credit, blushed prettily and smiled at Will with adoring eyes. Helen said little but seemed to know which fork and spoon to use with each course. Katherine fought tears when the subject of her own wedding arose; she would have been married eleven years come November if Henry hadn't died. Emmett and Will speculated when the war would end; Emmett had been part of a reserve naval unit at Harvard during his freshman year and considered himself an expert. Both sons agreed the end would come soon, then Emmett mentioned that Louisiana had passed Prohibition, the fourteenth state to ratify the amendment.

"Twenty-two more," he said. "And we'll be out of business."

It was strange and gratifying, Mary thought, to hear her youngest discuss politics with such confidence.

"There's little doubt it will pass," said Will, inclining his head and shoulder to the right while peering at her intently, just as John used to. "Heinrich and I have been preparing for this inevitability for the past year. I've arranged to sell most of our reserves to Canada, and some to Mexico."

"Mexico," Emmett said, wonderingly. "I've always wanted to visit Mexico to perfect my Spanish."

"Maybe you'll get the chance. And what we haven't sold will go to Julian Van Winkle at W.L. Weller and Sons to be bottled in pints and sold as medicinal whiskey."

Will said, "It will be strange to be out of the whiskey business."

Mary nodded, then glanced at Margaret, who looked dismayed by the turn of the conversation. Mary said, "But let's not pollute this happy occasion with talk of Prohibition. There will be time aplenty in days to come."

Emmett raised his wine glass; they'd moved to a claret for the beef course.

"To the next Dowling." He smiled at Margaret. "Welcome to the family."

My, Mary thought. *But he's grown up fast at Harvard.*

On October 1, Mary, Margaret, and Will took the train from New York to Washington, so the young people could be married the next day in a side chapel at St. Matthew's Cathedral. They couldn't be married at the main altar or by a priest because Margaret was a Protestant and intended to remain one, although she'd promised to raise any children Catholic. St. Matthews wasn't as impressive as Saint Patrick's Cathedral in New York, or nearly as old as the Basilica of St. Joseph in Bardstown. But the church and its altar, Mary thought, especially the large paintings of the saints, were inspiring. For Margaret, who'd traveled little and had likely been inside few, if any, Catholic churches, the experience must be overwhelming, notwithstanding it was also her wedding day. Whatever the explanation, Margaret *beamed*, like the faces of saints and cherubs in old paintings.

She dressed well, if simply, and seemed genuinely excited about spending her honeymoon in Washington, DC, which Will had long wanted to visit because of his interest in politics. Washington might not be as thrilling or dramatic as Niagara Falls, but you wouldn't know it from the conversation of Mrs. William E. Dowling at the wedding lunch Mary hosted before boarding her train to Louisville.

Mary liked to keep her children close, and there were some who said she was too involved in their lives. But she knew enough not to be in town on their honeymoon night, when at long last she could stop paying for separate hotel rooms for Will and Margaret.

The newlyweds accompanied her to Union Station. Seeing her off on the platform, Margaret addressed her as *Mother* for the first time and shed a little tear when they hugged goodbye. Mary took Will aside and pressed two one-hundred-dollar bills into his palm.

"Show her an extra good time, Will."

"I shall."

"I really like her."

Will smiled. "So do I."

Somewhere behind her a conductor shouted, "All aboard!"

"And if you decide New York's not for you, and you want to return to Lawrenceburg, I'll help you get re-established."

Will nodded but said nothing. Mary turned and mounted the steps into the first-class sleeper. Her last image of the newlyweds was of them holding hands and waving goodbye.

CHAPTER FIFTEEN

War and Armistice 1918-1920

Heinrich arrived from Chicago for his semi-annual visit a week after Mary returned from Washington. He looked older, more haggard, as if he hadn't been well. He presented her with a bracelet, another gift, he said, from Grommes and Ulrich. The bracelet matched the diamond-and-sapphire ring he'd given her a year and a half ago; she'd chosen to wear it this very evening.

"It's beautiful, Heinrich. Look how well they match."

He helped her fasten the clasp on the bracelet, which she'd placed on her left wrist. "They do, don't they?"

She shifted her wrist, and the gemstones flashed. "Too nice for an old woman," she said.

"You're not old."

"Sixty in January, Heinrich."

"I'm seventy-two."

"You don't look it. John died at sixty-one."

"I know."

"And I know, this is too nice a gift from a business associate."

Heinrich looked away, and Mary fretted he might think she was trying to elicit a declaration of affection, which she wasn't. She knew he cared for her and she for him, but her feelings had limits. Still, she wanted to acknowledge the bracelet was an exceptional piece of jewelry.

"I'm afraid it *vill* be the last such gift." Their eyes met, and this time, he did not look away. "On January fifteenth, when all the states voting this fall announce results, Grommes and Ulrich *vill* exit the liquor business."

"January fifteenth is my birthday."

"Some present."

She smiled. "We saw this coming and did a good job selling high."

"*Ve* did." He sipped his bourbon, the best she had. "*Haf* you applied for a medicinal license, as *ve* discussed?"

"Of course, but I'm not a good old boy, so have been told not to expect one. Van Winkle, at Weller, believes he'll receive one of the six and has offered to sell whatever remains of Waterfill and Frazier, although I'd have to re-bottle in pints."

"And then *vhat?* I don't see you as retired."

Heinrich knew her so well. "I've had an offer accepted on a large bluegrass farm. Two hundred and thirty-three acres overlooking the Salt River. I plan to raise purebred sheep, cattle, and hogs. I have a lot of experience over the years feeding mash to livestock."

"If you don't mind my asking, *vhat* did you pay?"

"I never discuss money with anyone else, Heinrich, not even my children. But I do with you." Her acknowledgement of intimacy scented the air between them. Funny, she thought, how money could almost be love. "Thirty-two thousand."

He whistled. "It must be very fine land."

"Some of the best in Anderson County. I'll name it 'Shonraugh,' Irish for Big Hill, after the place John came from."

"His family was wealthy?"

"Oh no. *Shonraugh* was the estate where his family worked."

"You still miss him."

She nodded.

Heinrich said, "So, you'll be a gentleman farmer."

"Hardly a gentleman, Heinrich. More bourbon?"

He nodded.

"What about you?" She poured him another two inches, adding ice from the bucket.

"I can stay on selling expensive foodstuffs, or maybe I'll retire. I'm certainly old enough." He sipped. "And if you're bored on the farm? *Vhat* then?"

"Maybe I'll move Waterfill to Canada. Or Mexico. Some place right on the border."

He laughed. "*Vhat* an idea. Do you speak Spanish?"

"I could learn. Or hire a translator. That's an easy, practical problem."

They sat in silence. Then Mary said, "You know what really angers me? Kentucky was one of the first states to ratify. All over Anderson County, even here in Lawrenceburg, people voted to put me out of business and throw my workers out of their jobs. Don't they know what's going to happen, especially in Tyrone? Tyrone will be a ghost town!" She shook her head. "Are these people idiots, or just mean-spirited?"

"Probably both."

They looked at each other and laughed.

In October 1919, Will and Margaret returned to Lawrenceburg for the first time since their marriage. Because they'd had no reception and because their visit coincided, more or less, with their first anniversary, Mary decided to host a grand soiree in their honor, inviting Will's political friends from Frankfort, their neighbors on Cream

Street, Margaret's Lillard relations, and every Dowling from Louisville to Lexington, including Will's uncles, as well as her own sisters, Sallie and Jessie, whom she rarely saw. Everyone was excited, because after months of avoiding crowds and staying indoors, the Spanish influenza epidemic seemed to have ended, and people were emerging from their houses, like snowdrops coming up after winter.

Everyone, that is, except Mary Bond. After the terrible fights when she was state president of the UDC, it had taken years for her relationship with her mother to return to its frosty equilibrium. Mary Bond did not appreciate being thwarted, nor was she accustomed to being opposed. In that respect, they were similar. Mary had made all the business decisions for the distilleries, warehouses, and cooperage since John died, and she was accustomed to being obeyed. She expected no less in Dowling Hall, where she paid the bills. But like many a firstborn child, Mary Bond didn't see things that way. She believed she owed her mother love, not obedience.

On the evening John Cody brought Will and Margaret home from the station, Mary Bond wouldn't even look at Margaret, and though she made a show of hugging and kissing Will, Mary observed she didn't congratulate him on his marriage or anniversary. Compounding the insult, the next morning when Margaret entered the breakfast room, Mary Bond stood and left without a word. Will took off after his older sister and caught up to her in the front hall. Although Mary couldn't hear *what* they were saying, their angry voices made clear they were arguing.

That afternoon, while reviewing party plans with Will and Margaret—who was such a slim little thing, barely five feet tall—Mary asked, "Is there something I should know about you and my daughter Mary? Some unpleasantness between you?"

Margaret glanced at Will, and Will, who was rolling a cigarette, turned his shoulder toward Mary before answering. "You know how she is." Will placed the cigarette between his lips and lit it with his left hand. He did everything left-handed. "Come on, Mother. You haven't noticed your firstborn is self-absorbed and jealous?"

Margaret placed her hand on his shoulder. "Now, Will."

Mary said, "Of course, I've noticed *that*."

Will exhaled a cloud of smoke. "When my wife enters a room, my sister flounces out."

"I've noticed that too," Mary said.

"I don't take it personally," said Margaret. "At least I try not to." She waved her hand, clearing cigarette smoke away from her face. "To be honest, I doubt Miss Mary would have approved of anyone Will married. She liked having him available to accompany her and Ida to parties."

Puffing happily, Will said, "I was content to escort her. She's my sister, and I love her. But I did get tired of her preening and snobbery, the way she insists on being called Mary Dowling Bond, as if it's one word."

Mary said, aloud, but almost to herself, "I don't understand why she didn't get Jim to take her to parties."

Will, whose hair, she noticed, was beginning to thin in back, cut his eyes. "I'm not going anywhere near that, if you please."

That sentiment dawdled awkwardly, and for once it was Mary who looked away. Then Will inhaled and held the smoke, before exhaling violently, as if trying to purge his anger. "I also think she blames Margaret for my move to New York."

"Should she?"

"Oh no," Margaret answered. "That was all Will."

Will said, "Katherine encouraged me."

"Of course," Mary replied. "She misses family."

"She could always move back," Will offered. "But I doubt she will."

"Why is that?" Mary asked, then added, trying not to seem so eager. "Do you think?"

Will's face assumed a familiar, bemused expression. "She likes being on her own."

And what about you? Mary wondered. Though she knew better than to ask.

The reception was a great success, and two days later, Will and Margaret were packing to return to New York. Mary planned to accompany them to the station and spent the morning reviewing pledges from the final Liberty Bond drive. She'd been the woman chair of Lawrenceburg's bond drives throughout the war, and that was another thing she'd no longer be doing once the calendar changed to 1920. Mary wondered if this meant she would take things slower, devote more time and not just money to charity, and spend afternoons and evenings with her Stewart grandchildren; Bobbie and Dr. John now had a fourth, another little girl. Mary hoped not. It made her twitchy even to contemplate a slower, less productive life. Still, if Will and Margaret would become parents and move home, she'd love it. From little hints Margaret dropped, Will wasn't happy at his job, which barely paid enough to get by. She knew he aspired to be a success in New York, and while she didn't want to root against him, it would be worth a lot to have him home. She'd also love to have Emmett back in Lawrenceburg after he finished Harvard, but that was almost two years in the future. She'd worry about that some other day. She no longer had to worry about him dying in the war, and that helped her sleep at night.

Someone knocked: *two soft, one loud, two soft, one loud,* which she recognized as John Cody.

"Missus Dowling, we ready to leave for the station."

"I'll be right out."

She closed the ledger, straightened her desk, and emerged from her office. Will and Margaret waited in the front hall, dressed to travel, surrounded by luggage, saying goodbye to Johnnie and Ida. Mary Bond was nowhere to be seen; what a self-important fool she was. Bill James, whom the other servants called Mr. Big Jack, entered through the front door dressed in the bib overalls he always wore. He snatched up Will's two largest valises, one in each hand, as if they weighed nothing, which she knew they didn't. Bill smiled, and she nodded her thanks. He'd been employed at Dowling Hall for decades, long before his hair and whiskers turned white.

Mary followed Will and Margaret, then watched Bill help John Cody load the luggage into the trunk of her Packard. After she joined Margaret in the rear seat, John Cody closed the door, then circled to the driver's side, getting in behind the wheel, alongside Will up front.

Johnnie and Ida came out onto the porch, waving goodbye. Just as they were about to drive off, Mary Bond appeared on the porch: unsmiling, not waving, but not wanting to appear in the wrong. *Just like her*, Mary thought.

John Cody shifted into first, and the car bucked a little.

"Excuse me, Missus Dowling. She's a bit touchy first thing."

They started down the long drive towards South Main. It was 10:22 on October 19, 1919. In a little less than three months, the Volstead Act would be the law of the land. But Mary wasn't worried about Volstead or the official beginning of Prohibition, though she should have been. After all, she'd prepared well. Instead, sitting in the back of her Packard, she worried they'd left the house seven minutes late, rather than worrying about the unseen locomotive bearing down on her and her family. But who can know the future? Not even someone as prescient as Mary Dowling. Once they were off Cream Street, she told herself, she'd ask John Cody to speed up. It wouldn't do for Will and Margaret to miss their eastbound train.

PART THREE

Enemy of the State

CHAPTER SIXTEEN

Prohibition Takes Hold 1920

It didn't surprise her, though Mary took scant satisfaction in being right. She'd warned Ed and Mike the first time in December 1918. "Find a buyer for your two thousand barrels. Later, it will be much harder. Try Canada, try Van Winkle, maybe Brown-Forman, or one of the others with a medicinal license. And do it now."

Did they listen? No. Mike was already ill, heart trouble, and he'd soon move from the wilds of Burgin to Ed's grand house in Lexington. Ed, a widower since Frankie died in 1912, after eight years an invalid, was focused on his coal and oil interests and didn't esteem a woman's opinion, least of all hers. Maybe he never got over how young she was when John brought her home; she was thirteen years younger than Ed. Or he never forgave her for speaking up publicly about the railroad, about which he'd been so wrong. Or hated that John weighted her opinion higher than his.

What was certain was that instead of getting out, Ed had appointed his younger son, Herbert, to manage Dowling Brothers. Together, they dithered and dawdled through 1919. And when the Volstead Act became the ludicrous law of the land in 1920, they had the same two thousand barrels in their warehouse. *Fools,* she'd thought then, and thought so even more strongly today. *Fools and bumblers.*

The first break-in occurred in February 1920. The second and third came in March. During the first two attacks, thieves breached the wall and rolled out a barrel. The third time, two barrels. Each theft happened between midnight and dawn on nights with no moon. Dowling Brothers was so remote, down a dark road in the woods of Burgin, there was nothing to do but hire an armed guard, equipped with a revolver. The fourth break-in led to six arrests, but even that didn't stop the attacks. Ed and Herbert hired a second guard in June, and after four barrels disappeared in September, they hired a third. All in all, during the first ten months of Prohibition, nine break-ins targeted Dowling Brothers. Five were foiled, guns blazing; four succeeded.

And now this, Mary thought, standing in front of Major Mike's open grave on a gray November morn. Beside her, Ida, Mary Bond, Gentleman Jim, and Johnnie, dressed in black. Major Mike was a worthy man, if not the brightest of the Dowling brothers. He'd never complained about the mandatory scrub-up before entering Dowling Hall. She could see him clearly, Dowling hair darkly wet, brimming with love for his nephews and nieces. He used to promise to write them all into his will, and she remembered, it must be ten or twelve years, how he'd importuned Will to move out to Burgin and take over the business, said he'd leave his share entirely to Will if he did.

Will said, *No,* or knowing Will, *No, thank you, Uncle.*

It turned out he hadn't written a will at all—*Just like him,* she thought—which meant his estate would be divided equally between his next of kin: Ed and his family, Mary and hers. *Major Mike, as badly organized in death as in life.* Which brought them to this cold dark day. Who could say if the stress of the break-ins had hastened Mike's passing? Too much for his damaged heart? Only the Blessed Mother knew, and really, what did it matter? Mike's heart had been failing for years, yet he'd attained the ripe age of seventy, while John died at sixty-one. It didn't seem fair.

The wind gusted, and Mary shivered, like a tree shorn of leaves.

Ida whispered, "It's so cold."

Johnnie answered, "That it is." And blew on his fingers.

Roused from her reverie, Mary watched Mike's pallbearers approach carrying his mahogany coffin. *Vanity*, she thought, yet Mike had spent so little on himself in all the years she knew him; likely Ed had selected the coffin's costly wood. She didn't know the pallbearers, who were Mike's friends from Burgin. The six strangers set their burden down; then, using ropes, two burly gravediggers lowered Major Mike to the bottom of his grave.

Mary glanced past the priest to Ed, surrounded by his children. There'd be a hosted meal at his home after the funeral, where she'd again suggest Ed empty the warehouse just as she had done at Waterfill. After selling thirty thousand barrels in 1918, she'd moved the last five to the basement of Dowling Hall. It was her whiskey, tax paid, nothing illegal about it. According to the monumentally stupid Volstead Act, private parties could store pre-Prohibition whiskey in their homes and share it with friends and family, just not distill or sell it. She imagined there would be whiskey aplenty at Ed's house.

The wind gusted again. Mary pulled her coat and shawl closer to her neck. *Damn Prohibition*, she thought, *and its dislocations*. A third of Tyrone was already gone, seeking work. The Klan was organizing in Lawrenceburg. Without whiskey to tax, the Anderson County budget was going to be halved. Nine break-ins at Dowling Brothers. High-speed chases through the hills and hollers. Will had told her a wild story about a Cincinnati lawyer, George Remus, who'd bought up distilleries with contracts to sell medicinal whiskey. Remus's trucks were regularly hijacked, and Will's friend in the know swore Remus's men hijacked the same trucks of an afternoon they'd packed that morning. Selling his purloined whiskey on the black market quadrupled its value, and Remus had grown rich as Midas. His mansion, Will said, made Dowling Hall look like a shanty. And because it was all so blatant, Will was certain Remus bribed the revenuers. *Damn them! Damn them on both sides.* And did she think Ed Dowling would heed her now? No, she did not.

Mary struggled to still her mind and remember Major Mike with grace and love. She glanced between her children, standing on both her left and right, grateful to have them beside her. Then Ed stepped forward and stood beside the priest, his hair still thick, though mostly white.

"I'm the last of the Dowling brothers," he shouted to be heard above the wind. "And I miss them sorely, I do! Our Johnnie gone seventeen years, and now our baby brother too. A finer, kinder gentleman never walked this earth."

Then Ed broke down and could not go on but extended his hand to Mary. She took it and stood beside him, staring out at the assembled Dowlings.

"Please, Father," she said to the priest whose face she knew but whose name escaped her. "Some words of comfort and remembrance."

Yet when the priest began to speak, his words blew past, nearly unheard, on the frozen wind.

When they returned to Dowling Hall, Margaret was in the living room, holding her infant daughter. Ann Elizabeth, Will and Margaret's first, was ten weeks old. Margaret had delivered in Lawrenceburg; ever since, she and baby Ann had dwelled in Dowling Hall. Ann was beautiful, blond, and blue-eyed, and Mary was as smitten as any first-time nannie, although Ann, in fact, was her sixth grandbaby. Mary had redecorated the nursery and hired a night nurse so Margaret could get some sleep. Will remained in New York, though not, Mary hoped, for much longer.

"Did Ann nap?" she asked, handing her coat to Rose. "And Rose," she added, "please bring chamomile tea."

"Yes, Missus Dowling."

When Rose left, Margaret said, "She slept two hours, then I fed her, and now she's happy as can be."

Mary Bond, who had little interest in infants, frowned as she approached the couch on which Margaret sat. Gentleman Jim entered behind her, sipping a whiskey. *That didn't take long*, Mary thought.

Mary Bond said, "I read in last week's *Scientific American* that new mothers can't access half their brains, they're so flooded by maternal hormones."

"Did you read that?" Mary snapped. "Or invent it?"

Mary Bond cut her dark eyes at Margaret, whose blue ones brimmed with tears. "I read it, Mother." She shook her head fussily. "Come on, Jim. We're not wanted here."

Mary Bond departed in the direction of the main staircase. A moment later, Jim followed, nearly colliding with Rose, who was returning from the kitchen with the silver tea service.

"Watch where the hell you're going," he snapped.

Rose's eyes met Mary's, sparking with anger, then she looked down and away.

Turning to Jim, Mary said, "Don't talk that way to Rose. We are all God's children, aren't we, Jim?"

He flushed, then stole from the room.

Mary sat beside Margaret and took Ann in her arms.

"I'm sorry. My daughter wasn't always so mean."

Margaret dabbed tears from the corners of her eyes. "It's true I can't think very well right now. The slightest thing makes me cry."

Mary patted Margaret's cheek. "I gave birth nine times. Baby brain will pass, and then you'll have your beautiful children."

"Oh, Mother. Thank you."

"You miss Will terribly, don't you?"

"I do." She started to sniffle again. "See what I mean?"

Rose set the tea service on the coffee table in front of Mary and Margaret.

"Missus Dowling, would you like me to pour?"

"If you think it's steeped enough."

Rose's eyes brightened, knowing Mary was complimenting her judgement.

"I believe it has, Missus Dowling."

Mary said, "I'm sorry my daughter's husband snapped at you."

Rose poured a cup of tea for Margaret, then one for Mary. "You know what *we* call him?" she asked boldly.

Mary supposed that by *we*, Rose meant the servants. "Please tell me."

"Lucky Jim."

"Why is that?"

"'Cause he don't have to do nothing for himself."

Mary was surprised by Rose's frankness, and though she would have preferred if Margaret hadn't heard, she replied, "Do you really think my daughter's husband is *lucky*?"

Rose allowed herself a small smile, matching Mary's, then excused herself. When she was gone, Mary began, "When Will visits next month?" Mary gazed at Ann's tiny face then bent and kissed her forehead, inhaling her sweet newborn scent. "Let's see what we can do about convincing him to move home. From what you've said, he might be ready."

Margaret nodded. She seemed shocked by the frank exchange with Rose, but Mary knew she wouldn't comment. "Mother, I think Will's used to being a big fish in a small pool, I really do. In Lawrenceburg, Will's *someone*. In New York, it's get up and take the subway to a job where they don't value him enough."

"That's terrible."

"It was thrilling, *really* thrilling, to stand on Fifth Avenue in the cheering crowd on Armistice Day. Everyone was going plumb crazy. I'll never forget it, and Will won't either. But I believe he's ready to come home."

Mary Dowling circa 1902, photographed in Manhattan.

Photo Courtesy of Bland Byrne

John Dowling circa 1890.

Will Dowling, circa 1910.

Margaret Lillard, Will's future wife, circa 1909.

Photos Courtesy of Bland Byrne

The Dowling family circa 1896, from L–R. *Front:* Will, Robert, George, John, Katherine, Ida, Mary Eileen. *Back:* Mary and John Dowling.

Dowling Hall.

Photos Courtesy of Bland Byrne

EMMETT AMBROSE DOWLING

Born November 1, 1898, at Lawrenceburg, Kentucky. Home address, Lawrenceburg, Kentucky. Prepared at Phillips Exeter Academy. In college four years as undergraduate. Instrumental Clubs, 1917–1918, 1918–1919, 1920–1921. Lambda Chi Alpha Fraternity, Secretary, 1920–1921.
Naval Unit.

Above: Bill James, Christmas 1954.

Left: Emmett Ambrose Dowling, Harvard Yearbook, class of 1921.

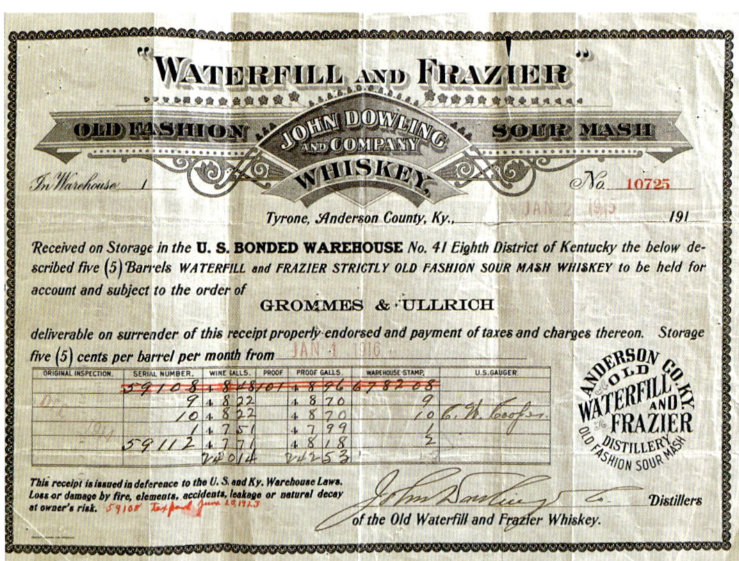

"WATERFILL AND FRAZIER"

OLD FASHION — JOHN DOWLING AND COMPANY — SOUR MASH

WHISKEY

In Warehouse 1 No. 10725

Tyrone, Anderson County, Ky., JAN 2 1915 191

Received on Storage in the **U. S. BONDED WAREHOUSE** No. 41 Eighth District of Kentucky the below described five (5) Barrels WATERFILL and FRAZIER STRICTLY OLD FASHION SOUR MASH WHISKEY to be held for account and subject to the order of

GROMMES & ULLRICH

deliverable on surrender of this receipt properly endorsed and payment of taxes and charges thereon. Storage five (5) cents per barrel per month from JAN 1 1916

ORIGINAL INSPECTION.	SERIAL NUMBER.	WINE GALLS.	PROOF	PROOF GALLS.	WAREHOUSE STAMP.	U.S. GAUGER.
	9	48 22		48 70	9	
	10	48 22		48 70	10	C. W. [illegible]
	1	47 51		47 99	1	
	59112	47 71		48 18	2	
		240 14		242 53		

This receipt is issued in deference to the U. S. and Ky. Warehouse Laws. Loss or damage by fire, elements, accidents, leakage or natural decay at owner's risk. 59108 Tax paid June 20, 1923

John Dowling & Co. Distillers
of the Old Waterfill and Frazier Whiskey.

ANDERSON CO. KY. OLD WATERFILL AND FRAZIER DISTILLERY OLD FASHION SOUR MASH

Waterfill and Frazier receipt for bonded whiskey, January 1915.

Top left: Courtesy of Harvard Yearbook Publications; *Top right:* Courtesy of Bland Byrne; *Bottom:* Courtesy of Allen Barteld.

Mary's D & W Distillery, Juarez, Mexico, circa 1930, front above and back below.
W.E. Dowling thirteenth from right.

Top: Photo Courtesy of Bruce Beam Phillips

Mary in Juarez, Mexico, 1928.

Joe & Katie Beam with their granddaughter, Katie Lou.

D&W Distillery, Juarez, Mexico. Mary's original doubler from Waterfall & Frazier distillery, transported from Kentucky. The doubler now resides at Vendome Copper & Brass Works in Louisville, Kentucky.

Photos Courtesy of Bruce Beam Phillips

The Dome Bar in Hotel Paso del Norte.

Hotel Paso del Norte, El Paso, Texas.

Photos by Chris Konikee, CK Milestone Photography

Joe and Katie Beam with their sons. *Back row L–R:* Desmond, Wilmer, Otis, Charles Everett, and Harry. *Front row L–R:* Elmo, Katie, Joe, and Roy.

Above and left: Kentucky Club, Juarez, Mexico, interior today and exterior circa 1927.

Top Photo Courtesy of Bruce Beam Phillips

What a dear sweet girl, Mary thought. "We'll work on him, you and I, and convince him it's his idea. That's the secret of a good marriage." She smiled at Margaret and at Ann, whose forehead creased in concentration. She sniffed. "I believe your daughter needs her nappy changed."

Margaret rose and carried Ann from the room. It had been a long, eventful day, Mary thought, bridging Mike's death and joy in this innocent life. The dowager of Dowling Hall sipped her tea, smiling at what Rose had called her son-in-law. *Lucky Jim.* That was even more apt than *Gentleman Jim,* since it cut both ways.

As much as the insult pleased her, Mary Bond and Jim's behavior rankled. *Enough is enough,* she thought. She poured and downed a small dram of bourbon, then marched upstairs, turned left at the second-floor landing, and walked to the closed door of Mary Bond's quarters, which were the finest in Dowling Hall, except for Mary's own suite.

She knocked loudly, and after a moment, heard footsteps. A moment more, and Gentleman Jim—it was hard not to think of him as *Lucky Jim*—opened the door.

"Why, Missus Dowling," Jim began, as if surprised to see her.

"Where's my daughter?" Mary asked, though she knew Mary Bond was behind the bedroom door, at the other end of the sitting room.

"In here, Mother," Mary Bond called, "lying down."

Mary started towards the closed door, then turned back towards her son-in-law. "Please don't go anywhere. I want to talk to you after I finish with her."

Mary entered without knocking. Rather than being in bed, Mary Bond sat at her make-up table, in a gown and matching wrapper applying Pond's Cold Cream to her forehead. Their eyes met in the large mirror above the make-up table.

"I'll get right to it," Mary said. "Your treatment of Margaret is abominable. I won't have it."

"I don't know what you're talking about."

"Yes, you do. I don't expect you to like her. As far as I can tell, you only like yourself and the rich ladies on South Main."

Mary Bond swiveled on her stool. "Who do you think you are, Mother?"

"Shanty Irish, which you can't stand."

"I never said that."

"Actually, you did. If you weren't ashamed of where you came from, you wouldn't have accepted that poor excuse of a husband."

Mary Bond's eyes narrowed then swelled, like mushrooms after a hard rain. "How dare you!"

"We've spent many years not speaking truth to each other, you who is most like me in temperament and intelligence both. We're too damn old for that. You're forty-five and still living in your mother's house!"

"How dare you!" her daughter shouted. "Father would never let you talk to me that way."

"We both know John loved you over the moon, but he's been dead these seventeen years. And I don't think being loved like that was good for you."

Mary Bond began to cry softly.

"Cry if you must. Lord knows I miss him too. But I won't have you being such a monster to Margaret. You don't have to like her. But there'll be no more walking out of the room when she enters. And you must keep a civil tongue in your head. Do you understand?"

Mary Bond raised her chin, looked her mother in the eye. And nodded.

When Mary exited her daughter's bedroom, Jim was seated on the divan at the far end of the room, closest to the door to Mary Bond's suite, a *Collier's* in front of his face. Although he was pretending to read, the magazine was upside down. *He's been eavesdropping,* Mary thought. *As would I if married to Mary Bond.*

"I'll get right to it. I won't have you cursing at people who work for us, no matter the color of their skin."

"Missus Dowling." Jim set down the *Collier's* and came towards her. "I'd hate for you to think I was harsh to Rose because she's colored. I was mostly raised by colored women, and I love them dearly. I haven't a prejudiced bone in my body."

Or a thought in your head. "Be that as it may, you snapped at Rose, and I won't have it."

"Understood, Missus D, if I may call you that." He smiled. "Completely understood."

She nodded and stepped through the door. It never failed to astound her that a man so attractive on the outside, could be so empty within.

CHAPTER SEVENTEEN

The Boys Come Home 1921-1922

Will agreed to resign from his New York firm during his visit to Lawrenceburg in late March 1921. Mary was overjoyed. She and Margaret had conspired to convince Will it was his idea, but he knew her too well. Maybe it was the suggestion of a stipend for help managing her three main properties: Dowling Hall; Shonraugh, her breeding farm; and the summer camp on Gilbert Springs Road—seventeen acres on the river, with a three-story house large enough to host the entire family and guests. Or maybe it was her offer to help them buy Judge McBrayer's house, a few doors away on South Main, which had come on the market.

"Oh, Mother," Will said, the night before he'd return to New York to settle his affairs. They sat alone in the parlor, which doubled as her home office. Margaret and the baby had gone to bed. Will filled a cigarette paper with tobacco raised and cured on her farm. He rolled expertly, plucked a loose strand from the open end, inserted the finished product in his mouth, and lit up. Although manufactured cigarettes had become much more popular since the War—even women were smoking now—Will insisted on rolling his own, which were more economical, he said, and better-tasting. He exhaled the first mouthful of smoke. "Who do you think you're fooling?"

"What do you mean?"

He aimed his shoulder before he spoke. "I know you and Margaret have been scheming since Ann was born."

She didn't deny it.

"But you're right. I'm ready to move back, though not thrilled about accepting a stipend."

"I've bought George a hardware store, and I'm looking for a business for Johnnie. And let's not even talk about the cost of Exeter and Harvard."

Will cast a wry eye in her direction. "Nothing's too good for Emmett."

She ignored the insinuation of favoritism, which she knew was true. Emmett was the future. "Besides," she said, "I'll be using the money your uncle Mike left us."

"Didn't he die intestate?" When she nodded, he added, "You could just as easily give each of us our share."

"Why are you challenging me? I would never give George a lump sum. It'd be gone in a week. I already help Katherine every month. Bobbie doesn't need money, while it appears Mary and Ida will never leave Dowling Hall, which means I'll be supporting them forever. So, each of you have different circumstances and needs."

Will exhaled through his nostrils, and cigarette smoke filled the space between them. "Are you implying you'd make better decisions with our money?"

"Not necessarily."

"But you believe you would."

"Your father trusted me to make those decisions, so I suppose I do."

She looked Will in the eye; after a moment he turned away. When his gaze returned, he said, "I know that look: the Dowling stare. I've used it myself when negotiating terms and conditions." He sighed. "Mother, I love you very much, and you've always been generous, not just with me but with all of us. But frankly, sometimes it's hard to be your son."

She felt stabbed. "What do you mean?"

"I'm almost forty-two, and you're still in charge of everything."

"I'm not sure I understand."

"I think you do. It's how you like it."

"No one's forcing you to move back."

They took each other's measure. Will inhaled and exhaled smoke. Mary felt attacked, but was honest enough to admit, at least to herself, that what Will said was true. She did expect to be in charge.

She continued, "But if you ask me, it's the right decision. And you don't have to worry. You're very much your own man."

Will stubbed out his cigarette, then joined her on the settee. "Forget I said anything. I'm sure Margaret and I will be very happy in the judge's house." He leaned forward and kissed her cheek. "And just so you know, I'm delighted to move home. So, thank you." He started towards the door then turned back. "It's just that you and Father set such a high standard. It's impossible to live up to."

Mary remained on the couch long after Will went upstairs, thinking of what she might have said, instead of simply nodding. *Would you have wanted us to set a lower standard? We had nothing, but that's not how you were raised, so you can't understand. Would you want me* not *to help you buy the McBrayer house? How does that make sense?*

After she felt certain she wouldn't encounter Will on the stairs or in the corridor, Mary went up to bed.

In early April 1921, Heinrich called to say he had to be in Louisville, then asked if it would be okay if he stopped to visit.

"Of course. But I thought you'd retired."

"I *haf*, mostly."

When he didn't offer to explain, she answered simply, which was the truth of both her mind and her heart, "I'd love to see you. When shall we expect you?"

"*Vednesday*, I'll be on the ten-thirty train from Louisville."

"This Wednesday?" It was Sunday evening.

"I hope it's not too soon."

"Of course not. John Cody will meet your train."

She replaced the mouthpiece on the receiver; she now kept a phone on her study desk. She reopened the novel she'd been reading but closed it. She hadn't seen Heinrich in more than a year, not since he'd given her the farewell bracelet from Grommes and Ulrich. It was out of character for Heinrich to call so close to a visit. When they were in business, they arranged his semi-annual visits months in advance. The timing was awkward. Katherine and Helen were visiting from New York during Helen's school holiday, and of all her children, Katherine, who hadn't remarried after Henry died, would be most opposed to Mary having a suitor or, God forbid, a second husband. But Heinrich wasn't either—just a friend. And she was eager to see him.

Wednesday dawned sunny and warm, promising a fine spring day. The magnolias had dropped their blossoms, but the purple lilacs in the side yard remained in fragrant bloom. She'd had Bill James cut bouquets for the hall and dining room tables. At breakfast, when Katherine remarked she seemed unusually cheerful, Mary admitted she was excited to see her old friend and business associate Heinrich Heinsohn. Katherine's lips pinched together.

"Remind me, Mother. Who is he?"

Mary wondered how best to explain without bringing up Henry's death. "You moved to New York not long after Heinrich became part of our lives. He was my agent at Grommes and Ulrich for sixteen years."

Later, when she heard the Packard's tires crunching up the driveway, Mary hurried to the front hall. Heinrich looked much the same. Tall and thin, perhaps a touch more stooped, but with the same lively eyes.

"I'm delighted to see you, Mary."

"As I am to see you." She extended her hand, and he shook it warmly.

Katherine entered the hall, accompanied by Helen, her twelve-year-old look-alike and shadow.

"This is my daughter, Katherine O'Brien."

"Ah, yes," Heinrich answered. "The one who lives in New York. I'm delighted to meet you, Missus O'Brien, after hearing about you for so many years." He smiled. "And this lovely little lady must be Helen."

Katherine looked wonderingly at her, or perhaps, Mary thought, with disapproval. After a moment, Katherine recalled her manners. She said, "Mother's told me about you, Mister Heinsohn." Then, turning to her daughter, Katherine said, "What do you say, Helen, when someone pays you a compliment?"

Helen, a shy child, glanced at her mother, then at Mary, who leaned down and whispered in her granddaughter's ear, "Thank you, Mister Heinsohn."

Helen curtsied and repeated, "Thank you, Mister Heinsohn," then allowed herself to be led by her mother to the front parlor to resume their game of cards.

In part to escape Katherine's anxious regard, Mary took Heinrich to Shonraugh. It was a splendid day, fair and sunny. In Shonraugh's hills above the Salt River, it felt five degrees cooler than in Lawrenceburg, and spring wasn't as far advanced. Jonquils still bloomed, while air scented by a multitude of flowering trees wafted up from the river.

Mary led Heinrich past the main house and barns to a viewpoint overlooking the Salt. She'd had a bench built in the shade of an oak; the lush hillside, carpeted by Kentucky bluegrass, descended towards a bend in the river.

"Mary," Heinrich murmured, "this is gorgeous."

"Thank you."

"So, maybe you *vill* be content as a gentleman farmer?"

"You're right to doubt it." She smiled. "But I wanted to show you what our years together helped me buy."

"You're *velcome*." He glanced her way then looked again at the green hillside sloping down to the river. After a moment, eyes twinkling, he said, "Maybe I should *haf* advised you to hold onto a few thousand of your barrels to sell to these bootleggers. *Haf* you any idea *vhat* fortunes are being made?"

"I hear rumors." She smiled, which he met with one of his own. "But seriously, though we may have cut a few corners."

"Very few."

"We were honest and straightforward, and that's why customers liked buying my whiskey from you." She hesitated. "We made a good team, you and I."

After a moment, Heinrich answered, "You're *vondering*, no doubt, *vhy* I visit *vith* such short notice."

"To be honest, yes."

He nodded. They were always honest with each other.

"During my last visit, *vhen* I gave you the matching bracelet from Grommes…"

Mary shook back the sleeve from her right wrist to show Heinrich.

"A few things *vere* left unsaid. So, I am here to say them. And," he reached into his pocket, "I *haf* a final gift, this one from me."

"You shouldn't have."

"I *vanted* to."

He handed her a yellow satin jewelry pouch, three inches square.

"Go ahead. Open."

Mary un-snugged the pouch and found a small gold locket, an inch long and three-quarters of an inch wide. She recognized the raised gold symbols on the front: Greek letters twined around a cross, which symbolized JESUS. The cross and letters were surrounded by a cloud border.

When she pressed the side button, the locket sprang open. Inside, resting on a blue velvet lining, lay a gold rosary, seven inches long from the top of the chain to the tip of the crucifix. The chain was gold, as were the five decades of hollow beads and the disc where the two strands of beads met. The disc was embossed with *IHS*, the Greek letters for JES, an abbreviation for Jesus, much as Chas was short for Charles. A short final chain consisting of five gold beads descended to a crucifix. It was the finest rosary Mary had ever seen.

"It's beautiful."

"You're not going to tell me I shouldn't *haf*?"

She shook her head.

"Please," he said. "Look on the back of the crucifix."

She turned it over. Engraved in cursive on the long post of His cross, she found, *Mary from Heinrich 1921*.

Before words could form in her mind, Heinrich began, "The last time *ve* met, Mary." He took her hand. "There *vere* things I couldn't say."

"I know."

His eyes, so wise and loving, looked into hers. "I *haf* feelings for you."

"I've always cared for you."

"But not in the way I *vanted*."

It was a question, and she answered. "That's right."

"*Ve've* always been honest."

Mary removed her hand from Heinrich's.

"So, I return bearing a gift that reveals the truth of our friendship. My love for you, and the limits of your feelings for me."

"I've never owned a rosary, though my mother did." Their eyes met. "Thank you. I feel certain I'll use it more than this lovely bracelet." She moved her wrist around, and the sapphires flashed in the sunlight. "Though I love it too."

"Ach, Mary." He stood. "It's so good to see you."

They started back towards the house and barns where John Cody waited, because as he'd already told her, Heinrich had a train to catch.

She thought of taking his hand but didn't. Instead, she said, "I'll keep you in my prayers."

Emmett graduated from Harvard in June 1921, a month after Will and his family moved into the McBrayer house. After spending a luxurious month on Cape Cod at the family compound of a classmate, followed by three weeks in Newport learning to sail at another friend's cottage, Emmett drove back to Lawrenceburg in the roadster Mary had given him as a graduation present. After he unpacked, he came to see her, his face as tanned as Spanish leather. Blond highlights sparkled in his sandy hair, and his blue eyes shone with confidence. Mary concluded that his years at Exeter and Harvard had been time and money well spent—even if he had majored in Romance languages, rather than something practical. She wouldn't be surprised if he'd be in demand at society parties in both Lawrenceburg and Frankfort, as Will had been, and perhaps even in Lexington. There weren't many Harvard men in this part of the world, and good-looking bachelors were always welcome, whatever their educational pedigree. She only hoped he wouldn't get serious too soon with any young woman. She'd missed him terribly and would prefer to have him home for a few years.

During his eight years in the North, much of Emmett's Kentucky accent had been worn away, although the soft local consonants and familiar phrases (especially *You-all,* as pronounced in Lawrenceburg, with the accent on *You,* rather than the elided *Y'all* further south), had crept back into his speech. By early 1922, a casual listener wouldn't be able to tell he'd been away, although as a party trick after a few bourbons, Emmett could be prevailed upon to "talk Yankee." Then there'd be a lot of *Pawk the caw in Haw-vahd Yahd,* much to the delight of the young men, and especially the young women, gathered around him.

He slipped back in with childhood friends from the Five Families, but Mary was grateful Bobbie included him in her Sunnyside parties. Lexington relatives and friends also added Emmett to their invitation lists, and as the spring of '22 merged into summer, her two youngest, Ida and Emmett, began to host parties at the Dowling river camp on Gilbert Springs Road. "Camp," of course, meant a mansion. Mary had built it for $12,000 in 1920 and early 1921: 4,500 square feet; she'd been cash-rich after selling her whiskey. There was a dock and a boat lift on the river below the house, and Mary had okayed the purchase of a wooden powerboat from the Chris Smith company in Algonac, Michigan, which Emmett assured her was the finest made. His Newport friend owned two.

Summer evenings, Mary would often sit on the second-story wrap-around screened-in porch. She loved it there. *So peaceful.* The floor and paneled ceiling were planed from longleaf southern yellow pine, notable for its hardness, ability to take a stain, and resistance to rotting. She'd had the floor stained dark but kept the ceiling paneling light. She'd been told this species of pine grew slowly, which explained why the wood was so straight-grained, hard, and lovely. It was more expensive by half, but far the best for building on the river.

Six-inch around red cedar saplings still covered with bark supported the ten-foot-high ceiling. As a special treat, Mary had paid Bill James, on his days off, to construct a double-wide swing suspended between two saplings. For sitting? A repurposed black leather seat from a 1905 Winton Flyer. Mary loved to sit on the comfortable seat as the sky indigo-ed and the summer heat came down. She'd swing, and whorls of scented cedar bark would poof into the air. Below her, crickets chorused while on the dock young people talked and laughed. She permitted Emmett and Will, all her boys, really, to draw on the bourbon stored in the basement of Dowling Hall. They'd begun bottling the last barrels, although two yet remained, still aging. In addition, she owned two hundred bottles of French wine and champagne, gifts from Grommes and Ulrich.

She didn't care for either, so they remained in her basement, except for a few she'd given to friends. Without an inventory, she estimated Will, George, Johnnie, Emmett, and his friends had drained eighty or perhaps one hundred bottles of bourbon since Prohibition began two years ago.

At this rate, she thought, *I'll have enough for two hundred years, though surely this damn Prohibition will end before that.*

Two young women she didn't recognize stepped onto the porch. Backlit by electric lights in the house, they could have been anyone. Emmett's parties were getting larger and louder. Frankly, she didn't know where all the young people came from—Lexington, maybe—or how Emmett fed everyone on the allowance she gave him. Maybe the young people brought their own food in exchange for the free alcohol Emmett provided. Or maybe young people didn't eat. The young women coming towards her, talking loudly, seemed quite tipsy.

"Good evening, girls," Mary said, as they were about to sit on the swing, apparently not seeing her in the dark.

"Missus Dowling!" one of the girls exclaimed, a Bond, Mary believed, while her friend, unable to change direction in mid-air and not sit in Mary's lap, stumbled and fell. "You gave me such a start!"

The girl on the floor stood up.

Foolish little things, Mary thought, *and clearly inebriated.* They apologized a second and then a third time, and re-entered the house. She heard them bumbling down the stairs, then the front door opened, and the girls headed towards the dock to rejoin the revelers. There must be twenty at least. How *was* Emmett feeding them? Then wild laughter rose from the dock. Perhaps the girls were recounting how they'd nearly sat on Mrs. Dowling's lap!

Above the dock, a full moon floated, reflecting on the dark water below. In the distance, carried on the breeze, came the growl of a motorboat. Mary swung her legs, and the large swing shifted. Alone on a seat meant for two—and very nearly three!—she felt the stab of John's absence. He'd be gone twenty years next April; she'd be sixty-four in January. *Lord, Lord. Where had the years gone?*

She decided to join the crowd on the dock, but just then, the door opened, and Emmett stepped onto the porch.

"Hello, Mother."

In the half-light, he walked towards her, smiling. His collar was open, as were the top buttons of his shirt. His right hand clutched a drink.

"I must apologize." He couldn't stop smiling. "I gather Mary Ellen and Louise nearly plopped down in your lap." She could smell the bourbon on his breath.

"In my day," she said, "young women didn't drink in public."

"In my day they do." He grinned. "Especially when the bourbon's free."

She was growing annoyed, even more so when a storm of laughter rose from the dock. "When hosting a party your father used to say, 'One to begin, savored and slow, and just another to end.'"

"That's not what I heard. I heard Father liked to drink."

"Who'd you hear that from?" Mary asked, remembering the night they conceived him.

"My brothers."

Just then, a loud crash and splash, then hooting on the dock.

"Sounds like someone jumped in."

"Or fell," he replied, grinning.

"Damnit, Emmett, it's time to send the drunks home. You need to be more discreet."

That wiped the grin from his face. "Yes, Mother."

"We need to discuss your future. One Gentleman Jim in the family's enough."

His face showed he felt the insult she'd intended. "I'll go see what happened."

Emmett hurried downstairs. Was this what it felt like to be put out to pasture, sitting alone in the dark while life went on someplace near, but out of sight? She didn't like it. Heinrich was right. She was neither a gentleman nor a farmer, although she did love the river's beauty and liked to think how it would amuse John to know they owned such a place.

She swung her legs, and the swing moved. She swung harder. The chains creaked, and whorls of bark flew, scenting the air. Then Emmett stood in front of her again, breathing heavily. He must have run up the stairs.

"Louise, that's the girl who nearly sat in your lap, fell off the dock."

"Is she alright?"

"Her pride's hurt, and maybe her bottom, although I doubt she'll remember. She's been put to bed, and those who can drive, I've sent home."

The full moon shone on his face through the screens.

"Listen to me, Emmett. Bourbon built this house and sent you to Harvard. But it's not the having or spending of money I embrace, for many scoundrels are rich, but the making of it with your father. That's what I want for you, to make something of your own. That's what I can't abide about Jim Bond and your sister. The idleness. The waste. Do you understand, Emmett?"

"I do. But I can't talk about my future now."

"I know. Go back to your friends. But we need to talk soon."

He turned to go, but she called him back.

"With the way the world is, people's eyes are on us. You must be careful."

"Prohibition?"

"And the Klan."

He nodded. After a moment, Mary added, "What your brothers told you was true. Your father drank a dram or two each night before bed, and I drank one with him. And the night we made you, we might have had three."

They smiled at each other, long on long, then Emmett was through the door and down the stairs. Alone, she remembered the strength in John's hands and the warmth of his body beside her in bed. Lord, the man was a furnace on cold nights. He'd burned strong and bright, if not long enough, and left her to carry on. Bossy, controlling, as Will had complained to her in the spring. She'd always been so, that's part of what John loved. Or so he said. Mary looked out at the moon, lost in memory, once again the precocious shopgirl pursued by an older man.

CHAPTER EIGHTEEN

A Knock in the Night 1923

Looking back, she should have noticed. Signs, after all, were abundant. And she had noticed. Emmett's large parties at the river. Late night comings and goings in his roadster. Frequent invitations to black-tie soirees and dances. Nights at the ballet and symphony with girls from good families in Lexington, Louisville, and Harrodsburg, but never a request for funds or an increase in his allowance, a request she would gladly have granted.

But her attention was elsewhere. Will and Margaret's daughter Ann, now just down the street, had turned two at the end of August 1922, and Mary tried to see her every afternoon. Will, delighted to be back in Lawrenceburg, had joined the Rotary Club, been invited onto the bank board to vote Dowling shares, and had assumed a new position: Anderson County attorney. There was no fixed salary; county fines fed his compensation. George's hardware store was making money, or at least breaking even, but he often needed assistance with practical matters: bookkeeping, inventory, and payroll. She'd changed tenant farmers at Shonraugh, and in January and February, they'd lambed forty black-faced ewes bred to a new ram.

Mary spent one and sometimes two evenings a week at Bobbie's newly remodeled home, enjoying her four grandchildren. Bobbie and Dr. John had added a new wing facing the lake, nearly doubling the size of the original ground floor. Constructed in the Greek Revival style, two-story limestone columns, floated down the Kentucky, adorned the new front entrance. Although they hadn't asked for assistance—the Stewart Home and School was thriving—Mary contributed to the renovation by purchasing a banquet table and matching chairs, as well as a Waterford chandelier for the new formal dining room. She had also given Bobbie the matching Harvey Joiner portraits commissioned a few years before John died. The paintings by the well-known artist hung in Sunnyside's new first-floor living room, a reminder of their younger selves. Mary looked forward to seeing John, who looked especially handsome in Joiner's painting, each time she visited.

And then, in late February 1923, to cap off a wondrous twelve months, Margaret confided she and Will were expecting their second child come August.

"Mother." Margaret beamed as she was wont to, her blue-gray eyes catching the fire's light. "You're the first to know." She laughed. "Except for Will."

Mary was delighted. Still, underneath all the joys of a large and growing family, she keenly felt a lack of purpose. She considered asking Lee Campbell if she'd want to stand again for school superintendent, or perhaps recommend another qualified woman, whose campaign Mary would organize and fund. She needed an outlet for her enormous energy, little suspecting that it would soon be met in a way she could not have foreseen or wanted.

Monday evening, March 26, 1923, began like many another weeknight. Mary Bond and Ida went out with friends. Mary dined at home with Johnnie and Emmett, then they left. Her daughters returned at nine, Johnnie a little later. After bidding goodnight to Ida, who retired early, Mary moved to her study and settled in with Edith Wharton's *The Age of Innocence*. If Charlie Shelton, a no-account Lexington bootlegger, had knocked on the carriage door and asked to speak to Emmett, she knew and heard nothing about it until eleven p.m., when several vehicles raced up her driveway. Headlights swept her window. Brakes squealed. Boots thundered up the steps, then half a dozen male voices were outside shouting, "Open up! Federal officers. Open the door!"

Mary rushed to the hall just as Johnnie descended the main stairs, followed by Emmett, Mary Bond, then Ida in her night clothes. Live-in staff, led by her cook Mary Margaret, arrived from the servant wing. The pounding grew louder, more violent.

"Don't make us break it down. Open up, damnit!"

Mary met Johnnie's eyes. He threw back the bolt and opened the heavy door. Four armed officers flowed in, followed by two older men, wearing suits and ties.

"Mary M. Dowling?" asked the oldest of them, silver-haired and bespectacled.

"Yes," she answered, flanked by her sons.

"You're under arrest for violation of the National Prohibition Act."

"Nonsense."

"I assure you, it's not." He glanced at the paper in his right hand. "In addition, I hold warrants for the arrest of any and all adult children domiciled in this residence, including but not limited to, John H. Dowling, Emmett A. Dowling, Ida Dowling, and Mary Dowling Bond."

Behind her, Ida gasped.

"Who are you?" Mary demanded.

"Sam Collins, perhaps you've heard of me." He grinned repellently. "Federal Prohibition director for the Commonwealth of Kentucky. And now, my men and I would like to search your cellar."

Before she could form a response, Emmett asked, "Do you have a search warrant?"

"Which one are you?"

"Emmett Dowling."

"Ah," Collins replied, showing his teeth. "My associate, Federal Commissioner Wiard, holds the warrant."

Wiard held up a single sheet, which he did not offer for inspection.

Making sure her voice sounded as strong as ever, Mary said, "Leave my house and return in the morning."

The armed officers smiled. Collins shook his head. "Not tomorrow. *Now*. Before you remove the bourbon we know is stored in your cellar."

"I do not deny there's bourbon there, moved legally from my warehouse, all taxes paid."

"We'll see about that."

"Not until my son, Judge William Dowling, examines your warrant."

Collins folded the paper in his hand, then placed it inside his suit coat. "Does William Dowling live here too?"

"No," Mary replied. "Down the street."

Collins motioned to Wiard and whispered behind his hand. Wiard nodded. Collins said, "We're not required to do so, but in deference to your white hair, you have fifteen minutes to get him here. Then we're entering the cellar."

Mary Bond stepped forward. "How dare you talk to my mother that way! Show some respect!"

"I show the respect bootleggers are due. Which is none."

"What a disgusting ill-bred man you are, banging on doors in the middle of the night and insulting my mother. You have no idea how decent people behave."

Collins said, "Watch it, sister, or I'll run you in."

Mary said, "My daughter is *not* your sister." She glared at Collins, whose eyes behind his glasses were gray like his hair. "I'll call my son now. Given the hour, I'm sure he's asleep. Nevertheless, he'll be right over."

The next afternoon, Mary, Johnnie, Emmett, Mary Bond, and Ida were charged with conspiracy to violate the Volstead Act. On the advice of her attorney, Ed O'Rear, former chief justice of the Kentucky Court of Appeals, they waived their right to a preliminary hearing. Each was required to provide a $5,000 bond to guarantee their appearance during the September term at the federal courthouse in Frankfort. That night, over dinner in Dowling Hall, Margaret told the story of the terrible night, from her perspective.

"Will and I were fast asleep when the telephone rang in the hall. Will rose to answer it, and when he came back, he said, 'There are revenuers down at Mother's house, including the head man. And Mother wants me to come down.'"

Johnnie broke in, "That bastard Collins."

Mary frowned. "No swearing at the dinner table."

"What else should I call him?" Johnnie demanded.

After an encouraging look from Mary, Margaret continued, "Will was gone a good while, and when he came back, I was in the front room where we run the fire, because it was cold last night. I asked him, 'What did they want?' He didn't answer, and if I live to a hundred, I'll never forget. Instead of speaking, he leaned on the mantle and sobbed like his heart would break. 'What's the matter, Will?' I said. 'Those revenuers have arrested Mother, Emmett, John, Mary, and Ida for bootlegging.' And I said, 'But she moved that whiskey in broad daylight.'"

Mary smiled at her daughter-in-law. "That's right, I did."

"Then I don't understand, Mother."

Mary answered, "They said we were selling whiskey out the back door, but that's a lie."

"No matter." Will grimaced. "It'll be front page news in every Kentucky paper, starting tomorrow."

And it was. Citing Commissioner Collins, inch-high headlines declared it was the largest haul of confiscated whiskey in Kentucky since the beginning of Prohibition. Estimates varied from 4,900 quarts of bonded whiskey to 6,820. In addition, there were twelve to fifteen cases of French wine and champagne. Estimated value of fine whiskey had shot up to one hundred dollars a case, meaning the cache in Mary's cellar was worth approximately $50,000 ($900,000 in 2025 dollars). For several days, Prohibition agents guarded Dowling Hall to secure "the contraband," then the whiskey and wine were moved to a government warehouse in Frankfort, there to be stored until its "status was settled by federal court."

And just like that, a five-year legal battle began. On one side, the US courts and Prohibition agents, determined to convict a prominent family. On the other, an equally determined and increasingly outraged Mary Dowling. If she'd been feeling a bit bored and put out to pasture by the advent of Prohibition, which had turned her into the lady of leisure she'd never aspired to be, those days were behind her. For the rest of her life, Mary would have a project on which to focus her considerable energy and intellect. The fight was on, and that suited her. She'd always been a fighter.

Four months later, on a scalding July afternoon, Mary met in her study with Will and Ed O'Rear. They were going to represent her at the hearing Friday next before Judge Bethurum, legal advisor to Commissioner Collins.

Mary said, "I don't see how they can blacken our reputation on the say-so of some soda-shop bootlegger."

O'Rear and Will exchanged glances. O'Rear said, "I've heard from a confidential source—"

Mary understood he meant someone in the Prohibition office.

"—that the last time Charlie Shelton was arrested before the raid on Dowling Hall, he asked, 'Why do you always pick on the little guy instead of the big fish?'

"The agent conducting the interview, replied, 'We'd go after the big fish if we knew who they were.' Shelton piped up, 'I've bought whiskey plenty of times from the Dowlings in Lawrenceburg.'

"Right away Agent Field took him to Collins, and they hatched a plot to stop Shelton on his way to Lawrenceburg, search his car, let him go, then stop him again, and search his car a second time. Otherwise, Shelton continuing to Dowling Hall makes no sense. Not a man with seven priors."

"Don't you see, Mother?" Will asked. "It was a frame-up. What police call a sting."

"Of course I see. But a *sting* assumes he'd previously bought whiskey at Dowling Hall, which your brothers and sisters say is a lie."

Will focused his dark eyes on her. "You've asked *everyone*?"

"I have."

O'Rear said, "This wouldn't be the first time Prohibition agents have lied, nor the last. And I have it from that same source, Collins is under considerable pressure to land a big fish. And there's none bigger around here than Mary Dowling."

"I'm not sure I like being referred to as a fish."

"The point is," Will said. "A great deal of whiskey confiscated by Prohibition agents has disappeared. Collins wants people to forget that."

"I'm sure he does," Mary said. "I wonder into whose bank account the whiskey money is disappearing?"

"I very much doubt it's going into a bank account, Mother. More likely a mattress."

O'Rear sipped a glass of bourbon and branch, then set it down. "We can speculate, but it's not relevant to this hearing or the case against you in the fall term."

O'Rear's frank sentiment darkened the mood in the room. The men sipped. Mary pondered her options. After a moment, Will said, "Ed, correct me if I'm wrong. But it doesn't look good that the whiskey in Shelton's car was wrapped in the same gunny sacks as the bottles in our cellar."

Mary glared at Will. "Those gunny sacks are common as dirt."

"But not if the newspapers around the bottles are the same day as ours."

"Those two sacks," Mary said, "could have been stolen out of our cellar. And who's the jury going to believe, that soda-shop bootlegger, or all the character witnesses who will testify for us?"

A little later, O'Rear, who was stout and gray-haired, excused himself. Will and Mary accompanied him to the door, where she again thanked him for coming. The former judge climbed into his car and drove off.

Will said, "I'll be going too."

"Please come inside for a moment."

When they were again in her study, Mary said, "I don't think you should have been putting ideas about the gunny sacks in Ed's head."

"Mother, he's on *our* side. I'm sure the same thing has occurred to Collins. We need to be prepared."

Mary's outrage bled out of her. "Of course, Will. You're right."

Will looked at her with sympathy and love in his eyes. "This is all so new. You've never been accused of anything before."

She nodded.

Will continued, "In the long run, I believe we'll be all right. But as for next week's hearing, we should expect they'll revoke our licenses."

"I agree. Otherwise, they'd have no excuse to proceed to a trial in September. It will be strange not to have a license after all these years, even if there's no distilling to be done. But now, Will, you best be going. I'm sure Margaret's expecting you."

"That's not all she's expecting." He grinned. "And she says hot days like this are the worst."

"She's right about that."

Mary stood when Will stood, and though she did not hug him or any of her children very often, she did now. He was a good son, close to her heart. They walked to the door, then she watched him stride down the drive. When he turned left onto South Main, Mary acknowledged the source of the guilt she was feeling. Although she said she'd spoken to all his siblings, she hadn't quizzed Emmett, or for that matter, Mary Bond. Since the summer started, Emmett had been living at the river camp on Gilbert Springs, while talking to Mary Bond was unpleasant at the best of times.

But she needed to talk to them soon. And she would. If not tomorrow, or after Mass, scheduled for her house on Sunday, then before the hearing next Friday, although as Will said, the outcome was certain.

CHAPTER NINETEEN

Spider Cochran's Courtroom 1923

When the Dowlings' indictments were unsealed on September 26, 1923, two days before the scheduled start of their trial, Mary, Will, and her legal team were caught off-guard. Instead of a single, relatively simple charge of selling twenty-four bottles of whiskey to Charlie Shelton, Sawyer Smith, the young, ambitious district attorney for the eastern district of Kentucky, had charged them with a vast conspiracy. Smith, who'd been DA for less than two years, alleged that the Dowlings had illegally transported 1,600 gallons of whiskey to Dowling Hall for the purpose of sale; that on March 26 and 27, 1923, the day of the raid and the day after, they had conspired to sell that same vast amount. These infinitely more serious charges were in addition to alleged sales to Charlie Shelton.

All in all, there were six counts: two for illegal transportation, two for conspiracy, two for sales.

As Ed O'Rear explained, if convicted of all charges, Mary and her children could face significant time in the federal penitentiary in Atlanta. Mary, Will, O'Rear, and two of his younger associates, recently added to the team, were seated in the conference room of the Frankfort law firm Ed had joined after leaving the Kentucky appeals court.

Mary said, "Before I moved those barrels from the free warehouse at Waterfill, I checked with Elwood Hamilton, then the Prohibition commissioner. He said I was within my rights, and the whiskey would be safer in my locked cellar. So, when did it become illegal?"

O'Rear replied, "It's not. But it makes a better story."

Will, who wore a dark suit and tie identical to the other lawyers in the room, said, "And even if they allege that the whiskey was moved after Prohibition started—"

Mary broke in, "But it wasn't."

"That doesn't matter," Will said. "Volstead provides an exception for transporting pre-Prohibition whiskey to a private home for noncommercial use."

O'Rear glanced at his younger associates, who nodded. Then he said, "I'm not sure what their angle is. But I've known Judge Cochran two decades or more. Smart fellow. Harvard Law. Seventy years old, on the bench a long, long time."

Even older than I am, Mary thought.

"Unfortunately," O'Rear continued, "he's a true believer in this dry laws garbage, a teetotaler for many years. To make matters worse, he's one of those judges convinced he's the smartest person in the room. He goes on and on and likes to see his name in print." O'Rear grimaced. "I shouldn't disparage a fellow jurist, but you should know what we're up against. Since Sawyer Smith became DA, they've worked hand in glove on quite a few dry law cases.

"And one more thing," O'Rear added. "Facing such a sweeping indictment, we're not prepared to defend in two days. With your permission, I intend to petition Cochran to move the trial to the spring."

"Why would he," Mary asked, "since he's clearly not impartial?"

"Because it's the law," Will answered.

O'Rear, whose bushy eyebrows remained dark, though his hair was mostly gray, nodded. "Don't worry, Mary. By spring, we'll be ready, and I'll have a much better sense of what they're up to."

Then the meeting broke up, and the Dowlings, mother and son, headed for the door. Two days later, Mary and her four indicted children were seated in Courtroom A, in the high-ceilinged, marble-floored federal courthouse in Frankfort. Mary dressed somberly in a long black dress; her attire hadn't changed much in thirty years, though her face and figure were fuller, her thick hair no longer quite so thick. In her early forties, she'd colored her hair, but had given up that vanity when John died. She'd never been very concerned with her physical appearance, and now that she was nearly sixty-five, most days she couldn't be bothered with how she looked.

But this wasn't most days. Her children and Ed O'Rear had assured her every eye in the courtroom would focus on her, and it would be a crowded courtroom indeed, so would she please allow Mary Bond to apply powder and rouge.

"Think of it as protection, Mother," Mary Bond said, "from all those prying eyes."

She'd consented, and now, seated at the defendants' table, she felt as if she wore a mask. And that was fine, because the courtroom was even more closely packed than she'd imagined, like opening night at the theater. There was a full bank of lawyers beside her, and a table of newspapermen from Louisville, Lexington, Danville, even one from as far away as Owensboro. O'Rear had instructed her not to talk to any of them, and if possible, not even to make eye contact. From inside her masked face, Mary stared straight ahead or down at her hands.

Shortly after they'd been seated, Judge Cochran entered, and everyone rose, then sat a second time. The lengthy charges were read aloud, a mortification for which nothing in life had prepared her. Ed O'Rear stood, as she knew he would, and asked to approach the bench. Judge Cochran, tall and lean, almost gaunt, looked a great deal like a spider, though in his youth, she'd been told, he was something of a dandy, sporting a dark beard and muttonchops that joined at his moustache. The Spider, now gray and clean-shaven, nodded his permission, simultaneously motioning forward Sawyer Smith. Smith was also tall and lean, Emmett's height, but with dark hair and eyes. The physical contrast between short, stout Ed O'Rear and Cochran and Sawyer Smith, made her uncomfortable.

After a brief conversation, Smith, O'Rear, and Cochran retired to the judge's chambers. The courtroom buzzed, yet Mary remained focused on the wall behind the court stenographer, neither standing nor conversing, though all four of her children stood and spoke amongst themselves.

Mercifully, Cochran, Smith, and O'Rear returned soon. In a loud, lightly accented voice revealing his origins in Maysville, north and east of Frankfort, Cochran said, "Upon the request of lead defense counsel, I have agreed to continue to the March term, the proceedings which we have started here this day."

The Spider looked pleased with the sound of his own voice and the grandeur of his words. His gaze fell directly on her, and against O'Rear's advice, Mary met his eyes. "I may be doing them an injustice," Cochran smiled, "but I believe they did not realize until now that they would have to face a *regular* trial."

Cochran glanced at the all-male jury, encouraging them, Mary thought, to contemplate what sort of trial a family as wealthy as the Dowlings thought they were entitled to.

"Make no mistake," Cochran continued. "I believe the defendants ought to be tried, and they will be. But attorney O'Rear argued eloquently, and I am satisfied that they are not prepared to meet trial today.

"With that in mind, and so that there will be no question of preference for or against the defendants, I have granted a continuance until March, when their *regular* trial will commence." Cochran pounded his gavel. "Thank you, Mister Foreman and gentlemen of the jury. You are now dismissed."

In the crowded hall outside the courtroom, Mary walked between Emmett and Johnnie on one side and Ed O'Rear and his team on the other. O'Rear, who was only an inch or two taller than Mary, whispered behind his hand, "I guarantee you everything Cochran said will be in tomorrow's papers. As he intended."

"What of it?" Mary asked. "We got what we wanted, didn't we?"

"We did." O'Rear eyed her with admiration. "That we did."

CHAPTER TWENTY

Mistrial 1924

In February, Mary added a second prestigious lawyer to her team. William Fowler, formerly Kentucky's assistant attorney general, joined Ed O'Rear in time to help with jury selection. Like most men Mary admired, Fowler, who was fifty, had started out with little in life. Formerly a schoolteacher—he read law in the evenings—Fowler had risen to wealth and influence. Working closely with Mary, O'Rear and Fowler put together a list of eighteen character witnesses, including Mrs. Campbell Cantrill, recent widow of the congressman, and State Senator Bell, principal of Lawrenceburg High School when her children attended. Others included Dr. John Stewart, Bobbie's husband; Drs. Kavanaugh and Gilbert of Lawrenceburg; Mr. Jean, deputy tax collector for Mary's distilleries; and Mollie Shelton, wife of Charlie Shelton, the prosecution's star witness.

The trial was scheduled to begin Wednesday, March 12, and the night before, Mary couldn't sleep. She sat up and reached for her rosary. She knew she was innocent. But she also knew Smith and Cochran were the sort of men who didn't like rich women, and it didn't help that she was a prominent Catholic. The Klan had recently rallied in Lawrenceburg, vilifying Catholics as well as Blacks. She wondered what Mary Bond, who still belonged to the UDC, thought about that? Did she still think being married to a Bond would protect her? Did she *really?*

Mary wasn't certain the judge or DA were Klan, though maybe they were. She especially suspected the DA, and who knew about the jury? She fingered the ten beads of each decade of her rosary, saying a Hail Mary after each bead. After each decade, she prayed, *Forgive us our sins, save us from the fires of hell; lead all souls to Heaven, especially those who have most need of your mercy.* Then she replaced the rosary in its locket and closed her eyes. It was midnight, and she despaired of sleep.

Mary, all four sons including Will and George, who were not on trial, Mary Bond, and Ida swore Wednesday they had not sold whiskey to Charlie Shelton. Ida testified she was asleep at the hour Charlie Shelton alleged she'd answered the doorbell. Moreover, there was no doorbell at the side entrance so Charlie Shelton could not have rung one. When Smith asked Mary Bond, "Isn't it true Charlie Shelton gave you two hundred dollars for two gunny sacks of whiskey?" her face turned firetruck red.

"Why, I've never seen that piece of trash before today!"

"Objection, Your Honor," shouted DA Smith.

"Sustained. Strike the witness's response." Cochran peered down his long nose. "Keep a civil tongue, Missus Bond, or you'll be cited for contempt."

Seated thirty feet from the witness box, Mary watched her oldest daughter glower at the judge, who glowered back.

"Let me re-phrase," Mary Bond said, eyes flashing. "The honorable, upstanding Charles Shelton, he of seven prior bootlegging arrests, did not give me or any member of my family two hundred dollars, because we would never have admitted him to our home."

Later, when O'Rear challenged Shelton to identify the Dowlings he'd purchased whiskey from, he pointed at Emmett and Will, whom everyone knew hadn't been there.

One for our side, Mary thought.

On Thursday, Mollie Shelton, a waspish little woman, testified, "Johnnie Hampton at the Phoenix Hotel told me, 'Charlie fell out with me because I would not swear in court against the Dowlings.' I told him I did not and do not know anything about the Dowlings and therefore cannot say anything against them. Charlie tried every way to get me to swear." She smiled at Mary. "I couldn't and would not."

Throughout both days of testimony, Smith pushed a line of attack that surprised Mary and her high-priced lawyers. In cross-examination, he hammered Mary, Ida, and Emmett about a home office. "Wasn't it true," he'd ask, in as many ways as he could phrase it, that you did distillery work at home? And isn't it true your children helped, by performing clerical or secretarial tasks?"

"It is true," she admitted, trying to catch O'Rear's eye for guidance. "That when the distilleries were operating, we kept carbon copies of correspondence."

In his closing argument, O'Rear declared that the gunny sacks of whiskey had been planted on the grounds of Dowling Hall so Shelton could place them in his car to frame the Dowlings and thereby escape punishment for his many arrests. Smith countered—in her mind's eye, Mary saw him under the cowl of a Klansman—that the purchase was not a "sting operation" but merely to confirm Shelton's claim that whiskey was being sold at Dowling Hall.

By eight-thirty Friday morning, the courtroom was nearly full. By nine, when Cochran entered, looking like an emaciated spider, there wasn't an empty seat. After acknowledging that the two ludicrous charges of illegally transporting liquor had been dropped, Cochran continued his charge to the jury. "As you know, gentlemen, under the National Prohibition Act, it is unlawful to sell intoxicating liquor. It is also unlawful for anyone to have in his possession intoxicating liquor.

"There is one exception, and that is anyone may have intoxicating liquor in his possession in his private dwelling if used only for a private dwelling, occupied by him as his home for personal consumption of himself, his family, and by his guests entertained by him, if the liquor was obtained before the National Prohibition law went into effect.

"If you believe beyond reasonable doubt, the Dowling dwelling was used as an office of the distillery, you are to find the defendants guilty. If, however, you believe the Dowling home was used as a home, you are to dismiss the charges."

Of course, it was used as a home, Mary thought, *every day and damn night for thirty-seven years.* She glanced at O'Rear and saw that he looked worried. After that troubling insight, she kept her head down while Spider droned on and on, not only explaining the charges, but as her father used to say, *Beating a dead horse.*

After haranguing the jury for forty minutes, Cochran gave them the case, and the twelve men filed out. Mary did not feel optimistic, nor did her children. Emmett, especially, looked ill with worry. Will speculated that if the jury returned quickly, that meant they'd had little trouble deciding; since the case was complicated, that worked in their favor.

Minutes ticked by. Mary worried about Cochran's emphasis on whether Dowling Hall had served as an office of the distillery and berated herself for admitting she stored duplicates of business correspondence. But really, what successful businessman didn't work at home? By Cochran's logic, every business owner's home was an office!

After being out an hour, a cry went up that the jury was returning, and the crowd rushed back into the courtroom. Cochran entered, then asked the foreman, a red-faced butcher, if the jury had reached a verdict.

The butcher stood. "I'm sorry, Judge. We're hopelessly hung."

Cochran's features darkened. Sawyer Smith looked as if his nose had been sawn off.

Trying, but badly failing to sound impartial, Spider said, "Why don't you go back out and see if you can't reach a verdict?"

The twelve men filed out.

"If the jury's evenly split, or in your favor, this might be the end," O'Rear whispered.

Mary didn't believe that.

"But if there's only one or two votes for acquittal?"—O'Rear glanced at Fowler, and the younger lawyer nodded—"Sawyer will move to retry, I'm sure."

After twenty-five minutes, word spread the jury was returning. Spider returned, looking dyspeptic, and asked the foreman to rise.

"I'm sorry, your Honor. We're still hung the same. Ten for conviction, two for acquittal."

"Thank you," Cochran said, though he clearly wanted to say, *Damn you*. "The jury's dismissed."

Mary met and held Cochran's gaze. "The DA has informed me he intends to re-file in the September session. I'll see you and your family then."

Watching Cochran sidle out, Mary considered how much she loathed him.

CHAPTER TWENTY-ONE

Fire, Lies, and Bourbon 1924

Four months later, on July 21, a brutally hot day, when all fifteen employees were outside eating lunch, a fire ignited in Warehouse B of the Hinds and Baker distillery in the Forks of Elkhorn, just east of Frankfort. Newspaper accounts in the *Lexington Herald, Owensboro Messenger, Louisville Courier Journal,* and *Danville Advocate Messenger* concurred that the blaze began at twelve-thirty p.m., and, despite heroic efforts by the Frankfort fire department, the seven-story building burned to the ground. Firefighters managed to save adjacent warehouses in which government-owned whiskey was stored, but from Warehouse B, said to contain 2,200 cases and 1,500 barrels of whiskey, only thirty cases survived. Prohibition value of the lost whiskey was estimated at $1 million.

Most of the whiskey in Warehouse B was owned by Hinds and Baker and fully insured. But the building also contained the whiskey confiscated in the raid on Dowling Hall, which is why, while the fire yet blazed and bottles were exploding like artillery shells, Mary, Will, and Emmett had themselves driven to the Forks of Elkhorn where they watched firefighters hose down Warehouses A & C, while Mary's 450 gunny sacks, each containing twelve quarts of fine bourbon, allegedly went up in smoke in Warehouse B. Also lost was the French champagne and wine Heinrich had given her on behalf of Grommes and Ulrich.

Some accounts speculated extreme heat sparked the flames, or perhaps nearby orchard grass, scorched sere by the summer sun, was the culprit. Others cited faulty wiring on the seventh floor where the Dowling whiskey was stored. But as Mary watched the conflagration from a safe distance, she seethed with anger. She couldn't be sure what had happened. In the coming weeks, she'd receive what she considered proof: rumors of a bacchanal hosted in Lexington by Prohibition agents flush with cash, swilling Dowling whiskey. Yet as she watched smoke rise in a scene from Hell, the heat of the blaze firing her face and hands from hundreds of feet away, she knew in her bones that Prohibition agents had stolen her bourbon then set the warehouses on fire to obscure the theft.

"I've never told you," she said to Will and Emmett, then waited for their eyes to leave the blaze in front of them. "And I'll ask you not to repeat it. But when your father and I were starting out, some of the other coopers and distillers were none too happy. This was just before you were born, Will, so we had only two children and lived beside the cooperage. Over a few weeks, some of our barrels had gone missing, then one night, a fire started. Your father, Uncle Ed, and the night watchman managed to save the building. When your father returned, hands singed, face black with soot, he said, and I'll never forget the look in his eye. 'If they *foock* with you, Mary, *foock* with them twice. Do ye understand?'"

Will, and especially Emmett, looked shocked. They'd never heard her speak that word, and never would again. But she wanted them to understand how things used to be. Because this was war.

Will asked, "Did he find who set the fire?"

"Maybe he did, but he'd never say."

"Why not?" asked Emmett, always eager for insight into the father he'd barely known.

"He feared my temper, and what I'd do if he told me."

"What did Father do?" asked Will.

"I'm certain there were beatings administered." She looked from son to son. "Yes, I'm certain there were quite a few, and heads split aplenty. The harassment stopped."

Just then, something stupendous exploded inside Warehouse B. With an enormous crash, the roof fell in, and John Cody came running from the car, calling her name.

"Mother," Will said, taking her arm.

She was so angry, she pushed him away. Then she relented and let herself be led.

That evening, a reporter from the *Lexington Herald*, who'd covered the trial, rang Mary at home. Perhaps intending to rile her up, he said, "I expect you've heard about the fire."

"I have."

"But have you heard the insurance on the building was allowed to lapse a few days ago?"

She moved the mouthpiece away from her mouth and swore. After a moment, she responded. "No, I hadn't."

"I thought you might also want to know the fire commissioner has announced they'll only investigate the blaze if someone asks for it, but so far, no one has."

In her raging mind, Mary counted to three, then all the way to ten. "I hadn't heard that either."

"I wonder," asked the reporter, "if you have any comment?"

"None that you can print."

The reporter laughed. "Are you sure?"

What the hell. "I can tell you I carried no insurance on the whiskey they confiscated. It was insured in my cellar, but not there."

"Would you care to explain?" She could hear the excitement in his voice.

"I kept whiskey safely in my cellar for twenty-five years and treated friends in my house, as was brought out at the trial. But when they took the whiskey away, I said, 'I will never see it again.'"

The reporter waited a respectful moment, then, hoping for something even more sensational, he asked, "Why is that, Missus Dowling?"

"I've heard some people *steal* whiskey."

"Are you saying the whiskey in that warehouse was stolen?"

But she wasn't born yesterday, nor even sixty years ago. "I think I've said enough, don't you?"

He laughed. "Good luck at the trial come September."

Mary replaced the earpiece. She was going to need more than luck and hoped she hadn't been imprudent. But it had felt good to disclose even a little of what she felt.

Jury selection was set for Thursday, September 25. The Monday before, Mary and Will set out in her Packard for Ed O'Rear's office. It had taken Mary two months to regain her temper after the fire. She'd heard too many accounts from too many people of the Prohibition agents' drunken party in Lexington not to believe it was true. She'd begun studying the Seven Sorrows of Mary, hoping to find guidance in the Blessed Mother's example of dealing with sorrow. She was not, after all, nor did she care to be, in the business of administering beatings. She was sixty-five, a bit plump. She knew she should walk more and eat less. Still, her heart was good, and she could climb the grand staircase without having to pause on the landing, which was better than George, who seemed to have inherited the weak heart that killed John.

"Will," she said softly. "I should have asked before. What do you think of our chances?" Their eyes met. "And be honest."

He exhaled heavily. "Not good."

"Why?"

"With the jury hung ten to two against, a retrial works in the prosecution's favor. If you, Emmett, or any of the others change your testimony, Smith will go after you for perjury. But you can bet, he's studied the first trial to hone his strategy."

"So, what should we do?"

"I'm not a criminal attorney. And neither is Ed O'Rear."

She took that as the criticism Will intended. He'd mentioned before she needed a true criminal attorney, but she'd chosen Ed because he was an old friend and had been a prominent judge.

"I know. I'm still waiting on your advice."

"Which you'll likely reject. But I think you should plead guilty—"

"Never."

"—in exchange for no one going to jail."

"*Never,*" she repeated. "And you know why?"

"Because you rarely take my advice?"

"Will!"

"I'm sorry, Mother, but it's true."

"Because the charges are false. And because I won't give in to the corrupt bastards who stole our whiskey!" She realized she was shouting, and John Cody could hear every word.

"And *because,*" she lowered her voice, "they mean to demonstrate they're not as corrupt as we know they are. So, if we plead guilty, you know damn well someone named Dowling will go to jail."

"If they insist on jail, you can have O'Rear turn down the deal."

She saw the wisdom in Will's advice but couldn't stomach it.

A new attorney joined them in O'Rear's conference room. Introducing Wallace Muir, O'Rear explained, "Despite his youth, he has more experience in criminal trials than I do. Objections, points of order, all that. He'll be our attack dog."

"Woof," said Wallace Muir and grinned.

"Mary, apparently with Cochran's blessing, Sawyer Smith plans to argue that because you stored duplicates of distillery paperwork in your study, it turned the entirety of Dowling Hall into a business. Therefore, your cellar could be searched without a valid warrant."

"Why?" Mary asked, though she knew the answer.

Muir explained, "Pre-Prohibition whiskey for private use can only be stored at home. To search your home, they needed a valid warrant."

Will broke in, "Which they didn't have."

O'Rear said, "We now know their warrant was written on March 27, the morning *after*, meaning any evidence obtained on the twenty-sixth is inadmissible. Therefore, we'll win on appeal, even if we lose at trial.

"In the United States we have what is known as the 'Right of Castle,' meaning a man's"—O'Rear winked—"or a woman's home cannot be searched without a warrant."

Will asked, "But Ed, based on Cochran's charge to the last jury, wouldn't you say he supports Sawyer's line of reasoning? For all we know, he suggested it."

O'Rear and Muir exchanged glances. The younger lawyer said, "I wasn't at that trial, but from what I've heard, I agree. That doesn't mean the court of appeals will support it."

O'Rear added, "If we get that far. We may yet prevail at trial."

Mary asked, "Tell me, Ed. What do you think of our chances?"

O'Rear looked offended. "This isn't like handicapping the Derby."

"Why not?"

"It's a trial, not a horse race."

"So, you can't estimate the odds of acquittal?"

"No."

She turned towards Muir. "What about you, young man?"

Before he answered, a flicker of *something*—candor?—sparked in Muir's eyes, then blinked out. "Not really."

Mary said, "I wonder if I've chosen the right jockeys for this horse race you say isn't one."

O'Rear shot back, "I'm sorry you feel that way."

Mary glanced at Will, who shook his head.

Mary said, "Excuse my frankness, but I feel like we're being framed."

A gloomy silence settled over the conference room, and Mary left feeling enraged all over again.

The next morning, forty-eight hours before jury selection, Emmett knocked on her study door. She hadn't seen him much over the summer. He seemed always to be at the river camp or visiting friends in Lexington.

"Enter," she answered, smiling when her favorite closed the door behind him. Although she needed to believe she loved her children equally (a phrase included in her last will and testament), Mary couldn't help what she felt. Emmett was different, her comfort and joy after John died. Gazing at his still boyish face, she was often overcome by a strong feeling, especially when, like now, sadness darkened his blue eyes.

"I'm sorry, Mother. I should have told you before. Long before."

"What is it?"

"I sold whiskey to Charlie Shelton."

If her heart could have stopped without killing her, it just had.

"Not that night. That's a lie. But three or four times in November and December. Just like he testified."

Mary folded her hands and eyed her short, manicured nails. She'd broken one the other day, and there it was.

"I'm not going to explain or justify what I did. But I have a plan to make it right."

She squeezed her hands together and felt pressure build under the broken nail. "And your plan is?"

"To tell the truth."

"And what," she asked, furious, emphasizing every word, "*do you think* that *will accomplish?*"

"Only I'll be punished."

"Don't be naïve! You will not be pleading guilty to those bastards!"

Now Emmett's temper rose, matching hers. "You can't stop me!"

"Yes, I can, but I'd rather it was your own decision. If you bare your throat, don't you know what they'll do? Slit it!"

There was a knock at the door, and without waiting for an answer, Johnnie entered.

"Am I interrupting…something?" From the look on his face, Johnnie clearly knew he was. "I heard shouting." He hesitated. "Do you want me to leave?"

"No," Emmett answered. "I've just told Mother I sold whiskey to Charlie Shelton months before the raid."

"Oh, God." Johnnie's eyes widened, and he ran his right hand across his forehead, then dropped into the chair beside Emmett's.

"Your brother wants to plead guilty, but I forbid it." She glared at Emmett and then, eyes softening, turned towards Johnnie, the kindest and gentlest of her sons. "There's no telling what those bastards will do if he does."

"If I plead guilty, then Johnnie and my sisters will be in the clear."

"Nothing's going to happen to your sisters," Mary said, "no matter what happens to the three of us."

Still, Johnnie did not speak.

Mary continued, "Just yesterday, Ed O'Rear, the new attorney, Wallace Muir, and Will agreed, we have a good chance of winning on appeal, even if we lose at trial."

Emmett asked, "What about the truth, Mother?"

"I don't give a damn about *their* truth. My truth is: keep the Dowlings safe. And the larger truth is that rotten judge and DA, and all the agents who stole our bourbon, want to paint us as dirty Irish bootleggers, which you know is shite and nonsense."

"Please, Mother," Emmett said.

"No. I mean it. *No*."

At last, Johnnie spoke. "Little brother, it's commendable you want to fess up, and I appreciate you wanting to save my skin. But we're a family, and we're in this together."

Emmett said, "Listen to me, Johnnie. It was immature of me to sell that whiskey, because we *are* a family, and I put everyone at risk." He looked from Johnnie to Mary, then back at his brother. "But I'm not that Harvard whelp anymore. I've grown up since the trial started, and I can't let you or anyone else in the family be punished for something only I did."

Johnnie looked at Mary and smiled proudly. He had such a good heart, and she loved him for it.

Johnnie turned to Emmett. "You have grown up, little brother. And that makes me proud. And I also say, *it's about time*. And one more thing, and my apologies to you Mother for taking the Lord's name in vain. We're the *goddamn* Dowlings, and we stick together. So, keep your mouth shut, little brother, and let this play out."

Emmett didn't answer, but when Johnnie frowned at him, he nodded.

"Not a word about this to the others," Mary said, looking at Johnnie. "Not even Will."

After a moment, her sons excused themselves, leaving Mary alone, her dark thoughts subsuming the love and pride she felt for her sons.

CHAPTER TWENTY-TWO

Outrageous 1924

Despite an hour of telling the beads, while importuning the Blessed Mother to teach her acceptance, Mary slept little that night or the next one. Each time her eyes closed, she'd startle awake. If she allowed Emmett to plead guilty, he'd go to prison, no question. Who knew what terrible things might happen to him surrounded by all those criminals? George Remus, who everyone said made millions, had only been sentenced to two years in the Atlanta penitentiary, but Cochran clearly hated the Dowlings. What was to prevent him from sentencing Emmett to five years, ten years, or longer? Would he still be Emmett when they released him? Would she even be alive?

She told the beads, turned and tossed, tossed and turned.

But in another, less maternal part of her mind, she wondered. If Emmett did plead guilty, testifying he'd sold only a few gunny sacks, and no one else in the family knew, wouldn't that eliminate the conspiracy charge? Last spring, Cochran had explained to the jury that conspiracy required more than one person. That was one of the details that most enraged her. The very idea that she and her children had conspired to sell a few gunny sacks! Anyone who knew them *knew* that was a lie.

And yet. Mary refused to ask Ed's opinion; she didn't want him to know. She understood attorney-client privilege but wasn't sure it would hold. And YET! If Emmett pled, maybe no one else would be charged? But if he went to prison, she might never see him again. And those *bastids*—she liked hearing it in her head as John had pronounced the word—those BASTIDS had stolen her bourbon and set an arson fire to cover it up. And now they wanted her son? *Never.*

By Thursday morning, Mary was reeling from lack of sleep. Her stomach was upset, and she couldn't keep anything down except toast and tea. When Rose, who now helped her dress, glanced at Mary's face, she said, "Missus Dowling, you're not well."

"I'm fine, Rose."

Then she stepped towards her dressing table and fainted. Rose ran for Mary Bond, who called Dr. Gilbert and demanded he come immediately. When Gilbert arrived, Mary was conscious but light-headed, again in bed. He listened to her heart, checked her pulse and temperature, then sent everyone out of the room.

"Missus Dowling." Gilbert was gray-haired, although twenty years her junior. He was also a skilled doctor. "You're unwell. And your fever's a hundred and one. Have you been sleeping?"

She considered lying, but her hands wouldn't stop shaking.

"No."

"Eating?"

She couldn't bear his eyes and closed her own.

"Very little. My stomach's upset."

He grasped her wrist. "Missus Dowling, open your eyes. I'm going to give you something to help you sleep, but first, you must eat."

"What I need," she balled her hands to stave the shaking, "is to dress for the courthouse."

"You've got a flu, which is going around again, and you're in no condition to go anywhere. Except possibly the hospital."

"No hospital."

"Then you'll eat and take the sedative I prescribe. I'll send word with Will to Judge Cochran. They'll have to do without you today."

"But I must—"

"What you *must* do is take care of yourself. You're this close"—he pressed his thumb and second finger together—"to being quite ill. You'll do no one any good, least of all yourself, by appearing in Frankfort."

An astonishing thought rose in Mary's tired mind. It was strategic for Dr. Gilbert to send a note. In fact, if she pretended to be sicker than she was, Gilbert would send subsequent notes, and the trial would be continued to spring. After Emmett's revelation, she was certain they'd be convicted, not of selling a few bottles, but of the whole vast conspiracy. Best to delay that as long as possible.

"You win, Doctor Gilbert, I am feeling poorly." She sighed and glanced surreptitiously at Gilbert, who looked pleased she'd given in. "Please send that note. And thank you."

Although Mary did not appear on Thursday, a jury was selected. In his opening statement, Sawyer Smith assured them he would prove all six counts. As Will explained that evening, Smith had reinstated the bogus charges for transporting whiskey, to again make the case against them sound more serious than it was.

The jury was sequestered Thursday night, but when, at Mary's request, Dr. Gilbert sent word Friday morning, Cochran continued the trial to Saturday. Late Friday, after she again feigned exhaustion, Gilbert alerted Cochran, reaffirming the seriousness of her condition. With little choice, Spider postponed the trial to March 1925.

Saturday morning, still officially confined to bed although miraculously improved, Mary requested three fried eggs, home fries, buttered toast, and jam. Rose set the breakfast tray in front of her. Before leaving, she asked, "How are you, Missus Dowling? You gave me such a fright."

"Don't tell anyone, Rose, but I'm fine."

Rose patted her hand. "I'm glad."

In her servant's eyes, an unasked question: *By touching you, have I overstepped?* Mary replied by squeezing Rose's hand. "Thank you, Rose." And then: "How's Aunt Ida?"

"She doing fine, 'specially for her age."

"If you don't mind my asking, how old are you?"

Now it was Mary's eyes that wondered if she'd crossed some invisible line.

"Fifty-nine my next birthday."

"You look younger."

"Working keeps me young." Rose smiled. "And my grandbabies don't leave me no time for getting old."

Before she could pose another question, Rose was out the door, and Mary started in on breakfast. It felt good to be hungry again. She imagined the scene late yesterday in Cochran's chambers. DA Smith, who'd started referring to her publicly as "the old woman" must have been in a snit. And Cochran? She could imagine his thoughts: *It wouldn't do for the old woman to faint, or even worse, expire on the witness stand. That would generate too much sympathy. Why, it might even lead to another hung jury, and then, where would we be?*

In Hell, where you belong. Mary sipped her tea. She had no illusions about Spider's motivation in granting the postponement: ensuring her conviction. What he didn't know was that a delay of six months would allow her to put an outrageous plan in motion. She was not going to let this trial destroy her family. If she had to pretend to be old and weak, she would. Anything to gain an advantage.

She'd decided to reach out to Lee Campbell for business contacts in El Paso. In particular, she wanted Lee to ask her brother-in-law, Judge Buckler—whom Mary had met several times—about a whiskey wholesaler named Antonio Bermudez. She'd sold Bermudez a thousand barrels in 1918 but knew very little about him.

Dreams of Juarez consumed her. Now that she had finagled six months, she was bursting with energy—*My,* she thought, *but these eggs taste fine!*—and she wanted to act immediately. She'd learned from a friend in Bardstown that there was already one successful distillery in Juarez, which was just across the border from El Paso. Fort Bliss, the second largest US Army base, was only seven miles away. Soldiers and every other stripe of American, the infamous and the famous, streamed across the border day and night. El Paso streetcars stopped in front of Juarez bars and cabarets. She'd been told by that same friend that Juarez whiskey flowed freely across the Rio Grande. Legally distilled, illegally smuggled, with great fortunes being made.

She needed to talk to Emmett, to share what she'd been obsessing about since yesterday. Truth be told, she'd been considering it for weeks, months, even years. Immediately after their arrest? Just a pipedream. When her bourbon was stolen? Something to consider. But since Emmett's confession? It occupied her day and night, and she'd reached a stunning conclusion.

She picked up the intercom, dialed Rose in the kitchen, and asked her to send Emmett to her room. He arrived faster than she expected, her breakfast at most half-eaten.

"Mother." He hurried to her bedside. "Is everything all right?"

"Better than all right." She filled her mouth with lukewarm but still delicious home fries, crispy and studded with peppers and onions. "How would you like to go to Mexico and work on your Spanish?"

"I'd love to."

"Then let's go."

He eyed her suspiciously. "Why?"

"It's time to teach you some lessons Harvard didn't."

"Like what? Accounting?"

"Risk-taking. *Big risks.* I don't mean selling a couple cases of bourbon to a two-bit bootlegger."

He looked chastened, then his jaw stiffened, and he looked her right in the eye. "What do you mean, Mother?"

"The government, Cochran, Sawyer, the revenuers—they have all been treating us like we're some kind of terrible criminals, when they stole our forty-eight hundred bottles of bourbon, and in

Louisville, New York, Cincinnati, Chicago, all the big cities, there are real criminals making hundreds of thousands or millions of dollars bootlegging. So why are they spending so much time and money trying to get us for two cases?"

"You tell me."

"Because I'm a woman and a Catholic, and because they think people are stupid, and mostly they're right."

She filled her mouth again with potatoes and a bite of egg, savoring the rich flavors.

"Emmett." She set down her knife and fork. "You realize we're going to be convicted."

"What about winning on appeal like O'Rear said?"

"Yes, I'll have them file in district court to suppress the search and seizure because the warrant was illegal. And I'll ask for our whiskey back. How do you think that will go?"

She watched him think his way through it. "Badly. They can't give back what's gone."

"That's right. So even if Smith and Cochran need to bend the law, you can bet your last dollar, which is something you've never had to worry about, that someone or several someones named Dowling, will spend time behind bars. Their reputations as Prohibition stallions depend on it."

For a moment, he looked frightened, then he didn't. "So what are you proposing?"

"These past couple of days, I've been doing a lot of thinking. And I realized, I've been so worried about clearing our *good name*, and keeping you and Johnnie out of prison, that I haven't been thinking right. I've been playing by their rules, when their rules are a pile of shite."

"So what do you mean to do?"

"We're going to set up shop in Mexico."

"*What?*"

"We're going to make bourbon in Juarez, right across the border, where it's legal."

He looked shocked, then he started to laugh. After a moment, he said, "You mean it, don't you?'

"Damn right. We're going to make of *lots* of bourbon, and you're going to get really good at Spanish. Now leave me alone or my breakfast will be too cold to eat."

Emmett closed the door behind him, and Mary sliced into her last egg. It was lukewarm. Then her mind moved to what worried her. By law, Americans needed a Mexican partner to own a business. To invest the large sums required, she'd need someone who spoke good English. Someone she could trust. Someone hungry and on the way up, just like she and John had been forty years ago.

My, she thought, *this egg is delicious,* and she helped it along with a forkful of potatoes. Sawyer and Smith had no idea who they were dealing with. She'd get even, she thought, *more than even.* As John had taught her years ago, she'd teach Emmett now. *If they foock with you once, foock with them twice.*

I might be old, Mary thought, and cleaned the last smear of yolk on her plate with a crust of toast, *but I ain't dead yet. In fact*—she smiled to herself—*I'm still hungry.*

PART FOUR

Back in Business

CHAPTER TWENTY-THREE

Dashing Antonio Bermudez
January 1925

For New Year's Day brunch, 1925, Mary asked Rose to prepare black-eyed peas. Other family favorites would be served, but Mary insisted on black-eyed peas because all around the South, they were said to ensure good luck in the coming year. Why? Near the end of the War Between the States, that's how people survived; Yankee raiders took everything else. Mary didn't much sympathize with the Confederacy, but growing up, she knew about hunger. Some oldsters believed it was necessary to eat 365 peas, one for every day of the year, but Mary doubted her digestion could handle that many. Still, she planned to make an effort—she needed to change her luck—and she'd invited Will, Margaret, and their girls, because she wanted Will to hear her big announcement.

After the dishes had been cleared, and Margaret left with her girls for the short walk home, Mary led Will, Johnnie, Mary Bond,

Emmett, and Ida into the front parlor. George wasn't feeling well, and he'd gone upstairs to rest. After everyone had settled comfortably, Mary said, "I'm planning to re-open Waterfill and Frazier."

"*What?*" Will exclaimed. "Don't we have enough trouble?"

Mary Bond said, "Have you lost your mind, Mother?"

"Hold on, you two." She smiled to see how easily they could be riled. "I'm not re-opening in Tyrone." She glanced at Emmett. "But in Juarez, Mexico, where it's legal, and there's a fortune to be made."

"*Mexico!*" Will exclaimed, looking even more aggrieved. "You're moving to *Mexico?*"

"*I'm* not moving. I'm planning to open a new distillery with a Mexican partner."

In the voice her younger siblings had feared when she had charge of them, Mary Bond demanded, "Where the hell is Juarez?"

Emmett replied, "Across the .Rio Grande from El Paso." He glanced her way then added, "Mother and I are taking the evening train from Louisville on Saturday."

"*This* Saturday?" Ida asked quietly. "In two days?"

Mary nodded.

Will said, "So you've been planning this for some time."

She nodded again.

"If you don't mind my asking…" Will continued.

"That will depend on what you ask."

"How much is this Mexican adventure going to cost us?"

She turned towards Emmett, indicating he should answer.

"*If* we go ahead," Emmett began, and from the expression on Mary Bond's face, Mary saw Emmett's use of *we* annoyed her. "In round numbers, as much as one hundred thousand."

Johnnie whistled. "That's a very round number."

For a moment, Will and Mary Bond maintained an angry silence. Then Will exploded. "Couldn't you have warned us or, Heaven forfend, asked for our input into such a major investment?"

"And with Father's money," Mary Bond insisted, "which is meant for us."

For a moment, full silence, under which a bomb *ticked, ticked, ticked*. Mary counted to three, then ten, then replied angrily, "It's not your father's money, it's *mine*! For twenty years, I've run the business, trebling our fortune. Someday, as Will knows, everything will be yours, to be divided equally. That time isn't now. Nor have I decided about Juarez. It depends on what I find there. But when it's time to decide, I'll do what *I* think best, as I always have, for all of us."

"Then why are you telling us, Mother," Will asked, "if your mind's made up?"

"Because I thought you'd want to know." She looked straight at Will then Mary Bond. "And because I don't want you telling anyone, and I mean *anyone*, where Emmett and I are headed. No one needs to know our business, except the family."

"So, now you're censoring us," Will declared.

"That's right, I am."

In years to come, society columns in the Lawrenceburg and Lexington newspapers would report Mary and Emmett's travels "to look after business interests in El Paso." But not in 1925. This journey, begun in secret, took more than forty-eight hours to complete: two overnights in a first-class sleeper, all meals in a white linen dining car. Emmett brought an advanced Spanish textbook from senior year to bone up on verb tenses, and *Don Quixote* in the original. Mary brought financial projections for building a model distillery, less the cost of land, which she expected her Mexican partner to provide. She carried a line of credit from Lawrenceburg National to establish her financial bona fides and a great store of hope for the enterprise.

On their second night, over dinner in the first-class car, served by well-spoken servants wearing black suits and white gloves, Mary asked, "Are you ready, Emmett? Because ready or not, here it comes."

"Ready for what, Mother? Dinner? Definitely ready for dinner."

"If we move ahead, your days of leisure are over."

"I'm more than ready."

"We'll work together on everything. You'll be my right-hand man."

"Thank you for trusting me."

"I especially need you to work on your Spanish. I don't want to get cheated."

"*No problema*."

"As I told you when I first took you to Exeter."

"Eleven years ago."

"You're the future. And the future is now."

She stuck out her hand, which Emmett shook. And the deal was done.

Twenty-four hours later, Mary met Antonio Bermudez over dinner in the Hotel Paso del Norte in downtown El Paso. He was thirty-three, six years older than Emmett, and very much on the rise. His middle-class family had moved to Juarez during the Mexican Revolution. Antonio attended business college across the border in El Paso, where he befriended sons of politicians and influential families. He later studied in Los Angeles, perfecting his English. After he returned, he married Hilda Mascareñas, daughter of a wealthy, well-connected family.

In 1927, two years after partnering with Mary, Antonio would be elected president of the Juarez Chamber of Commerce. In 1942, he became mayor. In 1946, he was chosen as senator from the state of Chihuahua (which included Juarez), but never served because in 1946, he was also named managing director of PEMEX, the Mexican national oil company. He'd remain in that position until 1958. In addition to becoming extremely wealthy, he'd be credited with modernizing the Mexican oil industry.

But that first evening, Antonio was still wholesaling whiskey, refurbishing railroad cars, and investing in bars and cabarets that catered to the huge influx of Prohibition tourists. Lee Campbell's brother-in-law, Judge Buckler, had highly recommended him, and when Mary and Emmett entered the Hotel Paso del Norte's formal dining room, she was delighted to see the Bucklers; she hadn't known they'd be joining them. Antonio impressed her immediately. He was not only tall and handsome but impeccably dressed in a gray worsted suit and matching cravat. She wasn't sure what she'd expected, but everything about Antonio put her at ease, especially the way he looked her boldly in the eye, shook her hand when offered, and said, with just the faintest of accents, "I'm delighted to meet you, Señora Dowling. I've heard wonderful things about you."

"As I've heard about you." Gesturing towards Emmett, she added, "This is my son Emmett. We work together on everything."

Antonio sized Emmett up quickly, but politely. *A gentleman,* Mary thought.

"*Mucho gusto,* Emmett." Antonio extended his hand.

"*El gusto es mio,*" Emmett replied, flawlessly.

Antonio turned towards a smiling Mary, who said, "Emmett majored in Romance languages at Harvard."

They sat down. Because of Prohibition, they were unable to order drinks to break the ice. Mary plunged ahead, anyway.

"Have you been able to secure a suitable parcel for the distillery?"

"I have," Antonio replied.

"How many acres?"

Antonio smiled. "South of the border, we measure in hectares. There are approximately two and a half acres to a hectare."

She turned to Emmett. "Did you know that?"

Emmett shook his head.

Mary continued, "I'm sure there's a lot we don't know about Mexico. But I can assure you, we're quick studies."

"I've no doubt." Antonio smiled. "Our site is four hectares, so more than large enough for the ten-thousand-barrel warehouse you requested."

"Rail service?"

"There could be."

"I'd like to see it tomorrow."

Antonio nodded.

Over the next few days, they would finalize details of their partnership. Who'd own what percentage. When construction could begin. Labor costs. Necessary licenses and whether bribes were needed to secure them. Mashing capacity. The need to import all grains from the United States since Mexican law forbade the use of Mexican grain for whiskey. How much quicker bourbon would barrel-age in Juarez because of the year-round heat. The need to bring a distiller from Kentucky since there were none available in Juarez. The size of the local market. The thirsty soldiers at Fort Bliss. The built-in competition from DM Distillery, already open and established.

But most details would come later, in large part because it would be indiscreet to discuss them in front of the Bucklers. What Mary would remember from the first night was how comfortable she felt with Antonio. She was an excellent judge of character, and she trusted him immediately. *He'll go far,* she thought, *and we'll prosper together*. There was one thing more, however, she'd always remember. When the main course was being cleared, she said, "I'm prepared to invest what's needed."

He nodded. "You have to spend money to make money."

Forty years earlier, John had said the same thing about bringing the railroad to Lawrenceburg. After a moment in the past, she returned forcefully to the present. "And I expect to make a great deal of money."

"*Claro*. We both will."

Then he sealed the deal by grabbing the check for the entire meal.

"No," she protested. "I invited you."

"I insist. This is my world, so I must be the first host. Besides"—he smiled—"we'll have many opportunities, as we build the business, to spend your money."

Everyone went home happy.

CHAPTER TWENTY-FOUR

Don't You Dare Cry
March 1925

The second Dowling trial began on March 11, 1925. Cochran's courtroom was again packed with Dowling supporters, newspapermen from around the Commonwealth, and as many curiosity-seekers as could squeeze into the limited number of seats. Sawyer Smith looked as if he ought to be twirling a handlebar moustache. Cochran so resembled a spider Mary had to remind herself he didn't have eight legs. Seated alongside her increasingly large and expensive legal team with her co-defendant children, with Will, Bobbie, George, and her daughter-in-law Margaret behind them, Mary endured Smith's long-winded opening statement without displaying any emotion.

She remained equally stoic throughout Wallace Muir's forceful rebuttal in which he assured the jury the trial would come down to whom they believed. A known bootlegger and convicted felon trying to secure a lighter sentence, or these pillars of Lawrenceburg society—he gestured in their direction—about whom anyone who knows them, and many do, will speak only of their integrity, as well as Mary Dowling's unstinting generosity to the less fortunate.

During Commissioner Collins's testimony, Mary's mind wandered to Juarez. She'd heard Collins's lies before. However, when he declared, "Despite Missus Dowling's protests, my men entered the cellar and found therein 478 gunny sacks identical to the ones Charles Shelton had purchased from Emmett Dowling," Wallace Muir leapt to his feet.

"Objection. DA Smith has not proven Charlie Shelton purchased anything from Emmett Dowling."

Spider pounded his gavel. "Overruled."

Moments later Smith attempted to introduce into evidence a gunny sack of whiskey purchased, he said, by Charles Shelton from Emmett Dowling. Again, Wallace Muir objected.

Cochran peered over his spectacles. "What is it this time, Counsel?"

"DA Smith has not proven this gunny sack was purchased from Emmett Dowling."

"Overruled."

Smith handed one of the newspaper-wrapped bottles to Collins and asked him to unwrap it. Which he did, revealing a bottle of Waterfill and Frazier.

Smith said, "Commissioner Collins, please read the date on that newspaper."

"March 25, 1923."

Smith faced the jury. "Let the record show, March 25 was one day before the search and seizure of approximately forty-eight hundred similarly wrapped bottles in the palatial home and offices of Mary M. Dowling."

Muir leapt to his feet. "The *illegal* search and seizure of legally possessed pre-Prohibition whiskey in the *home* of Mary M. Dowling."

"Sit down, Mister Muir. Do that again and you'll be cited for contempt."

Cochran turned to the court stenographer, an emaciated older man, seated just below the bench. “Strike defense counsel’s outburst.”

As the morning dragged, Mary’s attention wandered. Muir was a bulldog, but since she believed a guilty verdict was certain, it was hard to pay attention. Sometime later, she looked up and watched Muir and Sawyer Smith snarl at each other. It was odd to watch them battle when she already knew the outcome. But that’s what came of living so long. Nothing surprised her.

In the morning, a parade of witnesses testified to the Dowlings’ honorable and upstanding natures. Eyewitnesses averred Emmett had received no phone call asking him to return home from the pharmacy. Agent Wiard admitted that when Emmett was arrested, he did not have $200, or for that matter, any cash at all. Mary’s neighbors testified that from South Main, where Collins said he’d been parked, it would have been impossible to see Shelton’s car at the side entrance of Dowling Hall; large trees obscured the view. Therefore, neither Collins nor his men could have seen Charlie Shelton allegedly enter the Dowling home or flash his lights upon leaving it.

When Mary was questioned by Ed O’Rear, she emphasized she had not sold any whiskey since the dry laws took effect. After O’Rear finished, Smith began cross-examination.

“Missus Dowling, please state your age.”

“Sixty-six my last birthday.”

“Isn’t that rather old to be running distilleries?”

“Is it?” Mary smiled sweetly. “I’ve known older.”

“Please explain why Commissioner Collins and his men found forty-eight hundred quarts of whiskey in your cellar, much of it behind a locked steel door?”

“Certainly. For more than thirty years, I’ve stored whiskey in my cellar, which I serve to family and friends. As for the lock, in the first year of Prohibition, there were eight attempted robberies in the Dowling Brothers distillery in Mercer County. *Eight in a single year*. The lock was to deter thieves, of which there are many." Her eyes found Collins in the back of the courtroom. "And you may have heard that last July, the forty-eight hundred bottles of my whiskey that were *illegally* confiscated disappeared in a warehouse fire. Some people believe that whiskey was stolen too."

A gust of whispering blew through the courtroom. Cochran hammered his gavel.

Smith said, "Of course, I've heard about the fire. Terrible misfortune. Fortunately, no one was injured."

"I was significantly injured," Mary said, "by the loss of my property."

"*Missus Dowling*," Cochran broke in angrily. "You may speak only to answer the district attorney's questions."

"I didn't hear any question."

"That's *enough*, Missus Dowling."

Smith glared at her with undisguised hatred. "As for your intention to serve forty-eight hundred bottles to friends and family? You must have a very large family."

"I do. And quite a few friends."

Laughter subsided only when Cochran pounded his gavel. Smith faced the jury. "I had not realized that at sixty-six years of age, Missus Dowling is not only a woman of means and a bootlegger, but quite the jokester."

Muir leapt to his feet. "Objection, Your Honor, to the use of the term 'bootlegger.'"

"Sustained."

Smith's lips twisted. It was easy to imagine him behind a white cowl and hood.

"You've testified to moving your last five barrels to your cellar, *not* to sell the whiskey, which is what this court believes, but to avoid paying a possible federal tax increase."

"Correct."

"And you further testified, and your children Emmett, John, and Ida confirmed, that from time to time you bottled the whiskey, and I quote, 'as the barrels became too hot and leaky.' Your son Emmett testified to personally bottling twelve hundred bottles."

"Also correct."

"Given your advanced age—"

Muir jumped up. "DA Smith's constant mention of Missus Dowling's age is irrelevant and insulting."

Cochran snapped, "I'll allow it."

Smith continued, "Given your advanced age and ill health, is it fair to assume you did not inspect the barrels or do the bottling yourself?"

"Correct."

"Is it also fair to assume you discussed the leaky barrels and the decision to bottle with your adult children?"

She nodded.

"Missus Dowling, you must *vocalize* your answer."

"Correct."

"And where did those discussions occur, in one of your shuttered distilleries?"

"In my home."

"Where in your home?"

"In various rooms."

"Including your study?"

"Including my study."

"Is that the same room where you store duplicate distillery records?"

"Yes."

"So, you stored distillery records in the same room in which you discussed bottling. That sounds like a business office, wouldn't you agree?"

"It's my study."

"Business records, business decisions. An office by any other name, is an office."

Muir stood. "He's berating the witness."

"I'll allow it. But wind this up, Mister Smith."

"You're a smart woman, Missus Dowling. Everyone knows that. So, you tell me. You store business records in your study. You have business-related conversations there. It's where you conduct business, isn't it?"

"No," she said, losing her temper. "Have you never worked on a case at home? Does that make your home a business?"

"I ask the questions, old woman." He aimed a finger at her. "You *answer*."

"I will not. They're dishonest, misleading questions. Just like this trial is a heaping pile of manure intended to cover the smell of the corrupt Prohibition administration."

Cochran pounded his gavel. "Missus Dowling!"

She ignored him. "There's not been one shred of evidence that my family conspired to sell the forty-eight hundred bottles in my cellar, which would be there today if they hadn't been illegally confiscated then stolen from the government warehouse."

Cochran shouted, "One more word, Missus Dowling, and I'm going to charge you with contempt!"

"Go ahead. Lock up the old woman! But it doesn't mean storing records and having conversations in my home makes it a business, any more than putting a tutu on a pig makes her a ballerina!"

After a short recess, during which Mary paid a fine for contempt of court, O'Rear asked that Collins' testimony be suppressed. Cochran refused. O'Rear requested that the whiskey seized using an illegal warrant be returned and stricken from the record. Cochran again refused. After summations and Cochran's explanation of the four remaining charges—the frivolous ones related to illegal transportation had again been dropped—the case went to the jury.

As she was leaving the courthouse, O'Rear and Muir took her aside. O'Rear said, "I informed Cochran if the jury finds against you, which, I might add, is certain after your outburst, we're going to appeal."

"How long will that take?"

"Six to nine months."

"And if the circuit court decides against us?"

"We could appeal to the Supreme Court," Muir offered. "But it would be costly."

Antonio had estimated the distillery could begin operating in a year to fifteen months once they found a distiller. The timing might work.

"Sufficient unto the day," she said.

"By the way, Missus Dowling," Muir said. "That was one hell of a summation. Have you ever considered reading law?"

"I have not."

She smiled, then started towards her Packard, where John Cody and her children were waiting. She expected to be cheered by some and chided by others. But whatever they said, the hundred-dollar fine was worth it.

Just before noon the next day, the jury sent word they'd reached a verdict. Looking neither right nor left Mary advanced slowly towards her place in the courtroom. Margaret sat on the aisle one row back beside Will, already fighting tears. Mary stopped beside her. She was very fond of Margaret, but needed her to be strong, as she needed all the Dowlings to be strong. She bent and whispered in Margaret's small ear.

"Don't you dare cry."

Mary continued to her seat. Moments later, Cochran asked the jury foreman, "Have you reached a verdict?"

"Yes, Your Honor. We, the jury, find Mary M. Dowling, John H. Dowling, Emmett A. Dowling, Mary Dowling Bond, and Ida Dowling—guilty of all charges."

A hubbub began in the back of the room, where someone shouted, "For shame!" Someone else cried, "It's an outrage!"

But she did not turn her head, though her face grew hot.

"Thank you, Mister Foreman. Please be seated."

Cochran sneered at her, then turned his gaze to the jury box. "It would have been a great miscarriage of justice if you men had decided otherwise. You have done what I would have done. You have not neglected your duty."

Mary was appalled, but not surprised, by anything Cochran said. From the beginning, he'd made no attempt to appear impartial. But this. *This,* she thought and glared at her lawyers. *What the hell was this?*

"I will not fix judgement because I have been informed that in the event of a guilty verdict, defense counsel will appeal to the Sixth Circuit, challenging the validity of the search warrant."

Cochran looked at her again, as if to say, *Good luck with that.*

"Until we hear from the honorable members of the Sixth Circuit, defendants will remain free on five-thousand bond each, already paid."

Cochran struck his gavel, then exited through the door behind the bench. Mary walked from the courtroom, accepting well wishes but engaging no one until she reached the sanctuary of her Packard. Safe inside, she said to her children, "To hell with those bastards. On to Mexico."

CHAPTER TWENTY-FIVE

Enter Joe L and His Boys 1925-1926

As the spring of 1925 sped towards summer, Mary turned her focus increasingly to Juarez. She'd put out feelers from Frankfort to Louisville to Bardstown that she sought a distiller willing to relocate to Mexico on a three-year contract. Primary responsibility: set up and run her new Waterfill plant. One hundred percent legal, all expenses paid, top-drawer salary. Independent nature a must; some Spanish a bonus, but a lack thereof no impediment. Time of the essence.

She heard not one word and wondered if her outburst and the verdict had ruined her reputation. Most owners, except the few who'd acquired a medicinal license, were living off what they'd made when times were good. She could easily have done the same. She'd set enough aside for the rest of her life and her children's too. But even at the time, that plan had sounded dull.

No danger of that now.

John used to tease her about her temper. He'd say people thought she was a lady because she wore fine dresses and fancied expensive rugs. But scratch beneath the surface and you'd find the scrappy shopkeeper's daughter he'd fallen in love with. After flashing back at Spider Cochran and being cited for contempt, she guessed the whole world knew that too.

When she couldn't find anyone else, she decided to offer the Juarez job to Lester Elliot, her tenant farmer at Shonraugh. For many years, Lester had worked at Bond's Mill, barely three miles away, rising from mash hand to distiller. Dark-haired and blade-thin—Mary suspected he drank more than he ate—Lester had struggled after Prohibition started, like so many local men. But since early '23, when she'd hired him, he'd been doing much better. He and his wife had several young children, and in the two years he'd been tenant farmer, Lester had worked hard, rarely lost an animal, and seemed grateful for the chance to live at Shonraugh, with its lovely view over the Salt River.

"Lester," she said, on the warm May afternoon she called him into the living room of the big farmhouse the Elliots never owned enough furniture to fill. "What would you think about going back to distilling? It'd pay a lot more than farming."

Like everyone else in the county, Lester knew about the trial, though, of course, she'd never discussed it with him.

"Well, Missus Dowling, I'd love to, but I'd be afeared of getting caught."

"Not here, Lester. In Mexico."

"*Mexico?*" A look of befuddlement crawled over his features. "Mexico, Missoura?"

She thought he was pulling her leg, but a closer look convinced her otherwise. "No, Lester. Mexico, Mexico."

"Ohhhhh." He grinned. "I'll have to ask the missus."

Lester's missus didn't take long. "She'd miss her kin," Lester reported. "And anyway, she'd heard there ain't much to eat in Mexico."

Mary thanked him, and when he walked away, counted herself lucky he'd turned her down. But she was no closer to finding her Juarez distiller.

Two months later, still without a distiller, she prayed to Blessed Mother Mary at the Sunday Mass at Dowling Hall. Maybe the plan to move Waterfill wasn't sound. By letter, Antonio had confirmed that the cost of the distillery, including disassembling and transporting her still and doubler from Tyrone to El Paso by train, was $80,000 to $90,000. And because Mary had been in the bourbon business for more than fifty years, she knew to add another 10 or 15 percent. So, say a round one hundred, confirming her original estimate, which would include land, warehouse, a three-story distilling tower, and a bottling plant, everything first-rate. And though that was a small fortune, Antonio pointed out that DM, established in Juarez by two Virginians, but now owned by a Spaniard named Gomez, was making a very large fortune, supplying all the bars and cabarets in Juarez, including the ones Gomez owned, with its primary brand, Straight American. And though they hadn't talked in specifics yet, she knew a great deal of DM's production was smuggled north across the Rio Grande. Mary hadn't seen it with her own eyes, but on her trip to El Paso, she'd been told a spur track went straight to DM, that barrels were rolled onto boxcars, then shipped across the border with cash payoffs in dollars not pesos to ensure corrupt US revenue agents looked the other way.

Mary knew all about corrupt agents. Every time she thought about the confiscated whiskey the revenuers had stolen, it made her furious. Sitting in her front parlor, listening to Father Judemann invoke the gentle spirit of her Savior, she prayed not to be ruled by anger. But most of all, she prayed for a distiller willing to move to Juarez.

The next morning her prayers were answered. While reading Lexington and Louisville morning papers, relieved and grateful to find no mention of her legal problems, Mary heard the doorbell ring. Likely a friend of Emmett or Ida; a large group of young people was headed to Gilbert's Creek for the weekend. Moments later, Emmett entered her study, dressed for the river, to announce two men wanted to see her.

"Their name's Beam. They say Tom Moore sent them."

Tom, an old friend, owned distilleries in Bardstown, forty miles southwest. The last she'd heard he was in Europe. As for the Beams, there was a passel of them, all involved with whiskey.

"Send them in."

Emmett returned with the men, one old, one young, likely father and son. The older was five seven or eight. Large ears stuck straight out from a long face that finished in a strong jaw. He was lean and hard-muscled. Like so many whiskey men these days, he looked as if he wasn't getting enough to eat. His short gray hair verged on white, though his brows remained dark. Glasses could not conceal the intensity of deep-set eyes, which were appraising the size of the room and the richness of its furnishings.

"Missus Dowling, thank you for seeing us. I hope we didn't come too early."

"Not at all." She stood and offered her hand, which he shook firmly. *Good for him.* His palm felt hard and calloused. "Which Beam are you?"

"Joseph, but they call me Joe L. This here's my son Everett."

Everett looked about Emmett's age, dark-haired and even-featured. The young men clapped hands, then Emmett shook Joe L's.

Everett said, "Mister Tom Moore, he said you was looking for someone to take down your still and ship it to Mexico."

"I am." She sought Joe L's fierce eyes, which held hers. "Did he also say I need a man"—she turned towards the son—"or two, to reassemble the still in Juarez and stay on as distiller?"

Joe L said, "Yes, ma'am, he did."

They took each other's measure. "You've been a distiller?"

"Since I was nineteen, which weren't yesterday. I started in Gethsemane, for my brother Minor. That would've been eighteen and eighty-seven."

"So, you know your bourbon?"

"Like mother's milk. My great granddaddy was Jacob Beam. Jim's my first cousin. It's what we Beams do and have always done. I was one-third owner and distiller at F.G. Walker, down Bardstown way, till Prohibition landed on our necks like a stone, and I lost everything,"

If she'd heard it once, she'd heard it fifty times. *Proud men ruined.* "I'm sorry, Joe L."

"I'm sorry for your troubles too."

She appreciated the grit it took for Joe L to mention *her troubles.*

"What are you doing now?"

"Four years ago, I owned a thousand acres. *Now?* Working on a five-dollar-a-day road-roller crew."

Mary glanced at Emmett, who stood half a head taller than the Beams. Like her, he looked appalled.

Joe L continued, "Tom Moore will vouch, anything needs doing? Me and my boys can do it right. Back when plants ran only a few months a year? I distilled several such each fall. So, setting up and shutting down presents no problem."

"It might be we'll have to shut down during the heat of summer. I'm not sure about water for cooling."

Joe L nodded, as if he'd thought as much. "One thing more. I could bring my own yeast, if'n you need it. I've made a real study of yeast, all us Beams have."

"What about your family?"

"Seven sons, plus two who died. I'd need to bring my youngest, who's only fifteen, maybe one other to help with the work."

"And your wife?"

"Of course, Katie."

"She wants to come?"

"I reckon."

Thinking about Lester Elliot's wife, Mary said, "I should meet her, if she'll be moving too."

Joe L's deep-set eyes glinted. "You'll like her. She says you might have known her father, Meverel McGill."

"I did. A fine man and a fine distiller."

"Katie's the smart one in our house. She taught school afore we married. I only completed third grade with the monks at Gethsemane."

"Maybe I should hire Katie as distiller."

"Maybe you should." Joe L grinned. "She knows most everything 'bout setting up a still. Tell her how many bushels you aim to mash, she'll figure everything else faster'n you can say Jiminy Cricket. Water, yeast, piping, you name it."

Mary turned to Everett. "That so?"

"Everyone says she's the brains behind Pa."

The men laughed, including Joe L, and Mary felt a heart-piercing sadness that John had died before Emmett could bask in his love, as Everett clearly did in Joe L's.

"Why don't I come meet Katie tomorrow morning? I'm up early."

"She'd like that. We live right near the Cathedral, the old house folks say Bishop Flaget dwelled in."

"I'm guessing you're Catholic?"

"Nine boys, ma'am, what do you think?"

She laughed. "One last thing, Joe L, which I don't tell many people. Third is the last grade I finished too."

"Looks like you done okay."

"Yes, I did."

They took each other's measure one more time, then the Beams left.

When Mary entered Joe L and Katie Beam's old house in Bardstown, she discovered she looked enough like Katie to be taken for her sister. Katie was nine years younger, with shorter hair still more gray than white, but there was no mistaking the similar shape of their faces, which sang *daughter of the auld sod*. And they'd each delivered nine times, which had shaped their bodies and their minds. Nurturers their entire lives, they also knew the pain of losing a child. Most importantly, perhaps, Mary found in Katie another strong, smart woman. Virtually none of the wealthy wives in Mary's social world had used the intellectual gifts God had given them.

It didn't take long for Mary and the Beams to strike a bargain. Joe L and his boys would disassemble the still and prepare it to be shipped. Harry, the youngest, would travel with Joe L and the still to El Paso when the distillery building was far enough along, likely sometime in March, according to Antonio. Katie and another of her sons—either Everett, who it turned out was only eighteen but looked considerably older, or Otis, twenty-five and recently married—would come a few months later when the distillery was up and running.

Money wouldn't be a problem. She planned to pay the Beams well and rent them a house on the Texas side of the border, where the demands on their non-existent Spanish wouldn't be so constant. That's another thing she'd liked about Katie Beam. When they were finishing the crumb cake Katie served in the dining room of their big house, Katie said, "Don't you worry, Joe L may never learn a word of Spanish, except *gracias*, but I was good at French and Latin, and I aim to learn Spanish before we head down."

Mary said, "I believe you."

Joe L beamed. "I told you she was the smart one."

Later, when Joe L and Katie walked her to the door, Joe L said, "I want to thank you for taking a chance on us."

"I don't believe I'm taking much of a chance."

"You're not," Joe L replied. "Just the same, this is the first time I feel like I can breathe in five years."

"I know what you mean," Mary said, and left it at that.

Instead of heading home, Mary asked John Cody to drop her at the Basilica of Saint Joseph, which was close enough she could have walked. She passed under the roof and soaring bell tower supported by three-story-high white columns. The Proto-Cathedral, as they called it, was completed in 1819, when this part of Kentucky was wilderness. Bardstown had served as the seat of the first archdiocese west of the Alleghenies for decades, until the archdiocese moved to Louisville. She'd read that Bishop Flaget, a Frenchman, didn't want to be here, but he was such an effective archbishop, the Holy See wouldn't let him leave.

Mary entered the main sanctuary. Behind her, there was a two-story organ balcony, supported by more pillars. The arched ceiling, several stories high, was whitewashed. An enormous painting of Our Savior on the cross, with Mary Magdalene embracing his feet, hung over the marble altar. Smaller images of her Redeemer and the Blessed Mother adorned the upper reaches of the walls, just below the ceiling.

Mary sat in an empty pew midway between the vestibule and the altar. The cathedral was empty. She fingered the beads of her rosary, said a Hail Mary—*Holy Mary, Mother of God, pray for us sinners*—and her mind stilled. She prayed to the Blessed Mother for guidance and forgiveness, for the wisdom to lead her family through this crisis. She prayed she was not allowing anger, however righteous, to cloud her judgment and thanked the Virgin for her many blessings, including sending Joe L Beam her way, then sat in silence, basking in Her Love.

When Mary rose and walked toward the light of day, the heels of her sensible shoes clicked on the marble floor, echoing in the

Proto-Cathedral's vast reaches. Outside, she waited for her eyes to adjust, then started towards her Packard, where John Cody was already opening the rear door.

CHAPTER TWENTY-SIX

The Viciousness of the Righteous 1926

In December 1925, before her case went up to the Sixth Circuit Court of Appeals, Elwood Hamilton, the Kentucky Prohibition director before Collins, submitted an affidavit recounting his advice to Mary regarding the legal status of whiskey stored in a free warehouse. "There would be no protection. Move it to a bonded house, or better yet, to your own cellar, if you have room."

When Ed O'Rear read Hamilton's affidavit in court, Sawyer Smith objected to adding it to the court record, announcing, "Commissioner Hamilton's advice was incompetent." Cochran allowed the affidavit to be filed but declared in open court, "I do not believe a word of it."

Mary had known then, as surely as she loved Emmett and believed the Holy Mother was her second redeemer, that her appeal would be denied. And she was right. On January 6, 1926, the Sixth Circuit denied her appeal to quash the illegal search and return "the liquors seized thereunder to Mary M. Dowling, the legal and rightful owner." In the final paragraph of their ruling, the circuit judges opined, "We may add, however, that we concur fully in the findings of the trial judge that, *irrespective of the validity of the search warrants,* the search and seizure under the circumstances was not unreasonable. It was not the *private dwelling, but the business building, that was searched,* and it was in the basement of the business building that the liquor was found."

Dowling Hall, her home since 1886, was *a business building?*

Ten weeks later, in Cochran's courtroom, Mary, Johnnie, Emmett, Ida, and Mary Bond waited for Spider to announce their fates. An emergency motion to delay sentencing, submitted by junior members of her team—O'Rear was in Florida—had been denied, and it had come to this: Judgement Day. Would Cochran send her sons to prison? Her daughters? One look at Ida and any fool would know she could barely swat a mosquito that was biting her, much less bootleg whiskey. Or Mary herself, sixty-seven years old, her hair gone white since this travesty began, but with her fiery temper intact.

Mary stared, expressionless, at the door behind Cochran's bench. Her children's faces showed the strain of the past few years, while beneath the table Emmett's foot tapped nervously. She touched his hand, motioned with her eyes.

"Don't."

"I can't help it."

Cochran entered.

"All rise," cried the clerk.

Cochran settled on his bench. With a great deal of shuffling and coughing, the crowd found its seats. Mary had cautioned Margaret as she had a year ago. *Don't you dare cry!*

She'd said it to Ida too, but not Mary Bond, who was more likely to bite off Cochran's head than weep. *Good for her*. And what had Mary advised herself? Appeal and delay until D&W was up and running, then damn them all.

Cochran pounded his gavel. "Before I pronounce sentence, I have a short statement to read."

She stopped paying attention during Cochran's long, sanctimonious remarks, then resurfaced when Spider said, "The real question is whether they were selling whiskey from that residence."

Residence, she thought. *Residence!*

"Evidence was presented to show that they sold two sacks, each containing twelve quarts of whiskey, to Charles Shelton."

Judas.

"Officers then found 478 sacks in the cellar of the Dowling residence—"

Residence!

"—identical to those sold to Shelton. It is an insult to a man's intelligence to claim they were not selling whiskey from that house. Anyone holding to the contrary is either ignorant or wanting in integrity.

"It is an extremely painful thing to impose these sentences, but I must retain my own integrity."

Liar.

Cochran motioned to his clerk. The clerk intoned, "Defendants, please rise."

Mary and her children rose.

"Miss Ida Dowling and Missus Mary Dowling Bond, this court orders you to pay a fine of one hundred dollars each."

Not bad, Mary thought. Their bond, to be returned, was $5,000 each.

Ida and Mary Bond sat down.

"Missus Mary M. Dowling, I fine you the sum of ten thousand dollars."

Around the courtroom, people gasped. *Ten thousand dollars?* For two sacks of whiskey? When the average working man's salary was twelve hundred a year? Maybe she should have kept quiet, but she'd said nothing but the truth. She glared at Cochran, *the bastid,* and her heart froze, fearing for Johnnie and Emmett.

"Emmett A. Dowling and John H. Dowling, for your crimes I sentence you to a year and a day in the federal penitentiary in Atlanta."

Not just Emmett, but Johnnie, who'd done nothing.

"Defendants' sentences will be enforced when your last appeals have been heard, which your counsel tells me will be to the Supreme Court. Until then, you will remain free on the five-thousand-dollar bond already posted."

Cochran struck his gavel twice, then a third time, and disappeared through the door behind his bench. Mary and her co-defendants started towards the rear of the courtroom. Standing at Will's side, Margaret appeared red-eyed, having failed to obey Mary's injunction against tears.

Mary walked stony-faced from the courthouse, remembering what some dead poet had penned: *Living well is the best revenge.* Opening D&W was her surest path to living well, so she had best get on with it. Damn them for their lies. She had a new business to build.

CHAPTER TWENTY-SEVEN

The Twenties Roar in Juarez 1927

On March 17, 1927, the year in which Babe Ruth hit sixty home runs, Mary and Emmett disembarked at El Paso's Union Station. Like the Babe, Mary was swinging for the fences, because unlike the other passengers, she was there to make history. In contrast to their quick visit two years before, she and Emmett planned to stay for two or even three months. They'd each brought a steamer trunk and a valise of supplies. Although Mary had scoffed at Lester Elliot's food fears, she'd packed a country ham for Easter, a month away. She'd reserved a long-stay residence on the second floor of El Paso del Norte and planned to host the Beams for a holiday celebration. Only the first, second, and tenth floors were electrified, and because she didn't cook and never had, she'd have the rest of the meal sent up from the hotel dining room. But the centerpiece, an authentic country ham, must come from Kentucky, even if it meant some of her clothes would smell smoky until hung and aired.

They retained two porters, then followed them across the packed waiting room of Union Station, which soared four stories and burbled with more than one foreign tongue. Spanish, but also something Middle Eastern? Their first visit she'd scarcely noticed. This time she planned to study El Paso and Juarez, and she'd been reading everything she could find. The cross-border region was thriving. El Paso had become the most important commercial city in Texas and a regional rail hub. Six different lines converged, linking El Paso west to Los Angeles, east to Miami, north to Chicago and the Midwest, south into Mexico. The Mexican Revolution had chased many Mexican elites and their money north to El Paso; several big battles had been fought in and around Juarez, with General Pancho Villa commanding the Revolutionary forces. But Villa had been assassinated in 1923, and fighting was over. Boom times had found El Paso, and especially Juarez. A golden age, the papers proclaimed, of spending, vice, and tourism, all enabled by the idiocy of Prohibition.

For months, Mary had been hearing nothing but positive reports from Joe L and Antonio, who'd promised to send his car and driver to the station. She'd invested a fortune in D&W, which was already distilling bourbon, and though she'd been traveling two full nights and days, she thrummed with excitement. Mother and son emerged into the morning light. Better than his word, not only did Antonio's long black car wait at the curb, Antonio himself waved from the polished hood.

Mary hurried towards him. "How's the business? How's construction?"

"Ahead of schedule. And how are *you*, Señora Dowling?"

"Glad to be here. Please forgive my manners. How are you, Antonio?"

He smiled. "Also glad you're here."

Mary took the Beams to dinner that night in the Paso Del Norte main dining room. In addition to Joe L, Katie, and Harry, Otis, a middle son, taller than his brother and father and rounder-faced like his mother, joined the group with his infant daughter. Katie Lou Beam looked to be eighteen months. Her fine brown hair was cut in a pageboy; she wore a hand-embroidered little girl dress of Mexican cotton; her dark eyes shone.

"I'm pleased to meet you and your daughter," Mary said, when Katie Lou had been placed in her highchair, which Katie Beam had requested in Spanish. Mary sat next to Katie, the *silla para bebe* placed between Katie and Otis.

"The last I heard you were getting married."

A silence descended, then Katie said, "Otis's wife, Louise, was taken when Katie Lou was but ten months. A finer young woman never walked the earth."

"I'm so sorry."

Otis looked down, as if embarrassed by his loss. *Men,* thought Mary.

"I've been pulling *abuela* duty," Katie Beam said brightly, "when the men are at D&W. If you want, I'll teach her to call you *Tia,* which means Aunt."

"I'd like that very much. I already miss my granddaughters, who live down the street."

From his chair on her right, Joe L said, "You ain't asked yet, but I know what you're thinking about. Things is going right well. It's so hot, whiskey'll age in two years instead of four. We'll be hard to market this time next year."

"That's good, Joe L. Emmett and I want a full tour tomorrow."

"Yes, ma'am." Joe L tore a roll in two and smeared it with butter. "But something right curious, you should know. The area where we built? Was known as *Waterfill* 'fore we came. I heard a story more than once, says Pancho Villa was hurt bad one time, but found by two Kentucky brothers named Waterfill, who saved his life. Ever since, people in Juarez are right fond of Kentuckians." Joe L savaged his roll, swallowed, and grinned. "That side of the river? Just say Kentucky, and they'll buy you a drink. And let me tell you, there ain't no shortage of whiskey nor bars to drink it in."

Mary said, "Well, I don't know if it's the same brothers John and I bought Waterfill from, but it's charming to think so."

Emmett, who seldom spoke his first time around strangers, asked, "Can somebody recommend what's good?"

Harry Beam, who was always smiling, piped right up. "You're in Texas, Emmett, you can't go wrong with steak. They serve 'em big as your arm."

Everyone laughed, even Emmett.

The next morning, even though she expected it, it was odd to see her Tyrone still and doubler. She could say the same about herself, an Irish-Catholic Kentuckian in Old Mexico. The Catholic part fit: most Mexicans were Catholic. But her pale Irish skin was ill-suited for the Mexican sun, and hers stood out in a sea of dark faces. Just for a moment, Mary reflected on how everything was upside down compared to Lawrenceburg. No one was prejudiced against Catholics, and it was uncomfortable to be white. Strange, indeed.

But there was good strange and bad strange, and seeing her still here was definitely good, like encountering an old friend on a train. Antonio and their plant manager, Enrique, had done a fine job with construction; everything was first-rate. A three-story tower accommodated the still. The walls were brick and stucco; floors concrete; the roof corrugated iron to concentrate the heat and speed up aging. By Kentucky standards, D&W wasn't huge; as presently constructed, the warehouse could hold 2,200 barrels, racked ten high.

Joe L pointed to the four five-thousand-gallon fermenting tanks she'd told him she wanted. She'd also told him who to buy them from. They were bubbling away, and in all this heat, even in March, the smell of the mash was overpowering.

"That how you wanted them laid out and piped, Missus Dowling?"

"You know it is, Joe L. It's exactly like the plans I gave you."

He grinned.

"And while we're on it, since I'm calling you Joe L, why don't you call me Mary?"

"I'd be right pleased."

They continued their tour, Mary peppering Joe L with questions and instructions. Twenty years ago, she'd avoided telling men directly what to do around a distillery and had used Will and Johnnie as intermediaries. But she'd gotten too old and crusty to bother with such nonsense, and anyway, Joe L acknowledged Katie was the brains of their duo, so he must be comfortable taking orders from a woman. Even if he was half-kidding about who had the brains.

"Let's have a look at the grain," she said.

They walked to the bins, where the next mash load had already been measured.

"I don't like the look of that barley. Find a new supplier."

"You know what I think?" Joe L responded.

"You'd like to reduce the barley. But we already hashed this out and I'm not changing my mind."

"You're hard-headed, Mary."

"Always have been."

"Who's the distiller here?"

"You, but I'm the owner. I'm not changing what John and I worked out forty years ago. Seventy corn, fifteen rye, fifteen malted barley."

He led her towards their first barrels. She'd designed their system to yield roughly fifteen barrels a day, requiring the six boxcars a month of American grain she'd budgeted for. She'd also factored in two cents a pound duty, which she didn't like. But compared with the enormous cost of Prohibition to her family, she'd take two cents a pound every day of the week and twice on Sundays. She planned to make the two cents back and way more.

They passed a group of warehouse workers. Mary nodded and smiled, and the workers nodded and smiled at the strange white woman, *La Patrona,* who knew about borbón. Mary found it passing strange—*strange* was the theme—that all her workers except the Beams spoke Spanish, which made touring her warehouse feel like walking through a dream. Even the weather was strange. Cloudless blue skies and scorching afternoons without a speck of humidity. Everything familiar—she'd been making bourbon most of her life—yet different, down to the signs over the loading dock doors: *Bodega 1 and Bodega 2.*

Bodega meant *Warehouse.*

Late in the afternoon of their fourth day, Antonio took her and Emmett on a tour of the bar and cabaret district, which was even larger than Mary had imagined. Electric streetcars entered Juarez over the Stanton Street Bridge, which connected to Avenida Lerdo on the Mexican side. The streetcars turned right onto 16 de Septiembre for a few blocks, then turned right again onto Juarez Avenue, continuing north across the Santa Fe Street bridge, which led straight to their hotel. Antonio was delighted to report a million and a half passengers rode the streetcars every month. The entire route, especially the intersection of 16 de Septiembre and Juarez, was lined with bars and cabarets catering to an American clientele. The most upscale cabarets featured dance bands, gambling tables, and white-linen restaurants. Antonio was co-owner of several, which they'd soon supply with Waterfill and Frazier. A businessman at El Paso del Norte told her that bordellos located just two or three blocks east of Juarez Avenue catered to the American GIs from Fort Bliss. Now one of the largest US bases, Fort Bliss had recently absorbed more than a thousand new acres.

After the tour in Antonio's car, they ended up at the Kentucky Club, one of Juarez's better-known establishments. There was a long, polished bar and a beautiful dark wood back bar. Tables and booths lined the opposite wall. Like most Juarez bars, it served Straight American, the bourbon produced by their primary competitor, DM Distillery. DM had been founded in Virginia by a man named Pigg, who moved it to Juarez in 1909, then sold to local interests. The current owner, a friend of Antonio's, was a Spaniard named Gomez, married to a Mexican woman. Like Antonio, Gomez had started out as a wholesaler, importing liquor into Juarez from around the world.

"He does very well," Antonio said when they were seated at a table across from the bar. "Very, *very* well."

After the waiter dropped off menus, Emmett asked, "*La comida está bien?*"

Antonio smiled. "I'd forgotten you spoke Spanish."

Emmett replied, "*Entiendo mas que puedo decir. Falto practica.*"

"You'll have many opportunities to practice." Antonio turned to Mary, "Shall I order? The food is safe, if relatively simple, and quite good."

"Thank you," Mary said. "Nothing too spicy."

Antonio laughed. "I think I knew that."

When they were halfway through their enchiladas and something called guacamole, made from avocado, whatever that was, Antonio asked Emmett, "What do you think?"

Emmett, who'd been eating with gusto and washing down his food with Straight American, answered, "*Muy sabroso.*" Turning towards his mother, he translated, "*Very delicious.* Except for the bourbon, which is rough."

Mary had ordered Straight American to judge the competition. "I agree, this isn't very good."

Antonio smiled. "That's right. And that's good for us."

Just as they were finishing, the front door opened, suffusing the dark bar with light. A group of five men and a lovely young woman entered. The door closed, and the light dimmed. The young woman held the arm of a pie-faced, balding man in a dark suit. The men spoke English, though the girl looked Mexican: skin the color of café con leche and thick black hair, halfway down her back. Leaving the beautiful girl and his associates, the balding man approached their table.

"Mister Bermudez," he began. "A pleasure to see ya."

He sounds like a gangster, Mary thought.

Antonio replied, "As it is for me. Allow me to introduce my partners in D&W, Missus Dowling and her son Emmett, from Kentucky. Mary, this is Mister Caponay from Chicago."

Mary glanced at Emmett, who was trying to look as if he were someplace else. "A pleasure to meet you, Mister Caponay."

He took the hand she offered and pressed it to his lips. Very courtly and European, and a practice Mary loathed.

Caponay said, "Let's talk business some time. I think we have, you know, mutual interests."

Mary nodded.

"Enjoy your meal, Missus Dowling. I look forward to hearing from ya."

Caponay rejoined the beautiful young woman at his own table.

Whispering, Emmett asked Antonio, "Is that who I think it is?"

Antonio said, "I don't know who you think it is. But yes, I think it is."

Then he laughed.

"Mother," Emmett said that evening when they were seated in the living room of their hotel suite—which also included two bedrooms, two bathrooms, and a small kitchen—at El Paso del Norte. "Do you know who that was at the Kentucky Club?"

"Why don't you tell me?"

"Al Capone, the Chicago gangster."

"Why didn't Antonio say so?"

"He did. Caponay is how Capone is pronounced in Spanish. The final *E* is sounded as an *A*."

"Do you think that young woman was his wife?"

"*Mother!* I'm sure his wife is in Chicago."

"She was very beautiful, wasn't she?"

Emmett blushed. He had such fair skin. "You're teasing me, aren't you?"

"Maybe she's his daughter."

"Antonio told me she's the madame of one of the top bordellos in Juarez, which is where Capone met her. They call her La Bandita."

Mary was feeling a bit wicked. Maybe the whiskeys at lunch and the week they'd been away had at last lifted the trial from her shoulders. "Why didn't Antonio tell *me?*"

"Mother, he doesn't know you as well as I do."

"We do know each other very well, don't we?"

Emmett nodded.

"You know you can tell me anything, or say anything, and I won't be offended."

"I know that." He smiled the loving smile she treasured. "You're not just my mother. Sometimes I think you're my best friend."

He'd never said such a thing before, and she didn't know what to say. But it was true, they were friends, and now business partners, not just mother and son.

"Emmett, were you angry when I said I wouldn't support you being an aviator?"

"Yes," he answered immediately, and with heat. "I was."

"I'm sorry. Would you like to try now?"

He didn't answer, and she could see he was choosing his words carefully.

"First," he said, "there's the little matter of a year and a day."

"We're still appealing."

"Mother, we both know, the appeals are a waste of money."

She felt slapped, but she had encouraged him to be honest, so she bit her tongue.

"What about *after?*"

"A friend told me Halley Field, to be run by flying ace Ted Kincannon, will open this summer on Meadowthorpe Farm in Lexington. *After*, I'd love to take lessons."

"Then you should."

Emmett nodded and a moment later announced he was going down to the Dome Bar. Watching him head for the door, she nearly called out, *I love you so very much*. She didn't, but when he was gone, she wished she had.

Antonio invited them to Sunday dinner at his palatial home. He and Hilda had no children, but he had invited his brother, who had several, including a very bright and energetic five-year-old named Jaime. Mary was very impressed by Jaime and told Antonio, who smiled. "Maybe someday, he will visit you in Kentucky."

Antonio had also invited several business associates, whom he wanted her to meet. Since they'd started D&W, Antonio had become head of the Juarez Chamber of Commerce, and he knew everyone.

One of his guests was a loud, charming, large-headed young man named Carlos Villarreal Ochoa. Mary remained vague on Mexican naming practices, although Emmett had explained several times that a Mexican's middle name was his father's last name, while his last name was his mother's surname. That was the opposite of Kentucky, where a woman's maiden name was often used as a child's middle name to keep it alive in the family, as in John Dowling Stewart. Still, it was a good thing she had Emmett with her, whose Spanish seemed to improve every day. It was especially useful with Carlos Villarreal, who spoke as much English as she did Spanish, which was very little indeed.

After conversing with Villarreal for quite some time—he seemed rather *rough*, Mary thought—Emmett led her to a quiet corner of the large room where the crowd was enjoying cocktails and appetizers.

"You'll never believe what he told me, Mother."

"Try me."

"When I asked him what he did? He said he was a *contrabandista*."

"What's that?" She was hoping to return to the appetizer table for guacamole, for which she'd conceived a great fondness.

"A *smuggler*. I'm not naïve, but imagine telling that to someone the first time you meet."

"He probably told you," Mary said, "because he wants to smuggle *our* whiskey."

"He said many people smuggle, and they're all getting rich."

"Then we'll get even richer."

She headed back for more guacamole.

Smuggling came up frequently during their two months in El Paso and Juarez. When they visited the DM Distillery, Julian Gomez showed them the spur tracks that came straight to his warehouse. As they watched barrels being rolled into freight cars, Mary and Emmett said little, but she was sure Emmett had a million questions, as did she, although only one mattered: *Where were those barrels headed?*

Later, sharing a delicious dinner with Antonio in a quiet corner of Café Central, an elegant restaurant across the street from their hotel, Mary asked, "Where were those DM barrels going?"

Handsome Antonio, with his high cheekbones and knowing eyes, cut another square of ribeye, fed it through his lips, then put down his knife and fork.

"Why, Señora Dowling." He smiled. "Where do you think, when a barrel is worth twenty times more in the US?"

She cut her eyes at Emmett, then turned again to Antonio. "Why isn't the *freight* stopped at the border?"

Antonio took up his knife and fork, then sliced another morsel. "Pardon my manners, but I'm *famished*." After swallowing, he continued, "I thought you and your children, including Emmett, had been convicted of bootlegging."

"It's not what you think."

Antonio's eyebrows rose, then he patted his lips with a white linen napkin. "As I'm sure you know, there are ways of persuading American border agents to look the other way. Mister Caponay, whom you met, is very skilled at persuasion." He paused and met her eyes. "These are strange times, Señora Dowling. Prohibition will not last forever, though it would be better for us if it did. Until then, there's a great deal of money to be made by people motivated to do so."

She looked at Emmett, then back at Antonio. "In Kentucky, I was accused of being a bootlegger when I wasn't. Now," she thought how best to phrase this, "I have no such qualms, but I don't want any trouble."

"I guarantee there won't be any. I plan to run for mayor as an anti-vice candidate after all this is over. So, it wouldn't do for me to be arrested."

"In that case," Mary said, "arrange for rail service before we complete our bottling plant this summer. And let's add two more fermenting tanks as soon as possible, which will allow us to increase production by fifty percent."

"Señora Dowling, you have the soul of a businessman, and perhaps a *bandita*."

Mary knew that's what they called Caponay's girlfriend but didn't want Antonio to know she knew. "In for a dime," she replied, "in for a dollar, and I intend for there to be many. But there's just one thing."

"What's that?"

"I'd prefer you think I have the soul of a business-*woman*."

Antonio grinned, clearly delighted by the strong-minded *Norteamericana* whom fate had made his partner.

"Bandita," he said again, then returned to his ribeye.

Mary touched Emmett's hand, and his eyes came to hers. The meek might inherit the earth, but they wouldn't do well distilling whiskey south of the border.

CHAPTER TWENTY-EIGHT

The Klan Empowered 1927

Mary and Emmett kept extending their stay. Mary ate with Katie Beam and her namesake, Katie Lou, several times a week. They shared memories of Kentucky before cars and electricity, long-ago days when they each cared for a large family with their husbands gone all day—a simpler time, when their biggest fears were fires and their children's futures. Of course, even forty-five years ago, Mary could afford household help, while Katie could not. Still, Mary and Katie saw the world through similarly wise and thoughtful eyes, and it was a surprise and delight for Mary to make a new friend at her time of life—she'd be sixty-nine her next birthday—when many of the men and women she'd known best, especially the ones closer to John's age, had gone to their Maker.

Emmett busied himself at D&W. For the first time, he seemed to take genuine interest in whiskey-making, and she spent long hours with Joe L, Harry, and Otis Beam, teaching Emmett first the basics and then the finer points of distilling. It turned out he had a fine palate, likely inherited from his parents, but also refined by his years at Exeter and Harvard. He confessed to his mother that Exonians and Harvard men were hard drinkers. And though the future remained murky, with prison hanging over him and Johnnie, she could more realistically imagine a time when Emmett, married and with children of his own, would run the Dowling empire.

In May, Mary heard from Ed O'Rear that he and Wallace Muir had filed another appeal. In a bizarre development, J. Grey McLean, the court stenographer who'd looked at death's door, had, in fact, passed through without transcribing his notes. The old man's handwriting was so jittery and faint no one could read it. Her attorneys were thereby denied a court record to examine for errors. She'd given O'Rear permission to proceed, although she believed, as did Emmett, that it was likely a waste of money.

Emmett went out several nights a week to dance at the best cabarets in Juarez, catching the streetcar outside their hotel. His favorite was Lobby Café No. 2, which broadcast its orchestra on the radio. He also liked the Mint Café, which he frequented with Carlos Villarreal. The Mint was owned by American Harry Mitchell, once a soldier at Fort Bliss, in partnership with Enrique Fernandez, who, according to Antonio, was a notorious smuggler and counterfeiter. Mary occasionally went along, because the Mint had an excellent kitchen with a menu that included caviar canape, lobster cocktail, wild duck, halibut, and French lamb chops with peas. And if the Mint catered to smugglers? Who was she to turn up her nose?

On July 10, Mary arranged a business lunch at her hotel for Emmett, Antonio, and Joe L. She also invited Katie, although she wasn't officially an employee. But she knew how much her friend had helped with the initial set up of D&W and wanted to thank her in front of the men. Women's contributions so often got erased, which is why those damn McGregors had called her loan as soon as John died. If she hadn't become sole proprietor, everyone would have assumed she was "just the wife," though John had told everyone they were partners. *Maybe someday*, she thought, sitting beside Emmett in the El Paso del Norte dining room, *things will be different*. She'd also insisted Katie come because she was so fond of her. Sometimes you don't know why someone touches your heart; they just do. Take Ida Lyter and Rose. It had been that way with Katie too, since the day they met.

By July 13, when they left El Paso for Kentucky, the temperature kissed one hundred most afternoons. When they reached Lawrenceburg two days later, it was only ninety, but so humid and uncomfortable Mary didn't go out for days. Not so for Emmett, who resumed his life of hosting parties at the river camp. But he also worked to keep up his Spanish.

Not much had changed in the months they were gone, with one huge exception. Ida no longer lived at home. She had moved out shortly after Mary and Emmett left for Mexico. In December, at the age of thirty-nine (the same age Mary had given birth to Emmett), Ida had married Wallace Camp, three years her junior. Mary didn't respect Camp, whom she thought of as no-account and disreputable. Originally from Perryville, a small town thirty miles south, he'd lived in Lawrenceburg for quite some time. Several years ago, he'd become a regular at Emmett's parties, and that was how he and Ida became acquainted.

Camp, who'd worked as a government revenue agent at the old Dedman distillery in Mercer County, was arrested in 1923, when whiskey with an estimated value of $280,000 went missing. Along with two associates, Camp was sentenced by Spider Cochran to two years in the same Atlanta penitentiary Emmett and Johnnie faced. But Camp and his associates never served time, or maybe only a few months. Ida claimed she didn't know, and she certainly didn't care. She'd been one month shy of her thirty-ninth birthday when

Wally, as she called him, proposed. She'd thought no man would ever love her. Mary wasn't convinced Wally Camp wasn't in love with the Dowling name and Dowling money, but she had the good sense not to say so to her daughter.

Still, Ida was no fool, and she likely suspected what her mother thought, for she did not ask to be wed in Dowling Hall, as had her three older sisters. Instead, there'd been a private ceremony in Versailles, where fifty-one years earlier, Mary and John had spent their wedding night. The nuptials weren't announced in the society pages of the Lawrenceburg or Lexington papers. Mary held her nose and paid for a wedding brunch and a wedding night stay for the newlyweds at the Rose Inn. In lieu of a big wedding, and fearful of another Gentleman Jim in the family, she offered to buy Ida and Wally the Shell station on Bush Avenue across from the First Christian Church. They accepted, happily, which made Mary happy too.

On her wedding day in December, Ida had looked radiant. When she welcomed Mary and Emmett home from El Paso, she was still glowing. Wally was running the service station, and the newlyweds were living full time at the river camp, which they'd taken to calling the Camp house, as if it were theirs. When the weather turned in the fall, they planned to rent or maybe buy a small house in town.

"Mother," Ida said, when they had a moment alone, a few nights after Mary returned. "For years I thought, and I believe you did too, that I'd always live at home."

Mary smiled at Ida, who looked genuinely happy. Her narrow cheeks glowed, matching her auburn hair, and there was a different smile on her thin lips than had been there before.

"It's true," Mary admitted. "I did."

"For years I feared, and hated it so, that on my fortieth birthday, I'd still be at home, an old maid." Her eyes flashed. "And a virgin."

"Ida!"

"And people would say, as they always had, 'Poor Ida, poor Ida, couldn't catch a fella.'"

Mary had never seen Ida like this, and she rather liked it. "I don't think they were saying 'Poor Ida.'"

"Oh yes, they were. You don't know, Mother. You had eight children and Father, so you don't understand. They *were* saying it, and when they weren't, they were thinking it! *I* was thinking it. Always the maiden aunt, awkward to seat at the table"

Ida looked away and licked her lips, as if trying to taste whether she dare say more.

"I know you don't think much of Wally, Mother."

"I never said that."

"You don't have to. I know he's had troubles in the past. But no more trouble than we're having now."

Mary locked eyes with her daughter.

After a moment, Ida continued, "And he's not from the Five Families, but I don't care. I love everything about Wally, except his age. It's embarrassing that he's three years younger."

Mary thought so too but bit her tongue.

Ida said, "Wally loves me. *He* loves *me*."

"I'm happy for you. I really am."

Tears welled in Ida's eyes, her daughter last and least, so often overlooked.

"On my fortieth birthday, Mother, I *won't* be at home. I *won't* be an old maid, and I *won't*—"

Mary broke in. "I know what else you won't be."

Mary hugged her daughter, and with her meager arms, Ida hugged her back.

In September, the Lexington and Danville newspapers published articles mentioning that the court of appeals would soon rule on the Dowlings' request for a new trial based on the illegible notes of the deceased stenographer. Mary hated to see her name again in the press. Bootleggers raced revenuers through the Kentucky hills. In the cities, fortunes were being made in speakeasies where whiskey flowed faster than Bailey's Run, but Smith and Cochran had caught their "big fish," alleging a vast conspiracy, when all they'd ever proved was the sale of twenty-four bottles.

The US Supreme Court had declined to hear her appeal based on the illegal search of her home. This request for a new trial was their last chance. But based on what she'd been told by her lawyers, it was a slim chance at best. Johnnie and Emmett were likely headed to Atlanta in the spring. Apart from concern for her sons, Mary no longer cared about the case. She had a business to grow, and it wasn't in Kentucky. She was sick to death of Prohibition's false morality. In her mind, the revenuers were as evil as the Klan. One group hid under white hoods, the other behind sanctimonious *bastids* like Cochran.

On November 9, and to no surprise, her last appeal was denied. Mary fell into a three-day simmering rage, emerging only when Will knocked on her study door to announce the Klan was rallying in Lawrenceburg next Saturday.

"Come in," she said. "Please."

She sat at her desk, Will opposite, as they'd sat so many times before.

"I know you've been taking the end of the appeals pretty hard."

"I'm furious," she said. "But only because I'm worried about Johnnie and Emmett. Otherwise, I don't much care."

"That's new."

"I've mellowed."

She smiled, and he smiled back, recognizing a joke when he heard one. Then he rolled and lit a cigarette. "There's something else I need to tell you, Mother. It's ugly."

"What?"

"A boy was lynched yesterday, south of Harrodsburg." Will hesitated. "He's a relation of Rose."

"Omigod. May the Lord have mercy on his soul." She took a moment, then asked, "Who would do that?"

"Our friends in hoods."

Her mind reeled. "But why?"

"The usual reasons." Will puffed his cigarette then exhaled. "They said he was having relations with a white gal."

"How do you know?"

"I hear things, Mother."

She supposed Will knew Klan members. "That's so evil."

She needed to talk to Rose, inquire if the family needed money for the funeral. *People are monsters,* she thought. *Monsters.* For a time, they sat in gloomy silence.

"If you hear things, Will, what do you hear about us, now that the last appeal's been denied?"

"Some folks say we're dirty rotten bootleggers and got what we deserved. There are rumors you had a tunnel dug under South Main from your house to mine, and we roll barrels back and forth. I've also heard you reinforced the attic floor and built an elevator to move barrels to the attic to hide them."

"You're making that up."

"I wish I was." He stubbed out his smoke. "But most people think it's a damn shame Emmett and Johnnie are going to the penitentiary. Especially Johnnie." Will stood up. "I best be getting to my office."

"Don't go yet."

Will sat again in the chair in front of her desk.

"Do you think I should have let Emmett plead guilty? He wanted to."

"Johnnie told me."

"Is he angry?"

"When have you ever known Johnnie to be angry?"

Mary's heart filled with warmth. And guilt. "Are you?"

Will leaned towards her. "Did Emmett do what he was charged with?"

"Does that matter?"

"Yes," he said emphatically, "it does."

"More or less," she admitted.

"Then you should have let him plead guilty. It would have saved you a great deal of money. And it would have saved the rest of us a heap of humiliation."

"I was afraid of what they'd do to him, with Smith and Cochran hating us so. I couldn't put that weapon in their hands." She reached across her desk. "I would have done the same for you."

"I know, Mother. I know."

Then he departed for his office, and Mary sat alone in hers, thinking about her grief and anger, but mostly about Rose and her family. *Those poor people,* she thought. *Those poor people and those lousy bastids.*

The next morning, when Rose didn't come to work, Mary summoned John Cody and asked if he knew where Rose lived. John Cody, who rarely looked directly at her and never spoke three words when two would do, looked up, startled. Then his eyes returned to the floor.

"I do, Missus Dowling."

"I want you to drive me there later, just before lunch."

John Cody looked up again. "They in a world of pain, Missus Dowling. That boy was her sister's son."

They set out at noon, with a basket of fruit, a country ham, and two roast chickens, warm from the oven. Mary Margaret had fixed the chickens according to Rose's own recipe, accompanied by dumplings, gravy, and a pan of yams. They drove out Lincoln to the Grove, less than a mile from Dowling Hall, but a world apart.

John Cody pulled over in front of a small white house with blue shutters shaded by a large sycamore. Carriages and cars filled the driveway. A black cloth was tied around the trunk of the sycamore. Another mourning cloth hung from the porch roof. Mary instructed John Cody to park as close as he could, then climbed out of her Packard and started up the driveway. She wore one of the long black dresses she'd been wearing for the past forty years; she'd fit right in on a sympathy call.

When she knocked, no one answered, though she heard voices inside. John Cody came up the walk behind her, carrying the fruit basket in one hand, the country ham in the other. When she knocked a second time, a tall, narrow-faced old woman with white hair opened and asked, "May I hep you?"

In a heartbeat Mary recognized Ida, who'd saved Johnnie all those years ago. "I'm so sorry about your grandson. I came to see if there was anything I could do?"

"Thank you, Missus Dowling. We so sunk in sorrow I can't hardly see the light."

"I can only imagine. Or really, I can't." They stared at each other. Heartbeats ticked past, and in her mind's eye she saw Ida the day she saved Johnnie. She owed Ida so much! Surprising herself, she reached forward and hugged her. Then, stepping back, she asked, "Is Rose here? I hope I'm not intruding."

"She's just inside, Missus Dowling. I'll just—"

But before Ida could turn inside, Rose appeared. When she saw who it was, she looked shocked. Or frightened.

"I had John Cody bring me. We brought…fruit. And food. Food's always good. People need to eat." She was babbling, hardly making sense. But she wanted to say…something. "There's more in the car."

Rose stepped around her aunt and stood in front of Mary.

"Thank you for coming, Missus Dowling."

"Oh, Rose," Mary said, "you don't have to thank me. I'm just so very, very sorry, and angry."

And fearing she might cry, and that would never do, she followed Rose into her house.

The service for Wilson Freeman, twenty-two years old, was held on Friday at the Evergreen Baptist Church on Lincoln Avenue, a few blocks from Rose's house. The College Street church destroyed by fire decades ago had been rebuilt here. The young man's coffin remained closed. Mary tried not to speculate why. In addition to the minister, several family members spoke, including Rose. No one directly mentioned the particulars of his passing. Will Freeman, as he was known, was eulogized as a loving son, brother, grandson, and nephew. An outstanding young man, everyone agreed, strong in his love of family and strong in his love of the Lord, in whose loving arms he lay.

Mary attended, accompanied by Will, Emmett, and Johnnie. Mary's friend and neighbor, Mrs. Frankie Saffell, who knew Rose well, came with them. Theirs were the only white faces in a church full of Black ones. After a long, tearful service, highlighted by a full-throated, full-choir rendition of "Amazing Grace" during which Mary thought her heart would break, Will Freeman was transported to the Colored section of the Lawrenceburg cemetery, where he was laid to rest.

Mary and her sons did not go the cemetery, uncertain they'd be wanted there, but Mary made sure to find a private moment with Rose alone after the service, both to give her an envelope filled with cash to help the family with the cost of the funeral and to tell Rose not to come to work for the next few days. Instead, she should take time at home to grieve with her family.

Rose tried to return the envelope. "There's no need for money, Missus Dowling."

"Please, Rose. It's the least we can do." Their eyes met as they each considered who Mary might mean by *we*. "Give it to your sister."

Rose nodded and placed the envelope in her purse. "As for tomorrow, aren't you having the whole family to dinner?"

"I am."

"Then I'll be there. Just like you were here today for me."

Later, Mary would wish she'd cancelled the meal. Of course, she did. But after avoiding her children since the last appeal was denied,

Mary had invited Will and his family, Ida, and Wally. Emmett, Johnnie, Mary Bond, and George would attend as well.

Saturday dawned clear and cold, as if it were January, not November. She'd asked Mary Margaret to prepare a hearty pumpkin soup, followed by beef and lyonnaise potatoes. Soup had been served and soup bowls cleared. Will was carving the roast at the head of the table, with Rose helping him plate, when through the glass of the bay window, near where the children sat at the opposite end of the room, came a cacophony of chanting voices.

Before they could stop her, Will's older daughter Ann ran to the window. Will's second child, who'd been given her grandmother's name, Mary Dowling, followed her big sister as she always did, four years old to Ann's seven. And that's when they saw the six-foot cross burning on the lawn.

"Get them away from the window," Will shouted, abandoning the carving knife and fork.

Before Will could reach them, the girls' favorite uncle Johnnie snatched them from the big bay window glowing with hatred. Mary glanced up at Rose still at the sideboard, fear rampant on her features. *If I were Black,* Mary thought, *I'd be terrified too. And after what happened to her nephew!*

Will, Johnnie, Emmett, and George rushed outside, followed by Wally Camp. Mary and Mary Bond were close behind. Ida, Margaret, and Rose remained inside with the crying children.

Fifteen or twenty Klansman lined her lawn: hooded and garbed head-to-toe in white. They stood twenty feet from her porch steps, chanting. In front of them, the cross flamed and smoked, throwing shadows on their faces, reflecting red and gold on the bay window. Mary stepped forward, beside her sons.

Someone shouted vile racial epithets, and Mary's mind flashed to the funeral they'd attended. Others took up the familiar cry, shouting words she'd heard her entire life but had never used for she knew the pain they imparted.

"Come in front of the cross so we can see you!" Johnnie cried out. "Come in front of the cross!"

"Papists! Bootleggers! Nigra lovers! Irish scum!" the Klansmen answered. "You got what you deserved!"

For a moment, Mary feared her sons and Wally Camp, who, to give him his due, stood at the front beside Emmett and Johnnie, were going to rush the mob even though they were outnumbered three to one. Mary glanced at Mary Bond, the flames of the cross reflected in her eyes.

"Catholic scum!" the mob shouted. "Got what you deserved!"

Just when she thought a brawl would begin or someone in the mob would draw a pistol, Mary recognized one of the voices.

"Jimmy McGregor!" she thundered, advancing to the front edge of the porch. "Step forward and show your damn face!"

The shouting stopped. Mary's sons moved up beside her. Will shouted, "You think we don't know who you are?"

The Klansmen muttered amongst themselves, then, turning their backs on the burning cross, started down the driveway, headed for South Main, where they disappeared into the darkness from which they'd come.

CHAPTER TWENTY-NINE

The Jail Doors Close 1927-1928

Mary and Emmett returned to El Paso in mid-December 1927. D&W's first barrels would soon be ready to bottle, and there was a great deal to arrange. Although she would have preferred to travel after the first of the year, Mary was not going to miss seeing the first bottle filled. Besides, with penitentiary awaiting Emmett, there was little time to waste.

They celebrated *Noche Buena* with a feast at Antonio's house, followed by Midnight Mass at the Juarez Cathedral. She hadn't known—why would she?—that in Mexico, Christmas Eve was more important than Christmas. There must have been seventy people at Antonio's hacienda, including politicians from both El Paso and Juarez. Everyone wore their finest, and there was enough food to feed a small city, including a soup called *pozole*, which was unlike anything she'd ever tasted. She enjoyed the *pozole*, some sort of popped hominy, more than she would have guessed—she was getting used to spice—but not nearly as much as guacamole, which remained her favorite. And she'd loved Midnight Mass in the Juarez Cathedral. So many people, all of whom Antonio seemed to know. So much joy. And all the children staying up late to celebrate the birth of their Redeemer.

They spent Christmas Day with the Beams, a much quieter celebration. Harry missed Kentucky and intended to move home to live with one of his brothers. He'd be eighteen next summer, and Katie confided she and Joe L were of a mind to let him go.

"That's fine with me," Mary said, when she and Katie were talking privately.

"Sometimes," Katie offered, "you have to let young people make their own decisions, even if it's the wrong one."

"That's true," Mary answered, "though not something I've been good at."

On December 28—they'd return home in two days—Mary and Emmett arranged to meet with Antonio at D&W. During the six months they'd been gone, a spur track had been laid leading to the distillery doors and bottling equipment had been installed. With Antonio, Emmett, Joe L, and his sons beside her, Mary gave the signal, and they watched whiskey flow into the first bottles of Waterfill and Frazier, SA. Their caps and bottles were manufactured in the US, but the labels, bearing the Spanish words, *Hecho en Mexico*, came from Juarez.

As the first bottles were capped, labeled, then packed in cases, many of her Mexican workers began to cheer. Mary felt a wild surge of pride. They'd done it. She, Antonio, Joe L, and Emmett. *They'd done it!*

"Señora Dowling," Antonio said. "Would you like to say a few words to the men?"

"I would, but I don't speak Spanish."

"I'll translate," Emmett said.

Antonio raised his arms. "*Amigos, hagan silencio por favor. Señora Dowling quisiera decir unas palabras.*" He nodded at her.

"Joe L and your sons. Antonio. And all you men"—she pointed at them—"whose hard work has made my dream of making Kentucky bourbon in Mexico a reality."

She paused to let Emmett catch up, understanding just a word or two in translation: *trabajo, sueño, realidad.*

"I'd like to thank you from the bottom of my heart."

When Emmett said *corazon*, she raised a fist above her head, and as she did, a strongly built worker in the front rank called out, "*Madre de Borbón! Madre de Borbón!*"

Mary turned towards Emmett and asked, "What's he saying?"

"Mother of Bourbon."

Mary smiled, placed both hands over her heart, then pointed them towards the worker. He bowed, then the other workers took up his cry. In a moment they were all chanting, "*Madre de Borbón! Madre de Borbón!*"

After a moment, beaming inside and out, Mary raised both hands, as if blessing them, and the men quieted.

"May D&W," she declared, "not only make great whiskey, but may it make all our lives better and richer! *Muchas gracias. Muchas gracias!*"

Later, Mary, Emmett, and Antonio retired to his office, where they sipped a ceremonial dram. "We already have more orders than we can fill. In Juarez, further south in Mexico, and, of course, further north." Antonio smiled. "Emmett tells me his friend and mine, Carlos Villarreal, has asked to purchase one of our first barrels once it's bottled, and we've agreed. Señor Caponay has sent word through La Bandita, asking to sample Waterfill and Frazier when he next visits with an eye towards a significant order, perhaps as early as March."

"Did he give you an idea how large an order?"

"One hundred cases to begin." Antonio smiled. "*Each month.*"

Mary calculated volume and dollars in her head. One hundred cases was slightly less than five barrels. At fifty dollars per delivered case, that was five thousand a month just from Capone.

"While we're on the subject," Mary glanced at Emmett then again at Antonio, "I want to confirm that our terms for these *special clients* is cash, not net thirty or sixty, whatever it is local customers receive?"

"Señora Dowling, remind me never to underestimate you."

"I don't think you have, Antonio. Nor I, you."

"Thirty days for locals, although they sometimes ask for sixty, and we grant it if they're selling in Juarez. Cash only for *clientes especial*." He turned towards Emmett. "Your mother misses nothing."

Emmett said, "Not that I've noticed."

Less than three months later, Emmett and Johnnie arranged to surrender to US Deputy Marshall Flint Davis in Lexington on the evening of March 16, 1928. He would escort them to the Atlanta penitentiary, where they'd begin their terms of a year and a day. After weeks of anguished conversations, the family agreed, honoring Johnnie and Emmett's wishes, that John Cody, and only John Cody, would accompany them on the ride to Lexington. Family members could say goodbye at Dowling Hall, over lunch before they left.

Mary asked Mary Margaret and Rose to prepare Johnnie and Emmett's favorite foods. Rose's chicken and dumplings, Emmett's favorite. Mary Margaret's beef Wellington, Johnnie's. White and green asparagus. Hot Browns, a delicious invention of Chef Fred Schmidt from the Brown Hotel that was all the rage. Three-layer chocolate cake and pumpkin pie, which was Johnnie's favorite Thanksgiving food, although Will, in charge of coordinating with Ed O'Rear's office, said they were not to give up hope. Parole was possible after six months, which would have them home for Thanksgiving.

Sitting down to lunch with her seven children resident in Kentucky, her daughter-in-law, Margaret, and Wally Camp, Mary was determined to keep the surface bright. She'd asked Margaret not to bring her younger daughter—Ann was at school—but Johnnie, who doted on his nieces, had overruled her, and little Mary Dowling spent the meal on his lap.

Later, she'd remember little of the luncheon, except that Johnnie, who had a tremendous sweet tooth, filled a plate with pie and cake and ate his way through it, sharing with little Mary. Emmett barely said anything and ate even less. He was so much younger than the others that when the family gathered, his siblings seemed more like aunts and uncles. Other than Johnnie and Will, Mary had never told them Emmett had confessed to selling whiskey to Charlie Shelton, but she sensed it was an open secret.

She felt worst for Johnnie. She suspected there had been a closed-door, pre-sentencing hearing after the verdicts were handed down. Although she couldn't be certain, she believed Judge Cochran had required a second, sacrificial Dowling to serve time, perhaps in response to her outburst. How else to account for Johnnie's sentence? Charlie Shelton had implicated Emmett, but there was nothing to link Johnnie. She wouldn't be surprised if Sawyer Smith, whom she still suspected of being Klan, had said, "If you don't want the old woman heading to Atlanta, you have to give us something."

Johnnie was a good son, loyal and self-sacrificing.

As the meal was winding down and the moment she dreaded was approaching, she heard Johnnie say to Margaret, "I want you to know, I never sold whiskey to anyone."

"I know that," Margaret cried. "You who never cared naught for money."

Conversation stopped, and all eyes turned to the anguished couple.

Then Emmett said, "It's true. *I'm* to blame. *I'm* the one." Then he stood and left the room.

Somehow, they patched things up before Johnnie and Emmett departed. Of course, her other children had known, and the love at the heart of the Dowling clan had guaranteed their silence. So maybe it was a good thing, Mary thought, that Emmett confessed to the others. Perhaps it was even better that they already knew. And maybe best of all was that Johnnie and Emmett were going off together so that neither would face the nightmare alone.

Soon enough, it was time. Mary stood on the porch, surrounded by her children save Katherine in New York: Johnnie, Emmett, Mary Bond, Bobbie, George, Will and Margaret, Ida and Wally Camp. Johnnie and Emmett handed their valises to John Cody, then faced her.

"Come back soon. And come back healthy. That's all I ask."

She hugged Johnnie first, then Emmett, swallowing her tears. She cursed Smith and Cochran. Then she thought of the bourbon aging in Juarez. She'd be damned before she let anything, or anyone, keep the Dowlings down. The children would share the Juarez money. Then her sons climbed into the Packard, and John Cody steered them down the drive and onto South Main.

CHAPTER THIRTY

Home Again, Home Again
1928

A week after Emmett and Johnnie were transported to Atlanta, Mary asked Mary Bond to join her in her study. On that March morning, Mary was sixty-nine years old, her eldest daughter, fifty-two. Still attractive, but growing pinch-faced, her lips and cheeks showing the first signs of the chronic pain that would shape her life twenty and thirty years in the future. Mother and daughter did not know it, but this meeting would mark the beginning of a new phase of their troubled relationship.

Entering the study, Mary Bond said, "You wanted to speak to me."

"Please close the door."

Mary Bond settled in the leather chair in front of her mother's desk. Since the cross-burning six months ago, they'd scarcely spoken. That wasn't unusual, but it was extreme. She'd always been more John's child, and ever since she'd married Gentleman, or more aptly,

Lucky Jim, Mary had had trouble respecting her daughter. For her part, Mary Bond had never forgiven her mother for refusing to support her when she was president of the Kentucky UDC. What she thought after the cross-burning, Mary didn't know.

After a brief silence, she said, "I need your help."

"With *what*, Mother?"

"Organizing a letter-writing campaign to get Johnnie and Emmett paroled. Ed O'Rear says they're eligible in six months."

"I know."

Can't tell you anything. "I think it would look better coming from you than me."

"Why is that?"

"I'm their mother."

"I'm their sister."

Mary Bond's eyes blazed, and for a moment, a long and increasingly awkward moment, neither spoke. Then Mary Bond said, "Do you trust me enough to contact your friends? And mine, of course."

"Absolutely."

"You haven't trusted my judgement in anything else." And then she was shouting, "Not once, Mother! Not once!"

Mary struggled not to shout back. "If I didn't trust you, I wouldn't have asked. Nothing is more important to me. *Nothing*."

"You should have let Emmett plead guilty." Mary Bond's eyes burned. "*That* was bad judgment."

"I did it out of fear for what would happen to him."

"And now it's happened to Emmett and Johnnie both!"

Damn her! "What was your excuse for promoting that disgusting book? Did you think it would make the UDC ladies forget you were Catholic? They're the same sort who burned that cross on our lawn!"

Mary thought her hot-headed daughter would storm out and damn the letter-writing to support Emmett and Johnnie. Instead, Mary Bond said, "That was an error in my judgment, which I regret."

This was the first time she could remember Mary Bond admitting she was wrong.

"Thank you. I know it's hard to apologize. In that respect, we're much alike."

They eyed each other across Mary's wide desk and the much wider gulf of decades of mistrust.

"I'll organize the letter-writing. Why don't you prepare a list of names you'd like me to contact."

"There's no need. I trust your judgment."

Mary resisted the temptation to add, *In this matter*. Her daughter squelched the need to fire back, *Since when?* They nodded at each other, then Mary Bond slipped out of the room.

In early April, after her brothers had been imprisoned less than a month, Katherine, accompanied by Helen, visited them in prison. Not to be outdone, Mary Bond visited at the end of April, but no one had seen them since; Emmett and Johnnie reported the visits were too upsetting and asked that they cease.

As they had when he was at Exeter and Harvard, Emmett and Mary corresponded. He was fine and hoped she was too. The food was tolerable. What he wouldn't give for one of Mary Margaret's apple pies. Mary was so worried she could scarcely breathe, and she prayed using Heinrich's rosary every night before bed. The Seven Sorrows of Mary, especially the third—the loss of the boy Jesus in the temple—seemed especially instructive now, with her own sons lost in prison. Contemplating the Blessed Mother's example calmed her better than anything else; without it, she didn't know how she'd ever get to sleep.

There was a positive morsel for which she was grateful. In the society columns that mentioned Katherine and Mary Bond's visits, neither "prison" nor "penitentiary" appeared, just that were visiting their brothers in Atlanta. *Society pages*, Mary mused, *the simple soul of discretion*.

In early September, Bobbie showed up unannounced and without her children or new grandson. After they finished lunch and were sipping tea, Bobbie said, "Mother, I probably shouldn't mention this, it's all so long ago."

"What is it, dear?"

"After I married John, and the Stewarts began to call me Bobbie instead of Margaret, why did you stop using Margaret?"

"I thought you preferred Bobbie. Was I wrong?"

Her elegant daughter shook her head. "For the longest time, Mother, I tried so hard to please you." Bobbie seemed to gather her nerve and continued. "Married John, birthed four children, built a house almost as large as yours. But no matter what I did, I felt you loved my sisters more than you loved me. Does that sound childish?"

"Oh, Bobbie. Or Margaret, if you prefer."

"After all these years, I *am* Bobbie."

"Of course, I love you just as much. It's just," Mary moistened her lips, "the other girls *needed* me more. Except for Mary Bond, who would say she needed nothing, but took the most." They smiled at each other. "But you, Bobbie. I've always been so proud of you and the life you've made. The one I didn't have to worry about. If you wanted my attention, maybe you should have caused more problems." She took her daughter's hand. "Or been less like me."

"I'll see what I can do."

They both knew she didn't mean it.

On September 30, Mary received word from Ed O'Rear that Emmett and Johnnie would be paroled October 7 after serving six months of their sentences. Mary Bond had been as good as her word and organized an extensive letter-writing campaign to the parole board; newspapers around the region reported that many prominent citizens in Lawrenceburg and Anderson County had recommended that the Dowlings be released.

After Mary heard from O'Rear, she felt as if two tons of sorrow had been lifted from her shoulders. Will, Mary Bond, and Ida accompanied John Cody to Lexington to meet the train, and when her prodigal sons came through the door, Mary was seated in the front hall, waiting. She rushed forward to hug them, Johnnie first, then Emmett. They looked and felt thinner, but exactly like themselves, with bad haircuts. Will, Ida, and Mary Bond left them alone, heading home, or in Mary Bond's case, up to her bedroom. Looking from one beloved face to the other, Mary asked, "Now, tell me the truth, how are you?"

Johnnie looked at Emmett, then Emmett answered for them both, "Ask us no questions, Mother, and we'll tell you no lies."

"That's all you're going to say?"

Johnnie nodded.

After a moment, Emmett asked brightly, "Mother, do you think there's any whiskey in Dowling Hall?"

"I'm sure I can find something."

Johnnie said, "I'm going up to take a hot bath."

Emmett said, "So am I."

Watching them climb the stairs, Mary thought, *Johnnie looks tired. And Emmett? I'll work on him later*. Then she went to find a bottle and inform Mary Margaret to hold dinner until the boys came down.

All eight Dowling children—even Katherine from New York—their spouses and children gathered for Christmas dinner at Dowling Hall. Mary Margaret, Rose, and the other girls outdid themselves. Christmas ham and a flock of roast geese weighted the banquet table, and spirits were light, at least Mary's was, because the worst seemed behind them. To be together with her entire family at Christmas, what could be better? Even Bobbie's husband, Dr. John, was on best behavior, and the whole evening long good feeling flowed, clear as Bailey's Run.

The only dark note was how George struggled to climb the stairs. Just forty-seven, he moved like a man of seventy. Mary, who would turn seventy in a few weeks, did much better than George, who needed to catch his breath every few steps.

Mary pushed George's health from her mind. She could usually control what she thought about. Strong-minded, strong-willed Mary Dowling. And this Christmas night she was determined to savor her blessings. So many children and grandchildren, and now a great grandson, one-year-old John Pogue Stewart II, from Dowling Stewart and his wife, Emma Adelia. Emmett and Johnnie were home. And there was so much good news from Juarez; even with increased production, they couldn't meet demand. As she accompanied her family to the door—kissing the children, embracing their parents—she kept returning to *A Christmas Carol*, remembering the piping voice of Tiny Tim in the production last week in Lawrenceburg: "God bless us, every one!"

Mary and Emmett boarded a train for El Paso on Thursday, January 10, her seventieth birthday. Friends and family had been feting her for days: luncheons, a dinner, presents, and too much cake. She was over-stuffed and glad to be going. When an older person reaches a decade-changing birthday, everyone wants to celebrate the past, while Mary remained focused on the future. As always.

There was a great deal to do in Juarez, and they planned to be gone a month. She liked hotel-living. She liked visiting with Katie Beam, and she liked El Paso. But mostly, she looked forward to working again. There'd been such a hurly-burly around her birthday, but enough was enough. She'd seen everyone except Ida, who'd moved into her new house, which was being re-plastered, and she was down with a cold. Her husband, Wally, never left her side; it seemed she'd misjudged him. Mary had missed seeing Ida but couldn't risk catching whatever she had before a long journey. She planned to recuperate from her birthday on the train; the train's motion was conducive to sleep. And maybe, on the train, or perhaps in Juarez,

Emmett would confide in her as he had before, re-establishing their former closeness. Since he'd returned from Atlanta, she'd found him as reserved with her as he was with the others.

When they arrived at Paso del Norte on January 12, the front desk manager handed Mary a yellow Western Union envelope before checking them in or sending their baggage to the second floor. Later, she'd wonder if he'd read the telegram or somehow knew its contents, alerted perhaps by the Western Union office.

She opened the envelope. *Ida died this morning of pneumonia. She did not suffer. So sorry, Mother, to send word this way. We await your return. Love, Will.*

Mary and Emmett headed home that afternoon. She spoke briefly by phone to Will and Mary Bond. After Mary Bond's work for her brothers' parole, something had changed. Mary Bond was now managing Ida's funeral; Wally Camp, she said, was useless, too grief-struck to function. He'd caught whatever Ida had, which the doctors now believed was influenza, but had thrown it off, while Ida succumbed. Or maybe it had been the wet plaster in their house. She'd never been strong, Ida. Why couldn't it have been Wally and not her daughter? Then she immediately felt guilty for her uncharitable thought. And then another surfaced. She supposed the service station she'd given them now belonged to Wally. Of course, it did, don't be a fool; they were man and wife, and Ida had been so very, very glad to be married.

She assured Mary Bond they'd be home in two days and disconnected. She sent word to Katie Beam to let her know; the Beams had no telephone. She did reach Antonio and promised to return in a few weeks, a month no more.

"Señora Dowling," Antonio replied, "I am so very sorry. All is well at D&W. Take all the time you need."

She and Emmett bathed and changed, ate a large lunch she could not taste, then returned to Union Station. They'd spent five hours in El Paso. Now they'd follow the same tracks north and east that they'd followed south and west the past two days, with sorrow replacing joy.

While Emmett slept, she began the Seven Sorrows of Mary. *I offer You this Rosary for Your glory, so I can honor your Holy Mother, the Blessed Virgin, so I can share and meditate upon her suffering. I humbly beg you to give me true repentance for all my sins.*

She found her thoughts dwelling on the fifth sorrow: Mary standing at the foot of the cross. It was going to be a long, dark night.

Ida's funeral service began at two p.m. on January 16, led by Reverend Father Judermann of Versailles, who'd married her. Three other priests assisted: Punch and Losterman from Lexington and Reverend Father McCarthy from Frankfort. Mary sat in the first rank of mourners, surrounded by her children. Wally Camp sat at the end of the row, beside his mother, sister, and brother. He seemed wholly undone. More than once she heard him say, "Why couldn't it have been me?"

Mary was thinking the same thing because in her mind there was no greater sorrow than losing a child. She'd long wondered about the Blessed Mother. How had she gone on? Mary herself had suffered terribly thirty years ago when Robbie died, but she had Emmett's birth to ease that pain and distract her attention. And now? It seemed certain that what came next was another death; George was worse than ever.

Dowling Hall was as packed as the courtroom had been in Frankfort. Everyone knew Ida. She'd grown up in Lawrenceburg and never left. She'd been named for the Black maid who saved her brother, a shocking story everyone knew, and many, she believed, disapproved of. No matter. The original Ida and her niece Rose were at the funeral. Damn anyone who said that was wrong. Despite Mary's initial misgivings, the town had cheered Ida's late marriage. Modest and unassuming, Ida had bloomed when watered with love.

Outside, the day was dark, barely above freezing, matching the mood within. All morning, the skies had wept rain and snow. The precipitation had recently stopped, and for that and that alone, Mary was grateful. Interment would follow immediately after the service at the family plot in the Lawrenceburg cemetery. A large stone monument—*Dowling*—stood at its center, topped by a Catholic cross. She and John had agreed that simple gray headstones laid flat on the grass—just name and dates—would surround the monument in orderly rows, emphasizing the importance of family. Robbie was first, then John, and now a third: Ida Dowling Camp. Mary, of course, would lie beside John, and Ida had asked before she died that space be saved for Wally.

Mary could feel herself getting upset and shook her head to clear her thoughts. Reverend Father Judermann was saying something about Ida being called home to Her Savior in whose sacrifice she'd found eternal life, but Mary couldn't help wishing Ida had been allowed to tarry longer in the arms of her husband, sobbing softly at the end of the row. In her hands, out of sight, Mary told the beads of her rosary, seeking guidance in the example of the Blessed Mother who'd lost and buried her own child.

Mary decided that when she ordered Ida's headstone, she'd bestow a final blessing on her daughter. Ida had loved almost everything about Wallace Camp, including his flaws, which she chose to forgive. There was a lesson here, Mary thought. She was less forgiving than Ida, and she should learn from her example and the forgiveness Christ showed sinners.

Mary had the power to annul the one thing about Wally Camp Ida couldn't forgive: his age. When she had Ida's headstone carved, she'd change the year of her birth from 1887 to 1889, making her two years younger. It was a white lie, but one that would ease her daughter's spirit when her husband was laid to rest beside her.

CHAPTER THIRTY-ONE

Death Knocks Again
1929

Mary and Emmett kept delaying their return to El Paso waiting for George to pass, but he lingered. When they could wait no longer—Joe L's contract was up—Mary and Emmett left on the first of June, planning to be gone a few weeks. But one thing led to another. Business was booming, and it looked as if they'd need to expand again. Joe L had been training a US Army vet, Bill Bezzell, from Tennessee, to take over as distiller, but he wasn't ready yet. Joe L had agreed to stay on through August, but that was the limit. He'd been promised work as the jailer of Nelson County beginning September 1. Little Katie Lou wasn't quite so little. Katie missed her family, and all in all, the Beams needed to be home.

Mary and Emmett worked on collecting debts, sometimes in cash and sometimes in goods: Mexican silver, and once, a painting copied from a famous one hanging in a church. The bars and cabarets in

Juarez buzzed even louder and wilder than in winter, and Emmett was gone several nights a week. Antonio was increasingly involved in politics, and she believed he'd someday be mayor, but until then, she was delighted with her partner, who had a golden touch, much as she and John had displayed in Lawrenceburg in the 1880s and '90s.

On the first night of summer, Mary accompanied Emmett to the Mint Café in Juarez. Carlos Villarreal met them. The large-bodied, large-headed young man still spoke little English. Mary never knew quite what to make of him. He laughed often and loudly and spoke rapidly in Spanish, which she didn't understand. She knew he was smuggling their bourbon across the river but didn't know how. She also knew he'd already re-ordered, and Emmett, now fluent in Spanish, enjoyed his company. The two of them spent the first part of the meal laughing and joking in Spanish. What she didn't know—nor did Carlos—was that years later, after serving time in a US jail for whiskey smuggling, he'd be elected mayor of Juarez. Later still, after building a bridge for the city across the same narrow ford where he once smuggled Dowling bourbon, Carlos Villarreal would be assassinated by a political rival in downtown Juarez.

But that night in June 1929, after finishing their first course—Mary always ordered a caviar canape followed by French lamb chops and peas—a large group was seated at the empty table next to theirs. After a moment, Mary realized it was Al Capone, his mistress, La Bandita, and several men Mary assumed were Capone's bodyguards. Carlos and Emmett crossed to the gangster's table to pay their respects. After a moment they returned, joined by Capone, who sat in the empty chair at their table for four: on Mary's left, opposite Emmett, adjacent to Carlos.

"I'd been hoping I'd be lucky enough to see ya tonight, Missus Dowling."

He looked for her hand to kiss, but anticipating he might, she'd folded her hands in her lap. Capone contented himself with a wide smile. Mary suddenly realized the empty table beside theirs was no coincidence. Emmett and Capone must have arranged it. She glanced at her son and saw she was right.

"I wanted to tell you, *poysonally*, how pleased we are with the quality of your hooch."

She could hear Emmett translating for Carlos. "Thank you."

"If a *poyson* didn't know better, that *poyson* wouldn't know it was made down here."

"We use the same mash bill we used in Kentucky."

"Tastes like it." He smiled and ran his hand over the thinning hair on the top of his head. "Compared to yours, the rest of the hooch down here tastes like piss. I mean, urine."

When Emmett translated for Carlos, the big man laughed. Capone shot him a look, and Carlos quieted.

"The thing is, Missus Dowling, we'd like to increase our order."

She looked directly at him, with anger. Emmett stopped translating. After a long silence in a room loud with conversation, Capone looked away from the Dowling stare. When his eyes returned, he was smiling. "Maybe dinner ain't the best time to discuss business with a lady such as yourself."

"I agree."

"You know, Missus Dowling, and I mean this as a compliment, you remind me of my motha."

"Why, thank you." Mary smiled. "I'm glad to see she taught you the value of good manners."

"And another thing," Capone said. "I heard from your partner Antonio that the workers at your plant have started calling you the Mother of Bourbon." He grinned. "I think that suits you. What do you think?"

"I like it too," she admitted.

"I also wanted to tell you, I think it was shameful what the revenuers, that no-good judge, and the DA done to you in that trial."

She felt her jaw clench. "What do you know about it?"

"I read the papers like everyone else." He eyed Emmett and Carlos, then leaned closer, so that only she could hear him. "I also got friends, *good friends,* who move a lot of product in Louisville and Cincinnata, and they told me three things about you when I inquired. None of their hooch came from you. You was on the up and up, just like my motha, and the revenuers stole a bunch of your hooch and lined their pockets with it. I hate those corrupt bastards, if you'll pardon my French."

"I do," Mary said, then added, "I hate them too."

They sat for a moment in comfortable silence, *thick as thieves,* Mary thought, suppressing a grin. Then, after a moment, once again all business, she continued, "Regarding pricing, availability, and discounts, ask Antonio."

"Absolutely, Missus Dowling." He eyed her shrewdly. "But in principle, you have no objection?"

She doubted Capone worried much about principles. "I do not. Of course, once you two have discussed terms, Antonio will need approval from me."

"Understood. You're the *Doña,* I got that."

He stood and smiled. Emmett and Carlos stood and shook his hand. Mary remained seated, insulated from the need to rise by her age and sex. Nor did she want her hand kissed.

"It's been a pleasure, Missus Dowling."

She smiled. "My regards to your friends."

The gangster returned to his table.

Four days later, Mary received the call she'd been dreading. George's heart had given out. She and Emmett would pack, leave the next morning, and reach Kentucky on Saturday. She asked Will to arrange a Sunday funeral, but he reported Mary Bond was already doing that.

On the long ride home, her second death train in five months, Mary initiated the conversation she'd been wanting to have with Emmett. He'd been avoiding her since his release from prison. She still treasured what he'd said after they met Al Capone and La Bandita the first time. *You're not just my mother. Sometimes I think you're my best friend*. She missed that closeness.

They sat alone in their first-class carriage. The moon was past full, perhaps three-quarters, rising in the east as they sped towards New Orleans. It was after eleven. They should have been in bed but knew they couldn't sleep. Mary was haunted by George's death and his life. The early divorce from Henryetta McBrayer McGregor. *Damn the McGregors*. His loyalty to Henryetta—he never allowed anyone to say a bad word about her in his presence—drove his decision never to remarry or have children. His inability to manage money, so much so that in her will, Mary had put his share in trust. Now that he was gone, leaving neither wife nor child, his portion would be shared by his sisters and brothers.

"Emmett." They sat at the small table in their compartment. "You never told me about prison."

His chair faced the direction the train was headed; moonlight bathed the left side of his face. He'd turned thirty in November, and though he remained baby-faced and very much *her baby*, he no longer looked as young as once he did, or maybe as she thought of him when he wasn't in front of her.

"I'm not sure you want to hear."

"I asked, so I do."

"Mostly, I was bored, as if I'd been sent to my room, or forced to listen to a physics lecture over and over."

Emmett grinned. All through school he'd notoriously disliked math and science, which was one reason, other than her sense of how dangerous it was, that she'd opposed his becoming an aviator.

"After I'd been inside about three months, a very large, strong, and violent inmate decided he wanted to have"—Emmett hesitated—"*relations* with me."

"What do you mean?"

Emmett looked out at the moonlit fields rolling past. "What do you think I mean, Mother?"

He met her eyes, and this time it was Mary who looked away.

"When I refused, this man and two of his friends beat the bejesus out of me, and I spent three weeks in the infirmary. Broken ribs. A damaged spleen. One or two other things."

"Why didn't you send word?"

"There was nothing to be done."

"Perhaps there was. Perhaps there still is. There must be someone in that godforsaken place loyal to the Dowlings. Someone who could retaliate. Someone with family on the outside we could pay."

"Let it go, Mother."

She didn't want to. She wanted revenge.

"After the infirmary, I was transferred into Johnnie's cell, although I asked them not to. I didn't want to put him in danger. But Johnnie being Johnnie, he insisted. We shared a cell our last two months. I made him promise not to tell you."

Mary thought about how to respond, and for quite some time, the only sound was the train's wheels click-clacking over the tracks. "What happened to the men who beat you?"

"Nothing, I won't name them."

"Even to me?"

He shook his head. She wanted revenge. Three children dead, counting Robbie, and Emmett badly beaten! She didn't think she could stand it. But her long life had taught her she could stand anything. Outside the window, the moon shone brightly on a broad expanse of fields. Cotton, or maybe rice. Something she didn't recognize.

"Is there anything else you've been keeping from me?"

"No, Mother, that's it."

"It's enough."

"It is," he said, then added, "I'm going to the smoking car for a cigarette."

"I didn't know you smoked."

"I didn't; I do now." He smiled. "So, I guess I have been keeping something else from you." He leaned forward and kissed her cheek.

"What's that for?"

"Just because."

"It's been a hard few years," Mary said. "But the worst is behind us. I see a lot of your father in you."

"Thank you, Mother. I wish I'd known him."

"As do I. I had to be mother and father both." They stared at each other, long on long. "We made mistakes, both of us, but I know your father would be proud of how you've grown stronger over time. I know I am."

Emmett rewarded her with a smile then headed for the smoking car. Mary took out her rosary. Her attention had turned fully to the last sorrow, thinking about the Blessed Mother and how she'd endured the loss of her son. She thought of George and gave him her blessing, staring out at the at the bright-eyed moon and empty fields. Then she rang for the porter and prepared for bed.

CHAPTER THIRTY-TWO

The Curtain Comes Down 1929-1930

After the final funeral guests departed and there were no longer crowds to feed or appearances to keep up, Mary unpacked with Rose's help, except for the D&W files and account books, which she carried to her office and put away herself, for only she knew where each should go. Then she spent several nights catching up on sleep because she was most dreadfully tired, in body and in spirit.

When she awoke on the third day after returning, she could scarcely leave bed, so deep was her well of sorrow. She had been sad before. When John died. When Robbie died. When she buried her mother, whom she had finally forgiven for marrying her off so young.

Her mother had been right, of course, and Mary now understood she owed much of her grit to her mother's example. She *had* led an extraordinarily rich life with John, and quite an astonishing one on her own. But once she left home, she never felt nearly as close to her parents or siblings, which was the price she'd paid for becoming Mary Dowling. For twenty years she'd barely seen her first family, and when her days and nights were again her own, she'd made a new life in which they scarcely mattered.

What Mary felt now was more than sadness. She knew why: the deaths of George and Ida. There'd been so little joy in George's life. He was neither as bright nor as healthy as the others. And Ida, always a bridesmaid, never a bride, until she became one, only to be carried off so soon. It wasn't right; it wasn't fair; and feeling abandoned by the Blessed Mother, Mary felt lost in every way. For the first time in her life, she couldn't pray. Why bother? Where was the Mother of God when George and Ida fell ill? Why pray if no one was listening? And unable to endure the unendurable, Mary Dowling slipped into darkness.

After she'd been lost for several months, the phone on her bedside table rang, and though she rarely answered, this time she did. His voice seemed older; they hadn't spoken in years. But there was no mistaking Heinrich's accent, the sibilance of his esses, the harshness of his vowels.

"Mary. How are you?"

They hadn't trifled with surnames in decades.

"To be honest, Heinrich," she replied, her eyes focused on the ceiling, as if the lost joys of life were concealed there. "I've been much better. My daughter Ida and my son George died—Ida in January, George in June."

"I know."

"Who told you?"

"*Vill* called."

"Will has a big mouth."

"Mary, I already knew. All your old friends know."

"I wish they didn't."

"Life happens, Mary. Sorrow happens."

She couldn't find a commonplace, and she suffered in silence, until her grief burst out. "I'll never get over this."

Heinrich said, "A *voman* who loves as deeply as you? It takes time."

"I doubt I have much time."

"Don't be morbid. I'm eighty-two. Compared to me, you're young."

"No! I meant to say, 'No matter *how* long I have, I won't get over this.' I'm sorry, Heinrich. I should have thanked you for calling. And for the gift of the rosary, which has been such comfort in my sorrow. And," she felt ashamed, "I haven't asked how you are."

He allowed he was fine. All the years she'd known him, Heinrich had been fine. She thanked him for calling, replaced the receiver, and felt no better. Or maybe a little. It was good to hear her old friend's voice.

Slowly, Mary's spirits rose. She read the months of daily papers she'd ignored and discovered the stock market was awash with speculation. In early September a man named Babson had predicted a "terrific crash." At first, the exchange went down, then shot back up, which reminded Mary of 1903, when she'd almost lost the distilleries, and 1907, when she lost thousands in a single day. And though she no longer kept much money in securities, Mary hadn't lost her financial sense. She sold all her shares and kept the proceeds in cash.

Reports from Antonio kept getting stronger. He now believed they'd turn a profit a year earlier than estimated. *Special sales*, as he called them, kept growing, and if he had 50 percent more bourbon, he could sell that too. Her friend, *Señor Caponay*, had returned to Juarez and asked after her.

"He's not my friend," she said.

"Don't I know it!"

And she could hear his laughter from thousands of miles away.

In November, a package arrived with a return address of D&W Distillery. Inside she found two metal whiskey trays advertising Waterfill and Frazier Co, SA, as well as menus from the Mint and Lobby 2 Cafés, listing Waterfill and Frazier as a premium brand.

On December 1, after six weeks of feeling increasingly like herself—able to pray, dining with friends, spending two nights at Bobbie's house visiting with her great grandson, and, best of all, planning a major expansion of the distillery to begin during her January trip to El Paso—Mary woke with a dull but persistent pain in her side and lower back. It continued for several days, sometimes worse, sometimes slightly improved. Just when she'd decided to see her doctor, the pain abated, and she resumed her busy life.

Emmett had been ill as well. Nothing serious, just colds that wouldn't resolve, a cough, sometimes a slight fever. Physically, he hadn't been himself since the prison beating, but he was young and heretofore strong, and on November 21, he traveled to Boston to attend the Harvard-Yale game played two days later. The Crimson won, 10-6, and while Emmett confessed to Mary upon returning that he little cared for football, it was grand to see old friends and classmates. He'd left a deposit to hold his place for the Class of 1921's tenth reunion in May.

In January, just after her birthday, Mary observed that her calves and ankles were swollen, and the pain in her side and back had returned. She decided to have breakfast in bed, the first time in months, and asked Rose to bring it up. After Rose arranged the pillows behind her and set the breakfast tray over her legs, she asked, "Will there be anything else, Missus Dowling?"

"Please sit with me, Rose."

Rose moved the chair from Mary's make-up table to the side of the bed.

"You know, Rose." Mary took a bite of toast then set it down. She hadn't been hungry for days. "Your family has worked for mine since before we moved into Dowling Hall."

"Must be forty years."

"Almost fifty. Your Aunt Ida and I were young." Mary sipped her tea. "And look at me now."

"I am looking at you." And she was.

Mary nibbled a slice of bacon and washed it down with tea. "I hope your family stayed, not because you had no options, but because we treated you well."

Rose looked alarmed, and in her eyes, Mary saw a fearful question. *What's this about?*

"You have, Missus Dowling."

"When I was young," Mary confessed, "I used to make Ida walk behind me on my way downtown, holding up my dress, to keep it out of the mud."

Mary watched Rose measure her response.

"I know," Rose replied. "Aunt Ida told me."

After a moment, Mary asked, "She hated it, didn't she?"

Rose nodded, and then, emboldened, she added, "It shamed her."

So, Ida had told Rose, and all the years she worked in Dowling Hall, Rose had known. *How shameful.* Mary felt her cheeks burn. These past few years, with all that had happened, her emotions were closer to the surface, as if layers of protection had been stripped away. "I was young," she explained. "Not thirteen years before, I was poor, Rose. Really poor. But I should have known better." She peered into Rose's large, intelligent eyes. "The truth is, I did know better, but succumbed to false pride."

"It's all right, Missus Dowling."

"It is not all right. Would you tell Ida I'm sorry? Or better yet, may I visit and tell her myself?"

"If you want, but I'll tell her." Rose re-filled Mary's teacup. "You should eat more breakfast, Missus Dowling. You need to get your strength up."

"Please put the tray on my dresser."

When Rose started towards the door, Mary called after her. "Thank you."

Then Rose was gone.

That afternoon, when Will stopped after work as he often did, he asked, "Mother, are you feeling all right?"

"Yes," she replied, though she didn't feel at all all right. "Why do you ask?"

He peered over his glasses. He was fifty, no longer young. "Your eyes look glassy." He reached over suddenly and placed his palm against her forehead. "And you feel hot."

She drew back, angrily. "So now you're a doctor, as well as a lawyer?"

"And a son, as well as a father." He met her angry gaze with one of his own, though his was tempered by concern. "And you're not well."

She held out for two more days then conceded when her three eldest, Mary Bond, Bobbie, and Will, converged on her bedroom at nine a.m. and demanded she accept a visit from Dr. Gilbert. Ten minutes later, Gilbert was taking her temperature. Her calves and ankles were frightfully swollen, and her fever, he declared, shaking down the thermometer, was 102.

He sent her children out of the room and palpitated her lower back and side. When she cried out, he asked, "How long have you been like this?"

She hesitated.

"I'll have the truth, Missus Dowling. I've been your physician and friend for twenty years."

"A week." She thought a moment. "Maybe ten days."

"And there's pain when passing water, I'm guessing?"

"Yes."

He glowered at her as if she were a child. "Is there any reason, other than your general stubbornness, that you failed to contact me sooner?"

She met his angry gaze. "I felt something of the same in December, but it went away."

Now he looked more concerned than angry. "If I'm right, and this is an infection of your kidneys, I can assure you it will not go away so easily this time."

He excused himself and sent in her daughters. Then Dr. Gilbert returned with Will, Johnnie, and Emmett, and the doctor announced he'd arranged for her to be admitted to Saint Joseph's Infirmary in Louisville. Will said John Cody would drive her unless she'd rather go by ambulance.

"I most certainly would not."

"Then it's decided," Will said. "I'll come with you."

"As will I," said Mary Bond.

"And I," added Bobbie.

Dr. Gilbert said, "Pack sufficient clothes for five to seven days." To her children he added, "I'll be down to check on her, but she's in good hands with Doctor Abell."

Then Dr. Gilbert departed, and her children bustled about readying her things. It wasn't until she was in the back of the Packard with her daughters, with Will up front beside John Cody, that she realized no one had asked if she wished to be transported to Saint Joseph's. After a lifetime of deciding everything for them, her children had at last decided something for her.

Later, when Mary considered why she'd hidden her symptoms, she realized she'd feared that if she allowed herself to be admitted to a hospital, she might never come home.

Without antibiotics, which wouldn't be available for another decade, Mary's treatment at St. Joseph's consisted of rest, a special diet to reduce inflammation, and, as her pain increased, doses of morphine. Dr. Irvin Abell, Sr., former president of the Kentucky Medical Association (and future president of the American Medical

Association), took over her case from Dr. Gilbert. With morphine masking her discomfort, she seemed gradually to improve. Soon, she was receiving a steady line of visitors and plotting her return to Dowling Hall.

But her symptoms lingered, and when Abell reduced the morphine, the pain proved unbearable. In early February, Mary's symptoms worsened, and her children increased the frequency of their visits. Conversations no longer focused on when she'd return home but on her days and nights. When her children gathered in the hall, they wondered, *Was there nothing to be done? How much longer could she stand the pain?*

Katherine and Helen arrived from Tarrytown and left Mary's room in tears. She heard them weeping through her door though pretended she had not. Katherine had always been a fashionable ninny, and Helen, though not yet twenty-one, looked and acted like a woman twice her age. Mary reminded herself to ask Will, who'd redrafted her will two years ago, if it would be possible to make a special bequest for Helen, who would likely need it. But alas, morphine addled her, and she could no more retain a thought than grow wings.

Mary Bond came often, as did Will and Margaret, but without their girls.

"Will," she asked the last time she'd remember seeing him. "Are my affairs in order?"

"Yes, Mother." He glanced at Margaret. "You've taken care of everything."

When they were preparing to leave, she asked again, "Will, are my affairs in order?"

"Yes, Mother."

"Where's Emmett? Why doesn't he visit?"

"He has a cold." Will glanced again at his wife. "Doctor Abell asked that he stay away until you're better."

"What nonsense." She looked hard at her son and then at Margaret. *Don't you dare cry*. To Will, she added, "Tell Emmett I need to see him."

But Emmett did not come, and though her pain increased and she barely ate, Mary lingered. Then one morning she awoke to find Emmett at her bedside. A mask covered his nose and mouth, and his face looked gaunt.

"Good morning, Mother."

"Take off that mask, I need to see you."

"But the doctor said—"

"I don't give a damn what the doctor said."

Emmett removed his mask. He sported a moustache, half grown-in. "What do you think?"

"I like it." She smiled. "Your father."

"I know."

"You're thin," she said.

"I don't feel like eating."

"You must."

"I will if you will."

She smiled again, and Emmett smiled too.

"Mother." They looked at each other, long on long. "You don't need to hold on for my sake. I know you're in pain."

"Are you giving me permission?"

He nodded.

"I don't need your permission."

"I think you do."

She said, "It's hard to say goodbye."

"I know."

"*Emmett,*" she began urgently then took his hand. His fingers were ice, and she was gripped by a terrible premonition. "What's wrong? *Tell me.*"

"It's just a cold."

"No," she said. "I forbid you to be ill."

"Like mother, like son. And best friend. It's too much to lose, all at once."

"No," she repeated. "You're the Dowlings' future. You must live so I can die. Promise me. I live through you now."

"All right, Mother. I will."

What was the point of all her struggles if Emmett wasn't there to take over? She'd birthed nine children. Built an empire. Withstood the Spider. Started again in Juarez. But what was it worth if Emmett died too? Maybe she was wrong. But she was seldom wrong, and never about something as important as this. And then it came to her. The lesson of the Blessed Mother's final sorrow. You cannot save Him. You can only endure the pain.

Moments later, sliding towards sleep, but feeling as if she had understood a terrible truth, Mary said, "Perhaps you should ask the priests to come today."

Emmett nodded.

"And when you leave my room, Son, put on your mask. I don't want you to get in trouble." And then, hoping against what she believed she knew, she tried one last time. "You must survive. Promise me, Emmett. Promise me you'll try."

He nodded.

"The family needs you. I need you. But no matter what, I want you to know." She squeezed his hand. "I'll always love you."

Reverend Father Losterman, a kind and pious man, arrived that afternoon, listened to her final confession, and offered the Eucharist, which she gratefully accepted. She'd eaten nothing for days, but the body of Christ would feed her spirit. Anointing her wrists and forehead, he prayed, "Through this holy anointing, may the Lord in his love and mercy help you with the grace of the Holy Spirit. May the Lord who frees you from sin save you and raise you up."

Mary closed her eyes, then reopened them. The Reverend Father continued, "I commend you, my dear sister, to Almighty God. May you return to Him who formed you. May holy Mary and all the saints meet you as you go forth from this life. May Christ who was crucified for you bring you freedom and peace."

But still, she did not go. She thought of her son and prayed the rosary. She remembered her living children, then blessed Robbie, Ida, and George, who'd died into a life everlasting. She blessed her children's children, then Bobbie's grandson, who represented another sort of eternal life. And because she was Mary Dowling, Mother of Bourbon, she thought of her still and doubler in Juarez, racked barrels aging in the heat. She smiled and drifted, yet remained.

Visits continued. Her pain worsened. Dr. Abell increased the morphine. On Wednesday, February 19, at 7:10 a.m., seemingly unconscious, with Will, Bobbie, and Mary Bond at her side, she felt her senses quicken. She stepped forward to be welcomed by the open arms of her Savior, but found to her delight that it was John, looking as he had the day they met. Black bowler, brown bow tie, twinkling eyes, and fine moustache.

"Mary, I've been waiting."

"As have I."

And with her spirit made flesh, Mary stepped into her beloved's arms.

CHAPTER THIRTY-THREE

After Mary 1930-1986

Mary was buried on February 21 in the Dowling family plot beside John on a perfect spring day come a month early. Reverend Father Losterman, assisted by Fathers Juderman and Murphy, led the service, and the pallbearers, active and honorary, were drawn from the best families in Lawrenceburg. John Cody and Bill James, Rose and Ida Lyter, and their families attended as well. Speakers praised her generosity to the poor, and more than one newspaper reported in her obituary that at the time of her death, Mary Dowling, widow of distiller John Dowling, and later an important distiller in her own right, was the wealthiest woman in Anderson County.

Her estate, left equally to her children, included: a large bluegrass farm along the Salt River; fifteen acres in Tyrone, comprising Waterfill and Frazier, as well as one of the finest quarries in all of

Kentucky; several other valuable parcels; Dowling Hall; the river camp; and a large distillery in Juarez, Mexico. The value of the estate was estimated at $300,000, which in today's dollars exceeds $5 million.

On April 17, 1930, less than three months later, Emmett spiked a high fever and died, likely of diphtheria. Family members said his health was never the same after prison. The following paragraphs, excerpted from the Harvard College Class of 1921 Decennial Report, conclude his only known obituary.

"In February 1930, Dowling's mother died. For a few weeks, he alone bore the burden of the responsibilities she had carried and, in addition, a heavy load of sorrow, for in his nine years' work with his mother the bond of affection which united the two had grown infinitely closer than is the case with most mothers and sons. A brief period of ill health culminated in his death on April 17, 1930.

Harvard, which draws so many of its sons from New England and the East, and so few from the South, sustained a real loss in the death of Emmett Dowling, for in him were found those qualities of which both Harvard and the South are proudest—unselfishness, courage, and modesty."

Wally Camp, Ida's husband, died in a one-car accident on May 26, 1930, six weeks after Emmett. It was late, just three miles from Lexington; he was on his way home to Lawrenceburg. Wally was the passenger; the driver walked away unharmed. He was buried beside Ida in the Dowling family plot. The headstone lists his year of birth as 1889, though he was born in 1890. This deception was likely arranged by Mary Bond, or perhaps by Will. Ida had entered the world in 1887, though her headstone says 1889. Though she was, in fact, three years older than Wally, in perpetuity, Ida is two months younger.

John "Johnnie" Dowling never married, though he was in love with and loved by Will's sister-in-law Jessie May Lillard (Margaret's younger sister). Johnnie had intended to propose after returning from prison, but showed signs of a degenerative disease, likely ALS. Will suggested that if he were seriously ill, it would be cruel to ask for Jessie May's hand, and Johnnie, ever considerate and kind, agreed.

In his last years, until he could no longer walk, Johnnie would have himself driven every night after dinner to Will's house to visit with his beloved nieces, Ann and Mary. He died in Dowling Hall in September 1936, five days shy of his fifty-first birthday.

Antonio Bermudez would remain a life-long friend of the Dowling family. In 1936, he enrolled his nephew Jaime Bermudez in the Kavanaugh School in Lawrenceburg, where he was known as "Jamie" and played on a Kentucky state champion basketball team. Will Dowling served as Jaime's legal guardian while he lived in Kentucky. In later years, Jaime, who attended Muskingum University in Ohio, helped create the *maquiladora* industry. These are factories on the Mexican side of the US border that assemble products for companies from around the world, but especially from the United States. Many of these factories now operate in the Antonio J. Bermudez Industrial Park in Juarez. Jaime would live until 2018 and died a billionaire several times over.

Will was the executor of Mary's will, yet never settled her estate. Instead, he allowed Mary Bond and Johnnie to remain in Dowling Hall and paid household expenses and the mansion's substantial upkeep with family money. Maybe he couldn't bear to sell his mother's possessions or evict his siblings. Or maybe, like his mother, he wanted the Dowlings as a family to own everything. It's also possible he feared Mary Bond's response if he ever told her to vacate Dowling Hall.

Will assumed responsibility for managing the family's interests in D&W and traveled regularly to Juarez/El Paso after Mary and Emmett's deaths. In May 1940, shortly after returning from El Paso, Will had trouble breathing and sought medical care, fearing the same heart trouble that had killed his father, uncle, and brother had come for him. Instead, it was his lungs. He died within weeks, not quite sixty-one, and was buried in the Dowling family plot in Lawrenceburg.

The task of telling Mary Bond to leave Dowling Hall fell to Margaret, who explained that without Will's salary, she'd need his share of the estate to raise her children. On September 30, 1940, Mary's Lawrenceburg properties were sold at auction, with all proceeds divided among the four remaining heirs: Mary Dowling Bond, Bobbie Dowling Stewart, Katherine Dowling O'Brien, and Will's widow, Margaret Lillard Dowling. All the sons were already dead.

Bobbie Dowling Stewart died in 1952 at the age of seventy-four, at St. Joseph's Infirmary in Louisville, the same hospital where her mother had died twenty-two years earlier. Bobbie was buried in the Stewart family plot in Frankfort, Kentucky. She was survived by three children, seven grandchildren, and three great-grandchildren.

As of August 2024, Mary Dowling's great-great-grandson (Bobbie's great grandson), Dr. John Stewart, is the fifth-generation family director of the Stewart Home and School, each of them named John Stewart. Bobbie's elegant home, Sunnyside, is presently owned by Milly Stewart, widow of the fourth John Stewart. Many of Mary Dowling's finest rugs and furniture, as well as the Harvey Joiner portrait of John Dowling, remain in Sunnyside. Unfortunately, the Harvey Joiner portrait of Mary Dowling vanished in the mists of time.

After her mother's estate was settled, Mary Bond invested her portion well and purchased her own South Main mansion. Although bedridden for many years, she survived until 1960, dying at home in Lawrenceburg at the age of eighty-five. She divided her substantial estate between her nieces and nephews.

Mary Bond was buried in the family plot, alongside her husband, James C. Bond. First in her own mind in death as she was in life, Mary Bond and Gentlemen Jim rest under the only large headstones in the Dowling family plot.

Katherine Dowling O'Brien, the longest-lived of the Dowling children, died in 1977 at the age of ninety-four in New York City. Her daughter Helen, who never married or lived on her own while her mother drew breath, died four years later at the age of seventy-two. Katherine and Helen are buried in the O'Brien family plot in Sleepy Hollow, New York.

Margaret Lillard Dowling, Will's wife, and Mary's daughter-in-law, died in 1986, at the age of ninety-seven, in Lawrenceburg. She was buried beside Will in the family plot. Many Dowling photos and heirlooms remain in her home, now owned by her grandson, Mary's great-grandson, attorney Bland Byrne. In 1983, to preserve family history, Bland recorded and transcribed extensive interviews with his beloved Nannie, never dreaming they'd one day find their way into this book. Without Margaret's eyewitness accounts of Armistice Day in New York City and the long, emotionally grueling Dowling trials, this book would be a pale and pallid version of itself.

Descendants of Ida Leyter have remained associated with and employed by Mary Dowling's descendants to the present day. Lucille Washington first worked for Will's wife, Margaret, in the 1930s. Forty and more years later, while Lucille's daughters cleaned, Margaret and Lucille, who'd served as the Republican chairperson for Lawrenceburg when Republicans supported civil rights and Democrats didn't, would sit together and gab. When Margaret died in 1986, Lucille was seated in the first rank of mourners alongside Margaret's daughters. When the service ended, she turned to Bland, who sat behind her in the second row. Lucille said, "You know she was my best friend."

Bland answered, "I know."

African Americans, both enslaved and free, have played prominent roles in Lawrenceburg's long history, yet their stories are seldom told.

Although Prohibition ended in 1934, Mary's D&W Distillery, SA, remained in business until the 1980s. After Will died, however, no one traveled to Juarez to look after Dowling family interests. In 1948, after Antonio Bermudez became managing director of PEMEX, Antonio's much younger brother-in-law, Rene Mascareñas, assumed control of D&W, which entered a long period of slow decline.

In the early 1960s, Mascareñas purchased a new still from Vendome Copper in Louisville; Vendome had also manufactured Mary's previous still and doubler, which Joe L Beam disassembled and moved. Tom Sherman, Vendome's president, traveled to Juarez to oversee installation of the new still. In the 1990s, after D&W had closed, Mascareñas offered to return the original still and doubler to Vendome if Sherman would pay the shipping. Mary's 1914 doubler remains on display at Vendome Copper in downtown Louisville, where it can be viewed today.

In 1964, the US Congress passed Joint Senate Resolution 19, which proclaimed that "Bourbon was a distinctive product of the United States." Very obviously aimed at D&W, Resolution 19 prohibited distillers operating outside the US from calling their whiskey bourbon. The only individuals to push back? Lawyers representing Katherine and Helen O'Brien.

Despite the new law, everyone knew that great American whiskey had been made outside of the United States for many years, bourbon distilled and bottled by a remarkable woman named Mary Dowling.

THE END

Select Bibliography

Books

Arreola, Daniel, *Post Cards from the Chihuahua Border*, Tucson, The University of Arizona Press, 2019.

Cruz, Francisco, *El Cartel de Juarez*, Mexico City, Editorial Planeta Mexicana, 2008.

McKee, Major Lewis W., and Mrs. Lydia K. Bond, *History of Anderson County (Kentucky) 1780-1936*, Baltimore, Clearfield Company, 1975.

Zoeller, Chester, *Kentucky Bourbon Barons: Legendary Distillers from the Golden Age of Whiskey Making*, Butler Books, 2014.

Newspapers.com

Newspapers.com has enormously simplified historical research for writers, offering full text versions of daily American newspapers published during the nineteenth and twentieth centuries. Long gone are the days of traveling to distant libraries to sit in front of microfiche readers. For me, newspapers.com was especially useful in uncovering details of: the long and drawn-out Dowling bootlegging trials; family weddings, deaths, and births; financial details of Mary Dowling's investment in D&W Juarez; the dates of Mary and Emmett's travels to El Paso, even the mash bill used to produce Mary's bourbon in Juarez.

Individual newspapers upon which I relied heavily include: *Courier-Journal* (Louisville), *El Paso Evening Post, Kentucky Advocate* (Danville), *Lexington Herald, Owensboro Messenger,* and the *Paducah Sun.*

Online Resources

www.twainquotes.com/July4-1886.html?ref=americanpurpose.com

Acknowledgments

Novelist Ron Hansen, in addition to penning the Introduction and commenting insightfully on the manuscript, has served as our unpaid consultant in all things Catholic. We hereby bestow upon Ron the right to append CC—*Catholic Consultant*—to his signature whenever he would like.

Many individuals with a familial or geographic connection to Mary Dowling and Lawrenceburg, Kentucky, have given freely of their time and knowledge of our protagonist and her world. What became clear, as we researched and wrote, is that many people not only wished this book to be born, but to be the best version we could make of it. We'd like especially to thank Bland Byrne, Mary's great-grandson, for sharing family photos, information, and artifacts, especially his extraordinary interviews with Margaret Lillard Dowling.

We'd also like to thank the extended Stewart family, headed by matriarch Millicent "Milly" Stewart, her son, the fifth Dr. John Stewart, and her daughter Cathy Stewart Brown and son-in-law Martin Brown, not only for speaking to us but for inviting us to visit their magnificent home, Sunnyside, on the grounds of the Stewart Home and School. Seeing the portrait of John Dowling, numerous family photographs, and many of the heirlooms Mary

Dowling gave to her daughter Bobbie Dowling Stewart helped bring their history to life.

Rose Cunningham, whose husband was the grandson of John Cody Cunningham, Mary Dowling's driver, and whose mother, Lucille Washington, was the long-time employee and friend of Margaret Lillard Dowling, shared stories of her family's long association with the Dowlings, helping us to provide a more complete and diverse vision of Lawrenceburg life.

Thank you, Bruce Beam Phillips, and your cousin Bruce Beam, for sharing information and photographs of your ancestors Joe L and Katie Beam. The images you provided are the only known photographs of Mary Dowling in Mexico.

Thank you, Thomas Ripy and George Geohegan, cousins and current owners of Ripy House, located across the street from Dowling Hall in Lawrenceburg. Your knowledge of Lawrenceburg history and the private tour of Ripy House were invaluable.

Thank you, Ed Smith, the present owner of Dowling Hall, for letting us in to look around. Thank you also for your gatekeeping challenge, which was answered honestly and correctly.

Thank you, Robbie Morgan, head of the Lawrenceburg Tourist Board, and Sharon Pike, former president of the Anderson County Tourist Board, for your help with research and for making interview connections around Lawrenceburg.

Thank you, Harold Peach, Sr., for sharing information about your ancestor, Lester Elliot, Mary Dowling's tenant farmer at Shonraugh. Thank you, Professor Harold Peach, Jr., for the introduction to your father and for alerting us to the existence of Mrs. Lee Hamilton, Lawrenceburg suffragette.

Thank you, Tom Sherman, of Vendome Copper, for your eyewitness accounts and photographs of D&W Distillery in the 1960s.

Thank you Andy Treinen, President and CEO of the Frazier History Museum in Louisville, for your support on archival research.

Thank you, Harvard University Archives and the Center for Archives and Special Collections, Phillips Exeter Academy, for your help with and permission to publish priceless information about Emmett Dowling.

Thank you, Carlos Villarreal, for sharing information about your grandfather, Mayor Carlos Villarreal of Juarez, and for the guided tour you provided.

Thank you, Jenna Pallecone of Rabbit Hole Distillery for your consistent good cheer and for all your help with practical arrangements.

Thank you to our wonderful agents and friends, Michael Carlisle and Michael Mungiello, of Inkwell Management. This one was a bit more complicated than the others, wasn't it?

Thank you to our fabulous editor, Jacob Hoye. Your sharp eye and engagement with the material added depth and detail to these pages. And it was fun.

Finally, thanks to our wives, Susan Morgan and Heather Bass Zamanian, for their thoughtful contributions and unwavering support throughout the writing process. So many drafts and iterations, so much insight into Mary.

About the Authors

Eric Goodman's eighth book, *Mother of Bourbon,* is his first collaboration. Previous books include *Cuppy and Stew* (2020), *Curveball* (2024), and its prequel, *In Days of Awe* (1991). He's published hundreds of articles and a handful of short stories in a wide range of publications; for a brief period, he also wrote episodic television. His work has been recognized with several Ohio Arts Council fellowships, and individual novels have been named Indies Finalist for General Fiction and Silver Book of the Year for Gay/Lesbian Fiction. For many years, he directed the creative writing program at Miami University (Ohio). Goodman lives in Sonoma County and Mecklenburg, New York, with his wife, Susan Morgan.

Kaveh Zamanian is a clinical psychologist and psychoanalyst turned master whiskey-maker. He fell in love with a Kentucky girl, moved to Louisville, and decided to take a leap with her down the rabbit hole of Bourbon, following his long-standing passion for fine spirits. He is founder of Rabbit Hole and Mary Dowling Whiskey Companies and serves as the Chief Whiskey Officer for Pernod-Ricard, the second largest spirit company in the world. In recognition of his achievements, in 2022, he was inducted into the Kentucky Bourbon Hall of Fame, cementing his place among industry pioneers and visionaries. He resides with his wife (Kentucky girl) and children in Louisville, Kentucky.

Ron Hansen is the author of fourteen books and several screenplays. *Mariette in Ecstasy* was nominated for the National Book Critics Circle Award and won the Gold Medal in Fiction from the Commonwealth Club of California. *Atticus* was a finalist for both the National Book Award and the PEN/Faulkner Award. *The Assassination of Jesse James by the Coward Robert Ford* was also a finalist for the PEN/Faulkner Award and was made into a movie starring Brad Pitt and Casey Affleck. He and his wife reside in North Bethesda, Maryland.